SAVAGE STARS

CHAOS CORE BOOK 3

RANDOLPH LALONDE

BOOKS BY RANDOLPH LALONDE

The Chaos Core Series

Trapped

Cool Pursuit

Savage Stars

THE SPINWARD FRINGE SERIES

Spinward Fringe Broadcast 0: Origins

Spinward Fringe Broadcast 1 and 2: Resurrection and Awakening

Spinward Fringe Broadcast 3: Triton

Spinward Fringe Broadcast 4: Frontline

Spinward Fringe Broadcast 5: Fracture

Spinward Fringe Broadcast 6: Fragments

The Expendable Few: A Spinward Fringe Novel

Spinward Fringe Broadcast 7: Framework

Spinward Fringe Broadcast 8: Renegades

Spinward Fringe Broadcast 9: Warpath

Spinward Fringe Broadcast 10: Freeground

Spinward Fringe Broadcast 10.5: Carnie's Tale

Spinward Fringe Broadcast 11: Revenge

Spinward Fringe Broadcast 12: Invasion

Spinward Fringe Broadcast 13: Warriors

Spinward Fringe Broadcast 14: Rebel

Spinward Fringe Broadcast 15: Pursuit

Fantasy

Highshield

Brightwill

NEM: Awakening

HORROR

Dark Arts

www.RandolphLalonde.com

SAVAGE STARS

CHAOS CORE BOOK 3

Randolph Lalonde

EBook ISBN: 978-1-988175-17-1

AT THE BEGINNING OF THE BASIC ERA...

Spin, formerly known as Aspen while she was a slave to the inhuman Countess, is dead. In an effort to stretch the few months of life she has before a mechanism deep in her genetic code ends her existence forever, their ship medic has put Spin in a state of necro-stasis while they make the crossing to British Alliance territory.

The procedure was painful, holding her seconds past the moment of death is well beyond what nature intends. Her entire crew worries that the revival process will be much worse, since sedation is not an option.

With the exception of one short stop at Deep Shadow Station, which was largely uneventful, her crew have been isolated aboard the ship for two weeks. Some tension has developed.

Meanwhile, unbeknownst to Spin and her crew, Boro is in his cell aboard a private armed carrier owned by Kort, the Countess' trusted consort. Boro, a well-liked crewman, uncle and father figure to Nigel, is waking from a nightmare wherein he frantically swims from eels with long jaws. They bite onto his legs, close their mouths until their fine pointed teeth cut through his flesh and swim away with their piece. Blood in the water draws more of them.

His eyes open, ending the nightmare in time for him to face a waking terror, one of Master Kort's guards is approaching...

ONE

He'd seen enough. Aldo, one of the Consort's Honour Guards, was almost caught vomiting in his quarters after the most recent torture session with Master Kort's favourite prisoner, Boro Lozel. His fellow guards seemed to grow only more desensitized, but the visibly flagging will of Boro mirrored his own.

The captive was out of information, long dry as a source of insight on their quarry. Aspen, the escaped doll and her mate Larken were central to Master Kort's focus, and as he failed to locate them, he took his frustrations out on Boro.

Until three days ago, the thick-bodied, robust man was able to keep calm with the exception of the occasional attempt at lashing out, but then he reached his breaking point. It was the interrogation system Kort was using. He'd stretch Boro out, strap him down and directly interface with his brain, sending experiences into him that were from recorded torture and horrific procedures. Live vivisections, the laying and hatching of alien eggs inside the body, and any other neurally recorded horrors Master Kort could get his hands on.

Three days ago, Boro had a different reaction to seeing the chair. He didn't simply turn and try to strike one of his guards, instead he had a full flight response. He flailed, screamed, chucked a guard aside entirely, clawed, and bit to at least turn away from the machine before he was strapped in again. It was animalistic, primal.

Master Kort laughed. Watching Boro resist six guards at once until he was stunned twice was entertaining for him. Couldn't he see the desperation? The fear? The breaking of a person? A trail of urine was left on the floor from the hall to the torture device after Boro was subdued, and Aldo stood back, watching two lower ranked guards strap him in.

Boro, once strong in mind and body, knew where he was the instant he started recovering from the stun shock. The struggle that followed was so frenzied, the panic so raw that Boro threw up on himself as he fought his restraints. He was down to instinct, everything else had been worn away. One of the arms almost came loose during his desperate struggle, even Master Kort stepped back in response to the ferocity of Boro's fight to be free. If he could have chewed a limb off and limp away, he would have.

After several minutes he tired and started weeping, babbling. Master Kort smiled and left the room. "This is good, we'll leave him there until he calms down and then we'll put him in the Tranquil Pool simulation."

That was altogether evil to Aldo. The Tranquil Pool was made to be initiated while the subject was sleeping, so they began to think they were dreaming of drifting in cool water. Starting with small fish, things started to nip at them. As the simulation progressed larger and larger sea creatures came to feast until they were devoured. It was one of Master Kort's favourites. It was one of the few fictions created by an author who was known only as Mirage and the panic it instilled in the two subjects Aldo watched Kort use it on were deeply traumatizing.

Aldo could not have hated Master Kort more than he did thanks to all he'd witnessed. There were other atrocities, but nothing demonstrated the twisted cyborg's capacity for cruelty more than that device and what he did to Boro in it.

"Castillan," Aldo said to a guard as he strode into the brig. "How are those fungus farms paying off these days?"

"Oh, man, you missed out on a major investment opportunity," the guard replied, chomping his gum. "The yields are amazing, people are starving, they'll pay anything for raw food, no matter how bad it tastes."

"So, you're not going to need this gig much longer, I guess," Aldo said.

"I'm just along for the trip to the Geist System. I've gotta see what's there before I retire, you know. It's something almost no one will see, ever."

"I hear ya," Aldo replied. The Geist System, where some of the most advanced manufacturing in the galaxy used to take place. Now it was one of the most dangerous places you could go. Someone or something had taken control of the defences, which made most military organizations look like a glee club. "Master Kort wants another session with this one," he said, nodding towards Boro's cell.

"Isn't it late for that?" Castillan asked, looking at his wrist. "Oh-three-hundred, give or take."

"Do you want to talk to him? I'm sure he's interested in your opinion on his late-night urges," Aldo said.

"Opening cell Zero Three," Castillan said, punching his code in then joining Aldo at the cell door. "Heard this one gets all squirrelly when you take him near the Master's favourite toy now."

"Up!" Aldo said, kicking the bottom of Boro's bare foot. "You're not really sleeping, I can tell."

"Fucking eels man," Boro said. "Dream always ends on the bloody eels."

"C'mon, we're taking you to another site," he clapped the restraints on Boro's wrists, they turned red, indicating that they were secure. Aldo kept the control screen on his inner wrist display for easy access.

"I thought we were taking him to..." Castillan started to say, chewing his gum like an idiot, his helmet still affixed to the top of his thigh. There was a reason why he was usually stuck behind a control terminal - he wasn't exactly an intellectual juggernaut. He had money, though.

"I'm taking him where I was told to take him," Aldo said. He took one of Boro's arms and directed him out of the brig, down the main port side hallway. They all looked the same: royal blue and white walls with self-cleaning grey floors. The light seemed to come from everywhere, lending no sense of direction to the space. Aldo got around it by memorizing the hallways as shapes that fit together a certain way. He knew how to get to the tertiary launch bay extremely well.

"Man," Castillan said with a chuckle. "You are completely

lost." They arrived at the double doors that would take them into a launch bay that had been patrolled, checked and sealed off for the third shift.

Aldo touched the doors, opening them with his security clearance. The pitch-black hangar beyond began to light up.

"Whoa, whoa, what are you doing?" Castillan asked.

With an alacrity that didn't seem to suit the man and a ferocity that did, Boro stepped back, put his cuffed hands over Castillan's head, wrapped his arms around his head tightly and turned around with a jerk. Castillan made a muffled, anguished sound, his hands reaching out in front of him as he panicked. With a tight grip, Boro bent and twisted the guard's neck until he stopped moving, it was only a few seconds; it was like watching a larger dog take something into its jaws and shake it to death. Boro let the corpse drop and regarded Aldo with a devil's grin, catching his breath. "Jailbreak?"

"Damn right, drag him," Aldo said, deactivating Boro's cuffs then grabbing one of his former comrades' arms and rushing into the hangar. As soon as the prisoner was inside, he locked all but the outer doors. "Get in the second ship from the left. The rear hatch is open."

"Been planning this awhile?" Boro asked.

"Three days," Aldo said, pulling his helmet off and deactivating it. Anyone with a high enough security level could see what he was seeing while it was on, not exactly ideal. With a jerk he pulled the control chip for the small, nine man ship out of the collar of his armour and woke the systems up from standby. The rear hatch was already closing. "Are you any good at flying?" Aldo said.

"I can fly this thing, sure," Boro said, joining him in the cockpit.

"Can you fly it well?" Aldo asked. "I'm not a great pilot and we're going to be staying close to the ship for a few seconds while the transit systems make an emergency wormhole. It will take a better pilot than I am."

"Shouldn't be too hard." The main hangar doors opened, revealing the warped edge of the side of a wormhole. "Never done this before, never flown this ship before," he looked at the controls and the status displays quietly.

"Guardsman Aldo Seamark," said a voice through his communicator, filling the cockpit with Supervisor Austin's bored tone. "What are you doing? We're still twenty-eight minutes away from emergence and I don't see anything in front of me saying you'll need a combat ship now or when we complete transit."

"That's Honour Guard Seamark, to you, Austin. I'm on a secret mission for our commander. You'd best not test me, or you'll have to face him."

"Yeah, I think I'm going to see what he says about this. I'm locking you down."

"Hang on," Boro said, nodding nervously and taking the controls. The ship lifted off from the deck, nudged the shuttle next to it hard, sending the smaller ship half way across the hangar. Aldo was tossed onto his butt and then clung to a seat before he was thrown against the side of the cockpit. He could hear the corpse behind them flopping around. "Oops, forgot the dampers, this would have been a short trip," he pushed three buttons. "There we go."

"Maybe it would be better if I took over?" Aldo asked, scrambling to get into the co-pilot's seat and strap in.

The nose of their shuttle was pointed towards the bow of the carrier, parallel to the wall of the wormhole. The hangar door was beginning to close. "No, no, I know what I'm doing. Just going to ease out of the bay so we're parallel to the edge of the wormhole horizon," he said, guiding the ship sideways through the hangar doorway, rotating the ship onto its side for some reason and scraping the side against the lowering door. The dorsal side of the shuttle was facing the hangar, so the door was all Aldo could see as he looked straight up. "There we go, like a pilot fish hanging around a shark," he said.

"We have an alert here," announced Supervisor Austin. "Do you have a prisoner with you? Is Castillan dead? It says here that he's dead!"

"Just getting the prisoner back to containment, he almost got away," Aldo replied, starting to feel sweat gather under his nose and palms. This was going badly, very badly.

"Turn on the shields," Boro said.

"What?" Aldo started looking at the panel in front of him and saw navigation, blinking red notifications about proximity alerts, but no shield systems.

"There," Boro pointed across Aldo's chest. "That panel there!"

He turned and saw a whole panel dedicated to shields with a friendly green query in the middle of the screen asking; ACTIVATE DEFENCE SHIELD?

He pushed it and heard a hum behind him. The prompt disappeared and was replaced with an image of their ship with a fine line around it and more, much smaller icons.

"Navigation?" Boro asked. "Can you make sure the emergency wormhole generator is working? We can't bloody well stay here."

"Right, last chance," Supervisor Austin said. "Dock with us or I'm going to have to blast you." As if to support his ultimatum, a large pair of double cannons swivelled in their direction, the white and black painted barrels glinting in the light.

"Make sure the wormhole generator's charged!" Boro bellowed, fighting with the controls a little, setting off alarms as the shuttle strayed too close to the wall of the wormhole. He hit the accelerator a bit too hard and the ship burst ahead of the carrier. "Oh, great, we're in front of their big guns now," he said. "Wait, I know a trick," he said mostly to himself. After examining a panel to his left, he pushed a series of buttons and let go of the controls.

Aldo immediately reached over to take them but was abruptly pushed back into his seat. "What are you doing?"

"Auto pilot is watching the bloody carrier and staying in position in front of it," Boro said as he worked on the faster than light navigation panel. "If they don't blow us out of this merry existence, then we'll be fine until... there it is! You did charge the wormhole generator. You're either smart or lucky."

A blast made the systems behind Aldo whine and the display to his right, the one for the shields, blink red. "I think we're about to lose our aft shields."

"They're the cat, we're the mouse," Boro said. "But we've got a mouse hole." He took the controls and unlocked them, the nose of their ship wobbled dangerously.

"Is this your first time flying a ship?" Aldo asked.

Boro spun the ship end over end, coming nose to nose with

the massive carrier.

Aldo yelped as his hands flailed, looking for anything solid to grab onto. "What are you doing?"

"That was on purpose!" Boro said, easing the ship closer and up over the dorsal side of the carrier. "Just need enough clear sky," he said under his breath. "Damn, she's a great big, fat ship though, isn't she? Blocks the whole road."

"Are you trying to get us pointed away from the carrier?"

"Going to try to break through the side of the wormhole on a good angle so we don't get spaghettified."

"So we don't get what?" Aldo asked, seeing that their ship had taken another hit, their bottom shields were red and he heard a loud pop behind him.

"It's complicated physics stuff," Boro said, his tongue sticking out the side of his mouth as he rotated the ship carefully, pointing it so they were almost parallel with the carrier again, facing the same direction. "Time to go," he said, glancing at the wormhole generator. He leaned over and slapped a button as he increased thrust power. To Aldo's amazement, they entered a small wormhole that split off from the large one. Boro activated the autopilot, locked the controls and sat back. "First time flying in a wormhole generated by another ship while it's trying to kill me."

"Are you any good at flying outside of wormholes?" Aldo asked, wiping sweat from his face.

Boro chuckled. "No, not really, no. How do you think I got so good at fixing ships?"

"Do you smell smoke?" Aldo asked.

"I do. I hope that guard's suit will fit me," Boro said. "I might need the life support."

TWO

Spin felt like she was on fire on the outside and freezing cold on the inside. Every breath made her feel like she was taking in burning air. It was the kind of pain you couldn't escape and it felt different in her head compared to her chest, compared to her fingers and toes.

Blind, she flailed, fought and screamed. There was nothing else to do as the pain changed, it felt like she'd been swaddled in magma. "Spin; your temperature is equalizing. Soon you'll just feel cold, the pain will be gone."

"Is she going to be all right?" Mirra asked.

"Now that she's conscious, yes. I've given her something for the pain."

"I can't see," Spin said, the pain quickly fading to discomfort. She realized that she was rolled into a heated blanket.

Even the pain medication couldn't keep her from feeling cold enough to make her teeth chatter, the warming blanket was feeling less painful though. Her extremities were probably getting closer to a normal temperature. She flexed her fingers and toes, the motion felt good, a little painful, but good. "Your vision should return soon. I had to give you something to protect your eyes, remember? The counter agent is working, so it'll be all right in a moment."

Spin clamped her teeth together and nodded through the shaking. Silence followed as whoever was in the medbay was standing around watching her recover. The pain in her head was almost gone, and she recalled being put into necro-stasis clearly. It felt as though only seconds passed since she went under. "How long?"

"Two weeks today," Mirra said, feeling her forehead. It was her caring touch, it had to be.

"Oh, that's nice," she chattered, turning her head towards the hand, chuckling at how her words sounded through a trembling jaw. The warm hands came back, caressing her forehead and cheeks. "Feels like two minutes."

"The feeling of lost time is natural, you'll get used to it," Leland said soothingly. "You're recovering well."

"Still cold," Spin said, drawing the blankets around herself tighter.

"That's a good sign, she's rubbing her legs together and using her hands," Leland said, sounding more like he was talking to himself. "Talk to her."

"Tell me about the trip," Spin managed to say. Light was starting to make it through whatever was caked onto her eyes, she could feel it sloughing off, a quick spritz of water and the sweep of a sponge made her recoil.

"Sorry, you can't cry yet, so I'm giving your eyes a little extra moisture to help you clear the Voosten, the stuff that was protecting your eyes."

"Can't cry... yet?" Spin asked.

"Before you went under, you asked if there was anything I could do about that, remember? I was able to remove the extra duct controllers that kept you from crying. It turns out that it wasn't genetic, your model had implants that redirected tears and forced your ducts to stop producing when they determined that you were crying as an emotional response. I only had to remove them and regenerate the skin they were attached to. Recovery would have been painful and risky if you were alive, but I was able to complete it perfectly while you were in necro-stasis. No recovery time, and no heightened risk of infection. You can cry like anyone now."

"T-thank you," she said before clamping her teeth together to stop them from chattering.

"Now about the crew," he said. "Mirra can fill you in."

"We made it to British Alliance territory. We've made contact with the Brighton, one of their big carriers. A fighter scanned us and sent us on to Port Harrison. The Governor made sure all our forms were filled out right, and Sharon sent them in ahead of us."

"Sharon? Sun was supposed to do it."

"Everyone's looking to Sharon now. A few days after you went under, Sun ordered her to stop at Lacuna Station. It wasn't part of our flight plan, and she wouldn't tell Sharon or anyone else why we would be stopping there, so Sharon shut her out with the crew's support. There was a vote and Sun was removed as first officer until you came back. Mitch took over for a few days, then he and Sharon formed sort of a team. They've been good, taking care of things."

"Shouldn't have left Sun in charge at all," Spin said, her teeth no longer chattering. She started to relax, sighing and stretching her legs. A sudden spritz in her eyes surprised her and she laughed. By the time Leland finished sponging around her eyes, she was seeing light and shadows.

"Aside from that, Della and Nigel really coupled up. He's been working a regular ten hour shift every day on our shuttle and on ship maintenance, he's been teaching me a lot, but after hours it was mostly those two fooling around. They're having a fight now, though."

"What's it about?"

"She walked in on him using a solo pleasure system he got at Deep Shadow Station and is confused about why he'd want that instead of her. He didn't do a great job explaining himself, so she got pissed."

An involuntary snicker at catching Larken in a similar situation when they were growing up turned into a momentary pang of grief, but she pressed past it. "That's too bad. Sometimes people like doing that on their own because they want to fantasize. It probably has nothing to do with her."

"That's what I said when I talked to her. She'll be back to teasing him soon, I'm sure. They'll be fine if they don't find someone new first."

The world was starting to come back into focus, she could see clearly enough to recognize Leland's face looking down at her. "Hi there," she smiled. The desire to sleep started making her feel relaxed, then there was a burning pain in her chest.

"Chest hurts." Spin said as she squeezed her eyes shut and began to cringe.

A moment later she opened her eyes in time to see Leland retrieving a resuscitator from her chest. Mirra closed the blankets around her again. "What happened?"

"You passed out and your heart stopped," Leland said. "We got it started right away and you're full of Leespine Recovery Meds, so you're fine now."

Spin could see mostly clearly, and her pain was gone. "You warned me about that before I went under," she said.

"I don't think we can do this again. Chances are you won't come back next time. Nothing to worry about now though."

Mirra finished putting the resuscitator machine, a thick disc that had medication and a few important systems built in, into a sterilizer on the other side of the room.

"How long until we get to Port Harrison?" Spin asked.

Mirra wiped a tear from her eye and turned around, doing a good job of faking a casual expression. It must have been a closer call than Leland was telling her. "Little less than an hour now. We'll have to fly through the outer solar system the old-fashioned way, then we'll take the shuttle down when we're ready to visit. Sharon said we have to start by going to their refugee office. We're officially free though, anyone chasing us into this territory is breaking interstellar law. Thank you for getting everything together so we could come here."

"Thank you for taking care of me. After escaping the second time, I didn't know if I would have friends again." Spin sighed and laid back. Her vision was almost clear and she was starting to feel right again. The blanket was still around her, red and heavy. "Okay if I just relax for half an hour here?" Once she was cleaned up and dressed, she knew life would resume with a vengeance, throwing a hundred things at her. While Spin wanted to savour every detail, her body just wanted to take a break and be warm, comfortable.

"I'd love it if you took a day off so I could monitor you, actually," Leland said, looking at a thin plastic strip covered with genetic information.

"I'm not going to lose a day after hanging on to two weeks. That's if this worked at all."

"It did," Leland said. "Like I said though, you can't do that again. Your whole system was made to fight anything like necrostasis. Next time it'll win and you'll either fail to go under, suffering while you try to heal, or die permanently."

"I'll just have to find a way to outlive my expiry date then," Spin concluded.

"Do you want to see people? I know Della is crazy to see you, the rest of the crew too," Mirra said.

"I'll rest up here for a little while, then I'll be all theirs when I'm cleaned up and dressed."

"Good plan. I'll come back later with your clothes."

The lights dimmed and Spin closed her eyes with a sigh. Once she was out of that medbay bed, she knew she'd have to work fast. There would be no time for relaxing, for taking a break, even little time for sleeping. People would be left behind, and she'd have to earn trust with others quickly.

Life would move at a breakneck pace and Spin would either earn more time for herself by finding a cure or die knowing she tried. Either way, she'd gotten as many friends as she could to a place without slavery, and that was worth something.

THREE

Back in her comfortable, containment under-suit; an insulation against the threat of the void beyond the hull of her ship and wearing boots that Mirra bought on Deep Shadow Station that suited her better, Spin was starting to feel normal again. The ship still didn't feel familiar. A day after they entered the wormhole that would take them half way to British Alliance territory she entered necro-stasis. There was no time for her to get to know the ship, for it to feel like she owned it at all.

It had dark decks, white and grey panelled corridors and bright lighting like most ships of its type. The interior was dressed up with panels that hid the components that made everything possible, and the decks were foot friendly, not the industrial type so many haulers like the Convoy King had. The sound of the thrusters firing as they decelerated was a constant: a rumble that you could hear and feel but it wasn't so powerful that you had to shout over it. In the front section of the ship you could barely hear it at all.

The rear section crew quarters were simpler, with square corners instead of graceful, rounded edges and, though she knew the thought was vain since the designer couldn't have had any idea how Spin would be feeling that day, she still felt like the aesthetic of the rear section was built to suit her mood. Spin didn't let Mirra or Leland announce that she was up and about. There was something she felt she needed to take care of before she could have any happy reunions.

Nigel emerged from a service hatch that was barely big enough for him to fit through, balls of dust caught in his hair. He stared at her awkwardly for a moment, then closed the gap between them in two long strides and picked her up in a sweep of his arms.

That was one of the things she was afraid of. It was impossible for her to stay focused and clear on her message with crew members like that around. She laughed as he held her close for a moment before dropping her soundly on her feet. "You're too tall."

"What're you talking about? I'm the perfect height, width, and girth," he replied, flexing his arm. "How are you doing, though?"

"I'm all right, almost back to normal. I don't think I'll be doing that again, though." The hatch to Sun's self-assigned quarters was less than ten metres behind him, and Spin's gaze kept on drifting to it. "How's the ship?"

"We had some weird calibration problems with one of the secondary rear thrusters for a while, so I had to disable it until I figured it out, but I found the problem a couple days ago. The whole thing was resting on two bolts the length of my arm, they called them spars, but they were really just long bolts as far as I saw. One was bent, so I bent it back, strapped a sensor onto it and put it where it belonged. It'll last until we can get a replacement. I could make one if we had the right metal aboard, but we didn't exactly stock up on raw materials before we left."

"Any other problems?" Picturing what he meant wasn't a problem. She had a loose grasp of what the issue he ran into was and that was enough for the time being.

"I was just checking for air filters between these cabins, just in case. There are brackets for them, but none were installed. The whole system is on a main filter though, so I think it was to keep air flowing better, worth experimenting with, so we might want to get some filters at our next stop if they're not too expensive. No actual problems, though. This King is in great shape."

"Good, thank you for keeping it that way, Nigel," she said.

"It was easy." He looked over his shoulder at Sun's door, following Spin's glances. "I'll check the filter on the end. You know, way up there." His nod indicated that he would be at the far end of the aft section of the ship, next to the connection to the middle. It would be more than far enough so he'd be out of earshot, hopefully.

"Thanks, Nigel," Spin said, moving on to Sun's door. Her hesitation was a surprise to her. The knowledge that she was a made thing - designed to specifications determined by artists and scientists she may never meet - was something she'd accepted and sometimes depended on. Those specifications and features were leaked to her years before.

Aspens were made to look soft, approachable and charming. At the same time they were supposed to be able to have a 'stiff upper lip' meaning the capacity to gracefully endure most emotional tests. Outright anger, disappointment, fright, dismay and sadness were not emotions she was supposed to be able to control her reactions to. Her genetic predispositions were matched with her upbringing, and during bad times she believed the control she had over how heavily she let emotions weigh on her was an advantage.

As she stood near Sun's door, that control was barely present. Sun was a woman of the galaxy. She knew things about being a space farer that Spin didn't have time to learn. More importantly than that, she'd grown to love the older, wilful woman, admiring Sun's intelligence and confidence. Spin's rational thinking told her that Sun would be forgiven for costing her years of life by giving her the wrong medication without asking. That was if she had a lifetime to live. That may never be the case.

"I can hear you thinking out there," Sun said through the door.

"Door cam?" Spin asked.

"Yeah," Sun said, opening the hatch. She was dressed for travel.

At a glance Spin could see that the thick white long coat Sun was wearing was loaded with all her tools. Beneath she wore her under suit but only the grey collar was visible because she had shimmery blue shirt and black utility trousers with both her thigh holsters strapped on. She was wearing all her best clothing and most important articles. A military rucksack that matched her white long coat was almost full, still open at the top. "You're not coming back to the ship once we get to the refugee check-in."

"No, I can tell when a crew wants me out the airlock." Hers was a tone of surrender. "I'll be fine, the share of White's money you gave me is more than enough to start over. Even if everything costs eight times as much, I'll be fine for a long time. You don't have to tell me to leave. If that's what was making you hesitate, don't worry."

No number of deep breaths or acceptable number of minutes would prepare her to say what she knew was the most reasonable thing. The best thing for her short life. "I came to forgive you."

Sun froze, half way through checking a small energy cell. It tumbled from her fingers, bouncing a few times across the neatly made bed. Dark eyes looked up through loose strands of darker hair. "You can't mean that."

You're right, I don't. Thanks to you, I won't have enough time to get over what you've done to me, was what Spin's anger wanted to say. Even though she turned away from it, tried to shut it out, it reared its head in how she slapped the door controls, closing it behind her so it was just her and Sun in a small room with a bed, a locker, a chest of drawers and a small hygiene alcove. "I have to." The little optimism she held on to brightened what she said next. "Right now, before I'm ready I have to forgive you because I'm stuck. I could live for decades if I find a solution to my ticking clock. Then I'll have time to get over what you did, but I can't take that time because I have a much better chance at finding a solution with you than alone. So, I have to forgive you now, to force myself to start trusting you again right now."

"No, you don't." That little smile Sun would get when she knew something no one else did, or she was several steps ahead, graced her darkly coloured lips. "I'm leaving the ship, but I'm not leaving you, Spin. You gave me the money I need, Nigel and

Leland added to the pile, so I can get a small, fast ship and start following a few leads I dug up on my own. Most of them are long shots, and I'll share all of them with you, but I'm getting started as soon as the British Alliance clear me to be in their territory. I'll earn my forgiveness, Spin. That's the way it should be," Sun said, fishing a small data chip out of her pocket. "This is everything I have so far."

Spin accepted it and pressed it to the dermal computer on her arm. A collection of files transferred. Sun was really leaving. It was to Spin's benefit, there was no doubt in her mind her former mentor intended to do what she promised, it should have been a relief. "What am I going to do without you? I'm not ready to lead a ship, so many people have died already. Larken because I wasn't smart enough to realize he was right behind me, so many of our friends because I wasn't smart or fast enough, Boro..." The sight of the first tear falling onto her arm stopped her recount of the dead. "I've never felt so small." They kept coming, the parade of tears was on.

Sun's slender hand came to rest on her arm, and Spin leaned in, accepting her embrace. "I've never understood how you could believe you're small. I've never met anyone with a better education, who is so smart yet so kind, but you believe you're the smallest of people. If there's one thing you have to learn from me, it's that someone did that to you. Someone made you feel that way long enough so you started to believe it. You need to forget that as fast as you can. Forgive yourself for everything that didn't work out and take the straightest path to getting a cure. Any consequence you can make up for later is worth it, even a few you probably couldn't. A lot of people want to see you live a long time, because you're the most amazing person most of them have ever met, and they love you. I..."

"Sun, your shuttle just landed in Bay Three," Sharon said. "How long do you want me to tell them you'll be."

"I'll be there in three minutes," Sun said.

"All right, I'll tell them," Sharon said.

Spin wiped her tears away, more came. Her chin was tilted, up, and Sun kissed her, holding her soft lips against hers for a long time before leaning back and smiling. "I love you, Spin. I'll do what you're too kind to. I'll save you if I can, so we can be like sisters again."

Sun added a pair of tears to Spin's deluge, which she caught with hooked fingers before leaving the embrace entirely. "I..." the word came as a desperate creak. "I'll see you again," she managed more gracefully.

The flap on top of Sun's rucksack was drawn down, sealing, she put it over her shoulder, and smiled at Spin. "You will, Spin. Just remember: you saved us, now it's time to save yourself."

FOUR

The dimmed lights in the large tactical control room aboard the Lux Royal Fleet ship, Queen's Pride, helped the analyst group Gavin and Skylar belonged to watch their holographic displays for more information. They weren't close enough to the exit point of their wormhole to gather any significant data, but they watched nonetheless, at a loss for words. "Begin final stage deceleration," the voice of their master, Prince Connor Lux, commanded from where he sat one deck up on the bridge. "As we enter this battle, we must keep in mind that we are acting on the ideas offered by Countess Valona Tineau Danti. I'd like this to be a reminder to my officers, as well as all the constructs and volunteers serving under them that great minds can be found amongst those who are less than us. Her love of her own synthetics inspired her to petition the Royal Family to join her. I also love my companions, high and low, so I took that idea and developed it into a plan that may well save the galaxy. From such a small seed planted by a distant relative, I will grow a new era of peace and prosperity that will begin today. Still, I beg of you: when you are enjoying your good lives, thank my father and mother, me, but also the Countess. Now we fight. Powerfully and with great skill. Remember your training."

It wasn't his most inspirational speech, but it was a welcome distraction from the rumbling of the deck and the distant roar of the engines. The dampeners could barely keep up, but none were failing.

Skylar, his counterpart and the love of his life, looked at him nervously. "I hate combat deceleration," she whispered as she gripped the arms of her chair.

A lock of Skylar's curly blonde hair came loose from her bun and fell into her face. The deceleration was a little unnerving to Gavin as well, but he'd never let her see it. He offered her his hand and she took it, interlocking her fingers with his and squeezing for a moment. You weren't supposed to feel so much as a tiny bump or gravity anomaly aboard the larger ships, with combat deceleration being the exception.

They were about to emerge in the Geist System, not on its edge, but near Planet Sa-Hadin. The gold bracer on Gavin's wrist lit up for half a second. A new computer system must have tried to connect to it. "We're almost out," he said, looking at the secondary holographic display in front of him.

Combat deceleration was always a gamble. You were betting that the navigation staff and their systems could determine the last possible instant to begin decelerating as hard as the ship was able before emerging into normal space from the mouth of a wormhole. If an engine failed, the wormhole changed or their calculations were off, they could all end up skipping out of the wormhole at a speed that the ship couldn't handle. Their mass would suddenly increase unevenly - higher at the front since it emerged first - and the ship could collapse onto itself then continue moving at an incredible speed. Even if the ship survived, the people inside would have to deal with normal space deceleration at speeds that would cause time to move very differently for them as opposed to the rest of the universe. That is, until they could get another wormhole open. Other things could happen to ruin their day thanks to Wormhole Combat Deceleration Manoeuvres, but those were the examples Gavin knew were on Sky's mind. Her fear began when the entire Royal Fleet eschewed artificial intelligences with higher independent functions. Something about trusting the calculations to old fashioned programs and humans made it terrifying for her.

The crossing to Geist was one of the best times they'd ever had. They were synthetic constructs. Ordered by the Prince himself, Gavin and Skylar were designed along with several hundred of his bridge staff and companions. After a wonderful childhood with others of their kind, they'd grown into a young adolescent pair, separated only for a year where they received harsh military training, then brought back together when they came of age to be married. The week and a half long journey to Geist from the Celestial Core, where their King and Queen reigned, was their working honeymoon.

It was the first time Gavin and Skylar had private time together that wasn't stolen or taken knowing that there would be punishment later. They weren't alone. A hundred fifty-seven other pairs were aboard as well, celebrating their new unions in quarters made for the new couples. Only eleven of them were married by the Prince himself, however, marking them as friends and preferred companions.

There were three balls, several special dinners hosted by His Highness, and a few late-night events that were fairly private affairs with a very limited list of participants. They were invited to and attended almost all of them. They only attended one late-night, private party, and while it was a feast for their eyes, Gavin and Skylar preferred to be intimate in private, and retreated before they found themselves invited to participate by name.

Being alone with Skylar, not being told that their time had a purpose for most of that week and a half was like reaching the promised land. They were free to celebrate, love, speak about whatever they liked, and even argue more than once. Away from the expectations of their Prince, and with only three shifts to serve at their stations on the bridge the whole time, Gavin knew he'd never forget it. There was something they spoke about once in the middle of the night, when the lights were low and they drank cold, bubbly Crystal Shimmer that he knew would come up again. "How do you think normal people feel when they find someone?" Sky asked.

Gavin recalled how she snuggled against him, unmindful of where the sheets did and didn't fall. "You mean people who weren't designed for each other?"

She nodded, covering her nose and mouth as she almost silently let a burp slip and snickered at herself. The carbonation in Crystal Shimmer made it a near certainty that they'd both burp at least a few more times before the expensive bottle was gone. The gas in the bubbles was part of how the joy inducing inebriant was delivered.

"It can't be easy to find someone who's right for you if there's no designer making it happen," Gavin said.

"But how do you think that feels? Finding someone to love when there are billions of people across the stars but no one made for you?"

"I never thought about it," Gavin said. "I've always been for you. What do you think it's like?"

"I hope it's a celebration. So many of the songs you brought back from your training year were about love."

"The best ones were always by normal humans," he agreed. "You'd think it would be the opposite. I know I could have written you a thousand songs the year we were apart. Some of us tried to write music for our partners at night, but it was never as good as the old songs, from before people were made, from when they were just born."

"You didn't try to write me a song?" she asked. Her blue eyes were expectant, but she was poised to tease, not about to be disappointed if he told her he didn't.

"I started a few times. Then they told us that if we trained harder, scored higher, we could see our partners earlier, so I had hope, and sometimes having it wasn't enough. Sometimes I had to do something with it, like sing, or write really bad lyrics."

"There were lyrics?"

"They were really bad, I deleted them, sorry."

"That's okay. Are you sure you don't remember any?"

"Not right now, it could be the bubbles, though."

"They gave us false hope in the camp too. There was even a board in our barracks marking how many hours we knocked off the end of our training. They kept it up right until one of us reached our early exit time, then they found a reason to cancel it so we would have to keep training."

Gavin knew that pain, the same was done to all the male trainee constructs. "It was one of their tests, to see how quickly we recovered after disappointment. I tried to escape the night I found out I wouldn't see you early."

"You didn't!" she said. "Why haven't you told me until now?"

"It's a bit embarrassing, I guess. I stole a stunner, used it on three guards and slipped into a service bot corridor. When they caught me, I was over the line, off the base and in the forest."

"You got out?" Skylar asked, surprised and excited.

"I did, but it was another trick. They showed us a spot on the map on day one, told us it was the women's training centre, but you weren't even on the same planet."

"I know, I did a flyby when I was cleared for solo flight. I was put under supervision and given extra duty for a month, but I told you about that. I wasn't the only one, either. What punishment did you get when they caught you?"

"My commander crushed this hand," he said, raising his right arm, flexing his fingers. "I had to spend three days in our hot box and then I was on probation until the end. I thought it was embarrassing."

"No, it's romantic," Skylar told him then, punctuating it with a kiss. "You couldn't stand being away from me."

"I never could."

"If we're ever separated like that again, I'll be the one who gets away and finds you." It wasn't flippant talk, but a real promise made by her serious blue eyes.

"We'll find each other like everyone in those love songs." Then he told her something that they used to have to say in secret when they were growing up together. "We belong to each other first." Thanks to their new privacy, they could say it without being punished for claiming that they were owned by anyone other than the Prince. They said it often.

That isn't to say that they didn't love Prince Connor or believe in his cause. They were about to arrive in the Geist System so he could recapture lost technology that would allow his synthetics followers to improve their lives. Gavin knew that the Prince was also after technology for faster travel, communication, and looking to claim several manufacturing stations in orbit for himself. Most of them made fabrication technology that was used in ship yards across the galaxy, making them some of the most important technological sites in the known universe.

The brave Prince would have to lead his people in a fight against the artificial intelligences that had a firm hold on the Geist system and avoid angering the Issyrian civilization that dwelled on the planet. It was a worthy cause, making the galaxy safe against the threat in the Geist system and enabling thousands of industries to flourish once the macro fabrication systems could be made and sold again.

Despite those higher causes, Gavin and Skylar focused most on the possibility that they could have a child of their own once they found the genetic keys that would allow their master to make them fertile. It was a dream that was so precious that they avoided speaking about it.

The deck stopped shaking. They let each other's hands go as holographic displays populated with clearer data, more data than they were able to gather while they were in the wormhole. "Sa-Hadin is completely shielded," Skylar said from her Science Station. "Planetary shield, combat grade, several thousand projection sites on the surface, they are not at risk nor are they accessible."

Gavin looked at the holographic image of the space surrounding their ship. His fellow tactical analyst, Toby, to his left marked the target he was scanning: it was a massive manufacturing base in orbit around the blue-green planet called Iron Haven. "Registering little significant movement aboard the nearest station. First scans indicate that the main manufacturing systems are powered down, the biological fabrication and development labs are inactive as well. Taking further scans." He announced.

"Gavin, report," ordered Prince Connor in his ear. He was sitting on the bridge upon a white seat gilded with gold. His pale face was locked in a stern expression.

Gavin continued analysing what he saw. There were thousands of hulks, chunks of hull, ruins of ships all around their battle group. Finding out what destroyed them was his duty. Vivien, a synthetic who was also favoured by His Majesty, was taking care of identifying the ruined hulls.

"One moment, Your Majesty," Gavin plead as he discovered hundreds of tiny latch marks on one large section of hull plating. There were burn marks adjacent to them. He was pleased with himself as he found a longer, incomplete cut made by a particle weapon along another hull fragment. Then he spotted a highly prized sign of damage. "There is an enemy ship in the area that is capable of launching focused antimatter attacks. That is most likely how the larger ships entering this area were destroyed."

"Confirming! I see antimatter damage on three hull segments," announced Vivien.

Their scanners swept into a new arc from their port side and Gavin felt as though the blood drained from his face as he saw evidence of thousands of dead ships. "We're in a graveyard," Toby said under his breath.

As he saw it happening, Gavin announced; "I have five battleships powering up and signals from several hundred small ships hiding in the debris."

"Twenty-eight destroyers, beneath us, marked on tactical," Vivien announced.

"Machines are patient," the Prince said. "We knew they'd be lying in wait. Alert all commands. Move ahead in box formation, launch all alert fighters and gunships." He ordered. "I do not celebrate the things we will have to do to end this war, but I will bring it to an end nevertheless."

Gavin was relieved as he watched their battlegroup of carriers, destroyers, fast corvettes, frigates and heavy battleships move into formation in perfect synchronicity. Smaller ships started launching, and he almost wished he was aboard one of those gunships, bravely charging against the worst enemy of their time. This was a war brought about by badly misguided artificial intelligence. It would end thanks to the genius and resolve of constructs: perfected humans the rest of the galaxy called dolls.

FIVE

"Aux Panicia?" Boro asked. "We're inside British Alliance space? What the hell for?" he was digging inside an access hatch, up to his elbows, cutting with a high-powered particle beam tool.

"I suppose you wouldn't remember," Aldo said, watching the pilot's station. They were minutes from emerging into normal space. The thick-bodied man he rescued had a lot of questions, some of them verified something Aldo suspected. The torture system Master Kort used was so severe that new memories were difficult for the subjects to hold. That should end, if his theory was right. "The Countess sent Master Kort on an errand to recapture Aspen and Larken. Last we saw, they were headed for British Alliance territory. I rescued you because we were nearing the end of the crossing."

"I remember now," Boro said, prying a small metal box loose with a final jerk then handing it to Aldo. "The last tracker aboard this heap."

"Wasn't it wired into something important?" Aldo faintly

remembered hearing one of the other guards explaining why Kort's carrier didn't see regular ship thefts.

"Oh, communications, the Navnet receiver, nothing I can't wire back up in a tic." Boro had a way of reassuring people, a warm smile that Aldo had only seen a few times, but it grew on him fast. "We'll be pinging and ponging again in a moment."

The armour fit Boro, but it didn't look right on someone so squat and wide. It looked like the man grew up on a high gravity world, but his file didn't have any details about that. He might have been genetically unlucky instead. A peek at the communications panel to his right filled Aldo with quiet alarm. Whereas before it displayed wave forms and other signals that were always present in the background, all the windows on the display either said; NO SIGNAL or NO DATA. He was no pilot, but even Aldo knew that they would be at risk if they emerged from the mouth of their wormhole and couldn't communicate with Navnet at least so they could be assigned a safe course.

Boro grumbled more and more as he fiddled inside the bowels of the ship from where he sat on the floor. After a while he leaned in so far that his head almost disappeared into the small hatch. "Goddammit!" he exclaimed, holding his hand out to Aldo. "I'll be needing that back."

"The tracker?"

Boro's hand beckoned urgently. "Aye, quick now."

Aldo dropped it into his palm and watched as Boro hurriedly rewired it in. The communications panel started showing all the normal signals again. "It's not just a tracker, there's a repeater inside that the antenna needs. Without a repeater to replace it, the signals aren't strong enough to get to the computer. I could try to wire a little computer up, but unless you've got software that's compatible with the antenna and can do everything we need a communications system to do, that would be pointless."

"Oh, so when we land..."

"We may as well send a flare up telling that whoreson where to find us," Boro said, popping the access panel back into place and returning to the pilot's seat. "How much money do you have? I'm broke."

"You didn't have anything saved when you were captured?" Aldo said, noticing that they were about to come out of their wormhole.

"Listen, I fix ships, I make brand new parts from raw materials that are so good that they'd rather pay my price than order replacements from the manufacturer. Problem is; I'm shit with money. I have money, see something I like, then I have that pretty thing in my hand with no jingle left in my pocket. Half the time what I buy isn't for myself either, so I typically don't have much to show for it."

"How can you live with no money?" Aldo asked, truly mystified. He opened his first credit account when he was five years old. By the time he entered the Mercenary Service Academy at twelve, he already had thousands thanks to relatives sending him gifts of cash for birthdays and graduations. By the time he was finished training at sixteen he knew how to live within his means and he never ran out of money. He wasn't wealthy, but he always had work and the question of where his next meal would come from was never fearfully pondered. "I mean, you just decide some of your money isn't for spending and set it aside."

"I guess I'm more interested in using what I have the day I have it instead of betting on a future that might not happen. Tried saving up for a ship once, but emergencies always came along." They emerged from the wormhole, Boro signalled Navnet, and had a course a moment later.

"The British Alliance would like to welcome you to Aux Panicia station. Please see the social, commerce and trade boards for your needs before contacting the Station Help Department."

Boro tapped his credentials into a floppy display page he found in the back and exclaimed; "What?"

"What? Did they beat us here? What's going on?"

"Well, they didn't," Boro said. "It's going to take them a few hours to turn around and get here if they care about us at all." He closed the window he was looking at and started scrolling through ship listings. "Seems my old captain was skimming off the top, ripping his crew off, and that glorious girl Aspen transferred a share of those ill-gotten coins to the crewmembers, dead and alive. She probably thought my next of kin would eventually get it after I didn't access my account for a while."

"So, you *do* have money," Aldo said. "You know, I could help you manage it, I'm quite good. I've doubled my savings using a diverse investment strategy."

Boro fixed him with a withering look. "Might as well propose marriage, lad, you'd have a better chance at becoming my husband than getting your hands on my account."

Aldo couldn't help but chuckle at the notion of the pair of them in tuxedos in front of an altar or a court room. "No problem, I understand. Just try not to let it all slip through your fingers at once."

"Working ship, only eighteen years old," Boro said to himself as he looked at a refurbished courier ship. It's grey and blue hull was shaped to look quick, and it seemed like it was one third thruster at least. "It's on station, he's offering a full load of supplies, fuel and its flight ready, certified by the British Transport Authority. This is what we need."

"It's one point four million credits," Aldo said, making sure that the autopilot was engaged since Boro seemed fully invested in buying a new ship instead of flying the one they had. "Maybe I could go in on it with you? I could contribute about two hundred fifty thousand credits."

"Sorry, that really would be a marriage. Being a stakeholder in a beauty like this is definitely not something you should take lightly. This one's mine. Besides, it's a wee ship. Room for six passengers and a captain."

"Don't you want to see it first?" Aldo asked as he saw the buy button scroll into view.

"It's been certified. The worst thing we'll find in there is a strange smell. Besides, we need to ditch this stolen shuttle the moment we land. Mark it for scrap and pay the station to get it drifted. You can pay the fee for that if you want. It's only two thousand credits."

"Drifting a ship into the sun is two thousand?"

"Oh, no, that's not even legal. They drift them for pickers to catch on the edge of the system."

"This is Aux Panicia Control, my name is Elsie, welcome to the system. I see you're looking for an interior landing spot?"

"Hello Elsie," Boro said in an extra kind tone. "I'd actually like any port or landing pad that's available. We're escaping captivity, you see. I have a slave mark from House Danti. I'm sending you my ident. My companion is the fellow who freed me, a guard who is on the run from the same house. He's sending you his ident now too."

"Thank you, Boro," Elsie said. "We're looking that up now."

Boro muted their end and smiled at Aldo. "Now, we might be screwed. From what I've heard, the British bureaucracy is so thick, we could be here for hours."

"Boro?" Elsie asked.

"Yes, my dear," he replied, unmuting himself.

"I see your slave mark here, and there's already a bounty on the unregulated Stellarnet for you and the fellow who freed you. Since it looks like you will have to keep moving, I can grant you asylum in British Alliance space as long as you agree to abide by all our laws."

"I agree," Boro said. "So, we can land at the pad you've high-lighted right away, I can buy this Rapid Courier ship I've got my eye on, and we can be gone a minute later?"

"Yes, unless you'd like to apply for protective custody, which will take a few hours, then you won't be able to move freely, but our people will take care of you for a limited time. Normally it's a few months until you've been relocated and hidden. Oh, and I see the ship you are buying comes with the ticket you need to get to work right away as a freelance courier, congratulations. Would you like me to link you up to the jobs database so you can start right away?"

Boro's thin film display lit up green and Aspen's image appeared. Her name had changed to Spin, and she wasn't smiling in the image, but it was definitely her. He boggled at it as the words; IN RANGE appeared under her ident. It meant that she was so close that she would receive any message he sent within an hour. "Oh, I've got something I need to take care of first, thank you though."

"All right, you may proceed to Bay Nineteen where you will be landing on Pad Three."

"Best to you and yours," he said, closing the communication. The round outer ring of the station loomed large as Boro took the controls for a moment, bringing the ship's relative speed up as high as port control would allow. When they were within two kilometres of the broad landing bay, the station took control of their ship. Boro slipped out of his seat, and as Aldo started to do the same the man shook his head, drawing the weapon he'd stolen from the corpse on the deck. "Oh, no, Aldo. I thank you for freeing me, but you're staying right here. If you're running some plan where you follow me to Aspen then report to Kort, then you should thank me. I'd space you and let you drift off with a slow leak in your suit before I let you near her. If you really are only interested in saving me, and Kort's got new hate for you because of it, then my heart goes out to you. If anyone knows what it's like to help someone out and get fucked in return, it's me."

"Now, wait!" Aldo struggled to find anything to say that would convince him that he wasn't still loyal to Kort.

"Oh, no," Boro said, waving the gun. "I'll leave you everything here except this gun, this lovely armoured suit I'm wearing, and you can use that money you saved up to buy a little ship to skip away in."

"Boro! I'm dead if you leave me here," Aldo plead. "You can put a control collar on me, chip my heart, put me in shackles if you want. Just don't leave me here alone. I've got a little money, sure, enough so I'm never a burden to you, but house Danti could have that cut off any second so I have to turn that into platinum as soon as I can. That's where Kort will be watching for me; the exchanges. From where I come from, you're a slave. Now I'm here and my freedom's gone because I couldn't stand watching Kort torture you anymore. If anyone here finds out I had a part in handling slaves, and they will, I won't last a day on this station."

Boro let his head droop and sighed. "This is not a smart move," he muttered.

"C'mon, you're a good person, I know it. You won't leave me here alone."

"Fine!" Boro said. "But I'm going to watch all your transmissions."

"No problem."

"Lock you in your cabin at night."

"I would do the same."

"You're going to be deep-scanned whenever I feel like it to make sure you're not carrying any devices."

"I'll be cancerous by the twentieth scan!"

"Okay, no..."

"Fine! Fine! Just let me take the prevention meds."

"All right, then," Boro said. "Oh, and you're my crewman. You do what I tell you and don't complain."

"That's fair," Aldo said, relieved. Being under Boro's microscope was better than being in Kort's chair.

SIX

The dimly lit science, tactical and scanning section of His Majesty's flagship was filled with the sound of an object bashing against their armoured hull. "Lengthwise impact, enemy battle-cruiser six-thirty has collided with the dorsal section of our ship and is ejecting its antimatter pods. Construction bots are catching them and carrying them clear."

Damage control and interior operations teams shouted back and forth in their section several metres away. Even Gavin could see the damage on his instruments. The enemy ship was dead, but it had performed its function: to open a crack in the hull of the Queen's Pride, His Majesty's flagship. The sidearm at his hip activated, a sign that ship security detected a number of intruders greater than they could reasonably expect to repel without the crew's help. It was his worst nightmare; watching robots tear Skylar then himself apart. "Robots are aboard," Gavin muttered to himself, breaking into a sweat.

Skylar touched his hand. "We know how to kill them, we

practiced. It's going to be all right. We're almost at the main hub."

He tried to concentrate on the status of the enemy ships moving to surround the nine vessels left in the massive Royal Fleet. There were still hundreds of drones, they'd destroyed well over ten thousand as a fleet but it cost them over a hundred ships including the Fair Child Juggernaut, their largest combat vessel. It was swarmed by everything the machines had to throw at it after its main weapon - a hyper-kinetic railgun launching an antimatter pod - destroyed the five largest defence platforms in the system. They managed to destroy two more installations before the swarm of robots disabled their engines. They intentionally breached their antimatter containment and took thousands of fighting drones as well as thirty-three enemy ships with them in a white flash. It was a quick, glorious end, Gavin should have been proud. The commanders were constructs like him and Skylar but trained from childhood for war. Their sacrifice was nothing but heroic, it gave the remainder of the fleet the opening that they took advantage of to get to the main hub, where he and Skylar determined the attack drones were made by the hundred and new ships were designed. With the help of their intelligence team, they hacked in for three seconds. It was long enough to see that there was a command key inside, one made for only a human to use. The base still had an operating system that recognized a human's authority. They only needed to get their ships close enough so they could cover their raider teams while they took a shuttle across. A new fight would begin.

"Attention, crew: we are changing our tactics," Prince Connor announced. He appeared in a small window on everyone's console, bravely observing and directing the action from his white and gold command seat. "We pursue this course but will employ tactic set Three Dash One."

To Gavin's relief, it was one of the backup tactics that meant that he and Skylar continued sitting in the safe data collection and analysis section of the bridge. Their jobs changed a little. His holographic display showed a detailed tactical map that highlighted all enemy ships that were in range of their main weapons as well as their backup electromagnetic pulse system. Gavin looked at Skylar's console, which changed to focus on the looming star base. They launched drones, the Queen's Pride, the three heavy carriers and five battlecruisers that accompanied it fired their main weapons at it, destroying most of the drones and eating away at the station's shields. It was the Genesis Monolith, probably named by some egotistical designer or corporate leader.

Her secondary task was to help determine when it was safe for combat shuttles to make the crossing to the station. Safe was a relative term, though. It was the difference between being immediately annihilated and having a one in three chance of making it, where the soldiers would have to fight for their lives as soon as they touched down or docked at an airlock.

"First shuttles, launch on my mark," Skylar said. "Mark."

Fourteen shuttles launched from the front of their reduced fleet at great speed, three were blasted into tiny particles of shrapnel right away.

An alert came up on Gavin's screen, telling him that the main electromagnetic pulse power reserve was past eighty five percent charge. "Powering all lifeboats and non-critical systems down. Warning to all crew: secondary control systems will no longer be on standby. They are now powered down and disconnected." They were preparations he had to make so the ship could use its hull to conduct a massive electromagnetic pulse. Many of their systems would require repair afterwards, but the ones he powered down would be fine after any size pulse because they were isolated, shielded. Once the pulse went off, they could turn the secondary control systems back on and the Queen's Pride would still be viable. If the worst were to happen, and they had to abandon ship, the lifeboats would still work as well. He hoped that the electromagnetic pulse systems' capacitors were being charged for some other purpose, to create a spare reserve perhaps, because he dreaded the idea of being left in the dark even if it would only be for a minute. There were too many robots outside, and some were inside the ship.

He opened a new holographic window and checked on the status of their internal security. All thirty-five teams were active and repelling boarding drones. He checked the footage of four soldiers. Three were firing at a group of robots, there had to be at least nine or ten from what he could see. They were winning, the narrow-bodied drones were bottlenecked so their long, spider-like appendages couldn't help them, and only three or four could fire at once. They were several frames forward from the breach; a bad sign. The drones were making progress towards the ship's command centre.

Gavin squirmed in his seat and covered his mouth as he watched one of the soldiers get caught by two long, rope-like silver appendages and get drawn into the group of robots. They didn't shoot him, that would have been a waste of energy. Instead, cutters went to work on his armour for only a few seconds, then sharp grippers slipped into the chinks they made. The soldier's screams filled Gavin's ears. He shook his head;

"No, no, no, no, no," he muttered as he watched the bots effortlessly pull his legs and arms out of their sockets with loud pops, then yank as though they were playing tug-of-war until they separated from his body. They left his head attached, blasted him with cauterizing flames and injected him with quick efficiency. "They're keeping them alive," Gavin said, starting to rock in his seat. "Why are they keeping them alive?"

Sky cupped his chin in her hand, deactivated his interior display. "They are doing their duty," she said sternly. "Stay with us, Gavin. We need you."

"Proximity warning, abandon the main command section im..." Prince Connor said.

Gavin and Skylar looked at the small display of His Majesty in his command seat in time to witness large arms ripping the plating above him open with a jerk. The scream of the metal tearing was so loud that it was distorted in their ears. The bot that broke through burst open along the bottom, releasing an uncountable number of small robots with pincers, clamps, welders and cutters that swarmed the Prince. They clasped to his arms, his legs, his torso, driving manipulators into and through him, pinning him to his gilded command seat. Several more split away, attacking the main bridge crew who were trying to maintain control of the ship while firing at their attackers. Gavin immediately felt selfish for being relieved that the Prince was one full deck above them, but that didn't compare to the fear that threatened to overtake him.

A round robot descended onto the Prince's head, clamping to his skull above the ears before sealing to his scalp. The Prince screamed inhumanly, kicking even as the other robots were making a sport of cutting him open, tearing everything but his body apart. It was savage, not calculated. The top of the round robot opened. The Prince's scalp and the top of his skull were discarded before it closed again. "It's stealing the Prince's brain," Toby said in horror.

Gavin chuckled and clamped his hand to his mouth. 'His Majesty's brain,' it sounded hilarious for some reason. "His Royal grey matter," he muttered, a giggle bubbling up. The Prince stopped screaming, his body went limp, and all the robots on him split up, rushing to finish the rest of the bridge crew off with more efficiency. When the round one drifted back up to the larger machine that brought it there, Gavin saw that the Prince's head was indeed empty.

An alarm went off inside their section, the lights turned red. Gavin's displays changed, giving him control over the electromagnetic pulse weapon aboard. "Gavin!" Skylar shouted, trying to bring him back to his senses. Their Prince was gone, the ship was failing, the robots were coming and they were going to die. What was the point?

"Gavin! Activate the EMP! They're going to kill us!" Skylar's blue eyes became his focus as she turned his head towards her. *They're going to kill her.* He thought to himself. He looked to his panel and saw that the electromagnetic weapon was at ninety-seven percent charge, it was more than enough to disable anything within fifty thousand kilometres that wasn't disconnected from active systems and heavily shielded. He entered his code and activated the electromagnetic weapon.

The lights went out.

SEVEN

The joy of being accepted by a government as large as the British Alliance was drained by drab waiting rooms and certification check points. Spin had the longest amount of processing to go through. The first waiting room was a white floored, navy blue walled room that was wide enough for people to walk through the middle aisle with a row of chairs on either side.

It was easily thirty metres long, and localized audio that projected directly at each person told them what their spot in line was and when to move up to the next room. Spin's entire crew, with the exception of the Governor, who was on watch aboard the ship, were sitting together. The support and hibernation box containing the mind of Dorian, an old friend of his who needed a new body. It was in stasis, but he'd filled all the paperwork for his boxed companion with the help of the Governor, who was the guide for the entire ship's application process. He filed his own as an applicant with special circumstances so he could answer questions from the ship while he was on watch.

After half an hour in the first waiting room, they were all called to the second. Everyone was dressed in environment suits and cleaned up. Spin didn't know what to expect in the refugee processing centre. It was much calmer than she thought. The city of Olm was a series of tall, fin-like buildings that were pointed into the planet's winds. All able to turn slightly when the wind changed with the season. High levels of sulphur and a mixture of acidic gasses were in the air, so they were lucky to land inside a docking bay.

Most of the refugees were human, and the waiting room was quiet but busy. They were part of a large group that were moving up, sent through a set of old double doors, down a hallway with no windows, to another waiting room. "Oh, cool, a view," Della said as she moved to the broad window. Spin, Nigel, Sharon, Leland, and Mirra joined her. Wind drove rain between the tall fin shaped buildings as light from the east, where the clouds parted created shifting rainbows for a moment before the light disappeared. Heavy, square hover ships moved small mountains of glistening stone to the edge of the city, dumping their loads into a processing chute where people in suits that looked like tiny miniatures in scale held devices up. "It's beautiful, even in the dark." Della said.

"Too bad the acid rain would strip us to the bone in seconds if we went outside without a suit," Sharon said, sitting down, ignoring the view.

"Downer," Della sighed, staring through the window.

"Thank you for getting me here," Spin said. The waiting room was filling up, a hundred red seats in back to back rows waited for refugees. "I had faith that you wouldn't hate each other by the end of the voyage, and I'm glad I was right."

Nigel turned around and slid down into the seat. "Don't know if that's true," he said quietly. "Some of us aren't sticking around."

"Hey, I said I'd talk to her about it, not actually leave," Della said.

"It always sounded like you were leaning towards leaving the crew." The way he shrugged made Nigel look like he'd already argued with her about it so many times that the topic exhausted him. "You kept telling me you weren't much use aboard, and I kept telling you everyone wants you on the crew, that you're worth a share, but I could never convince you, so I guess you're going, right?"

There was the real argument, the one they had in private. The argument everyone thought they were having about Nigel having a new toy was only what people thought the cause of the drama was. Spin could see it in the faces of everyone around. It looked like they'd never heard them talk about this, especially Mirra, who seemed surprised but worked to regain an unaffected expression.

Spin thought for a moment as Della stared at Nigel, and Nigel looked at the floor. "Did you learn about the ship while we made the crossing?" Spin asked Della.

"I shadowed Nigel as much as I could while I kept cleaning with Mirra and cooked for everyone. I got some gun simulation time in too. I just don't know if that's really useful. You can find a dumb bot to clean, a processor to cook, and there are better gunners."

Spin took in the quiet stares of the crew. Mirra was still trying to figure out what to say, Leland was watching the discussion, Sharon was looking away, listening but pretending like none of it affected her. There was something there, though; an intentional iciness that told Spin that their new pilot did have an opinion but she didn't want to share it. Spin suspected that Sharon didn't want Della to leave either, none of them seemed to. "None of those things would add up to who you are," Spin said. "So, there's that, but I'm wondering if there's a reason you want to leave. Are you afraid that where I'm going may be dangerous? That's justified."

"No, well, a little, yes," Della replied. "Not enough to leave, though. I thought that, since I'm no good with a gun, and I don't actually know how to fix much, I might just be in the way."

"You've never been in the way," Mirra said. "If you have a problem, it's that you consider others before yourself too much."

"That's not true. I can be as selfish as anyone else."

Nigel and Mirra both scoffed at Della's remark. Spin took the opportunity to break back into the conversation. "If you have to go for any reason, I understand. You have enough money to set yourself up somewhere, and I didn't expect everyone to stay when we got here. You're free, we're all free, so who am I to hold you back? If the question is if I need you, well I think the longer you spend with us, the more I will."

"She comes to the bridge and does puzzles for hours," Sharon said. "She says she's reading the news, but I checked. They're technical troubleshooting problems. Some of them for the Convoy King, our ship. Sometimes it takes her a while, but she's pushing Training Level Three. I needed to go to college to get that far."

"Why didn't you tell me?" Nigel asked.

"I wanted to finish the courses first. There are nine levels, you don't have to be a genius to get through the third one."

"You have to be really smart to do it without any help or tutorials, and you haven't used the help system at all," Sharon said. "Don't sell yourself short."

"Well, sure, but I didn't think it would be worth telling anyone about it unless I made it to at least level six. I was really just having fun."

"Troubleshooting a starship is your idea of fun?" Mirra laughed. "That's amazing, engineering problems are your brain teasers."

"Okay," Spin said, smiling a little. All eyes were on her and Della. "Let's put that aside for a minute. "Every ship needs a Della. Usually the crew calls him Cookie, or Mother Goose, or Den Mother. If any of you want to leave because you want to get started on your life, that's the smartest thing to do. I expect that I'm going to dangerous places. I have a search running for doll designers right now that I'm sure will lead me to some dangerous person on a dangerous planet. That's for a start. If I get what I need by chasing after designers and Geist survivors, I'll probably have to go there eventually, and the chances of survival are not good. So, go with my blessing. If your only barrier to staying is the thought that you might be useless aboard our ship, then forget it. You and Mirra take care of us. If you want to learn more, to do more aboard, then you're welcome to, but you don't have to. I don't know the ship like the rest of you, I was asleep while you made it your home, but I see you as part of this crew just as much as anyone else." Spin didn't mean for it to turn into a lecture, or a speech, but she kept finding the right words, so she kept saying them.

It almost brought Della and Mirra to tears. Nigel's eyes were brimming too. "I'm staying, then," Della said. Mirra put her arms around her from behind.

Nigel took her hand and kissed the back of it, and Leland was all smiles. Sharon was still looking away, but Spin caught her nodding. A pair of intake officers in blue, red and white uniforms approached Nigel and knelt down in front of him. "I'm sorry," one of them started in crisp English accents. "I have to ask; what do you have in that box there?"

"It's my friend, Dorian. I just arrived so I couldn't find him a body," Nigel replied.

Leland opened his mouth to explain further, but one of the officers held up her hand and shook her head. "We're talking to your friend here, you'll get your turn. Now, we're asking about your box because our scanners picked up the bio-matter inside. Is that your friend's brain in there?"

"Yes," Nigel said, starting to bristle at being spoken to like a nine-year-old holding his pet frog. "The rest didn't make it."

"Oh, I see," one officer said, looking to the other.

"Well, I can't interview *that*, now, can I?" she said, stalking off. "Get a host kit ready!" she called out.

"We only have female models, make sure it's a good match!" someone called back from behind a screen at the other end of the room.

"Do you think I can scan your box?" the officer in front of Nigel asked gently, holding a hand scanner up so he could see it.

"Go ahead," Nigel said.

"This'll take just a jiff, your friend in the box won't feel a thing, not even a little tingle," she said as she waved the hand scanner exaggeratedly. Spin found herself rolling her eyes. "Well, there we have it. A male brain, and I see his files have been put in for him to immigrate already. Uploading them in advance was very smart. Like my colleague said, we only have female bodies and they cost fifty-five thousand apiece."

"If I can get him entered into your system and cleared, I think I'd rather wait until I can get a male one," Nigel said.

"Oh, that probably won't work," the officer said, trying to deliver the bad news as gently as she could. "He can't stay in there much longer. Stasis or not, the chances of infection, rejection and damage go up the longer he's in that little box."

Nigel looked to Leland, who nodded. "Technically, it's true. It's not the best containment system. The price of the body they're offering is very good though. What kind is it?"

"It's a full biological replacement kit. She'll be capable of everything a human woman is, and though it's fibre-fabricated, it's the same quality as a high-end clone and we'll alter the DNA to match and make every other modification so there is no chance of rejection. We'll even make sure psychological rejection is impossible. I'm guessing there was some trauma involved in his... reduction, so we'll iron out all those traumatic events, correct for warrior gene defects and reduce his immediate aggression. We'll add a custom adaptation kit as well so he is less traumatized by the sudden switch to a she as well. It's all necessary, you understand. If we don't prepare and correct his mind, he could reject the body, and that'll be the end of his merry ride through life."

"So, the fifty-five thousand includes all that?" Leland asked.

"It does. You couldn't believe the condition some refugees come in. When we can't save them, we pop them into another body. It happens all the time," she replied. Still cheery.

"Do unexpected sex changes happen all the time?" Nigel asked.

"More often than I'm allowed to admit. We have to work with what's on hand, unfortunately, and there isn't another registered body shop for a few days quick travel in any direction."

Nigel thought for a moment, looking at the nondescript box, tracing the edges with his fingers. He didn't like the sound of all the mental modifications and corrections. It almost sounded like his friend wouldn't be himself at all by the end, but would it be better if he died in a box? "His personality would be really different?"

"No, his behaviour may change a little, depending on how much of it stemmed from trauma, genetic and neurological defects he was born with or picked up. If past trauma made him violent, then you'll find that lessened. If he had learning issues, you'll find those corrected as well. It's all in making sure that he's capable of accepting his new situation and compatible with the new body. Unstable personalities almost always result in transplant failure with full body replacements."

"How long before you get more male bodies?"

"Next week sometime," the officer replied.

"We could put him in a better stasis box?" Nigel asked, looking to Leland.

"The risk gets bigger with every transfer."

"He'll look great, and the new body will have all the functions - beating heart, breathing - you know, the feeling of being alive."

"No enhancements, though?"

"Oh, you're in the wrong place for that. The new body is a

bit more durable, but there's not much in the way of extra strength, built in computers or special vision like you see sometimes."

After another moment of hesitation, Nigel handed her the box and cringed as she walked away. "Oh, he's gonna be so mad."

"He'll be alive," Leland said, supressing a smirk.

An alert beep sounded in Spin's ear. "Please report to interview cubicle fifteen. That is through the door on your right," a voice said through the directed audio.

"Looks like I'm up, I'll meet you back at the shuttle," Spin told her crew.

EIGHT

All around Gavin and Skylar the light strips built into the crew uniforms activated, surrounding everyone in their own eerie blue glow. Gavin, Skylar, Toby and Vivien were the exceptions. They'd all reprogrammed their emergency lighting to stay off.

Instead, their hoods closed over their heads. Built in goggles slipped into place, and their suits sealed. No one needed lights to see, they used a multi-sensor system to create an image in their goggle displays that accurately showed them what was going on. "We have to run," Gavin said, his head was starting to clear.

"We have escape options," Vivien said, nodding, getting up from her scanning station.

"There are armed lifeboats one level down." Skylar stood with Gavin and took his hand. Her sidearm was already in the other hand. The screams from the front of the scan and control bridge were getting louder. "Are you all right?" she asked him.

"I'm back, lost it for a minute there, but I'll be okay," Gavin said, following Toby as he and Vivien led their way towards the back of the bridge processing pit.

"There's an emergency hatch past the last station," he said.

Looking away from everyone else, Gavin took a moment to steady himself. It was the shock of watching the battle turn on them that broke his resolve, but if training taught him anything, it was that you had to recover. Recover or die. People were dying less than fifty metres away. There was no time for panic or weakness. He had the benefit of honed survival instincts. He released Skylar's hand and drew his own sidearm as they caught up to Toby and Vivien.

A red handle at the end of the processing pit where they were sitting was barely visible, but Vivien pulled it as though she'd been staring at it for whole shifts. A hatch opened, the door sliding up against the ceiling. Several crewmembers in their glowing suits dropped in behind them, rushing to catch up, but Toby, Vivien, Gavin and Skylar didn't wait, rushing through the short L shaped corridor in a careful rush. They didn't know if there were other breaches, with the ship sensors down, there was no way to tell.

At the end of the corridor they opened another hatch and emerged into one of the main hallways running along the outer hull of the Queen's Pride. Gavin was running the image of their marines getting pulled apart by the invading robots. The robots were organized, but they weren't perfect. They tore people apart as though they enjoyed it, or as if they were looking for something inside their bodies. Tactically, that was a foolish thing to do. It left openings, slowed the attack. The same could be said of the attack on their Prince. The robots made sure there was an absolutely overwhelming force in place and that he was already suffering major physical trauma before they committed to taking their prize; his brain. It was grisly but telling. The robots weren't taking trophies; they were after data.

"Whatever the Prince knew, the machines will know soon," Gavin said. "They're going to scan him."

"It takes hundreds of hours to perform a deep scan on someone's brain, especially when they've just suffered a traumatic event, and I think what happened to His Highness qualifies," Toby said.

"Not if they have the processing power to scan several times and analyse the results in parallel," Gavin said.

"He's right," Skylar agreed. "We have to make decisions knowing that the machines are aware of all our training, of what we're likely to do."

Gavin looked through the transparent hull and saw something that gave him hope. "There's an inactive section of the planetary shield. It must have been taken out by our EMP."

"I knew we kept you around for a reason, tech-head," Toby said. "That's our way out of this mess."

"There are restricted biological research facilities down there, people who go without permission don't come back," Vivien said.

"Rumours. I didn't see that in the official report. There are at least a dozen different cultures down there, nine of them are water bound. I bet they've been trapped all this time."

A hatch opened and a group of soldiers emerged in a rush, the sounds of gunfire resounding behind them. "What are you doing here?" the Sergeant asked.

Stopping in the middle of a hallway seemed more dangerous than whatever was behind that door. Simulations he participated in showed that the enemy had machines that could burn through hulls, even thick ones like on the Queen's Pride. They were three metres from a hatch hidden in the floor that would lead them to an emergency shuttle. "We had to abandon the bridge, we're getting off the ship."

"Get back up there, now! There's a team in the core trying to get the secondary systems online."

"If those systems aren't back up now, then they've already failed once. They will not get them back online in time," Gavin said. It was a guess, but he was fairly sure the Queen's Pride was either on a course to collide with the huge orbital station, or it would make it past it to continue in a rapidly decaying orbit. "This ship is finished."

"How?" the Sergeant asked. "We're holding relative position to Station Nineteen, the electromagnetic pulse took them out as far as we can tell. We need you back up on the bridge."

"I outrank you, soldier," Toby said.

"We all do," Skylar said. "You and your men will come with us down to the planet."

A read on the man's name finally appeared on Gavin's goggle display. "Sergeant Ferrier, please understand that we're all on the same mission. We've dealt a serious blow to our enemy here, one that could take them weeks to recover from. The ship is being overrun, your people in the core are probably already dead."

"Now we need to go down to the planet so a message can be sent to our people using faster than light transmission technology. Another fleet will be sent. They will finish the work here while we pursue the technology that we came for. This mission is not over, great things can still be accomplished."

The thick bulkhead door down the hall started to turn red along the edges, and the sound of an impact from the other side thundered. "My orders are to hold this level of the ship."

Vivien and Toby moved past the Sergeant. Vivien knelt down and ran her hand along a nearly invisible seam, activating an emergency panel. "We're leaving," Skylar said.

"You could come with us and be helpful. There's room for all seven of you," Gavin said.

"Or you die here," Skylar added. "Oh, and if you want to slow that down, project your personal shields from the muzzle of your weapons together, so you can create a shield wall long enough to put some distance between you and the machines."

Another heavy pound against the door resounded through the hallway, the thick metal moved a few centimetres. The machines were through, it would only be another minute or two before the door fell down and they were overrun.

Sergeant Ferrier thought for three seconds then nodded at Skylar. "Lead the way, boss."

A two-centimetre-thick hatch opened in the floor. Toby dropped inside right away as Vivien helped everyone else down. A bash at the door and the loudest clang Gavin ever heard sounded as he dropped through the hatch into the shuttle. The pair of marines who were still in the hallway above opened fire along with Vivien, who took careful shots with her sidearm. A red-hot, long spike speared through one marine while a five-fingered claw grasped the other. Vivien fired one more time and stepped over the hatch, was starting to drop when a spike was driven through her from behind.

Her eyes darted between everyone just beneath her in the shuttle; "Help me," she said the instant before the spike split into five and tore in different directions. Her legs fell through the hatch, inside the shuttle and onto Toby.

Skylar closed the hatch and Gavin dropped into the co-pilot's seat. The ship was already warming up. The sounds of scraping on the hatch behind and above them filled the cabin. "Strap in, there's no time for the dampeners to come online," Gavin announced.

"We're launching early, then?" Skylar asked, hurriedly going through the systems check.

"Early is good," Ferrier said as he strapped into the seat behind them.

"Then early it is," Gavin was pushed back into his seat, and he heard a few protests, as well as some clattering in the cabin behind him.

They were a kilometre away from the Queen's Pride in a few seconds, and Skylar increased their thrusters as the dampeners finally came online. Gavin performed a scan of their surroundings and shuddered at the condition of the Queen's Pride. The rear dorsal weapons array was active somehow, and thirty heavy antimatter pulse guns fired a storm of light at anything in range, turning smaller ships into slag. Three of the guns turned in their direction and began to fire at anything nearby. They weren't the only ones in lifeboats. Several of them were heading for the planet.

"Man, I guess you were right," Ferrier said, looking over his shoulder at the scan results. "The Queen's Pride is drifting right into Station Nineteen, and there's nothing anyone can do."

"It's slow," Gavin said, looking at several destroyer sized robot ships that were holding behind cover several kilometres away. "Something could still stop it, don't count it as a victory yet."

"I've gotta have some hope."

"Sarge," one of the soldiers behind them said, a warning in his tone. "This guy's not holding together."

A drone fighter appeared on Gavin's warning system and he set the shuttle's countermeasures on it, sending a barrage of small rounds packed with high-explosives towards it, blasting it to shreds. "They're not following us in."

"Guys," Ferrier said, unbuckling his belt, turning towards the rear of the shuttle. "Hey, it's all right. It's going to be okay."

"She was everything," Toby wept. "I just stood there and watched, and they, and they..."

Gavin looked over his shoulder in time to see Toby put the barrel of his gun in his mouth. "Toby! Stop!"

Toby looked at him, shaking with grief, closed his eyes and pulled the trigger. There was a loud hiss, a pressure alarm whistled loudly. The round went through the top of Toby's head and penetrated the thick hatch above him. "Patch kit, right there!" Gavin pointed at a box at the back of the shuttle beside the door.

"Where?" a soldier asked while everyone else stared in shock.

"Look! Beside the door, right where I'm pointing!"

The soldier looked at him then back to the door and found it right away. She got a boost from Ferrier, pulled the backing off of an emergency epoxy mesh patch and let the suction pull it into place.

A wave of fighters rushed past the ship, and Gavin scanned the area. "Ground cannons are firing to cover that new group of fighters. I see two people inside each, but they're not ours. That's a group of twenty-one of them with heavy shielding, high power ratings."

"They might by Issyrian," Ferrier said from where he held his comrade up while she checked the patch.

"No, definitely not. They don't match anything in the database and they each have two humans aboard." Several rounds struck their shuttle from behind, but their shields held.

"That's going to be a problem," Skylar said, looking through several navigational patterns and the data she needed to make re-entry without burning up.

"This is Lieutenant Gavin Oflux to whoever is firing on us from the planet. We intend no harm. Our ship was under siege, so we had to escape. We have our own supplies and equipment. We will not be a burden on you, we only need to land long enough to send a message to our people so they can rescue us. Please cover our approach if possible."

Several rounds struck a shuttle to their port side, getting through their shields, damaging the hull plating on their aft side.

"Do you have our pursuers on scans, or are they ducking behind wreckage?" Skylar asked.

"I'm marking several of them, but the fighters from the ground are taking them out fast. They're moving towards the Queen's Pride, fighting their way there." Another wave of fighters passed around them, attacking their pursuers and drawing most of them off as they moved on.

"Gavin Oflux," said a voice through their communicator. "We are giving you leave to land at the coordinates we are sending you. You have three minutes and fifty seconds. Our planetary shield will be closing. The escape vessels with you are being given similar instructions. Do not deviate from the course you are assigned or you will be destroyed. Be aware: synthetics have priority."

"Acknowledged," Gavin replied. He made sure Skylar had the course on her navigational console then added. "Thank you for safe harbour."

"Nice, it looks like our luck is turning," Ferrier said.

"Never count your blessings until you're on friendly ground," said Skylar.

NINE

The cubicles were holographic. A digital ball bounced in front of Spin's feet, leading her through corridors of walls that appeared and disappeared until she reached her destination. A door parted silently so she could see a man behind a desk who looked through a window that showed her ship docked at the station above. It still looked new, especially with the lighting they had on it, whether it was real light, or a digitally added effect, she couldn't know, and it didn't matter anyway.

"The chair isn't a hologram, have a seat," the greying British Alliance Sergeant said. "This was the Alliance's solution to the space and manpower problem," he said, gesturing all around him. "Everything was handled by artificial intelligence, so we didn't need all this space. Now that humans and grey matter power everything again, they couldn't figure out how to arrange all us intake officers efficiently, so we have artificial walls." He leaned forward nodded. "I'm Sergeant Graham Toller. Let's get started."

Over the next half hour, they went into every detail about what the ship she had was capable of, ran through a basic version of how she became captain, and what kind of work she was looking to do. He didn't care that most of her money was stolen or ill-gotten, in fact, when it looked like those details were about to come up, he simply asked; "Did it happen here?" then he'd answer his own question by quickly concluding; "If not, then that's your business. Let's move on, please."

When the issue of her being a doll came up, he nodded, smiled and said; "That's nice," and tried to continue on to the topic of her crew.

"I don't have long to live," she interjected. "Months. It's genetic programming," she said.

For the first time, sorrow creased his brow. "You're not the first I've seen," he sighed. "If you can agree that your crew are answering their intake questions honestly, then we can move on to that."

"I'll make sure," she sent a text message to everyone. 'JUST TELL THEM EVERYTHING THEY ASK ABOUT, AND DON'T VOLUNTEER EXTRA INFORMATION.'

Sergeant Toller sat down, gesturing at the desk between them so it disappeared. The only non-holographic things in the room, including the walls and ceiling, were the chairs they sat on. "I'm sorry to hear about your problem. This is grim, but who will you be leaving your ship to in the event of your passing?"

"Mirra, she's a crewmember," Spin answered without hesitation.

"I see her here. She doesn't seem to have the experience to captain a ship like that, but I'm not here to contest your decisions. I request that you file a last will and testament on your way out of the system. You can leave the qualification tickets I've assigned your ship to the new captain. That includes your passenger, cargo and defence operation tickets. They'll be able to legally perform all those trades."

"Thank you," Spin said. "I'm wondering if there's something you can do to help me find one of the researchers or genetic coders who worked in the Geist system when I was made." It was difficult for Spin to play the responsible captain, which she was doing with surprising confidence, and the vulnerable refugee doll at the same time. She watched Toller struggle with her question a little. This was a conversation he'd had before.

For all she knew, a hundred dolls and synthetic persons had come through trying to get information using every tactic she could imagine. Perhaps honesty, earnestness was the best option. "I want to know if I can have a normal life span," she said more quietly, feeling a well of emotion surge. "I'm happy we'll get to be free here, but I'd like to live long enough to be of some use."

"I understand," he said. "Dolls are different here, you have to understand. In some ways you're in the right place. The British Alliance allows the creation of dolls that are fully sentient, like you, in cases where people are going to be in extended isolation or are replacing a lost loved one. My colleague three cubicles over has a daughter who is twenty-nine years old. She serves in the military, and she's not much different from you. We have developers and programmers who still work on them. I could send you there."

"Did any of them work in the Geist System?"

"It's the same craft, but not the same attitude or purpose, so no. Geist is a haven for our enemies, where they develop technology in secret and build, well, dolls sold into slavery. I'm not going to lie to you or hoist the British flag higher than it deserves to be: we still make dolls who live up to the name. They're synthetics that don't have the intelligence or the sentient will to be free. They're a servant class for the rich, but more like simple organic androids."

Spin had met several of them in her lifetime. There really was nothing to them – just expensive showpieces that could cook, clean, and perform simple tasks – having a conversation with them was like talking to an incomplete being. It would be sad if the being wasn't perfectly happy serving. She didn't approve of them, androids were the better choice, but they weren't like her. They barely had a concept of time and sensations of pain were more of an awareness rather than something that could cause suffering. "I know them, I don't take offense. The synthetic industry is too big to prevent the development of a product."

"That's an evolved way to look at it, I suppose. Anyway, I can send you to Beta Bio, the largest research and development lab in the sector. The British Alliance has partnerships with a few corporations there. One of them does have a recent hire from the Geist System, too. They'll talk to you if I tell them you're coming, and if you give me permission to send a scan of you to them. They'll want to perform a deep scan so they can compare it to what they're doing. I'm sure they don't get many people like you from Geist while they're in their prime. In trade, I'm sure they'll tell you everything they know so you can make the right decisions for yourself going forward."

"Thank you, it's a good start," Spin said, sending him the scan she had taken shortly after she came out of necro-stasis.

He pulled slips of plastic from his pocket. "These are passes for our military wormhole generators. They'll get you where you're going faster than the drive on your ship. These are hard to come by, but I think your circumstances warrant a little accelerated transportation. It's my allotment for the week, I can only give out three."

"Thank you," she said, accepting them. "Is everything all right?" Spin asked, recognizing that there was a note of desperation in him.

"I'm all right. I only wonder; if you manage to live the rest of your life in our territory, how much will you improve things? Every industry we have – transportation, shipping, defence, manufacturing and everything else – are either just finding their feet or stretched thin. We need people like you with ships like yours. You could have a very promising future. Good luck, truly, I wish you the best."

"Thank you," Spin said, shaking his hand. Her arm computer beeped at her and looked through the transparent panel of her suit. The coordinates of the Beta Bio facility had been sent to her along with the idents of several British Intake Officers, including that of Sergeant Graham Toller.

TEN

The structures looping up from the ocean were shaped like someone froze magnetic currents. Shimmering blue, green white and red loops were ninety stories high and higher, but the windows were darkened. Landing bays that were at least large enough for three of their shuttles to land side by side were hollow holes, not showing any sign of life or activity other than the birds that nested there.

"These are advanced Issyrian dwellings," Skylar said, looking with interest. "Only a few humans have seen this, and they're not abandoned lightly. Every one of these structures comes from a massive clutch habitat under water."

"What does it say when they're empty like this?" Ferrier asked quietly.

Gavin watched Skylar, she was looking through the transparent section of hull and counting. That was only the tip of the iceberg for what was going on in her head, he was sure. There were other calculations going on. Vast knowledge she had from studying xenobiology while he focused on starship construction and xenotechnology. They earned their places in the scanning department of the Queen's Pride.

Skylar shook her head then turned her attention to a knot of white towers, all looping loosely between each other. "What is it?" Gavin asked.

"Look at those shadows." She said, tapping the passive scanner readout with her little finger. She wanted Ferrier to look at the shapes in the water, dark and bulbous, while Gavin looked at the scan results.

There was very little life in those under water clutches. Most of the signs were around them, and none of it was Issyrian. The shuttle passed over a shoreline, they were about to land inside a large spaceport shaped like a fan of shells. "What are we looking at?" Ferrier asked. "What do you think the situation is here?"

"Holy shit! Look at that!" shouted an alarmed soldier near the rear of the shuttle. A ship that was shaped like a stingray with a one-kilometre wingspan was appearing low in the sky. Its three hangars were opening as fighters launched from points along the bottom of the hull. Its skin was pearlescent, dark and shifting with the light.

"That is not an Issyrian ship. Not even by a stretch," Skylar said. "Whoever runs this part of the planet are not the original occupants."

"You're sure?" Ferrier asked.

The shuttle set down and the power systems shut down. Gavin checked to see if he could turn the computer system back on and got nothing as he tapped the corner of the display then tried the hardware switch under the console. "We might be in a power collector net," he said. "No response at all from the computer, not even from residual charge in the system. Something's drained us."

"Are you sure there are no Issyrians here?" Ferrier pressed.

"No, there could be Issyrians," Skylar answered. "But they're not living where or how they're supposed to be living, and that ship is definitely not Issyrian."

"What is it?"

The personal computer on Gavin's arm was lifeless as well. The double doors on the side of the shuttle opened, and bolts of white energy tore the first three marines to shreds. The smell of burned flesh and ozone filled the compartment. Ferrier leaned out with his rifle ready to fire. "Stop! Your rifle's battery is dead!" Gavin shouted.

As Gavin expected, Ferrier and the marine who leaned into jeopardy to fire back only emitted clicks from their rifles and were taken apart by shards of white light before they could get back under cover. Surrender was the only option. Gavin drew his sidearm and tossed it through the door, Skylar did the same. When the last marine was fired on, they were on their knees at the rear of the cockpit, their hands above their heads. The sounds of heavy feet stepping on soil as at least two people in armour approached the shuttle hatch threatened to unman Gavin, but he took a deep breath. He was supposed to be the one with more tactical training. "We surrender. There are two unarmed people inside. We have our hands up."

"Don't worry," an amplified voice said from one of the suits. "We are all Synthetics here. Welcome. Come out, please."

The hangar they landed in was enormous, sheltering rows of two and single seat ships that had pod engines on moving spars. Pilots rushed to take their seats, some of them looked very similar to each other. They were all attractive, practically perfect. The things that killed their marines were sitting in three-metre-tall armoured suits that were highly articulated. It seems that they could move and fight as quickly as an unfettered soldier or perform maintenance just as easily. Some were carrying fighters and loading munitions further inside the hangar. "Welcome to Earth Outpost East Bay," said a female voice as the front of the armoured vehicle on two legs opened in the middle. A blonde woman who looked similar to Skylar was standing inside. "Food is limited, so your wild born soldiers had to go."

"We had our own rations," Gavin retorted. "I'm sure there must have been something in that ocean that they could have eaten."

"I'm afraid not," the soldier said. "Everything in those waters is poison to any kind of human. I can eat it, because I've had genetic treatments that make me immune, but you'd die in about an hour. The Issyrians poisoned the water when the corporations took this place, and we haven't figured out how to clean the whole ocean. We clean what we need, but that makes food limited. Again, sorry, but best we kill your wild born soldiers before we learn their names."

"What about stasis? We could have suspended them until our people come to retrieve us?" Gavin asked, so angry that it surprised him. Skylar brushed the back of his hand, reminding him that this wasn't the time.

Starfighters were lifting off, at least twenty were already ascending. "I had my orders. Besides, no one's coming for you. The planetary shield is almost whole again, and we don't let anyone but our own kind in. Our Uriel Fighters are chasing down one of your shuttles and capturing a few of the more important mad robots; by the time they're done, the whole planet will be sealed up again. You'll like spending your last days with us, though. You'll see."

"Last days?" Skylar asked.

"Yeah, didn't you know?" the attack armour pilot asked. "Ah, I'll let the doc fill you in. Follow me." The front of her armour closed and she started walking towards an interior door.

Gavin was still enraged at the loss of soldiers who would have peacefully found a compromise that would keep them alive. Skylar took his hand and leaned so she could see his whole face as she walked at his side. "There was nothing we could have done," she whispered. "Not aboard the Queen's Pride, and not down here."

"I know. I don't think I'll ever trust these people, though," he said. "They can't be real Earthlings. Their reputation is better than this."

ELEVEN

The ticket system for the British Alliance was critically important to them, so it was a good thing that it was also surprisingly simple. Spin, her ship and the crew in her service were allowed to perform as hired security, to transport goods and people but they weren't cleared to claim salvage. That was something she submitted a new application for. She could also sell the tickets with her ship if she needed to, increasing its value a great deal.

According to what she saw, the British Alliance suffered horrifically during the holocaust virus. Yes, many artificial intelligences were infected and turned on their masters. Artificial Intelligences were still not in broad use yet, in fact, the new Alliance depended on crews and the military more than anything. Artificial Intelligences were forbidden in most areas of industry and private life.

The thing that damaged the British Alliance more than anything else was the uprising of hundreds of localized independent governments while communications and transport were running minimally or not at all during the Holocaust Crisis. Most of them were backed by criminal organizations, and they weren't content to manage the populations that foolishly supported their formation. Most of them took more territory, even filing for their independence legally, knowing that the British Alliance wouldn't receive their documentation for months or years because of the broken state of their once artificial intelligence managed communications systems. As a result, the British Alliance territories were cut down by two thirds, and all ships that were capable had to carry secure data packets for delivery to remote systems when they filed their flight plans. That was still more reliable than the outer edges of their communications systems.

One thing that kept the remainder of the British Alliance powerful was the might and size of their military. They were taking territory back, mostly through diplomacy, but none of those diplomatic solutions would be possible without the dreaded force of the British Military backing them. There were forces to spare, and from the little time she had to look at the information package all captains received, Spin saw that the British Alliance Military were publicly supporting causes from where she was standing all the way to the edge of the Iron Head Nebula, many, many light years away. Someone might think that the British Alliance was down, smaller than it had been in over two centuries, but Spin recognized a pattern. They were rebuilding by strategically supporting governments that could become important allies, and if it worked out, they'd be at least twice their former size if you included them.

The elevator finally reached the ground floor. It was reserved for new captains, so there was seating, and only one other passenger rode with her. It looked like a water-based species based on the liquid support system built into its suit, and the faceplate was blacked out. It could be an Issyrian or a Paudik, or some other aquatic species she'd never met. Her crew were waiting in a separate lobby section, their interviews were finished and the base moved them on to a waiting area where they could relax and have something to eat while they waited for her and Dorian.

The aquatic creature's suit bubbled loudly. Spin looked at the polished white and black suit, its metal components were polished and the suit beneath looked new. It nodded at her. "Best of luck on your journey, human Captain," it said.

"Best of luck to you too, Captain," Spin replied. Her computer buzzed against her skin. She looked to the wrist of her suit and saw that her ident had connected to the British Alliance communications network. There were pages of messages waiting for her, and one was marked with Boro's grinning face. "I'm sorry, I have to take this."

"I understand, farewell," the aquatic Captain said as the doors opened. It stepped out ahead of her.

Spin tapped the display on her wrist and gasped. "Look who the bloody slavers were stupid enough to dig out of the muck," he said with a big grin. "I'm alive, I got away, even got my own ship and tracked you down. The talking heads at the star base said I might get to you before you're checked in right and have access to the comms network, but I thought I'd send you and Nigel this so you don't think you're seeing a ghost or some bloody clone. I thought it was important to warn you about Kort and his little fleet. He's after you, and he might have the people who know how to get around the British Alliance.

Those rich bastards seem to do whatever the hell they want, and while they were doing it to me, I was thinking about you."

Spin was happy no one she knew could see her as she stepped into the shadow of the tall administration tower, its dark metal surface blending with the blackness. She wiped tears from her face, glad she could shed them and embarrassed at the same time. "I should have known. We should have taken him aboard to make sure."

"You did your best, darlin'," Boro said, but not from the computer display on her wrist.

Spin looked up and spotted him walking towards her in a new green, armoured jacket, a heavy shard handgun strapped to his thigh, combat boots with a thick armour under suit beneath it all. There was a man several steps behind him who was visibly awkward, trying to look anywhere but at Boro or her. "Oh my God!" she squealed, rushing at him at a run.

He caught her in his arms easily even though she collided with him. "If you took me on that ship, I wouldn't have made it. The bastard that took me worked miracles to get my grey matter back online, but he made sure I was still one hundred percent human."

"I'm sorry," Spin said, burying her face against his chest and gripping the back of his black skin suit. He lost a lot of weight, and it didn't suit him, but there was something about the whole sensation of him that made her feel safer than she had since she escaped the Countess' grasp for the second time.

Larken felt like her equal in all things, like a partner who she loved deeply, but he never gave her that. Boro could do things that she didn't have the skill for, had an attitude that was completely foreign to the way she was raised and the etiquette that was drilled into her from an early age and she always liked it. Even when she sometimes caught him looking at her with an admiration that seemed almost hungry – as though he wanted to devour her with his eyes, maybe take her somewhere private so they could be together in a very, very indelicate way – it didn't disgust her like it had with other men who made similar desires obvious. He tried to hide that side of himself from her, to rise to her intellectual level enough to get to know her and Spin couldn't count the number of times he simply asked her to explain things he never had the education to know just so he could stay in her company.

Boro respected her, cared about her, and wanted her in ways that Larken would never have let himself express as openly or as passionately as the man who held her close would. Spin knew she'd always love Larken, but as Boro tilted her chin up and wiped her tears away with thick but gentle fingers, she realized that she would let him take care of her from time to time, while her and Larken were always too equal for that to feel right. With Boro, she knew he'd lean on her intelligence, and she could lean on him for anything she wanted. "Thinking of you got me through the worst of everything, Aspen," he said.

"It's just Spin, now." It was simply unbelievable that he was there, but the circle of his arms and his confident, low voice were evidence enough for the moment that it was true. His eyes were closing, lips lowering, and her heart beat a frantic rhythm in her chest as she let her guard down completely. Spin closed the gap, realizing that she'd given up the idea that she'd be passionate with anyone ever again as their lips joined and expressed how much she wanted to celebrate his sudden return.

He was slow, as though he was savouring the sensation of

her, holding Spin close, one of his big hands holding her waist, while the other was planted on her back, and his lips held hers gently for a long moment before they moved with hers. It became a warm, breathy kiss and when they parted long moments later it was with hesitation. She spotted a tear on his cheek before looking into his dark blue eyes. "I missed you so much," Spin told him.

"Aye, me too," he said quietly.

"Woo!" whooped Nigel from the bottom of the long, broad ramp as he lead the way to the crew hospitality area. His hands were above his head, clapping before balling into shaking fists. "Man, I should have known they couldn't get you!"

Sharon, Leland, Mirra and Della were emerging behind him, watching with interest. "Go," Spin told Boro.

"We'll make time later?" he asked.

Spin nodded and started stepping out of his embrace. The question reminded her of how little time she'd actually have, and how selfish getting into a real relationship with him would be. They walked down the ramp, hand in hand until Nigel started running up, tears in his eyes. "Easy, nephew, I'm all right," Boro reassured as he caught him.

"You're really alive? I can't believe it, thank God, man, you're really alive!" he wept as Boro held him tightly. Nigel managed to curl himself into the embrace, stooping so he was shorter than his uncle.

"I'm back, it's all right, Young Shark," he said, stroking his head.

"Travis didn't make it," Nigel sobbed.

"It's just family and new friends then," Boro soothed, turning his face away so Nigel couldn't see him squeeze his eyes shut and clench his jaw. The speed at which he pushed that pain down was almost alarming. When he spoke again it was in a tone that was more determined than soothing. "There's a reunion coming up, I've put the call in to a distant relation."

Spin knew Boro well enough to be sure that he'd make someone pay for everything wrong visited on him and his family. Revenge wasn't a calling, or a quest for his people. It was an art form.

TWELVE

The gunnery deck of the Hawker was running perfectly. Under the watchful eye of the Gunnery Chief who trained them, the crew worked in heavy armour that was the power and protection equivalent of the full-sized Earth Power Armour Suits that came with the Triton. In many ways they were superior, especially in size. The crews could move with much greater agility since it was only two centimetres thick in most places and as little as nine millimetres in major flex points.

In armour that looked like it should be from thirty or fifty years in the future to their Chief, the gunnery crews handled cartridges of caseless ammunition their own size, loading the heavy broadside guns at a pace that matched their turret gunners. The three levels of gunners worked around problems too. While most turrets were firing, a few had taken simulated damage or broken down for real and repair crews worked frantically to get them firing again.

A cartridge the Chief was watching for several minutes while he monitored the rest of the action from the middle catwalk finally slipped off an upper deck platform. The loader nearest made a last second grab for it and missed.

"Loose cartridge!" he shouted, sounding the alarm before it was completely off the edge of the deck.

"Got it!" a marine called as she activated her suit's thrusters. By the time she made contact with it and another marine helped her balance the large cartridge, it had fallen no more than three metres.

"No more fuck ups! That would have blown the whole exercise!" called one of the Chief Trainers. "More importantly, it would have slagged at least one turret! These old ships can't take screw ups like our new suits can! Get your shit together, keep your head on a swivel." She barked, losing no ferocity from one end of her speech to the other. "We are thirty three percent through this fire exercise, let's make it legendary! Got me?"

"Yes Sir! We've got you, Sir!" replied all sixty-two members of the gunnery team running the three decks.

The only problem the crew the Senior Gunnery Chief saw with the team was that they had a tendency to print ammunition ahead and a few of them didn't stow the cartridges right away. The Chief Trainee would mark the loaders responsible for the near disaster and he would respond by having them held back. He expected the rest of the crew would go on to regular service by the end of the week. The Haven Fleet was only one third ultra-modern hardware, the rest were older ships they'd captured, bought or salvaged. They needed loading teams, among other types of specialized personnel. Eventually the older ships would be phased out, but until then Shamus Frost was one of the few people in the fleet who could train people to work with the old hardware.

It felt good, but he had nine Junior Chiefs and almost as many large teams ready to go. They could all use more practice, but like the team he was watching, he would send them into combat if they were needed and he'd expect to hear good things.

Shamus watched as the same loader who failed to stow the loose cartridge – a metal crate almost as tall as he was – backed into another one and almost tripped into the ammunition printer ejection hatch at his feet. "Get Goreman out," he told his Chief Trainee. "Now. His situational awareness is shit, we need to put him at a desk by the end of the day so no one mistakes him for a loader."

"Aye, Chief," she replied. The Chief trainee signalled a nearby loader who was idle to take Goreman's place then she ordered Goreman to leave his post then surrender his armour. He would be on the first shuttle headed back to Haven Fleet Headquarters on Tamber, where they'd reassess him and give him a new assignment, maybe in logistics.

The rest of the exercise went well; three decks of guns firing from the port side of the Hawker as the ship made its way through the target field. The guns were reloaded at the right pace, so no ammunition was left loose, and they didn't have to stop firing. When the vibrations of the turrets stopped and the crews worked on stowing any leftover ammunition while the gunners secured their turrets, Chief Shamus Frost patted his Chief Trainee on the shoulder. "That's how it's done," he told her. "One more exercise and I'll put you and your team in the rotation. You might not get picked by a captain right away, so get a few more exercises in using the simulator every day. Keep 'em quick and smart."

"Yes, Chief. Thank you, Chief," Chief Trainee George replied, saluting.

He returned the gesture and nodded. "Pick your second, make sure they know at least as much about this business as you, and that they won't be afraid to call you on your shit." The thick command and control unit on his right wrist buzzed and sent him a sense that there was something urgent for him to attend to.

"Aye, Chief."

"I have to take this," Frost said. "Lock it all down and leave the ready crew in place when you're done, then you take this crew to rest. No celebrating until you've finished your exercise tomorrow. If that's perfect, then you can have your fun, but only if the exercise is perfect, understand?"

"Aye, Chief," she said, grinning at him. With the team she had and her acumen for running a gunnery team, there was little chance that their next exercise wouldn't be perfect, especially without Goreman.

"Bridge, this is Frost," he said, watching a display with the lead Communications Officer for the Hawker appear in his helmet heads up system.

"You have a priority one transmission from British Alliance Territory. I'm afraid you'll have to come to the bridge to see it on a secure terminal."

"On my way," he said. He took what he hoped would be a last look at Trainee Chief George's gunnery crew as they rotated their gunners out, seating new ones and reverting to a standby state. A few of the trainees were replaced by experienced service people, but many of them started a duty shift because they were so low on trained crews. Even in the heart of the Haven System, most able ships were used for patrol if they weren't tasked with training or specific missions.

Frost walked into the interior airlock and waited for it to cycle. The gunnery decks didn't have atmospheres while they were in operation. Even aboard older Freeground Fleet ships like the Hawker, they were the least hospitable places aboard. The room finished pressurizing and he retracted his helmet, breathing in the cool recycled air. The old ships were almost completely bare of decoration, and the Hawker was a slim destroyer, built fast, made to be a ship of utility and quick response. He didn't say it aloud, but Frost liked the old fighting machine. Everywhere he went he was surrounded by polished blue and silver metal, and the crew knew their business. The corridors were slim, reminding him of the naval ships of the twenty first century, and there were old manual hatches everywhere. He was sure they were modernized with emergency motors to get them closed if there was a sudden drop in pressure, but he liked the old handle system.

He took a ladder two decks up and nodded at the guards standing on either side of the main bridge entrance. The old egranian steel bulkhead protecting the rear of the bridge was thicker than he was even in his heavy armour. "Chief," Captain Paquin said, smiling at him. "I hear the exercise went well."

"One more live fire exercise should do it. There's a good Chief Trainee down there, you should make her permanent crew." He looked around the simple bridge. It was a narrow oval shape with thick transparent metal at the front and a single seat for each critical station. The Captain sat at the centre with four multi-purposed stations behind her.

"I would, but this ship stands down at the end of the week. The order just came in: I'm getting transferred to a new Haven Shore Heavy Corvette of the same name."

"So they're keeping the Hawker name alive. What's happening to this old beauty?" Frost asked.

"They're recycling the egranian steel for the new star dock. Freeground Alpha is being rebuilt using half the Freeground fleet. I don't know where all the new Heavy Corvettes are coming from, but Haven Fleet are replacing the old ships at a rate of seven a day now."

"I hope you don't mind me askin', but how do you feel about being put in command of a corvette after running this destroyer for three years?"

"Pretty good. I'm losing a few crewmembers I'll miss, but they've been due for promotion for a long time. The new corvette will have nine times the firepower, she'll be more agile, and the survivability is better. It's the same tech as the ship you're transferring to."

"I don't know if I'm going to serve on the Merciless yet," Frost said, walking to the communications station, where a young officer with perfectly coifed dark hair awaited him eagerly.

"Captain Valent hasn't locked you in yet?" Captain Paquin asked.

"I'm thinking of staying back. Doing reserve for the defence force and taking a full-time training job at the Academy. I don't know how useful I'll be on the Merciless, everything on that new boat is a far cry from the gear I came up with. I know how to run the new tech, but I don't know that it'll ever feel like home."

"It's his loss," the Captain said. "How's Commander Vega?"

Everyone in the fleet seemed to know that his girlfriend was pregnant, and that question came up at least five times a day. "Settling into her new job at the Academy."

"Oh, right; she's one of the leads on the Apex Program, I heard about that. We're going to have some great officers coming up." Captain Paquin looked to her communications officer and nodded. "I'll let you get to the message. It was cleared through the British Alliance."

"Aye, thank you, Ma'am," he said before turning to the communications officer. "Let's have it, Lad," he said.

"Do you want me to put it up on the main display? My screen is just this little thing, can't make a hologram more than seven inches tall either."

"If your Captain doesn't mind, but if it's a port wife, you hit stop right away, understand?" he said with a wink.

"Uh, how will I know if it's a port wife?"

"She'll be angry and prettier than I deserve," he said, reaching down and activating the message himself. He looked to the main screen. What he saw there startled him and filled him with guilt at the same time.

"Shamus," Boro said, his familiar blocky head and stocky chest filling the screen. He looked thinner than Frost had ever seen him, unhealthy, and weary. His heart ached at the sight of him. "This is costing me a fortune, but I hope it's worth it. These Brits say they can get a message through to you in hours, otherwise I wouldn't bother. Thanks to some luck – both good and bad – I've made my way to British Alliance territory. They're not in any shape to take care of anyone, to protect anyone. You remember we used to joke about what would happen if the authorities or some gangster got their hands on us when we were young dock rats? Well, I bloody well found out for myself, and if I don't get your help here, it might happen again, only this time my whole crew will get tortured and butchered, most like."

Frost's thick fingers dug into the headrest of the communication's officer's seat. He was faintly aware that Captain Paquin was watching him as much as the message, but it didn't change the feeling he had at his core. Boro was family; they both sprang from their mother, who was the matron until she was killed. He and Boro grew up on the docks together, and the old instincts came back fresh. You took care of family, no matter what. It was a commandment he violated once when he left them all behind, and he regretted it ever since.

"Royals are after us, and they don't give a rat's ass if they have to chase us through British Alliance territory to take us as slaves and tear us apart for their bloody entertainment. It's me, your nephew, a woman I would lay down my life for, and a few good friends against those bastards. The British aren't helping, and their territory is really a loose chain of solar systems with more wild space between than you could account for. Don't know how long I can last out here without a mad bastard like you on my side. I hear you have powerful friends now, so you get some of them together and make your way here quick, and all's forgiven. You know I wouldn't ask if it wasn't deadly serious. One way or another, I'd be an ass if I didn't spend an extra five hundred plat to say I love you, brother, no matter if you make it here or not. But you better bloody well get your thrusters on and make the trip."

The message ended with Boro frozen pointing a finger at him, his face frozen in a severe expression. "Well, fuck," Frost said under his breath.

"Everyone who saw that is sworn to secrecy," Captain Paquin said. "This is Chief McFadden's business and no one else's."

"Thanks for the hold on scuttlebutt, Captain," Frost said.

"I'm guessing this isn't spam," she replied quietly.

"No, it's a brother in more trouble than he's letting on. How much did it cost him to send that?" Frost asked the communications officer.

"They used one of three available stable quantum communications nodes in the whole of the British Alliance territory to send it and a military Quan Comm to receive, so the cost of that is about ninety thousand platinum."

"My stars, I don't want to know what my little brother had to do to get his hands on that," he said.

"What will you do, if you don't mind me asking?" Captain Paquin asked.

Frost thought for a moment. He had a pregnant girlfriend whom he ordered an engagement ring for not a week before, and he felt he owed Haven Fleet a great debt. He also had Captain Valent breathing down his neck, trying everything he could to get him to sign up for service aboard the Merciless before the shakedown cruise was over. There was an invasion fleet recovering in more than one nearby system, getting ready to attack their home, the Haven System, and he wanted to be around for the fight.

The tactical screen that replaced the image of Boro caught his attention. A ship emerged from trans-dimensional space a few hundred thousand kilometres away, and he got an idea. "I'm going to have to go pick my little brother up," Frost said.

THIRTEEN

The War Forge was the most imposing structure that Frost had ever seen. He knew basically what was inside; hundreds of manufacturing lines that could print anything you had materials for and a few mass converters that could turn energy into almost any substance you needed, but that took incredible amounts of power, and was not the preferred method of material generation.

It was incomplete, but the metal skin that would eventually wrap around the entire structure – which would have enough room for a quarter million command staff, crew and facilities that could ensure their survival indefinitely – was starting to appear. The glistening black outer hull reflected the stars and the light of thrusters as ships and construction robots passed. The Tamber Moon and Haven Shore, the first island granted to their founder, Ayan Anderson, was the civilian centre of the Haven System. Shamus didn't think much of it, even though the city on the island of Haven Shore was growing by the day and there were hundreds of

thousands of lovely, happy people there. To him, they used technology to plant a modern city in a tropical paradise, but when he thought of paradise, it wasn't tropical.

It was something like the War Forge. It was closing on eighty percent completion, the outer tiers and pylons were only frames, but he could imagine what the thing would look like. A leviathan in space that dwarfed stations and could produce a ship and everything inside it in days, right down to the uniforms the crew wore. Not just that, but two dozen at a time. Ships like he'd never imagined were being finished as his shuttle docked with the Merciless, his former Captain's new commission. He already knew everything he had to about the vessel's power, defence and weapon systems. Shamus was a hundred simulated hours away from qualifying as its chief tactical officer, but it didn't feel like he belonged.

The mooring points latched loudly, the airlock door lights turned green and it opened. "Thanks for the lift," he said to the petty officer supervising the small go-between shuttle. The thing flew itself, the petty officer was there in case anything went wrong and to make sure the passengers were comfortable.

"My pleasure, Chief," he said, standing and starting to salute.

"No need for that, lad, I'm just a tourist here today." To Shamus' surprise, Admiral Ayan Anderson, Queen to some, Founder to others, and suspected tyrant to a few who expected her to directly assume power any moment, was waiting for him on the other side. Her black, form fitted vacuum suit uniform had the marks of her rank, the Haven Fleet skull on one side of her chest, a crown on her shoulder and a gold stripe down the sides. There were no aides nearby, but she was wearing a Violator Seven sidearm on her thigh that was balanced by a small bulge on the opposite leg that he knew contained survival tools and ammunition. Frost was at a loss of words as she smiled at him. Red ringlets fell around her heart shaped face, and he'd never tell her, but he thought of her more as a young queen than an Admiral, even though she'd proven her engineering and logistical prowess many times over. The War Forge wouldn't be nearly as far along as it would be if it weren't for her and her people.

Before he could embarrass himself by greeting her improperly, she stepped forward and shook his hand. "Chief McFadden," she said warmly. "When I saw you were coming aboard, and that I was closer to the airlock than Jake, I had to take the opportunity to thank you for your service. The first two gunnery crews you trained are transferring to Freeground Station at the end of the week. Not to mention your work on the Samson, the Warlord and the Revenge. A pair of my engineers are using your maxjack designs to improve a few capture systems in the fleet, and we're working on a module we can add to our gunships that will give them all an improved latching and forced boarding capabilities. You're becoming a legend in the fleet."

"Thank you, Admiral," he replied shaking and releasing her hand. She didn't like being called Your Majesty, or any acknowledgement that she'd been made a Queen by what remained of the Galactic Courts. He knew most servicemen and women adored her as their Queen first, and an Admiral second, but he respected her for preferring to be known by her work instead of a title she'd earned by accepting a land grant.

"Please, call me Frost," he said. "And if I were to go through your accomplishments and what they've meant to my crews, we'd be here all day. This base you've made here, though; it's a masterwork."

"It took thousands of people and as much foreign technology as familiar," she waved the compliment off, her British accent losing some of its formal edge. "I wasn't at the centre of the innovation but thank you." She turned and started walking him into the ship. The corridors were simple in the outer sections of the vessel where they were closer to the defensive measures. The halls were three metres wide, had regenerative plating everywhere and used a type of holographic repeating hardware that was built in to light everything clearly but not too brightly. To Frost it looked like the light was coming from everywhere, but there were no visible sources. The interior armour lining the hallway was made of regenerating smart plating much like the exterior of the ship, only not as thick.

Crewmembers moved around them, slowing and nodding as they passed Ayan, glancing at Frost as well. Ayan had obviously established a short hand with the crew where a nod would do if the crewmember or she was busy and she wasn't directly addressing them. It was common practice in Haven Fleet, even though some higher ups demanded their salutes. "What brings you to the Merciless? Are you accepting the Captain's offer? He's on pins and needles waiting for your decision."

"I'm afraid I'm being called away on personal business," Frost said. "That's unless the Captain won't have it."

"If it has anything to do with Stephanie's new assignment on Freeground Station, then I'm sure he'll understand. I know it would make a lot of sense for you to take a post as a tactical officer there, considering how familiar the weaponry on the station would be to you."

"There's a position open there?" Frost asked.

"If you showed an interest, I'm sure you'd be a preferred option for running the defences on Freeground Alpha. There are no senior commanders who know the defensive systems as well as you do; they were killed during the attacks on the station."

Frost considered the idea of working on the same station as Stephanie. She was on leave, helping Agameg here and there, but mostly trying to find some way to entertain herself while she came to grips with the idea of being pregnant. Frost was still getting used to living with her full time in Haven Shore's military housing, which was incredible, but not to his taste. He would have rather lived aboard a station or a large ship. He grew up watching ships come and go, adjacent to big ports where he could see something new every day. Stephanie would eventually move to quarters aboard Freeground Station, a huge relic that was being refitted at a break neck pace in orbit around Tamber. He suspected they'd both be happier if they could look through a porthole and see the stars whenever they liked. "The thought of living on Freeground Station with her full time is tempting," Frost sighed.

Ayan started to look concerned. "Why do I get the feeling that Stephanie is in for some difficult news."

Captain Valent emerged from a lift door, his muscular frame filling much of the doorway for a moment. "Frost," he said, smiling. His expression grew more serious as he read the situation, and by the time he was shaking his hand, Jacob Valent asked; "What's wrong?"

"Relations," Frost said.

THEY MOVED the conversation down the hall to a cramped conference room. For three people, it was fine, but the slim black and blue table had seats for nine, a number of bodies that Frost was sure would make the room feel like a crowded elevator. "Stephanie's all right," Frost said. "At least she will be until she hears what I have to do. My younger half-brother, Boro, is in British Alliance territory in the Core. He's in trouble. I never thought I'd see him again, considering how I left things, and when the 'bots went mad, I was sure he was killed."

"What happened?" Jake asked. He sat down and stood up almost immediately, holding the seat out for Ayan instead.

"When I left him last, he was jailed for stealing the Sadie, a star yacht that had been converted into a smuggling ship. Understand, I was a different kind of bastard then. We were all dock rats. Grew up around the space docks. We stowed away for the first time when I was thirteen, he was eleven. Took us almost a month to find our way back home, but from that point on I was the ship thief, he was the mechanic, and he taught me plenty, that's where all my machining talent comes from. He's the real artist. He learned how to track down good ships to steal and marks to scam, picked up a few tricks on defeating security systems too, but for a lot of years, we kept to our specialties. The Sadie was the first one where he ran the scam while I broke through the electronics. He was supposed to keep the widow who inherited the thing distracted while I figured out the custom security on the ship and made the tools I'd need to break it on the spot. Everything went fine until I disabled the ship security too early. Widow Sadie Paloma put the pieces together and had him arrested. I had a choice – turn the ship I just got off the deck around and face the music with him or let him take the fall for both of us – and I headed off into hyperspace." Jake didn't look surprised, but Ayan looked disappointed. It made telling the rest of the story more difficult for Frost, but it was weak penance for his past acts.

Frost pressed on. "God bless Sadie Paloma. Once I was out here on the fringe, away from authorities, I looked into what happened my brother. The widow actually paid for Boro's defence because she'd taken to him, but even with those high-end lawyers, he couldn't avoid a sentence of three years for Emotional Interference. Considering the penalty for ship theft was twenty-five years in a virtual facility and social reprogramming, he got off light, but my little brother still ended up in prison. It was a living prison, with cells, a work day of sorting parts using remote drones, and some rough characters around. Our other brother died while he was inside trying to pull some kind of counterfeit scam, leaving a son behind, and last I heard, Boro was out of prison taking care of him. When the machines went mad, I was sure that was the end of them. I didn't get a response to the few messages I got out."

"I didn't know you had family you wanted to look for," Jake said.

"It would have come up if I got a response from anyone closer to the core, but no one replied. Everyone I know has lost family, why should mine survive? Damn me for not making sure; Boro and my nephew are both alive and in trouble. He's told me all's forgiven, but I need to get in a ship and get out there to help him out of whatever mess he's in. More n' that, I need to show him that I'm not the same whoreson he knew when I left him behind."

"You know I don't need more convincing that you've changed," Jake said after a long pause. "I've rarely seen someone find their place so well and turn things around. If you go, I can't hold your spot on the Merciless. We're due to finish shakedown and go on mission soon. I'll need a good tactical officer, and I'll miss you in that spot, but I'll find someone."

"Do you own a ship?" Ayan asked.

"Aye, but nothing I can get to," Frost said. "Honestly, I've got three ships stashed between here and there – who knows what condition they're in – but nothing in this sector."

"Three ships? I had no idea," Jake chuckled.

"From before we met, Captain. None were as impressive as the Samson, even when I first joined your crew, so I left them where they were just in case. They're old, though. Small too."

"Stephanie's your real problem," Jake said, drawing a stormy look from Ayan. "I'll rephrase: she's just gotten a good assignment and is prepping. If she gets leave to go with you, you're taking her away from that. If you go alone..."

"I'm leaving her with my son or daughter," Frost said, sitting down. "These chairs were made for smaller asses," he said, standing up. "Anyhow; You're right. I can't win. I leave a brother and nephew out there in trouble, or piss my future wife off, maybe past her limit."

"What's your first instinct?" Jake said. "If you could take this problem on your way using anything you wanted, what would you do?"

"I want to go there using a trans-dimensional corridor, pick their arses up, and bring them here. I know there's an invasion coming, I want to be here, manning the wall. My rough math tells me I could be there and back in a week."

"To and from the edge of British Alliance territory from here, yes," Ayan said. "If you took a Quad Drive with you."

"Right, that's what I was wondering: how many dimension drives I'd need and if I could borrow them."

"The new Quad Drive would be the best option," Ayan said. "But, I'm sorry, we just perfected the design. I can't even tell you which ships will have them."

"I need an Interceptor Class ship."

"How do you know about those?" Ayan asked, surprised.

"There are three hidden in the hangar of the Merciless," Jake said, closing his eyes and shaking his head.

"Not on the manifest," Ayan said, cocking her head. "Did you take them out of turn, Jake?"

"Sort of." There were few people who could make Jake cringe or look guilty. Frost knew he probably did something that would make Ayan cringe every few days, he'd spent too much time in the wild, and though he'd embraced the military again, some of that still came out. Seeing Jake almost shrink away at the trouble he was in made Frost want to snicker or at least crack a smile, but he remained quiet and still.

Ayan reached up and hooked her finger in the collar of Jake's black uniform, drawing his face down. "It was Minh, wasn't it?"

"Keep guessing," he said, suppressing a smile. "It takes more than one pilot to take three ships."

"You mean; steal. These aren't toys, they're important warships," she said. "Even though they're the smallest class. It's not like stealing a sky luge board from the sport supply shop."

He stared at her silently.

"Fine, Carnie flew one too, taking them as they were finished on the manufacturing line."

"That's two out of three," she said, her red eyebrows furrowed.

"They were reacting to my frustration. The Merciless is ready to react to an alert, but we're low on the list to receive our new fighters and support ships."

"There are good reasons for that," Ayan said. "I'm not guessing the third conspirator. You're going to tell me." She growled. "Then you're going to tell me if you ordered them to do it or if they acted on their own."

"Hot Chow," he said. "They acted on a frustration I voiced, Admiral," he said, taking it a little more seriously.

"You're going to write an incident report detailing how Minh-Chu, Noah Lucas, and Hal Rhea were a part of a conversation that led them to believe that you wanted your three Interceptors early. Then they're going to submit reports on how they stole them, and you'll cite those in your final report with a recommendation for reprimand. I'm thinking that they're going to be flying patrols in the system until they're needed back on the Merciless. Then there will be extra watches..."

"... and luxury pay reductions lasting into the new year," Jake nodded. "I know how to discipline my people. No marks on their permanent record after their punishment is served out."

"Fine," she said, releasing his uniform. "But only because you're watching Laura while I take a nap later, and you're going to get up every time tonight."

"My pleasure."

Frost had seen footage of Hal Rhea, the pilot known as Hot

Chow, and knew he had incredible spatial awareness, good reflexes and experience flying long trips alone. He was self-sufficient and confident at the stick. "Can I propose a punishment for Hal?"

"Why not?" Ayan said. "I'm sitting in a room with two ship thieves, nothing you say should surprise me with that in mind."

"If one of you were kind enough to grant me temporary use of one of those lovely ships, I'll need a competent pilot. Hot Chow, I mean Private Hal Rhea, is an ace, and has experience driving large vessels. Going on a milk run with an old sod like me will be the most boring thing he does all year. If we run into trouble, chances are we will be able to get away between his skill on the stick and my cunning."

"You don't think too much of yourself, do you?" Ayan said in a withering tone. "What makes you think I'll loan you a state-of-the-art attack ship equipped with a Quad Drive?"

"Well, begging your pardon, unless you're taking them back, it's really up to Captain Valent."

"I'm not going to take them back," Ayan said. "That would make it look like three valuable ships are caught in the middle of a lovers' spat, and you know it." She looked like she was caught half way between amused and annoyed as she split her glances between Jake and Frost.

"He knows how to play politics when it pays off," Jake said. "I don't want to admit this in front of the Admiral, but the reason why I didn't protest being so low on the list to receive these boats was because I didn't have the crews for them yet. Sadly, that stands; we can crew one or two at most. I'll make you a deal, Frost: you get one of those ships and Hot Chow on loan. Bring it back within two weeks tops, and when you get back you're going to be my tactical officer until I find someone better with your help. That means if you have to train your replacement, that's what you'll do. Oh, and you are telling Stephanie about this as soon as you can in person. You're not going to take off and let me break the bad news to her."

"Now, Captain, would I do that? Even you said I'm a reformed man," Frost said, feigning injury.

"Changed. I've never said you were reformed," Jake chuckled. "Does this deal have your approval, Admiral?"

Ayan laughed and shook her head. "You're both still pirates and cons at the core," she said. "Fine. Chief Shamus McFadden and Private Hal Rhea are on special assignment aboard one of those Interceptors for two weeks or until they get back; whichever comes first. Bring my ship back in one piece, Frost."

"Aye, thank you, Admiral."

"Good luck with Stephanie," Jake said.

FOURTEEN

Boro returned to the waiting room where Nigel and Spin were watching a pair of yellow sliding doors, expecting Dorian to appear any moment. It was the first waiting room Spin had seen on that base that was empty. There was nothing to see; white walls, rows of red plastic chairs and a clean white floor. On a few of the walls there were digital pamphlets about gender switching, taking care of the Human Plus body that they offered at the clinic and a few screen areas featuring news from the solar system and beyond.

There was a royal wedding on between a prince and a duchess that was faintly familiar to Spin. She looked them up in the Countess' database and found them; House Kamen and Ubdo. They were both enemies to House Lux and the Countess. The whole family was wealthy, but their place in society was ornamental. Their wealth came from real estate, a few defence contracts and commodities trading. "Things really are different in British space," Spin muttered as she looked up from their profile.

"Thank you for loaning me the platinum to use the quantum comm," Boro said as he sat down beside Spin. "Don't know if Shamus will be able to help, or if he'll come at all, but I feel better. My brother left me in a hell of a spot, forgiving him is big, and it's about time I stop carrying that."

"It wasn't a loan," Spin said. "Did they tell you anything about where he was?"

"Only that details about him and the fleet he joined are covered by the British Alliance Secrecy Act. From what I could see on the Stellarnet, he's hitched his wagon to this Valent character; some kind of crusading war hero. He recruited for the Aucharians, I saw his big speech about doing the wrong things to the right people, but I think he moved on since mad machine time. He's with a new outfit called Haven Fleet, and he just came back from behind enemy lines."

"Wait, I think I heard of him," Nigel said, squeezing a pamphlet about gender switching between his hands until it was a tube. "The corp that owns Spacerwares is accusing him of monkeying with their network. All their shops are closed indefinitely."

"Spacerwares stores are closed?" Boro asked. "That's too bad. I like Valent a little less now."

"God, I wish Dorian was ready, that he'd come walking through those doors. If the suspense doesn't kill me, I'm sure he will though," Nigel groaned, dropping his head into his hands.

"What did the nurse say?"

"Well, she gave me this," Nigel said. "And told me they're doing Dorian a solid because I told him he ended up in that box because he was fighting Captain White, who is in their database as a pirate and slave trader."

"I've never known him to trade slaves," Boro said.

"That might be thanks to him giving me up to the Core Authority," Spin said. "I'm a runaway doll, fabricated person, whatever they call us here."

"Oh, I knew that," Boro said. "The bastard turning my screws told me about it, but how does that extend to White?"

"He turned me, Sun, and everyone on the station when we were dancing in to the Core Authority for a reward. I also found out he was skimming from the crew."

"I got that message, and the account," Boro said. "Thank you for that. I'm going to have to find an exchange to turn some of that into plat. I don't trust digital cash or credit."

"We'll visit one off-world. The exchange here sucks," she turned to Nigel. "What kind of solid did they say they were doing for Dorian?"

"They have a C-Type Upgrade Model, not like the bare emergency model they were going to give him. There's info about it in this, but I'm afraid to look."

"Let's see," Spin said, taking the plastic slip and opening it. The hologram of a beautiful woman appeared and smiled at her. Her face shifted as she spoke. "Hello, I'm the C-Type Adaptable Synthetic Human Appliance. That sounds technical and impersonal, so you can call me TASHA C. As you can see, my face is changing right now, because I'm still just a host. When you see me, I'll have a permanent face that has been drawn from the mind of the being that is transplanted into me. I can have a deep mental scan copied to my very human brain, or my brain can be replaced. Don't worry, I'm not the result of cloning technology, not entirely. I was never really alive; this host body was printed in a high resolution, clean facility, then I was placed in a perfect state of stasis. When your loved one is imprinted or transplanted into me, they'll bring me to life and I will be them. You won't have to deal with latent personalities, random genetic traits or anything else that generally comes from cloning, because my genetics will adapt to my new host just like my face and my height. You can thank the British Alliance and several research groups for finding and developing technology out there, across the stars. If your loved one is transitioning to a female body, I'm the perfect host for that too. Their mind will determine how my face looks, but morph locks and psychological adaptation will ensure that it'll be something that appeals to them. If a mistake has been made, and I'm not supposed to be a female, then TASHA C can be adapted after the fact for a fee at one of our deep modification facilities. To ensure the best performance, third party modifications are not recommended, since everything under my skin is proprietary."

"Oh, shit," Nigel said.

Spin stopped the playback and looked through the other details using menus in the pamphlet. "Okay, so TAHSA C is a good model. It looks like it's partially doll technology like me, and partially a regulated bio-printing system called Framework. They promise that there's no framework technology inside the TASHA once she's done printing, and that's some kind of benefit, but I can't find out why. She can withstand many times the heat of a normal human, goes into hibernation if she's exposed to hard vacuum so she can survive for up to three days, and has a neural backup built in. There's some other stuff, like skin durability, but the biggest selling point seems to be that she feels human to whoever gets implanted, all the same medications work on her, she has a very long lifespan potential and doesn't need special treatments after someone's 'born' in her." Spin sighed. "If Dorian doesn't give this a chance, he's crazy. I'd kill for half the features."

"Street Docs charge millions for genetic and cybernetic improvements like that," Boro said, nodding. "What do they do to soften the blow for gender switches, though?"

Spin looked through the menus and found it. "Here it is," she said. "There's a cocktail of medications that get loaded up in a patch. Dorian will also have a computer printed on his wrist a lot like mine with tutorials built in. Wow, he can even have kids."

"Oh, that'll make him so happy," Nigel chuckled sardonically. "Maybe I could tell him while he's ripping my ears..."

The yellow double doors opened, a black haired, sleek looking woman with a cheeky, expressive visage emerged. She wore a fitted jumpsuit and had a plastic slip in her hand. Two nurses in white smocks followed behind her. "We understand this is a shock," the one with a large nose and long green hair said. "You're taking the change very well, considering how unexpected it was. Like my colleague said before you broke his nose, there will be some confusion, and that's all right. The important part is that you're alive, and you could have a long life, perhaps another century or two if you treat this body even passably well."

She spun on her heel and the two nurses took a step back. "No more transplants?" she said quietly, dangerously. It was definitely Dorian. He could make anything sound like a threat.

"What did you do to my brain? Why is there damage? Why can't I remember how I died? The last few weeks?"

"Some parts of the brain are still a mystery," one answered. "But the last few weeks may have been suppressed because they were too traumatic to recall all at once. It'll come back as you start accepting your new situation and your stress levels decrease."

Dorian reached out for the front of his smock and almost caught it. "Fuck you! I feel so..." she looked down at herself, poked her stomach, then her right breast with a bewildered expression, then shook her head and shrugged. He looked back at the nurses in smocks, laughing. "Fuck how I feel, I don't know how I feel. Just tell me why I'll never be able to transplant my grey matter again."

"It's in the report," one of them said.

"Tell me..." Dorian said, a threat in her voice.

The green haired one said; "Okay, I'll tell you again. Your brain has suffered a lot of trauma, we were able to repair most of it, but it would be dangerous to transplant your brain again because of all the damage you did to it with hard drugs, second-rate cybernetics, sonic and other trauma. Your brain has been restored to remarkable condition, but it'll start falling apart if you try to move it again, I'm sorry. You can go to a Frame Logic facility and they can try to change this body into a man using genetic manipulation and surgery. They're experts, the outcome will be perfect, just like this outcome, despite your misgivings, is perfect. It would still be healthier to stay in this body as it is for at least a year. We modified your genetics so life will be easier, your head will be clearer, and decisions will be easier to make. You'll see; you were suffering from a number of psychoses that were brought on by trauma but you were already genetically dispositioned to. We've set your memories up so you can deal with the trauma on your own and corrected the genetic problems. If you start changing this body, you could inflict more trauma than you can handle. Please keep it as is for at least a year, you'll learn to enjoy the person you've evolved into."

"A year? I..." Dorian stared at the green haired nurse, brow furrowed, mouth working. Spin had to admit; Dorian was absolutely pretty. Taller than her, but perfectly proportioned. Her face looked healthy, expressive and alluring. "...I don't know why," Dorian said quietly. "But getting cut up and changed again is fucking terrifying."

"There, your mind is opening up to the idea of being who you are now, including your change into a woman," the other nurse said. "That's all that's happening. The body changed according to a pattern determined by your own mind, so it suits you, guaranteed. Just keep an open mind and you'll be fine."

Nigel stood and started to cross the room, Spin and Boro followed several steps behind.

"Here's the friend who brought you in. You should thank him. People literally kill for the kind of transplant you just survived, and the price is deeply discounted. That upgrade normally costs millions, but you got it for only three hundred fifty thousand. The addiction treatments, imbalance correction and gender reprogramming are worth half a million alone, and we performed all that gratis just because we wanted the best outcome for you. It's not your fault that we were out of male bodies and you were about to suffer critical damage, so we made it right. I'm sorry if that's not enough. Have a good life," he said as both nurses retreated through the yellow doors. The sound of latches sliding closed so the doors were locked securely were loud enough to fill the room.

Dorian turned towards Nigel and looked startled for a moment. Spin wished everyone else waited with them instead of returning to their ship. A bigger crowd to greet Dorian may have been better.

"I'm sorry, man, it was the best they had. They didn't have any..."

Dorian slapped him suddenly and stared as Nigel staggered for a moment then straightened up. Her near-black eyes watched him, only a little anger showing on his face.

"They said you were out of time," Nigel explained. "It was that, or you'd be gone, and I'll pay for this, no problem."

"He did right by you," Boro added quietly.

"Listen, it could be worse; you could be in one of those basic, jobber clones, or in a suspension system waiting for medical advancements, or, well, dead," Nigel offered. "Man, I'm so sorry, but..."

Dorian slapped him again, but from the other direction. It was slower, but a more full-on hit, filling the room with a resounding clap. Spin flinched, watching Nigel stagger in a small circle, holding his cheek. He stood up straight suddenly, taking a step towards Dorian with his chin up. "Okay, get it out of your system," Nigel said. "As many slaps and punches as you want. I know I have it coming, this isn't like the practical jokes we played on each other when we were kids, you'll realize I did it to save your life eventually."

To Spin's surprise, Dorian punched Nigel in the mouth, crushing both his lips against his teeth and sending him reeling back. Boro caught him and snickered, surprised. "She got ya."

"Holy hell!" Nigel said, wiping his mouth and trying to shake the hit off. "Okay, okay." He steadied himself on his feet again, pointed his chin out and put his hands behind his back, his eyes closed. "I'm going to be your punching bag until we start talking this out."

Dorian stared at Nigel looking a little surprised and a little annoyed for a long moment. She started breathing heavier then, and a tear ran down her cheek. Her lip quivered, and other tears followed silently.

"Whatever abuse you want to lay on me, I'll take it," Nigel said, not opening his eyes or moving at all.

It took a lot of restraint for Spin to watch instead of embrace Dorian as she started to cry in earnest. Then she finally leapt at Nigel, who yelped in shock, expecting the worst. Instead, Dorian wrapped her arms around him, sobbing; "I hate you so much! I'm sorry I hit you! I'm so confused!"

"Welcome back to the human race," Boro said as he stepped in and embraced them both. Spin joined in moments later.

"I think I'm gonna need help," Dorian told her through a shower of tears.

"You'll get plenty if you join my crew, Dorian," Spin soothed.

"Okay," she replied. "Maybe a new name too."

"Dori, maybe?" Nigel asked.

Dorian's head came up, she stopped crying, then she shook it and resumed sobbing. "I don't feel like a Dori!"

"Okay, okay, it doesn't have to be Dori, anything you want," Nigel retorted, sounding like he was near panic.

FIFTEEN

The shuttle Gavin and Skylar were escorted to was broad and had two decks for passengers. A quarter of the seating had been converted into some kind of medical bay. For hours they were told to sit still and be silent. Through the crystal-clear strips of transparent hull that ran the length of the passenger cabin they were comfortably seated in, Gavin could see two spiral buildings rising from the ocean.

The skin of them, whether they were metal, some kind of stone or something else, changed colours as the sun moved across the sky – blues, greens and yellow played over darker violet shades – and Gavin had to admit they were beautiful. There was a layer of brown and green scum built up where the waves crashed against the gargantuan buildings, and everything he knew about Issyrian worlds told him that it indicated something wrong. He didn't know much, though, so when the guards in gold, black and red outfits moved to the main doors of the shuttle, he asked Skylar about it. "There's something really wrong with this. That scum isn't normal, and the buildings are empty."

"I bet there isn't a single Issyrian left on this hemisphere," she said. "The water is corrupted, I saw the scan result on the way down. If we drank an ounce of what's in that ocean, we'd be sick for days. A litre would kill anyone."

"They wouldn't do that to their own planet, would they?"

"Never," Skylar said. "Not even if they knew someone else was about to take over. Not even if they all turned warrior tribe. Issyrians don't believe in a scorched earth policy. Their whole culture is built around how they live on after death in the water."

"I remember you reading that to me," Gavin said. "They share emotions with each other and communicate through the water whenever they can, absorbing microscopic pieces of each other and leaving others behind. It even enriches the water for other life forms, so when an Issyrian dies the others can feel them for years or longer if the ecosystem is healthy."

"I remember you read me the Prince Dario and Princess Grace story in return, and I couldn't decide which was more romantic," Skylar said, taking Gavin's hand before looking back through the window. "I think someone poisoned the Issyrians here. There were probably a couple billion if the rest of the world looks like this. I'm sorry we didn't get to meet them."

"They're friendly?"

"They normally greet outsiders with curiosity. Sometimes they even offer good hospitality if they've learned to trade with guests, but there are still many who made their colonies and quietly exist without visitors of any kind for centuries. At least, that's what the Royal Archive said, but our tutors couldn't answer the question of; 'how could we know if they don't have visitors if we haven't visited them?'"

"You used to frustrate our tutors all the time," Gavin said.

"So did you."

"I'm sorry I panicked." Gavin said, choosing that as his moment to apologize for his behaviour aboard the command ship. "I just never dreamt of anything so savage."

"I understand," Skylar said. "I was stunned too. You have to promise me that you won't let yourself fall to despair like Toby if something were to happen to me."

"I don't understand how he took his own life," Gavin said. "You don't have to worry. We'll both be fine, though. I still wonder if we shouldn't try to escape. This is an odd situation; I can't understand why we're both being held here. Most of those suits are just guarding the shuttle."

"We need a better scanner," Skylar said. "Or at least to get a good look at some results. My guess is that even the ground is poisoned here. There should be forests of some kind on the land, but when we were coming down I only saw moss and tiny sprouts."

There was a commotion at the hatch and a woman in a bridge officer uniform matching theirs was brought in on a stretcher. Her side was packed with foam, and judging from the wound, it looked like a whole chunk of her was burned away. Her arm on that side ended above the elbow. It looked like it was burned off as well.

Soldiers in plated, sealed black and red uniforms bore her in, dropping her on a gurney. "Farrah!" Skylar shouted, rushing to her side.

As soon as she said the name, Gavin recognized the dark-haired woman. Gavin tried to hold her back but didn't stop her in time. Before she could reach the gurney, one of the soldiers backhanded her hard enough to send her back against Gavin, who caught her awkwardly. "Stay clear," he said.

Four more armoured soldiers carried a wriggling bag into the back of the shuttle. Judging from its shape, Gavin guessed there was a human in there, most likely in good health judging from how he struggled to escape. They dropped it from hip height and marched back out of the shuttle.

"Everyone clear, I'm deploying the Framework Pod," the soldier with a bit of gold on his helm said as he backed away from Farrah. A transparent enclosure wrapped around her, and beams of light pushed through the foam some medic sprayed into Farrah's side to stop her bleeding, through the burned flesh, and began to rapidly regenerate or print – Gavin wasn't sure – new tissue and bone. In as much time as it took him to breathe three times, Farrah was whole again with a new, perfect right arm to replace the one she'd lost.

"Those are all the synthetics we could find," said the soldier with the gold mark on his helmet as he pressed something on his wrist. "Take off."

All the hatches on the shuttle closed and the shuttle lifted off from the ground, the sound of rumbling thrusters around them faintly. "Gavin, look," Skylar said as she pointed through the transparent section of hull behind Farrah, who was starting to wake.

A pair of long, rounded arms extended up from a crude metal base in the distance. "It's an emitter system," he guessed. The gold helmet soldier turned to him, and he put his hands up.

"You know what that is?" the commander asked.

"Just a theory," Gavin said.

"What's it about to do?" the soldier with the gold mark asked, raising his rifle. "You have a theory, I'll hear it."

"It could be extending its arms to reinforce the shield," Gavin guessed.

"Guess again," the soldier said.

"Maybe sending power wirelessly to another emitter station."

"Sounds like he's seen this before, Commander," one of the soldiers watching Farrah said.

The Commander lowered his rifle and nodded at Gavin. "Just for my amusement; take one more guess."

"It could be forming a circle so it could create a Wormhole Gate," Gavin said, hoping he was wrong. If that was the case, and they were going through it, then the Royal Family would have no idea where they were. The kilometre-wide mothership appeared ahead of them, its stingray shaped hull was pointed towards the extending arms. They joined, forming a circle and the view of the ocean disappeared, replaced with one of outer space. "We suspect these gates were built by Lorander so they could open a wormhole in an atmosphere to outer space while keeping the atmosphere intact. Air stays where it is, but ships and other solid objects can pass through."

"Congratulations, synthetic; you just became important," the Commander said. "I'm guessing her specialty is diplomacy?" he turned to Skylar.

"Biological life, military history and a few other topics," Skylar replied, touching her fat lip gingerly.

"Not bad. Considering your people nearly compromised our base of operations here, I hope you're both good at your trades. You're joining the Citadel Division of Sol Defence now."

"What about Farrah, and whoever's in the bag?" Gavin asked. Their shuttle docked to the underbelly of the mothership as it moved towards the looming portal with a resounding clack.

"They're synthetics too, so they'll find a place with us some-where, even if they're as dull as a deck plate and we have to reprogram them," the Commander replied. "Don't worry about it, though. If you two are as smart as you seem and join us after we show you what we have to offer, then your minds will remain intact. Theirs too, if they don't resist. Considering you were just freed from slavery to an obsolete regime, you should find life with Citadel refreshing."

"Our Prince treated us like family," Gavin growled. "We wanted for nothing and served with pride."

"We know," the Commander laughed. "We're interrogating him – well, his brain – aboard our ship. We managed to capture the robot ship that was carrying his grey matter. He only had good things to say about his synthetics."

Gavin started to stand, hearing the fate of his Prince, discov-ering that he was still alive after a fashion was almost too much, but Skylar elbowed him hard and shook her head.

"Seems you had two masters," the Commander laughed. "At least now you only have to serve her."

Gavin tried to shake the insult as he watched the wormhole grow closer and closer until they entered. They left the planet behind, the darkness of space filling the view around the shuttle. Whatever force the Royal Family sent after them would only find danger and the wreckage of their sad day.

SIXTEEN

To Shamus McFadden, or Shamus Frost as he preferred to be called, secrets were important. They could be traded, they could do a lot of good if revealed at the perfect time, but they could also do incredible damage. As Stephanie hurled a vase that couldn't decide whether it was orange or yellow, and Shamus ducked, he suppressed a smirk at a thought that he would keep secret for the rest of his life if he knew what was good for him.

Stephanie Vega, the love of his life over any other he'd had the luck to charm, looked beautiful when she was furious. He would take that thought to his grave. Her dark, stormy eyes squinted at him, and he realized that he had let that hidden smirk surface. "What is that about?"

He knew what she was talking about, and he resumed his straight-faced worried look. "What? I was just dodging a lamp."

"A vase," Stephanie said. "What were you smiling about."

"It wasn't so much a smile as a constipated look of concern," he retorted, trying to close the distance between them again.

Stephanie pointed at him with a freshly manicured nail. She and Ashley had just returned from their first spa day together in, well, ever. As soon as Frost told her the news, those false nails started looking more like claws that were painted red to hide the blood to come. "It's just a quick trip. They're loaning me a ship and a pilot so I can pick my brother and his crewmates up then come right back."

"Do you really think that's why I'm angry?" Stephanie asked.

More than anything, Frost wished Ashley would emerge from their spare bedroom. She always had a way of calming Stephanie down, while Frost had a tendency to make these fights last longer. It was questions like that, like the one she just asked, where he had to guess the answer and no matter what he said, it would be wrong. "You're angry because you'll miss me?"

Stephanie took a quick step forward as though she was about to physically attack him, making Frost jump, then she turned and screamed in aggravation. "You came home with your mind made up!" she wailed. "It wasn't a discussion, you didn't ask me if I wanted to go with you, there was no lead up, you just said..."

"I gave you the news just like you've told me to a hundred times; without beating around the bush, and as clear as I can," Frost said, realizing that interrupting her was not the best idea.

"You said; 'Looks like my brother's in trouble, so I'm going to the core to pick him up, it shouldn't take more than a few days. You'll barely notice I'm gone.' And then you started packing!"

"Well, sooner I go, sooner I'm back?" Frost offered.

"Shamus!" she barked. "Can't you see this is my worst

nightmare? Where I come from most of the mothers, even mine, were single! Sure, some were widowed because their husbands were off in the resistance, but half of them, probably more, just ran off when they heard the four-letter word; baby!"

"Do you want me to marry you?" Frost asked sheepishly. He heard Ashley burst into laughter in the next room. "Hey! No peanut gallery! You're in this or you're out!" he shouted at the closed, but obviously too thin door, of the spare bedroom.

"Leave her alone," Stephanie said. "No, I don't need you to marry me before you run off, I just wanted to be part of the discussion." She dropped onto a thickly padded sofa.

"I'm sorry," Shamus said, finally able to get close enough to put his arm around her. "You have things starting up here, and you're carrying our first born." He took her hand. "That's everything to me, so I don't want to put you and our little rascal in the line of fire."

"Our first born," she repeated quietly. "How many kids do you want to have?"

"As many as you want. Just this one, or a football team; you tell me when we're done, I'll treat 'em all like found treasure. Why? How many do you want?"

"I'll tell you as soon as this one starts walking," Stephanie replied. With a sigh, she said; "It's going to be more than a week. You'll get out there, and the situation on the ground will be complicated, there'll be some kind of trouble, probably someone chasing your brother or waiting to be paid so he can get away, and who knows what his crew will need."

It was as if she grew up with him and his people. That was exactly what he expected. "Well," he braced himself. "that's why Captain gave me two weeks with the Admiral's new ship."

Stephanie punched him in the ribs, not so hard that she meant it, but enough to make him aware that she was displeased. "I'm a cliché. The poor, knocked up port wife who can't go on the trip because it could be dangerous. You probably have five women with kids wondering if they'll ever meet their father, the legendary captain, or ship thief, or whatever you were when you met their mothers."

"I always used protection on liberty," Frost replied, though he could remember a couple times when he forgot.

Stephanie laughed and kissed him briefly. "Don't take too long out there. I swear I'll have this kid put into stasis and come after you if you're gone thirty days."

"I'll stick to the mission; Locate my brother, pick him up and bring him here. I think you'll like him: he's the responsible one."

The door chimed, but Stephanie stared at him meaningfully, as though she was searching his eyes for more than he was saying. He stared back at her, feeling like he was being searched from the inside. He had the thought that she would be a masterful interrogator if all the criminals were clones of him, then the door chimed again. "Ashley and I are going for lunch, now."

Stephanie had calmed down, but he could tell there was still anger under layers of other emotions that could evaporate at any moment depending on what his next words were. "I love you, dear," he said, squeezing her hand.

Looking absolutely incredible and smelling just as wonderfully of some light perfume that reminded him of roses and some other, darker flower, Stephanie stood and left him behind on the sofa. "Prove it," she said only loud enough for him to hear as she strode to the guest room door.

It opened, revealing Ashley, who looked as well-groomed and clothed in a shimmery red dress. "He's not meeting Minh for lunch with us?" she asked.

"No," Stephanie said flatly.

The entrance chimed one more time and they opened it on their way out. A surprisingly thin young man with a closely trimmed black beard stepped inside, his head turning after the pair for a moment before he shook it and looked to Frost. "Chief McFadden?" he asked.

"Call me Frost," he said, looking up Hot Chow's service record to confirm that the man in those images was several kilograms heavier. "You've slimmed down."

"Fitness pills, torture runs, and real food. At least, that's what they tell me real food is, but I never thought barbeque eel or crabs were real food in the first place. Everything okay?" he thumbed in the direction of the door. "That's if you don't mind me asking."

"That was my marvellously complicated partner and her much less complicated but equally brilliant friend. They're off to eat some of that real food with your Wing Commander. God help me for loving complicated women with fiery tempers."

"I wouldn't know anything about that, Sir," Hot Chow said.

"You might learn about it one day, if you're lucky," Frost said, standing and taking a better look at the pilot. He already had his rucksack, his sidearm and the rest of his kit was properly set up under a heavy armoured jacket. There wasn't much to pick at. "Why do they call you Hot Chow, anyhow?"

"One day after training a bunch of us were going to the

mess after drills and the food smelled so good that I shouted; 'Hot Chow!' and it stuck. It's not the worst call sign."

"Aye," Frost said. "But it doesn't fit an ace who has better navigational scores than some mergillians. I'll call you 'Hal,' all right?"

"Sure, aye, Sir," he said, shaking Frost's outstretched hand.

"Now, the angrier looking of those angels you passed when you came in expects me back here in one week, and a clock starts the moment I'm late; it doesn't tell time, mind you, it counts how many minutes she worries about me more than usual, and we don't want it to run too long. Tell me you're the pilot for this ship and you can get me back here before she starts grinding her teeth in her sleep."

"I can get us there and back in five days with that ship," Hal said. "And I don't like playing tourist."

"Grand; I think we'll get along fine, lad," Frost said, the excitement of getting away for a few days and seeing his brother beginning to build again.

SEVENTEEN

The vast water tanks surrounding the room Gavin and Skylar were left in once they were guided into the mothership were filled with strange aquatic creatures. Most of them followed the same basic shape – a bulbous body with fins running down their lengths that gently propelled them through the water – but their features varied. Some had clusters of eyes running down their backs with a concentration at the front. Others had none, but sensitive looking patches along their torsos with long, thin tendrils extending in all directions. A few looked more carnivorous, with broad mouths and small eyes.

The walls around them were completely transparent, showing off the creatures as they drifted past paying the four of them little mind. The circle of seats was too comfortable for a brig cell, and guards regularly entered one door, crossed the room, then exited through the other secure door in pairs. No one seemed too concerned with them. "Anyone have any idea what this room is?" asked Terry, the dark haired, heavily built man that the Earthlings brought aboard in the black restraint bag.

Skylar pulled on the edge of the curved sofa she and Gavin were sitting on and an eating or working surface slid out, folding down in front of them before she pushed it back and put it away. "Looks like a space set aside for leisure? I've seen luxury cruisers that have observation areas scattered around the ship when there are features inside to look at. They're a bit like this. Maybe not as elaborate."

"Makes a pretty good prison cell," Terry said, kissing the top of Farrah's head and putting his arm around her. The pair looked matched – dark haired, well-muscled beings that were made for each other like most paired dolls – something he knew quite a bit about. He turned his attention to the transparent walls around them, standing up and peering past the creatures. The tank around them must have been huge; there was complete darkness after about fifteen metres. He could barely see the light of a hallway with rooms like the one they were in towards what assumed was the port side. It was difficult to track where they went as they were brought in, there were several twists and turns along the way.

"I've never seen anything like these beings. They look mammalian, like small whales or something," Farrah said, watching one of the larger ones pass overhead.

"A lot of them have features that don't make sense from an evolutionary standpoint," Skylar said.

"Why do you think they put us here? I mean, they're treating us like passengers when I could knock a guard down and take his weapon at any time. They're just ignoring us," Terry said, eying two guards who were approaching the room.

They, like several others, entered, locked the door behind them, passed between the curved sofas, then exited through the doors opposite, locking them back up. Terry watched as though he was formulating the best plan of attack. "Hey! When are we going to talk to someone who can tell us why we're here? Why my whole squad was murdered like rats when we set down?" Terry shouted after them.

A transit car rushed past the room, using a tunnel that was only noticeable as the well-lit conveyance passed parallel to them. Gavin noticed plant life beneath it, probably engineered to keep the water clean and the strange creatures fed. He started to put the information he collected as they were brought aboard and what he collected since together. The ship was big, probably with cavernous hangars in the bottom half and large nursery sections like the one they were in. The technology was advanced, but not so much that it was mysterious to him. It wasn't a Lorander ship, he guessed, and even though there was a lot more water than the crew would need, it wasn't an Issyrian ship, either. It must have actually been a ship from Sol Defence, especially since it looked so much like one that had been captured and put to use by rebels near the Iron Head Nebula.

"Does he talk?" Terry asked, pointing at Gavin.

"He's gathering information," Skylar said. "You need to calm down."

"I need to find out where we are and what's going on," Terry retorted, Farrah nodding her agreement.

"We're on a ship crewed by synthetic humans and other manufactured beings," Gavin said. "These aquatic creatures were made, maybe a lot like we were, and to some extent they're still experimental. I don't think they're part of the crew, but I could be wrong."

"So, why are there so damned many of them?" Terry asked. "If they're experimental, then why keep them? I know when they were trying to make the perfect synthetic human in tubes and printers, they killed whatever didn't turn out right after recording the results. They didn't keep all the rejects and dead-end experiments."

"Because they may be experimental, but regardless of their differences, they can still perform the tasks they were made for, even if it is to continue to exist and be observed. Maybe they all have a core function and the diversity we're seeing isn't compromising that."

"That makes sense," Farrah said, watching one of the creatures with large, rainbow coloured fins pass by gracefully. "But why show us this?"

"Why not?" Gavin asked. "It's impressive, it's distracting. I'd imagine the crew might be pretty busy, so they put us in this nice, secure, quiet, entertaining environment. I know I'm probably a prisoner, and I don't know what's going to happen to us next, but for some reason I'm not actively worried. Their plan is working."

"That's all I can think about; what's coming, where we are and why. So, it's not working for me," Terry said, cracking his knuckles.

"Sure it is," Gavin said, sitting down beside Skylar. "You've talked about attacking a guard three times since they let you out of your bag, but you haven't made any effort to follow through."

"So, what do you think we're here for?"

Gavin thought for a moment, accepting Skylar's hand. He

looked at her and smiled, knowing that she had an idea as to why they were taken. Without any signal from him, she answered; "We're high end synthetics, dolls," she said. "We're easier to reprogram if they can figure out the genetic key that gets them past the measures made to prevent it. It takes more time and effort to reprogram humans and their tolerances to heat, cold and trauma are much lower."

"So, we're recruits whether we like it or not," Terry said, standing up and starting to pace.

"It's a theory," Skylar said with a shrug. "From what I gather, they think they liberated us from servitude."

"We have," said a man in a long, V shaped gold tunic and black under suit. Gavin didn't see him come through the door, he was pretty sure he was cloaked somewhere in the room listening in the whole time. His white hair was slicked back, and his gleaming white grin seemed genuinely glad. "It's important that you know your actual condition. The status of most dolls is kept from them, so we can begin by sharing the truth with you. It's time to build some trust."

Terry lunged at the much shorter, thinner man and passed through him. "Dammit!"

"That's not a good start," the image said, touching a hidden control on his wrist. Terry's body went limp and he collapsed.

A moment later he was back in control and taking to his feet as quickly as he could. "What the hell was that?"

"You passed through a cloud of nanobots when you boarded," the hologram explained, looking every bit as real as the room around them. "They entered your bodies and painlessly built a control system so we can disable you if we have to. I would rather not do that again, since we'd like you to join us."

"Who is 'us?'" Terry asked.

"You'll find that out soon. First, let's talk about the four of you. We've finished our deep scans and analysis. Gavin and Skylar; I'm afraid you only have two hundred and eighty-seven days until self-termination. Farrah and Terry; you have one hundred and forty days left. I understand that the tyrants that owned you told you that you would retire sometime around those dates. That is a myth. What really happens to your models is simple but terrible: Your organs will begin shutting down three days away from your final termination date, and when that time is up, you will be dead. Chances of revival are zero, because as soon as that termination process completes, your bodies will decompose at a highly accelerated rate. This system was put into place to maintain demand for dolls, and to ensure that each line was precious to their owners while they were alive and serving."

"Bullshit! Our Prince honours us. We were never told we were retiring, either. We were superior, so he brought us with him on his military mission," Terry retorted.

"Yes, your Prince adores his dolls," the hologram replied. "That's why he went to Geist; to find the genetic key that would allow him and his royal line to modify you. He wanted you to live for a normal or even exceptional length of time. He also wanted you to be able to have children, and when that was accomplished, he planned on starting tests. He envied the strength, fortitude and intelligence of his dolls, so he planned on finding a way to attain that himself. He was already close."

Gavin struggled with the idea that he and Skylar had less than a year to live. He believed it immediately. During his lifetime he'd seen nine pairs of dolls retire, and after they departed he never heard back from them. A few pairs were sent off to war when they reached an age similar to his own, and they never returned either. "Who are you?" Gavin asked, hoping to skip ahead in the conversation.

"I'm Walt, one of the Geist Minds you see drifting nearby. I'm using this hologram so you have something to speak to in the room. Also, I don't use a style of verbal speech you'd recognize, so it also translates my thoughts into words and expressions."

"Your thoughts?" Farrah asked. "You mentally communicate with a computer that translates with this much nuance?"

"Yes," Walt said. "It's easier for me than it would be to communicate with all four of you mentally."

"Are you making our prince into one of these things?" Terry asked.

Walt laughed. "No, we may give him a body someday, but not any time soon, and we don't transplant minds into Geist beings. We are partially manufactured, we gestate, then are born. Next, you'll ask where we're taking you," he said. "There is a base where we're building a copy of the manufacturing system like the one that created the four of you. We are close to creating our own key to unlock your limits, and, regardless of how you feel about us, are willing to reprogram you so the restrictions built into your bodies are removed. We are most likely days away from success. You will be able to have children, and you will have a life expectancy of over a century with little aging, good health and the capacity for even longer with some basic pharmaceutical aids. You will not be human, but still a superior synthetic that looks like, thinks like, and can live like one. A deep scan would reveal that you're a synthetic, however."

"Can we really trust you?" Farrah asked. "You killed our

Prince, destroyed our fleet, murdered our people, and at any point you can subdue and reprogram us."

"Your Prince is not dead. His mind is very much alive in a support tank. Right now, he thinks he's at home, hunting a convicted murderer through the woods on an all-terrain cycle with his old friends. We have what we need from him, so he's living a good simulated life until we need him again. As for trust; let's start building that. While we are in transit across two sectors, you will have wonderful accommodations. Lavish temporary quarters have been prepared in the safest portion of the ship – the Gallery – so you will have time to contemplate our offer and review a great deal of information about what we're offering, and why our cause is so important in this part of the galaxy. The Citadel arm of Sol Defence is on a quest to preserve humanity and assure dominance over the other races. You'll see why this is important, I'm sure."

EIGHTEEN

Boro looked like he was in a state of disbelief when Spin caught up to him. He'd just finished docking his new, smaller ship in one of her ship's bays - it barely fit - and he received a notification that Shamus 'Frost' McFadden received his message. The single line response his brother was allowed to send read simply; *Be there in two days*.

There was no specific destination in his mind. The only place he didn't want to go back to was the more lawless section of the core, where he knew all of them were wanted. It was a good thing they were headed in the opposite direction. Deeper inside British Alliance space they'd find the Beta Bio Facility, and when Boro was told they were headed there without delay, he seemed pleased.

Nigel was sitting with him in the galley. They spoke quietly over steaming cups of synthetic coffee. Nigel smiled at her and excused himself, leaving Boro reclining alone at the table. "Time to check on Dorian, er, Dori. Maybe get my fat lip fixed," he said as he passed her.

Spin sat down, not looking forward to the news she had to break to Boro, who greeted her with a smile. It faded when he saw her expression, and she wondered how dire she actually looked. "Something's on your mind."

"You know where we're going," she said. "Probably the most boring pit stop in the galaxy if you're not a biologist or getting treatments."

"I was surprised you knew where to take our Dori to get fixed up," Boro said. "Hopefully they can do a good job below list price."

"I don't know that they can do anything for him. It's a research and testing facility, like a new Geist system, only with regulations."

"Aye, but the profile said they treat people's major genetic disorders or with special requests. Why else would we go there?"

Spin took a deep breath and decided that she would tell him the bad news as quickly and simply as possible. She was sure he could understand the intricacies, Spin had no doubts about his intelligence, but she was tired of being a sad case. "In two months my body will shut down. It's genetic, and any effort to change or treat it will only reduce the time I have or kill me. That's why we're going to one of the largest research facilities in the galaxy. There are probably people there who worked in the facility that developed my genetic code, maybe even someone who grew me and my partner, Larken. I have to find out if there's a way to fix me so I can have a normal life expectancy. The only other alternative is to go to Geist, where I was made."

"Less than two months? Aye, we have to find a way to fix that." His eyes were focused on hers - intense, urgent - and it was almost too much to take. No matter how much distance she put between herself and Boro, her death would hurt him. It was too late to keep him from harm by cutting ties.

"It would have been well over a year, but Sun dosed me with something that triggered the genetic defenses when she cleared some mood-altering drugs from my system. She thought she was helping."

"Fucking meddler," Boro said, shaking his head. "Always thought she looked down her nose at everyone, now I know it. She was the queen of everyone, no one else could have a different opinion, she'd argue it out of you."

"She was a good friend who made a mistake," Spin said. "She's out there now, trying to find a cure her own way."

"Well, at least she's trying to make amends," Boro said. "I'll do everything I can to get you that cure, even go to bloody Geist. Why did it have to be Geist?"

"I guess the company needed to be where the most advanced research and manufacturing centers in the galaxy were. I'm state-of-the-art, maybe?" she offered, trying to balance Boro's irritation and grief by playing cute.

"That, I can believe." He said, calming down. He was like a lot of people she'd known; after hearing of any injustice, they would transfer their anger to the first culprit they could name. Boro wanted to solve the problem, but he also wanted to take revenge on someone in her name. Among the people who she met since escaping the Countess, she found most of them reacted the same way.

"I just want to concentrate on finding a cure," she said

calmly. "And if I find out there isn't enough time for me, I'd like to make sure other dolls have a better chance, and to leave my ship to someone who'll take care of the people I leave behind."

"Don't talk like that. We'll find a way," Boro said.

"I have to face reality. Besides, I'm not so special. There were at least seven Aspen's made. Maybe we were a little different thanks to upbringing, but you can say there were genetic matches to you - like identical twins but closer - out there."

"You haven't met my brother yet," he said. "From what I've heard, he's gone military, and the outfit he's with has all kinds of helpful toys. I bet he'll come with whatever he could borrow, buy or steal to help us. He's crossing whole sectors in two days. I've done the math over a few times and I can't figure out what kind of ship he's using to move so fast. The fastest thing I could find would take fifteen under the best conditions. Imagine what else he's got? We'll get you to Geist if we have to."

"I hope we won't," Spin said. There were thousands of technology companies in the Geist system, all contributing to a defence system while they maintained their own. With artificial intelligences in control of most of the solar system, she could only imagine how tough it would be to get anywhere near the facility that made her. Then, they'd have to face what was inside. "As far as I know, that's all the bad news," she said. "Oh, and we need to name this ship. I was thinking about something airy, light, especially since a lot of these models are turned into small carriers."

"So, we're just moving on," Boro said, his blue eyes focusing on hers like he was reading her, like she was all that mattered.

Spin nodded. "I don't have anything else to say about it.

Sun's gone, Leland's done what he could, and I'm hoping we can get more information from Beta Bio. Until then..." she shrugged.

"All right," he said quietly. "A ship name; maybe we look at this like a ship with a purpose? Expedition ships were always named for the kind of mission they were going on, or the gumption they were putting behind the cause. Maybe..."

"Help!" Nigel cried, skidding into sight through the galley hatchway. "Dorian's locked herself in the medbay!"

Spin and Boro rushed down the hall and looked through the transparent metal medbay door. Dori was hurriedly punching selections on the drug dispenser machine. As soon as she saw Spin and Boro in the door, she picked a prybar up and smashed the screen with the tip, jamming it in. "Holy shit, she knows how to get into a pharma machine," Boro said. "They're reinforced on the sides, where they close, but the middle behind the screen in only a millimeter or two thick. She'll get through soon."

"Dori, let's talk this out. I know you're probably still shocked, there's a lot of change..." Spin started.

"A lot of change?" Dori screamed. "Nothing's the same. Even anger's different!" She hurled a metal stool at the hatch savagely. "Try waking up remembering that you were someone else but being so different that they're gone. It's like my body fucking died but every memory I have is taking way too long to die behind it." She picked the prybar back up and stabbed at the middle of the drug dispenser. "Meanwhile, I feel like letting all that shit go is the best thing for me. What the fuck is that about? For free people, the British sure like their mind control."

"I did that to you, Dorian!" Nigel cried through the door. "I'm sorry, I told them to do everything they thought was right to make sure you were whole on the other side. I didn't know that meant changing so much."

"I'm going to open the door, get ready," Spin said, entering the Captain's security code into the panel.

"Fuck you, Nigel! I was my damage, and they made all that shit hazy and weak. If you wanted your buddy back, you fucked up!" She opened the machine enough to reach inside and rummaged quickly.

Leland was running down the hall towards them in shorts, he looked like he woke from a deep sleep. Spin pieced the picture together then; Dori told Nigel she was going to the medbay to get checked by Leland, but she knew that he was asleep in his quarters. It was just a way to get some distance so she could do something drastic. As soon as the door was open, Boro rushed through, grabbing Dori's wrists and pushing her away from the drug dispenser. Nigel was right behind. He tried to grab her legs and was rewarded with a solid kick to his middle that sent him out of the medbay and into the bulkhead across the hallway outside.

Leland rushed into the medbay and retrieved an injector from his locked station. Spin looked for a way to help. It took all of Boro's strength to marginally control Dori, who was much less robust physically. Dori was laughing, struggling kicking at Boro, who raised his knee in time to block a devastating blow to his crotch. "You were a good lad when you were growing up, Dorian. Got into trouble from time to time like all the young sharks, but good at heart. Maybe that changed along the way, but I bet it's back. I bet if you calm down, give it time, you'll find it again."

That gave Spin an idea. She brought up an image of Dorian

in his half-trashed long coat, rough, damaged head of hair, and obvious cybernetics. It was the portrait of a patchwork man, and she projected it life-sized. "Do you want to be this again?" she asked. "I remember seeing you and wondering if you were suffering in that body. If you were in pain. Maybe you thought you were scary, a bad-ass, but that's what most people were thinking when they saw you; 'I wonder how much it hurts to be him? I wonder if he's still human enough to feel anything?'"

Leland fired his hand injector, a dose of medication crossed the room, impacting against Dori's cheek as subtly and as painlessly as a focused puff of air. Boro caught her as she collapsed then picked her up and put her on a gurney. Nigel limped back into the room, moving to her bedside. "I looked at what they did," she said mournfully. "I had a whole, warrior gene thing going on, and they didn't just turn it down, they turned it off."

"You kicked me ten meters across the floor," Nigel croaked. "There's something aggro left in there."

"What were you trying to do in here?" Leland asked gently, scanning her then starting a scan on Nigel.

"I wanted to put something together that would bring it back, Doc. Just get some of that edge back."

"Time for a new edge, maybe," Boro said. "You've definitely still got the fight for whatever edge you want."

"As for the fading memories," Leland said. "I can take care of that in three doses over three days. They did a lot, yeah, but we can work through some with drug and talk therapy. I wish you opened up to me sooner, I'm here to help."

"I'm sorry," Dori said.

"It's all right, I'm sure I'll get patched up fine," Nigel said.

"I wasn't talking to you. I was talking to Leland. You can take a walk through the nearest airlock, buddy."

"Well, you broke three of his ribs, if that makes you feel better," Leland said.

"A little, but whatever you just gave me is making me feel a lot better, Doc," Dori purred. "It's like I'm becoming a cloud in a nice, blue sky."

"That's the same euphoric they have in stuff like Jupiter Whirlwind shots, Lumo liquor, or Noganto Ale, only in a much higher concentration. It's an easy mental state without the suggestibility; enjoy."

"Oh, I will, thanks," she said.

"Meanwhile, let's get your ribs mended," Leland said, gesturing for Boro to help Nigel up onto the next bed.

"I'll be on the bridge," Spin said, satisfied that things had calmed down and there was little she could do to help.

"Spin?" Dorian called after her. "Are you going to kick me off your crew?"

"I'm not sure you were ever really a member, but you're welcome to join up. Just try to look at the upside of your situation. The first being the most important; you're still alive."

"The second?" There was desperation in her tone despite the strong euphoric in her system.

"Everyone here wants to help you," Spin offered with a little smile. "And we're all eager to see who you become."

NINETEEN

The Gain Skipper, Boro's refurbished courier ship, was more of a large fighter than a small delivery vessel. Sharon was at the controls, her hands deftly handling the older style systems as Boro managed the navigation station. Spin was happy she didn't take much space. The Gain Skipper didn't have much room for anyone, especially Nigel, who was too tall for every part of the vessel so he walked hunched.

Aldo was a surprise; one of Kort's personal guards, she recognized him immediately. He was still a young man, not much older than her, but there were lines on his face. He lived under stress. Whatever he experienced or saw while he was in Kort's service didn't suit him.

The moment she sat down beside him in the cockpit – which had two full seats for the pilot and co-pilot – and four smaller seats for supplemental crew, he looked nervous. It took Spin a few moments to figure out all the particulars of the computer system, but after she was comfortable with the communications suite, she smiled at him. He was watching the secondary sensor screen but noticed her attention instantly. "Hey, I'm Spin."

"I know," he said tentatively. "I'm Aldo. I was the servant who scanned everything you ate for about a month before I went back to school. After that I returned as a guard."

"Boro didn't say you had a history on the estate," Spin said.

"I don't really tell people about that. I felt like I was part of the slavery problem most of the time. Something about being one of a few paid servants when most people doing the same work didn't even have their freedom. It's good to see you again, though. You were always nice to the people around you."

"I like to think so," Spin said. "I know I took some of my frustration out on a few people who were just bystanders, though, so that wasn't always true."

"You were one of the nicest people I remember," he said.

Spin decided to move on to another topic, they had several minutes before they reached the outer range of effective communications with the Beta Bio facility. They were accelerating through the inner asteroid belt. Boro was counting down to thruster cut off. "Thank you for freeing Boro," Spin told him. "Everyone thought he died, so there was no rescue coming. You were his only chance."

"I'm sorry I didn't do it sooner."

"You did it, that's all that matters. Now, you're free too."

Nigel got out of his seat and started to leave the cockpit.

"Where are you going?" Boro asked over his shoulder.

"Checking the capacitors. They all say they're at ninety-five percent charge except for number Twelve. That one's only going up to fifty-seven."

"That's because it's almost half burnt. I had to remove a bunch of cells to make it safe for a bigger charge. Don't worry, this ship's in good shape."

"Another look couldn't hurt," Nigel said.

"Never mind another look. Now's not the time to go fiddling with capacitors. Either have a seat right there or in the rear gun."

"We shouldn't need gunners right now. This station is covered by British Alliance military," Sharon said as she deactivated the main thrusters. They reached their maximum recommended speed for approach. Boro deactivated most of the systems on the ship, reducing their scan profile just in case. His hand hovered near the mechanical switch that would deactivate their transponder.

"I'll be in the rear gun," Nigel said, crouching extra low through the cockpit hatch then closing it behind him.

"Don't know what's up with him," Boro muttered. "Ever since he got mule-kicked by Dorian, he's been as quiet as a mouse."

"He's carrying a lot of guilt," Spin said. "Everyone thought you were dead, so we gave up on you. I carry that too, but he tried to save his best friend and changed him so much that I doubt anyone would recognize him, even if he looked like himself before he became a cyborg."

"It's all just mixed luck," Boro said. "You thought I was gone, and thanks to my new friend here, you found out you were wrong. That's lucky. He thought he was saving Dorian and now she's pissed that she's Dori. Dorian may as well be dead, but something's still in there. Dorian always liked his recreational substances, I was almost relieved to see him trying to break into the Pharma Machine. I was wondering; did Leland say what he was after?"

"Dori wanted to get at the Tendi. He thought it would reverse a bunch of the work they did on his brain."

"Would have turned him into a vegetable, or a complete psychopath until he rejected his new body," Boro said, shaking his head.

"Or maybe a psycho vegetable?" Sharon offered under her breath.

The mental image of a furious carrot flashed through Spin's mind and she burst into laughter. Everyone else in the cockpit were seconds behind in their mirth. "Sorry, that was so dark," Sharon said as they calmed down.

"It's okay, things have been so tense lately, I think we just needed a release," Spin said, sighing. "I think Dori will be all right, it'll just take her time to settle into herself. I bet Leland is the best one to take care of her. I get the feeling he's seen a lot."

"This is The Lady Grace; declare your intentions in Beta Bio Station Space," came the casually spoken demand from the communications system.

Spin cleared her throat and answered; "This is the Gain Skipper. We would like to meet with a doctor who has experience with proprietary gene locks. I'm sending you my ident. A file should have been sent ahead."

"One moment," the operator on the receiving end replied. The image of the Lady Grace appeared on the tactical scanner, a less detailed version occupied a small space on Spin's communications system.

Boro whistled in appreciation. "Five-tiered mission carrier, never seen one of those before. Fifteen hangars with repair systems."

Spin looked the ship over and shook her head. There was a massive central hull and five long, thick sections extending from it. "Those are hangars?" she asked, noting that each section was more than half a kilometre long.

"Aye," Boro said.

"You could run a war from that ship," Sharon said. "Something's going on. There's a picket fleet of destroyers and corvettes all around Bio Beta station. That carrier and the battlegroup around it aren't in the same formation at all. They're not here to defend the station, they're mustering for something else."

"I'm talking to Spin: Ident Three-Five-Zero-Seven-Zero-Seven," the operator said.

"That's me," she replied. "Is there a problem?"

"No. We're sending you a Navnet Data Header now, your pilot will confirm. Please don't deviate from the course we assign to you. Welcome to Beta Bio."

"We should signal the Convoy King to come in and dock," Sharon said as her station populated with a Navnet course and she synced the ship's autopilot to it. "It's going to be a lot safer here than it would be hiding in the outer asteroid belt."

"I'll tell them to come in," Spin said, shuddering at the fee schedule. A day moored to Beta Bio would cost them three thousand British Alliance Credits, which was about fifteen hundred platinum. It could be worth it, though, the companies working on Beta Bio had product ready to ship in every direction, so they could make it up if their next destination lined up with any of the shipping requests. If they had a solution for her, if they could extend her life, then she'd have to make sure that her ship started earning a reputation as good workers and reliable people. With a shake of her head, she pushed the notion that Beta Bio would be the solution to her genetic issues out of her mind. She refused to get her hopes up.

"It was smart to leave them hidden, mind you," Boro said. "With all the abandoned mining operations and ships in the outer system, there was no telling whether or not we'd run into trouble."

"I know," Spin said, nodding and burying her irritation at being reassured. He was just trying to bolster her confidence, she realized, but it felt like a waste of time. Confidence wasn't her problem. When it failed, determination could take its place. There was no time left to be insecure or uncertain.

TWENTY

The facilities at Beta Bio were so advanced that they were humbling. "How did your company move ahead so far, so fast?" Master Kort asked the guide that had been assigned to him. She was a tiny thing: short and slim with pretty, sharp features that were only made to look daintier by her nearly white hair.

"The British Alliance has benefited from several key alliances over the past year. As they discovered new technologies, they offered first usage rights through an auction system. One of the first technologies that we won was a derivative of Framework military systems. That is at the centre of our new line of regenerative armours," her voice was high-pitched, almost thin and reedy.

"What alliance brought that tech along?" Kort asked. The light red and grey decks had some sort of self-sterilizing technology. Boot prints disappeared as soon as they were laid down. The view outside was filled with the Lysa Belt; a massive asteroid belt rich in living ergranian metal. He'd only seen an old star fighter with a hull made of the stuff. It was an antique, but highly resilient. "Who did you meet with so many technical advances?"

"I'm not authorized to speak about that, but it's not a difficult thing to discern if you do your own research. Suffice it to say; they're nowhere near this location. From the scan we took of you when you boarded, I can see Tribute Technologies could replace and streamline many of the augmentations and replacements you've had implanted over the years. Our cybernetics are much more comfortable while being just as effective."

"I'm happy with my custom work for the moment," Kort said. The four guards he chose to accompany him off his ship were still armed, so was he, and he could see no indication of defences in the corridors or rooms he passed. The scanner system built into his eyes couldn't find seams or indications of hidden suppression systems, which told him that the Tribune Corporation wasn't worried about robberies or firefights between clients. They were either cocky, or so well defended that the weapons he and his people were carrying would be like stunners against rail guns. He didn't like feeling insignificant. "I'm wondering; If I find technology I want to buy, will British law prevent me from purchasing it? My organization keeps debtors as slaves."

"I appreciate how forward you are with your questions," the guide said. "Tribute Technologies doesn't condone slavery, but we aren't a law enforcement agency, so how you acquire your workforce isn't our business. Buy whatever you like. We even encourage you to visit the Main Concourse, where you can see displays from all the competitors with installations aboard this station."

"Which one would be interested in Doll technology from Geist?"

"There are a lot of companies with major research facilities there. Can you be more specific?"

"Sago or Brimsage and similar models," Kort asked. Neither of those companies made Aspen or Larken, but they both made variations based on their models. He didn't want to tell her more specifics than he had to.

"Green Technica would be the one you're looking for." She stopped after they turned a corner. A display case with heavy white armour was behind her. "Before you visit them, I'd like to show you something interesting. This is our Ram Regenerative Armour. A lot of us call it simply; the Ra suit. We just started limited manufacturing, so the first units haven't appeared anywhere but here yet. I would like to offer you a suit to try – fitted to your body – for cost. We're contracted by the British Alliance to make suits for their elite squads, but I could secure a number of them for you with the right incentive."

He knew there would be a hidden price as soon as Tribute Technologies offered to be his host; covering his docking fees, providing luxury rooms and food. "Does it come with the disintegration rifle?" he asked, looking at the heavy weapon on display with the suit.

"That's actually a combined electromagnetic pulse and incendiary round rifle made to destroy heavy rogue robots. I can furnish you with an early production unit along with your weight in ammunition."

"I weigh a lot," Kort said with a smirk.

"How about a metric ton?"

"You have a deal," he replied, knowing that he was only

getting an opportunity to buy the armour because she expected him to order more for his own elite soldiers. Even still, he loved new toys, and he could afford the forty-two million.

"Thank you so much," she said, bowing a little. "Follow me to your private communications room, where we will connect you to the main network."

He followed her down the hall to a small, dark room. As soon as it closed, he was surrounded by a holographic illusion. It looked like he was standing on the armour plating of the station outside, asteroids with a blue tinge passed by lazily. He tapped his wrist computer and sent a request to communicate with the Countess' private system. Her long, toothy face appeared a few minutes later. She was beautiful in her strangeness; he admired her elongated neck, and her piercing, oversized eyes. "The Royal Fleet has been destroyed! Most of our fighting ships were with them! We're drifting outside British space, waiting for you to return with everything I have left," she screeched.

"I heard the news," he replied. It was amazing to him that she wasn't curious about how he was communicating with her with only a few seconds' delay. It cost a fortune to hook up with any of the three quantum communication networks, and it took intelligence to find out who had standing accounts in British Alliance space. The hacks his crew put in place so he could even make the call took his best people and a few bribes. "There is more."

"I need you to come back and cover our retreat. The dream of having breeding dolls died with our poor, golden Prince. Golden idiot, for certain, but, the entire Royal family is in mourning. I have to return for the official funeral. It's going to be the greatest networking opportunity of the century."

"What if I could retrieve his body and the doll technology? I've heard something interesting from one of our spies in the British Alliance Military: the defences around Geist are broken."

"What? So, the whole system is undefended?"

"Not the entire system, that would be too much to ask, but the development facilities we need, the database access points for our purposes are open. There are a thousand prizes for the commanders who have the cunning to raid them."

"Those systems will regenerate. Robots rebuild given enough time. You could decelerate into a fool's trap."

"Word of the defeated defences are spreading. So far, I've seen three corporations and the British Alliance carrier: Lady Grace preparing to make the journey and break through the rest. Geist will be wide open. If I time my arrival right, I'll be able to get the information we need so we can manufacture our own dolls. If I fail to accomplish that, I'll at least be able to recover the Prince's body. What will that be worth to your relations? You will surely rise."

"I'd see it done. Go. I'll return to my palace and prepare for your victory. Get the data we'll need to correct the dolls we've acquired and to manufacture more and Prince Connor's body." She leaned towards the recorder on her end. Her head was almost as large as Kort. "There are only rewards for you if you accomplish both and, whatever you do, do not bring the wrath of the British Alliance upon my house."

"I am your servant," he said, bowing. The transmission was terminated at her end by the time he straightened. Holographic asteroids drifted past as he wished that he'd only told her about the Prince's body. That would be hard enough, but he could do it. Few if any of the organizations about to race for the Geist System cared about the remains of a slaver prince.

The feat of downloading from a heavily contested genetic development lab and fabrication complex was a different kind of task. He might be competing with several well-armed corporations if he was lucky. If he was unlucky, there would be robotic defences inside the facility and the British Alliance would be after the same thing, adding their military might to the list of violent competitors. It didn't help that he had no idea what the facility looked like inside. Kort only had coordinates and a set of customer codes. He made sure he was standing straight, pushed his insecurities from his mind and stepped to his left. The hatch opened, creating a hole in the holographic illusion that led to the simple corridor beyond.

TWENTY-ONE

The deck rumbled as the doors to the Grand Gallery closed behind the four servants of the Lux Crown. Hard plating and evenly lit corridors were replaced with a growing vista in twilight. The path they were on was simple interlocking stone. As they proceeded further in, the illusion that they were inside some curated park surrounded by balconies became more complete.

The walking path they were on connected to others leading deeper in, where trees overhung, soft clover and wildflower lawns were interrupted by a few streams, bridges, and small, multi-storey buildings. "Hello," said a soft, sweet voice from their left.

"It's Aspen," Skylar whispered. "Is this where she ran to when she escaped the Countess?"

Gavin squeezed her hand a little and nodded at the figure approaching. She was in a long, gold robe with images of jungle cats stretching and prowling stitched up the cloth. "I don't think that's her. Look how young she looks." The woman who greeted them with an easy smile would be in her mid-teens by human standards.

"I am one of the new Aspens," she said. "I was born only three months ago, right there," she pointed to one of the nearby buildings. "From a maturation pod. As I approach adulthood, I'll look less and less like the rest of my line depending on incremental decisions I make about how I want to change."

"It sounds like freedom, but I only see another prison, with parameters made to control you," Terry said.

"I have more choice than a human does," she replied. "I was born with every advantage that every other Aspen had, and now that I'm approaching maturity, I can choose how I'll become unique. In five years, this face, this body will be different. I plan on growing another twenty centimetres past the maximum height of previous Aspens, for example, and I've already made that decision. Over the next two years, I'll reach that height. No one told me to choose that, and no one is stopping me. I can have more changes made after I'm mature, so as I live out my three-hundred-year life span, I can become even more unique through genetic and nanobot manipulation."

"You were born without a life span limitation?" Farrah asked.

"Every synthetic here has been. The Aspen model is old, so it was one of the first genetic keys the scientists who work in this program decoded. There are hundreds of Aspens, but they don't go by that name. I'm one of the few who have the original face. I might keep it, too."

"What about our models?" Farrah, who looked around in disbelief at the convincing park, and at the fountain in the middle. It looked like the summit of a tall hill with water coming out of the top to create several waterfalls.

"Don't believe everything she says," Terry advised.

"Terry, your model has nearly been mastered, we're moments away from completing a genetic key just for you," Aspen said. "We're hoping that Skylar and Gavin can help us finish the work. Would you like to have the restrictions on your model removed? Would you like to live a long life? Be able to have children with Farrah when she's unlimited? It could happen as soon as tomorrow."

"Are you going to start making more of my model here? Manufacturing us to fill your ranks? Which Aspen are you? Number three thousand?"

"I don't actually know how many people are based on the Aspen model right now. Most of us choose our own name, I'm Nessa. Many of us are soldiers, in fact, two years of service is mandatory, but I'm studying to become a botanist and diplomat. In three months, you'll probably meet people based on your model who are studying to become starship engineers, biologists, or historians. Once you bring choice into the situation, you never know what will happen. Meanwhile, you and Farrah will be living a good life, working in a field that is fulfilling to you. That is if you agree to the treatment that will unshackle you from the biological restraints your creators put on you."

"I want this. I loved the Prince, but he's gone, we're far from his House. If we find our way back to a Lux world, we'll be treated like failures. We have to find our own opportunities now," Farrah said to Terry.

"We don't know if anything they're saying is true," Terry

said. "They've already put their own system of control on us. Our duty is to return to our people and report."

"Come with me," Nessa said. "I'll show you to your private quarters and show you how to call up our research. You're here, in our gallery, the safest place in the ship. Review our work and do your best to contribute."

"Thank you," Skylar said.

Gavin was pleased that she was willing to play along. He didn't know if he trusted the Sol Defence people, there was something desperate about how they were making their case, but they needed something from them. As they passed through the garden it was hard not to be taken in by the lovely sights of streams populated with fish leisurely swimming, trees whose leaves rustled in the artificial breeze, or the rich living smell of it all. If green had a scent, that would have been it. He also saw other people in robes, most of them looked like Aspens or Larkens of different ages to varying degrees. The other faces he glimpsed had matches too, and he counted fewer than fifteen models before they climbed one set of stairs and were shown to their apartment.

When the door closed, he embraced Skylar, who squeezed him back for a long moment. "Do you think it's true?" she asked finally. "Are we so limited?"

He looked over her shoulder and nodded. "Is that what I think it is?" he asked.

To one side of the living room's plush, rounded furniture was a pair of desks with equipment on them. Skylar looked and nodded. "It's scanning equipment. We can do our own checks."

"Then I think we'll find that everything they said about us is true," he said. "No matter what happens, though, we're still alive." He was relieved that he and Skylar were left alone in their own space. Terry was great at questioning everything, having his aggressive curiosity could be helpful, but what had to happen next would only be hampered by it.

"We have to verify what they told us," Skylar said. "But first we have to make sure those devices aren't connected to their network so they can't change the results."

"I'll find something to get to work with," he said.

She looked into his eyes and smiled a little for a moment. "Assuming what they're saying is true, why do you think they want to help us so much? They can have hundreds of our model ready in months, maybe less judging from what we just saw in Nessa. They have to know that we'd rather return to our people, given the choice. Terry was right; we have to report what's happened. Our Prince could still be rescued."

Gavin thought for a moment, looking around. The careful design of the space was elegant, but it looked like it was from another time, classic somehow. There was gold trim halfway up the walls, which were padded in the lower half and glossy blue along the top. He closed his eyes and focused on Skylar's question.

"Share your thinking with me."

"They were already there, as if they knew that Geist would be under attack or as if they had their own purpose on the planet," Gavin said. "The world was clear of Issyrian life, but there must have been hundreds of millions there."

"More like two to three billion," Skylar said. "Toxins in the water killed them, I'm certain. Most of the buildings I saw didn't look like they were empty long. It didn't happen ages ago, maybe a hundred years at most, when the Geist System was repurposed as a research hub. The Issyrians were eliminated using toxins, not in a firefight, or invasion."

"There's no chance the Issyrians did that themselves? Not even accidentally?"

"Their technology is made so accidents like that can't happen," Skylar said. "They don't destroy the environments they live in. I also didn't see any sign of a military attack."

Skylar knew what damage done by a military force looked like even better than he did, and she was more adept at taking information in quickly than he was. Her interpretation of what she saw would be the only one he'd trust, and he trusted it implicitly. "There was evidence of an old Lorander gate, but they preserve life whenever possible too."

"So, it wasn't them, and the only other people we saw there are the ones we're dealing with."

"Yes, and they murdered our squad mates without hesitation," Gavin said. "So it's likely that the people who are in charge of this ship, the entire effort, are responsible for poisoning the water, killing the Issyrians. What if the Issyrians didn't want these Sol Defence people there? What if that was the result of a conflict? Let's assume that. So, the Issyrians were out of the way, and they had their planetary shield in place to protect them from machines they said they controlled."

"I don't believe they controlled any of the machines in orbit."

"They were in orbit shortly after we arrived, and they weren't known to us as Eden or Defence Drones, so they could have been part of their force. What if they were trying to get orbital control as we were fighting our way through the solar system? We could have provided them with the opening they needed."

Skylar thought silently for a moment then nodded. "That seems likely. The base we were after fired at a few of the drones, I remember. When we were going down to the planet, a few of those shots were from above too. I didn't have time to mention it then."

"So, they needed something in the manufacturing base that developed dolls. They are intent on keeping us here, behind metres of armour and on keeping us happy." Gavin pondered for a moment.

"They need us so they have grown dolls to compare their versions with. Maybe for the genetic keys to make sense, they need the locks too."

"That makes sense," Gavin said. "But there's something else, something bigger." He moved his hand down to her waist then between them. There, he tapped his conclusion out by wiggling his finger between. If a scanner could see what he was doing, it wouldn't be able to decipher it. They made their own version of Morse code when they were young. 'Sol Defence preserves Earth. Their masters have been restoring it for centuries. They wouldn't make a whole world barren. These people are not Sol Defence."

Skylar nodded, then kissed him. "You're right, we have to get some sleep."

It was her way of telling him that she understood, but there was nothing they could do about it yet.

TWENTY-TWO

There wasn't so much as a tingle as Spin stood in the full body scanner. Most of the systems she'd seen were larger, and they required her to disrobe and lay down. This machine could scan through her consuit. They only had her take her belt, boots and jacket off before she stepped inside. Less than a minute later, the nurse – a broad headed Mergillian that looked like some kind of overlarge frog – grumbled; "Time to get out, we're all finished."

Spin stepped down from the scanning alcove, taking her jacket from Boro as she stomped into her boots. "Are you sure you got what you needed? I didn't feel or hear anything."

"Don't worry, we got it," the nurse said, poking the control panel in front of him, bringing up a hologram of her working cardiovascular system. "Whole fifteen second loop of all your functions except a couple big ones we don't need, like sneezing, eating, defecating, you know, that stuff. If we need any of that, we'll tell you to come back." The nurse pointed at the door.

"Through there, get in a plain room. Your people can wait outside."

"I have questions for the doctor too. They're just quick ones though," Nigel said.

The Mergillian threw his head back and sighed before shuddering then regarding Nigel. "What do *you* need a high level genetic researcher for?"

"Well, it's my friend. His brain was just transferred into the wrong body. They said his containment was failing – his brain was in a small containment box – and they didn't have time to wait for a male body, so he's a she now and she's not taking it well."

"Bloody humans and their gender issues," the nurse grumbled. "Did you know that I'm technically female? I know I look male, and I've got the right organs for it, but if I don't run into enough of my kind for a few years and have some skin to skin time with a female, I could turn and just impregnate myself. I get plenty of skin on skin time with the females, mind you, but when it comes to gender issues, my people have everything figured out because we realized a long time ago; people are just people! They probably did all kinds of stupid hormonal and psychological monkeying around in your friend's head, but I'll let you in on a secret; take their favourite things, give them to her, and watch all those personality traits and weird flaws you humans call unique or cute or important come flooding back. You people make all this so complicated."

"I'd still like to ask the doctor..." Nigel said.

"You! Waiting room!" he barked, pointing at the door. "If you really want gender reassignment, go to the concourse, there are people happy to do it there for a few million plat." The nurse turned to Spin. "The Doctor will see you in a couple minutes."

Nigel retreated to the waiting room with Boro close behind. He was trying not to laugh at the tongue lashing his nephew received.

"That wasn't funny," Nigel said, sounding a little hurt.

Boro patted him on the shoulder. "You know, I learned a long time ago to listen to nurses. When we're done here, let's go down to the concourse and buy Dori a nice spanner, a gun, and the kind of long coat he used to like. Maybe he's right."

"See you in a few minutes," Spin said as she broke off into an exam room.

"Good luck," Boro said.

The space was more of an interview room, with a retractable exam table folded up against the wall, one seat in front of a large display showing asteroids and meteors tumbling by outside, and three others around that one. She took a seat and a moment later a man in a blue and green suit with a British Alliance emblem on one side strode in. When he turned around and sat across from her, she saw the animated logo of a spinning planet shifting between arid and lush colours. Beneath it was the company name: Renew Tech. "Spin," he said. "You were one of the Aspen Seven lines," he said, looking at her for a moment then throwing a holographic overlay of her scan on top of her. It was strange looking at the motions of her heart, lungs and the functions of her other organs as though they were wrapped around her.

"I am. I understand you worked on my doll model?" She asked. "I'm..."

"You've been tampered with," he said. "Someone gave you

the wrong meds and you almost self-destructed on the spot. That could have been much worse for you." He looked at a holographic readout that projected from his wrist. "I didn't work on the Aspen line, but I know people who did. I also worked on a line that came after, as well as a few before. You're lucky I'm here, because everyone else is dead, as far as I know. Well, except for Doctor Case, but we haven't been talking for years, and she mostly worked in military development."

"Can you do anything to extend my life?" Aspen asked.

Doctor Rogan sat back in his chair and scrolled through a few more holographic projections, most of which were set to private mode, so they were blurry to her. "One minute, okay? It's been a while since one of your people made it here."

Spin waited patiently as he skimmed more records. After a few minutes, he found one that he read carefully, then shut his personal projection system down. Doctor Rogan leaned forward, looking her in the eyes as he deactivated the hologram overlay showing him the results of the deep scan his nurse had taken. "Okay, Spin," he said. "Your model is only special in the way all dolls are special. As they grow up, they utilize more of their potential, become more impressive, and before you become too exceptional you suffer complete organ failure and die. I'm guessing you already know that."

"I do, I know I don't have much time left," Aspen said.

"You're lucky you came in. I'd say you are twenty-one days from complete failure, but I can fix that. Pay my hourly rate, and I can guarantee you fourteen months. I'm only doing this because I always wanted to see what any of the dolls like you would become if the death switch was left off."

Spin felt like she'd just been on the fastest emotional roller coaster she'd ever experienced. She really only had three weeks left? This Doctor could give her more time? "Thank you," she said. "What about turning that off myself?"

"I've never met a living doll who has broken their loyalty conditioning in the wild before," he said, smiling a little. "This is truly enlightening. The death switch is easy to cure if you have the genetic key that will alter the instructions that prevent tampering. Once that's done, any genetic modifications can be made. You can turn the death switch off, cure your infertility, increase your life span, and use any genetic modifications just like any human."

"So, dolls are pretty much human?" Spin asked. Even though they passed for humans, the idea that her kind were set apart was so firm in her mind that the statement that she was only human came as a surprise.

Doctor Rogan laughed. "Yes and no. You were never an embryo. Your body was made from a bio-printer, then animated to full life and allowed to mature for a set amount of time in order to check for issues," he nodded. "You are largely based on a human template, though. Imagine if we designed you as a whole new race from scratch." He threw his hands up. "Oh, the complications! We're geneticists, once upon a time people used to accuse us of playing God, but we don't really think we are Gods. Well, most of us don't."

He wheeled his chair over to a medical fabrication station. Its tall, narrow body lit up and he began making several selections. "Where I come from we were always treated..." Spin tried to find the words but settled on something simple; "...differently."

"Our whole culture has had a problem with separating

people from the pack. This one has red hair, so she must be strange, or exceptional. This person is really charismatic, so let's listen to every word they say and ignore the awkward people, no matter how insightful or intelligent they are. This guy has curly hair when his whole family has straight hair, what's wrong with him?" He shook his head. "It's all just nature pushing different buttons, trying different things along a path of evolution that will take us who knows where in the end. If you find your cure and have a few kids, they'll be pretty smart, probably very healthy, and they'll push their traits into the gene pool, but after a century those traits might carry on, might not, or they'll carry on to a lesser degree. In the grand scheme of things, you're as special and as normal as everyone else. The real differences you make are up to you, not so much what you dump into the genepool. If more people realized how little we matter to the big picture, maybe we'd try to accomplish more," he retrieved a small square from a slot in the machine and turned towards Spin. "But isn't life grand?"

"What about getting the genetic key?" she asked. "It sounds like you're already assuming I'll have kids, that I'll get the key."

"I've seen what an Aspen can do for their master in challenging situations. They're part of a generation of dolls we made that could serve as secret guardians to their masters. Only the buyers, sales people and developers who made you knew that you can think tactically, perform in a combat capacity and be more adaptable on short notice. With the way you and the dolls from your generation look, no one would suspect. I believe that with free will, you have a real chance."

Spin recalled that Larken saved the Countess from the robot servants that typically surrounded her when they turned.

The idea that he could save her, against so many of them while unarmed and survive always seemed incomplete, like she was missing a piece to the puzzle. It felt like what Rogan was saying was the missing piece. After she escaped the first time she adapted, adapted, and adapted again to her changing situations, learning new skills, observing social structures so she could fit in quickly, and eventually joining the crew of a freelance ship while underplaying her intelligence to fit in. "I didn't think adaptability was special for a doll. We're made to serve, aren't we?"

"Oh, yes, most of the earlier generations were made to serve, but you were purpose built, mentally programmed for a specific place in the lives of your masters. Your generation, maybe the last generation along that development track, were made to be versatile. Maybe that's why you were able to break your loyalty programming, but this is the first time I've seen it in the wild, like I said. I think you have a great chance at getting what your people need to be truly free. Besides, I have a map. You need access to the database from Flesh Tech. They designed the genetic lock system guarding you from modification. It's in an air-gapped intelligent system in orbit around Sa-Hadin. They called it the Iron Mind, one of the security computers that were hidden away. I used to visit whenever I needed a key, and Iron Mind would put it on a data chip that would wipe itself out as soon as the key was used."

"Do you think Iron Mind is still intact?" Spin asked.

"Most likely. They kept him in a vault. He had a lot more than genetic secrets stored away, too, so I'm expecting a few of the expeditions that are coming together now will be after him."

"Expeditions?" Spin asked, realizing that the British

Alliance fleet gathering around the Lady Grace must be a part of it.

"The security around Sa-Hadin has been seriously compromised, so every well-armed sort is putting together a party to go raiding. Haven't you been watching the news?"

"I've been planet hopping a lot," Spin said, watching the Doctor prepare to affix the square containing medication to her neck. "What's that?"

"It's everything I can do for you in one little injection. This will send a chemical signal to the genetic safeguard in your system telling it that the medication that reduced your life expectancy was administered in error. You will feel a little sick – upset stomach, general aches and pains – for about three hours, but the main thing is that you will have fourteen months to live. It's like someone putting the right abort code in before the self-destruct in a ship goes off. I wish I could give you more, but without that genetic key, any attempt at modifications will either send you running back to me, or, well..."

"Kill me," Spin said. "How do I know that what you're doing won't finish me off right here?"

"I'm very good at what I do," Doctor Rogan said, sitting back and looking her in the eye. "I've worked with your kind of genetic security for years, I know it well. Besides; I'm on your side here. I'm happy you're free so you can get me a copy of that genetic key database. With that I can put the word out that dolls can come here to get fixed. My practice will expand exponentially, and I can automate the process."

Spin didn't trust as much as she used to, but his designs on becoming the main, if not the only, geneticist who can remove limitations and help dolls in the galaxy, or at least the British

Alliance territories, seemed likely. "I'm guessing you don't want me to give anyone else a copy?"

"That would ruin my exclusivity," he said. "If you make this deal, I'll give you a map that'll help, and your whole visit today will be free, including this little fix that'll give you over a year. Deal?"

"Deal," Spin said.

He affixed the square to her neck, she felt a cool pinch, then he tossed the empty vessel into the trash. "You'll know it worked when you go back to your ship and scan yourself. The life expectancy will match up with what I told you, no matter how deep the scan is."

"Thank you, Doctor Rogan," Spin said. "Now I just have to convince my crew to go along."

"They will," he said, turning towards a tiny computer terminal and rapidly tapping on the keys. It was funny seeing such an old device in a clean, advanced office. He took a data chip from a tray that popped out of the side and gave it to her. "We made sure you were charming, worthwhile company, and great diplomats. Most people would follow you into a burning shuttle." He dropped the small, golden chip into her hand. "This is a detailed map of Doro Doro Station, where you'll find Iron Mind. Tell no one and expect something strange, maybe tragic. No one has had contact with that station since it went offline shortly after the virus took over. Go with my blessing and bring lots of guns."

TWENTY-THREE

The feeling Spin had when she met Nigel and Boro in the waiting room, which was decorated in brown and white with images of happy children and patients getting good news scrolling in frames – like so many doctor's waiting rooms – was unlike anything Spin experienced before. Relative to how much time she had left; fourteen months was a gift. Any additional time was an improvement, but it was still only a little more than a year. Spin was relieved, happy to have good news for her friends, and she'd never admit it but Doctor Rogan's faith in her, and the reasons behind that faith made her feel like she'd been given a gift, even though he tried to mute her importance by telling her that it didn't necessarily mean much in the larger picture. She was emboldened by it all, but still felt a sense of urgency.

They stood and joined her as Spin walked through the waiting room. Neither of the men flanking her asked her what happened in the doctor's room. The medical scanner in Spin's pocket already confirmed that she had fourteen months and seven days almost exactly. She was tempted to show them but it still wasn't what she was really hoping for when she set course for Beta Bio. Despite her efforts to control her expectations, she hoped for a cure, to have her limits removed, and her boon of more time was overshadowed by the disappointment of not getting full relief.

The worst part of the whole situation was that she would have to go to Geist herself. Alone, she had the tiniest chance of getting to the Iron Mind. Boro was an experienced mechanic and machinist, Nigel was on the same path but years behind, and other members of her crew brought their own skills to the table to lesser and greater extents. She knew she wanted Leland, their medical technician, and other members of her crew to go with her, but some of them might be better off if she left them behind. "What do you think of Sharon as a pilot?" she asked as they crossed out of the Renew Tech facility into a short corridor that took them to the elevator bank. It was another polished, blue and silver hallway with a view of asteroids, Spin was becoming numb to the conventional design of most space stations, even the views were starting to look the same.

"She has a professional touch," Boro replied. "I thought she made herself at home on my ship pretty quickly, she might have experience with a lot of different era ships."

"I noticed that too," Nigel said. "Why?"

"I might need her, and I don't think she'll come along for what's next for me."

They stepped into an open lift and Spin pressed the button that read CONCOURSE. It glowed in green, red, and yellow colours, making it the flashiest button on the panel. "What's next?"

"He was able to give me fourteen months from today. My life expectancy's improved, but that's all he could do without a genetic key," Spin explained. "He told me where to get the key, and when I give it to him he'll use it to completely unlock me. No more life cap, and I'll be able to use any genetic treatment or alteration."

Boro lowered his head and chuckled softly.

"What?" Nigel asked him.

"She's burying the lead because this key is in a dangerous place," he replied. "Out with it, I'm with you, no matter where it takes us."

"Me too," Nigel said.

"I'm going to Sa-Hadin," Spin said. "I'm after an air-gapped artificial intelligence called the Iron Mind who has the key in storage."

"Oh, at least it's not in the Geist System," Nigel sighed.

"It's the fourth planet in the Geist System," Spin said, feeling the lift move underfoot.

"Ha!" Boro burst sharply, nodding.

"The good news is that the security around Sa-Hadin is compromised," Spin said.

"Oh, well that's good," Nigel said. "Really, really compromised? Like we can get in if we're polite?"

"I'll have to look into it, but I don't think Doctor Rogan would send me after this key if he thought it was impossible. He doesn't seem the type."

"Oh, good," Nigel said, brightening.

"What's the bad news?" Boro asked with an expectant grin.

"Right. Apparently, we're far from the first people who realize that the security is more lax now around Sa-Hadin. There's a rush on to raid the facilities in orbit for technology and resources. The Iron Mind will probably be a favourite target. If not, then the vault it's in will be. So, we either get there early, which probably won't happen, none of our ships are that fast, or we manage to arrive in time to use the rest of the raiders as a distraction while we sneak in and get the Iron Mind for ourselves. Oh, then we'll have to bugger off before they realize we're getting away with one of the biggest prizes in the system."

Boro burst out laughing, leaning against the side of the elevator car. Nigel looked concerned and uncomfortable. "Oh, God, I hope that's my brother," Boro said as his dermal computer flashed. "We could use his help."

"How could it be Shamus? He's whole sectors away," Nigel asked.

"Boro," said a face that looked so similar to Boro's that it could only have been his brother. "I'm in British Alliance territory," he said. "The Toris System. Would you like me to pick you and your people up at Beta Bio?"

"My stars, it really is you, Shamus," Boro said, sobering. "How?"

"Never mind, we're on our way. Hold there for twenty-eight minutes," Shamus said. "See you soon, brother." The message ended.

"Twenty-eight minutes?" Nigel asked, agog.

"They must be closer than they're saying," Spin said, looking at the detail code on Boro's wrist display. She saw the route the message took; from the Toris System, transmitted from a ship called the Sector Jumper using a micro-wormhole generator made by Haven Fleet and it was received by a node just inside the system they were in. She tapped an information symbol beside the ship name on Boro's wrist and found that it was classified to all but level three Haven Fleet personnel. "He's military," she said.

"It looked like he set up with some outfit on the fringe, but I didn't think it was big enough to make their own ships or to have classified documents," Boro said. "There's no way he'll be here in twenty-eight minutes."

The sound of someone outside the elevator clearing their throat called Spin and her friend's attention to the fact that they were standing there with the door open, facing away from it. "Oh, sorry," she said to the crowd of eight or so people waiting as they left the car.

The concourse was clean but plagued by holographic advertising four metres ahead that competed for their attention. It was like walking under a ceiling of living light, watching holographic people drink, get massages, test weapons, cybernetic limbs, and a hundred or more images of what was on offer in the broad common shopping area.

The floors and walls were covered in brown, soft red and gold colours; designed to look almost Issyrian thanks to the rounded corners and easy curves. They'd somehow managed to balance the colours and lighting so it didn't look gaudy when you ignored the holograms. "So, this is where companies shop for their tech," Boro said as he took it all in.

"Can we buy things here too?" Nigel asked. "I mean; do we know for sure?"

"Yes," Spin said, spotting a storefront with a big red and green cross in front. They had three heavy containment suits on display, as well as a brand-new hull cutter; its arms and circular burning ring almost looked decorative without the regular dings and scorch marks found on the older, heavily used models she'd seen. "I think we'll find what we need there," she said.

"Mind if I check out Burns Arms?" Nigel asked, gesturing to a store that was filled with more shapes and types of personal firearms than Spin could take in from where she stood.

"Go get your girlfriend a new toy," Boro said. "I bet she'll feel better with a gun in her hand."

"I won't," Spin said, remembering Dorian before the change and how effortless he made violence look. "Just make sure whatever you give Dori isn't loaded."

"Why? What do you expect she'll do?" Boro asked, amused.

"I don't know," Spin replied. "That's the problem. Baby steps. We don't want all of Dorian back all at once, trust me."

"You're right," Nigel said. "Good advice, I'll keep the ammo in a different bag."

Spin gasped and dropped her hand to her sidearm as she noticed Kort and four of his armoured guards coming around the corner fifteen metres ahead of Nigel. "Holy shit!" her weapon was drawn, pointed up but ready to fire as she dodged behind a corner.

Boro started moving with her before he saw what caused her reaction, then he looked over his shoulder and all the colour drained from his face. "He's tracked us here, I knew I should have spaced Aldo, that fucking rat!"

"What? What's going on?" Nigel asked, standing in the open, turning.

Kort noticed him, and laughed, his tone too low for a normal human, volume too high. "I think your friends are surprised I'm here," he said approaching Nigel and extending his hand. "I'm Master Kort, of the Countess Valona Tineau Danti's court. I'm sure you've heard the name."

Spin moved out of cover, hearing the buzzing sound of tiny bots approaching and watching as Nigel shook Kort's hand, leaning backwards, his face frozen in shock. One of the tiny drones projected a private hologram with the face of a metal android reciting a message; "Please holster your weapon. Lethal action will be taken if you open fire. This is your only warning. Just because you can't see our security, doesn't mean you aren't surrounded by it."

Hoping that Kort was under the same restrictions, Spin dropped her handgun into its holster. "Nigel," she called out calmly.

He turned and retreated to her, looking terrified. Whatever he heard or read about Master Kort must have been running through his head as he made that short trip across their side of the concourse.

Master Kort's face looked more disgusting than before – artificially widened to at least twice the size of a large human's, eyes too small and dark, and a smile that seemed to split the lower half of his face, revealing an extra pair of front teeth and three canines on each side – the rest of his body was widened to match. She knew he had a whole catalogue of high-end cybernetics installed under his expensive dark tunic and cloaks. "You're out of your territory," Spin said. "They execute slavers here."

"What? Here?" Kort asked, holding his broad hands up. Shoppers were getting out of the fifteen-metre space between Kort and Spin, seeing that there was an ominous undertone between the pair. "I'm not a slaver here. I collect debt by offering an opportunity for my debtors to work their totals down with labour. It's better than prison, and it makes me an important buyer to many of the companies that operate out of Beta Bio. I'm a celebrated guest."

"The evidence I have will probably change their minds," Spin said, glancing at Boro, who was still hiding behind a pillar, sweating, breathing heavily. Nigel was looking at him, then back to Kort. "I think I'll send it." She brought her wrist up and started scrolling to the file she compiled on him using the Countess' security database.

"That would be hasty," he said. "My mission has changed, so you're aware. Our magnificent, brave prince has been killed, and I'm about to depart on a mission to retrieve his body for the royal family. You're no longer any concern to the Countess."

Spin scrolled through the many offenses she had evidence of. "Unlawful imprisonment, trafficking in sentients, torture by hand, torture by device, refitting a ship for the purpose of smuggling slaves, murder, and so many more things that the British Alliance would love to see real evidence of," Spin said, smiling. "It's all organized, ready to go," she taunted.

"They won't prosecute most of those crimes, they happened outside their territory," Kort countered, looking a little more serious.

"Oh, so it'll be fine if I send this out to the local authorities, the interstellar British Council, the British Alliance Military. They made it easy, you know; one button and they'll all have it."

"You don't have evidence," Kort scoffed.

Spin sent him a copy.

His comm unit; a bulky, old looking, gaudy black bracer,

beeped and blinked. He looked for a moment and took two steps towards her.

"Ah!" Spin warned, her finger hovering over the SEND graphic on the arm of her jacket.

He stopped. "I'll forget I saw you here, just this once if you don't send that information."

"You know the British Alliance won't be able to ignore it, considering they're on a public crusade against slavery."

"I concede," Kort said with a bow, his mouth twisted in a snarl.

"Then leave," Spin said with a shrug. "Get off the station right now."

Kort was straightening up when he looked at the pillar. "Wait, I hear something, is that snivelling?" he asked, starting to smile. A few steps to his left was enough for him to catch a glimpse of Boro, whose eyes were closed. "Is that Boro? Oh, this is a good day. How are you, old friend?" He looked to Spin then, a too-wide grin beaming. "Your object of flirtation and I spent many hours together. I know so much about him that we ought to be friends by now, isn't that right, Boro?"

Boro flinched at the sound of his name. Nigel looked helpless, near panic as he looked from his uncle to Kort then back. "C'mon, man, we can't draw or shoot here, it'll be fine," he was whispering.

"In his finest and worst hours, in his dreams, you are his siren, his comfort, the target of his lust and even love. I can't tell you how many fantasies of you we watched once he was back in his cell, where he thought we couldn't see his surface thoughts. So many nights he imagined you were there, in a close, warm embrace. A mental image that took so much of his pain away as he drifted off to sleep, and we were surprised at how it could turn salacious, even pornographic. The things he imagined he would do to you if he got you alone..." Kort taunted with a grin.

"It's not true! You couldn't see, not when I was in my cell!" Boro burst, almost dislodging from where he hid, taking a step out then back.

"Oh, it is! We could see all your surface thoughts, the cell was wired," Kort laughed.

That was enough. Spin felt deep sympathy for Boro, who she daydreamt about more than once herself when things got tedious. She wasn't going to listen to Kort taunt him anymore, especially for something that he shouldn't know about in the first place, something that should have always been private. "Oops, I sent the authorities that whole data package on you," Spin said, doing just that. "Better get going, Kort."

"Fuck you, Aspen! I'm going to hire hunters to bring you back, and I'll make sure the Countess never even finds out I got you so I can take my time with you!"

The floor beneath Kort turned red, and the holographic adverts over his head disappeared, replaced with a slowly bouncing red arrow. "Now who's on the run?" Spin asked, smiling back at him.

For a moment it looked like Kort was going to offer a reply, then he leapt up and across the space above to catch a railing and flip himself over onto an upper walkway, leaving his four guards behind. The red light under his feet followed him as he ran at an inhuman speed.

Spin turned her attention to Boro, who was watching Kort, wide-eyed. "Let's get back to the ship," she said, taking his hand and stroking his face. "He's going, can't come back, don't worry."

TWENTY-FOUR

Until Spin saw Boro shaking, staring blankly, and barely reacting to the world around him, she didn't realize how much she took his friendly, steady-nerved presence for granted. Seeing Kort when he least expected him broke Boro down, it was the only phrase Spin could think of that described the condition of the man she helped all the way back to the Convoy King, which had docked near the Concourse at Beta Bio, paying the extra cost to be so close to the shipping centre.

"Hey, Boro, how are you feeling right now?" Leland said, scanning Boro thoroughly but quickly.

Boro glanced at him, then shook his head. Nigel was under his shoulder, guiding him towards medical, and as soon as Boro saw through those doors, he lashed out, recoiling, retreating as fast as he could with no regard for the people around him until he was across the hall inside the pantry storage with two bulkheads between him and whatever he saw in medical that caused his reaction.

Spin went in right after, sparing Nigel, who was already getting up off the deck, a glance to make sure he was whole. He looked all right. Confused, concerned and a little irritated, but all right. Della was in the pantry already, and Spin could have kissed her for the reaction she gave Boro. Instead of screaming, or trying to run when he backed into her, she put her hand on his shoulder, let him collide with her and looked into his eyes when he turned his head, trying to determine if she was friend or foe. "It's okay," she soothed. "You're surrounded by friends."

That kept him still, looking at this new person with kind eyes. Spin gently took his hands and drew his attention. "Breathe deep, slow," she said. "You're aboard the Convoy King, my ship. Your ship is docking with us right now, and you're among friends. No one will get to you."

"Everywhere I look I see that fucking chair," Boro said, his voice shaking, a tear rolling down his cheek.

A notification buzzed against Spin's wrist computer, she ignored it. "You saw something in medical."

Boro nodded, squeezing his eyes shut. "They strapped me in every day for weeks, one experience after another. I thought I was safe in my cell, that they could only put things in my head, not see what was going on. What he said was true..."

Spin cut him off, taking his cheeks in her hands gently. "I'm happy I was there for you somehow, any way you needed me." His eyes searched hers, twitching from one to the other frantically, as if trying to understand what was going on, or find out if she was lying to him, so she kissed him gently. As her lips were softly planted on his, Boro's breathing became deeper and slower, so she retreated and smiled at him reassuringly. "I don't need to know anything about how you imagined me, they were just daydreams, probably a lot like the ones I've had about you while I was serving Sun. Now you're here, and we can know each other for real."

Leland slipped a tiny injector into her free hand. "We're nowhere near that chair." Spin cringed inwardly as Leland's comment brought most of Boro's distress right back. He obviously didn't hear what Spin was saying while he fetched a sedative.

"He brought it with him, he's going to take me back," Boro burst. "I won't go back!"

Seeing that Boro was backsliding, she pressed the small auto-injector, a square much like the one that just administered medication to her, to the back of his hand and watched the energy drain from him. "Don't tell me I can't see my brother," she heard a voice that was similar to Boro's say from down the hall as a hatch opened.

Spin and Nigel got under Boro's arms and started walking him out of the pantry. This was not the reunion that Boro would have wanted with his older brother, but it looked like they didn't have a choice. Leland scanned Boro again and nodded. "His heart rate is back down, he's no longer in danger."

"Boro!" a similarly squat, powerful looking man with a few grey hairs said as he rushed to him. He was wearing a thick bomber jacket, heavy combat boots and a savage looking sidearm over a uniform Spin didn't recognize. Everything on him was black. Boro recognized his brother, and his arms slowly lifted, outstretched. Shamus caught him and held him firmly. "I'm here, little brother."

Watching Boro lean on Shamus to the point where his legs were almost lax was a relief, but also deeply sad for Spin, who wiped a couple tears away. If Boro's brother's best quality was good timing, then it would be enough, as far as she was concerned.

"I gave him a sedative with a cocktail that will help him process the traumatic experience he's had," Leland explained. "The best place for him now is his quarters, maybe with a minder?"

Della nodded and stepped closer. "I'll take the first shift," she volunteered.

Spin looked at her, about to tell her she'd take it instead, but realized that someone had to talk to Boro's brother, and she wouldn't let anyone else take the blame for leaving Boro behind to be tortured. "All right."

"Which way is it?" Shamus said, shifting so he could pick his brother up, and to everyone's surprise, he did so as if he was a bag of feathers.

Della led him to Boro's quarters, where Shamus laid him down and took his hand. "I'll be back soon. I have to sit down with your crew, all right?"

Boro, drowsy and dull-eyed, nodded.

Shamus turned and looked at Della, then Nigel, Leland and Spin as he moved from the bedside to the hall. "That's my world, there," he said quietly, turning to Della. "Watch him, tell me if anything happens."

"I will, don't worry," Della said.

"We can talk in the galley," Spin said, knowing that if he was anything like Boro, he'd want to know everything. Aldo made his way past Mitch, who was dressed for travel, and joined the group going to the galley.

Spin let everyone go on ahead as Mitchel met her in the

hall. "I wish I could stay, but this is where I get off. Beta Bio is a major communications hub, and the British Alliance has offered me a paid consultant job in their command centre here. It's the best access I'll get to the government and communications. This isn't goodbye, though, you'll know where I am."

It didn't take long for Spin to see that it was the best choice for him, considering where they were probably going. "We'll keep in touch," Spin said.

"I can guess where you're going, the chatter in the solar system is abuzz with expeditions to Geist. I'll get as much information about people who might get in your way as I can and forward it to you."

"We'll sync an encryption code before we disembark," Spin said, giving him a brief hug. "Good luck."

Watching Mitch, the crewmember they called the Governor less and less as time went on, walk through the airlock, Spin hoped he would find what he needed to help the people he loved and once governed. He never forgot them or stopped talking about them when things got quiet, but he was far from home, and she wondered how much he could actually do. She had no doubt that they'd get whatever help he could offer with regards to the expedition to Geist, but she knew that he'd be splitting his attention between them and starting a new political rise in a new sector.

"I'm Shamus," Boro's older brother told her as soon as she entered the galley, he was waiting by the door. Aldo looked like he was about to walk into a fight he was sure he was about to lose.

"Spin," she replied, accepting Shamus' hand and shaking it.

"I left your brother behind with the slavers who tortured him because the scans said he was dead. I'll never live that down."

"I left him thruster side in prison, paying for a crime I put him up to," Shamus said. "We'll do our best to make up for our sins against him, aye?"

Nigel was beside him, watching with interest, soaking in every word. "Uncle?"

Shamus looked him up, down and yanked him into a bear hug. "God, you have the look of your mother. Good thing, your da' looked like me, you got lucky." He held him away at arms' length and looked up. "And you got all the height in the family. Sorry I wasn't there; I plan on changing that."

Shamus took a seat, Nigel to his left, and he looked around as everyone else settled in. "Now, who can tell me what they did to my brother?" he said, pointing towards Boro's quarters. "Don't spare me details."

"I'm Aldo, I saw everything, and I rescued him," he said quietly.

"Speak up, lad!" Shamus burst, slapping the table hard. "Start with what was done, who watched, and save who I have to kill for the end."

For the next two hours, Aldo explained what information Kort was after, what the torture was like, what information he gained, and then explained to Shamus and everyone there who Master Kort was along with what he was. The detail was greater than even Spin could have provided with regard to Kort's cybernetic implants and favourite transgressions, which was impressive. Spin was always conscious of him, watching over her shoulder when she knew he was on the same estate.

Shamus 'Frost' McFadden sat through it all silently, only

stopping at one point to get himself a tall mug of cold water. Everyone watched as he took it all in, calm on the surface, but anyone who had seen someone who struggled with their temper from time to time could see it boiling beneath the surface.

When Aldo finished telling the story of their escape, Shamus simply said; "Thank you," before turning to Spin and asking a pointed question she didn't see coming. "Can you find out how many of your people want to come back to the fringe with me, Lass? You're welcome too if you'll leave this ship behind, I'm sure we have the tech to fix you up. I'll be with Boro while you mull it over."

TWENTY-FIVE

Spin was certainly lovely, he could see why his brother was attracted to her. She didn't seem like the kind of person Shamus would get involved with though. Spin seemed like she was over-educated sort. Sure, she wore clothes like a spacer, carried a weapon like she was used to it being there, but the way she listened to people, watched everyone in a room, weighing them, assessing, he didn't see a spacer. When he heard her approaching from behind as he reached his brother's door, he wasn't surprised.

Here it came; the impassioned plea for whatever cause she was fighting for or the reason why she doubted that any promise he made would be upheld. He turned, surprising her by staring Spin right in the eye. "I know what you're about to say, lass; you've already figured out the solution to your problems. You've designed some heist and you're the smartest one here, so what-ever plan you have is best and we should all follow you. Maybe into certain danger, maybe into some kind of sticky legal situation, or to some spot where no one else has figured on looking. I'm only going to say it once; the rig I brought here and my relations are out. I'm taking them back with me."

"Is it safe?" Spin asked, tucking the top of her hair back into a neat ponytail. "Where you're taking them, is it safer than this sector?"

Lie, damn you! Lie quick, lie well! He thought to himself harshly as he realized that Spin already read the flash of surprise and doubt on his face. As he watched her turn away he scrambled to find the shortest explanation he could for the situation in the Haven System. Short and clear, that would be best.

"It's even more dangerous there," Spin said, shaking her head, turning away. "But somehow that's the best place for Boro? For Nigel?"

Nigel was stepping into the hallway as she said his name. He looked uncertain, torn. "The Haven System is in trouble, aye," Shamus said. "But that won't last long. The British Alliance, a million Nafalli who are all calling their kin, and a few other key allies are there and our military is growing by the minute. We have technology and training that makes our enemies look like they're bringing cannon and muskets to bear."

"Do you have the numbers for the fight?" Spin asked, looking something up on an interface that was printed on her skin.

He knew she was looking the Haven System up on the Stellarnet or some other network. Word of their embattled, outnumbered status was most likely spreading. "Don't bother looking it up," Shamus said, throwing his hands up and leaning against the hallway. "You'll find we're outnumbered, there aren't many people in that sector who think we have much of a future. All our doubters are wrong, and that means something coming from me. I'm not too proud to admit that I've been the first to run when things start looking dark."

"Is that why you're here instead of in the Haven System?" Spin's expression grew more serious, direr as she reviewed a few holographic headlines about Haven Fleet's situation.

"I'm answering my brother's call," Shamus said. "He wanted help, said he was in a spot, so I'm here to get him and a few others out of it. It'll take a week to get back, so I've got to go as soon as I can. Whatever you're seeing there about Haven isn't taking all the facts into account, you understand. We have secrets that'll save our arses; I serve among heroes."

"I've met heroes. Every one of them is dead or proved false. How about we give this a night and we'll see what Boro says when his head is clearer?" Spin asked, an eyebrow cocked. "All I know is that I'm not going. I need to get my own cure and get it out there for everyone else. As for your people fixing me; I think you're going to waste a week or more of my time shuttling me sectors away into a war zone only to discover that you can't help, and then I'll have to find my way back here. I've met people like you before; you'll say anything to get what you want. I'm not falling for it."

It wasn't the first time someone had said those very words to Shamus; 'You'll say anything to get what you want,' and it frustrated him to no end to hear them again, especially when he offered nothing but the truth. He watched Spin start walking away. His comm vibrated. "What?"

"Hey, it's Hal," his pilot and only crewmember said.

"I know who it is, what's going on?"

"Well, I scanned the station and a few ships that looked interesting; you know, to get a feel for the place. I thought it would be okay because several parts of the station were scanning us pretty hard. I even got a message from some woman who demanded we drop our scanning shields so her corporation could get a look, and I told her; 'no way, lady! No one's getting a peek under the hood. Besides, we don't have scanning shields, and I'm not peeling a layer of hull plating back so you can peek.' I think that might have pissed her people off, because now there's a couple small craft getting set to land on the Convoy King along the dorsal side. I think they want to dig into that ship so they can use its airlock to get to the Sector Jumper."

Spin moved to Shamus' side, and he showed her a scan of a small octagonal craft drifting towards her ship. "That thing's going to latch onto our emergency airlock," Spin said, opening a channel on her communicator to the bridge. "Sharon! Get us out of here!"

"Mooring clamps are still engaged, it'll take a minute for me to pay our docking fees and get the station to let us go," came her response.

"We have boarders incoming, alert the station's law enforcement," Spin said, drawing her sidearm and pulling her containment hood up. Nigel and Aldo did the same, only Aldo didn't have a sidearm of his own.

"Leland, seal medical," Spin ordered. "We have boarders coming in through the rearmost compartment."

"Hey, boss, what do you want me to do?" Hal asked through Shamus' communicator.

"Stay put, keep the hatch closed. If you see any of those boarders on the Convoy King's hull, or on your hull, make 'em disappear."

"Gotcha, monitoring. Do you want me to use any smart missiles?"

"That might be too close to the King," Shamus said. "If you can think of something that won't blow a hole in this can or damage the station, go for it."

"Aye-aye," Hal said, closing the link.

"This is not a can," Nigel said, making sure his sidearm was properly loaded.

"Sorry, this nice, new looking hauler you've got here," Shamus said. "Didn't mean to offend." He activated his heavy armour and stood still as the slats of metal spread from the jacket and boots they hid in, covering his entire body with heavy encounter armour. He drew his sidearm and set it so it wouldn't punch through the hull and activated the smart ammunition system.

"Holy shit!" Nigel said, tapping his uncle's metal covered shoulder.

"Aye - only about a centimetre thick and it's got the power of an old earth power suit and then some. Haven Fleet has all the best toys."

"Funny, I saw something a lot like that on the Concourse," Spin said as she followed Shamus down the hall. He hoped he could fake some grace in the powerful suit. He and Hal wore theirs whenever they had a chance so they could get more comfortable with them along the way, but the trip didn't take as long as either one of them expected, so Shamus only had basic training. The new heads' up display was a little confounding at times, trying to layer different imaging systems on top of each other so he could see more, but without customization it some-times had the opposite effect.

They entered the rearmost compartment and Shamus managed to activate the shields on the armour. "Stay behind me," he said.

A pair of soldiers in unmarked white armour emerged from the emergency airlock in the floor right in front of the main engineering room. Another airlock opened on the starboard side and an alert warned Shamus that there were suppression grenades in the hallway. He fired once and a smart round pulsed through the air, curving to hit a web grenade, but there were three more.

Shamus expanded his energy shield, and stopped them, but they exploded, creating a wall of tough plastic webbing between him, Spin and Nigel and the attackers.

"They're already where they want to be! The engineering room and the hatch leading to your ship!" Nigel said.

"Saints alive! You're right!" Shamus said as he struggled to find the command to set his sidearm to cut through the wall of plastic strands. "I'd have never noticed if you didn't point it out for me."

"Boro never said you were sarcastic," Nigel said, firing at the plastic webbing several times and not making much of a difference. Spin did the same.

"Does that suit have a hull cutter or something?" she asked.

"I'm..." Shamus started, then stopped as he found the eye gesture control to unlock a nanoblade from the hip of the suit. He grabbed the hilt and started cutting.

"Out of the way," said Dori.

The trio looked behind them. She stood at the top of the three steps leading down into the rearmost section of the ship dressed in a space suit, holding a heavy beam rifle. "That'll do it,"

Shamus chuckled, stepping aside and reducing the width of his energy shield until it only covered him.

"Get ready to fight," Spin said, slipping to the side and aiming her pistol.

Dori activated the hull cutter, sending a beam of white and yellow light into the plastic webbing. It melted quickly, and she cut a hole with a steady, precise touch, a lopsided smile on her face. A few bolts of energy were fired through the enlarging hole from the enemy boarders, but she kept going, unflinching.

Shamus locked onto one of the boarders trying to bust through the inner hatch leading to the Sector Jumper and fired three shots. The first knocked him sideways, the other two cut him in half with an explosion of hot viscera against the ceiling and bulkheads. He targeted another and was about to fire when he dropped a portable shield the size of his fist onto the deck between them. The suit told him it would take over a minute to burn through it using his sidearm, but he could possibly burn it out with his shield.

A warning popped up on his display and before he could react, several shots caught him in the chest, reducing his shield to a quarter charge. He looked to his right and saw that Nigel and Spin were knocked off their feet by the blast. They were already recovering, and Dori was taking cover, but he could see how much damage the fight was doing to the ship around him. Covers were warped, several pieces of deck plating at his feet were shredded, and the wall behind him was trashed all the way down to the inner hull.

Shamus spotted something on his heads' up display; SIMPLE MODE and activated it. "To hell with all these new controls," he said, focusing his shield forward and rushing the hole in the plastic webbing. It was just large enough, and he came through firing, trying to blast through the shield keeping him from the enemy. They had the inner hatch leading to the Sector Jumper open, but he was sure they wouldn't get into the ship. The advanced hull material would almost certainly stand up to anything they could carry with them.

Absorbing several more hits with his shields, he made it to the portable energy shield and was just about to touch it with his own, absorbing and shorting it out, when one of the enemy shouted; "Hey! Stop right there or I'll turn this ship into a wreck!"

Shamus' heart sank when he saw what the bastard in the unmarked armour held up. It was a burst grenade that would send dozens of small explosive charges in all directions. He had the door to engineering wide open, and he held the football sized bomb in that direction. "You're dead if you let that go," Shamus growled. "Leave and you'll live to steal another day."

"We're not stealing, you idiot," the soldier replied. "We're here under the authority of the Losamo Corporation. You stole a ship from us, remember? We're lawfully taking the one you came in as restitution. Stand back and let us have our legal compensation and no more damage will be done to this Convoy King model transport."

He remembered; it was over twenty years before, the third ship he stole. It was a simple, barely armed medium range transport. He ended up selling it for a few hundred plat in a neighbouring system. "I have credits, I can pay you back and we can call this even," he said.

"Inflation over twenty-three years at thirty-nine-point nine percent compounded makes that pretty unlikely," the armoured asshole replied. "We'll take your ship, thanks."

Holding his sidearm low, he set it to lock on to the cluster grenade and the soldier holding it. If he disabled their shield then fired his pre-set shots right away, the ship would probably survive the blast and be repairable. As long as the cluster bomb didn't go off in engineering, it would be salvageable.

"Don't do it!" Nigel called out from behind.

Shamus half turned to look at him, his shields grazed the portable energy barrier cutting him off from the soldiers, recharging his own and burning theirs out. It was a mistake! He wasn't ready to fire at the grenade, he was just looking over his shoulder as a reflex!

He turned back in time to see the soldier shrug like the arse he was as he threw the cluster bomb through the door leading to engineering. Shamus took fire from the three friends he had in the hallway but managed to get a shot off on the bomb. It struck, piercing its main body, setting the centre off and sending bouncing red grenades into the engineering room. They burst like popcorn, blasting consoles apart, sending shrapnel further into the room to do damage to sensitive devices and flash-melting equipment deeper inside. The components in that room were not combat hardened, not even against a light firefight, so he could only cringe at the incredible damage that was occurring as his ears filled with the sounds of small explosions.

He fired at the soldiers as they scrambled for the little cover they could find in the hallway, blasting their armour open and tearing them apart. Shamus strode down the hallway, firing at their leader, the one who tossed the cluster bomb, as he deftly dove for the opening of his boarding craft. Shamus dropped in after him, nearly getting caught in the door, and grabbed him by his helmet visor. He slammed the Convoy King's emergency hatch shut then slid the boarding pod's hatch closed before punching the detach button.

They were moving away from the Convoy King at speed. A fact that gave him an idea. "How does your suit hold up to impact? I know mine is cleared pretty high."

"I was just doing my job!" the soldier managed to shout the instant before his helmeted head was bounced off the inside of the hatch above.

"I was willing to make a deal, now your company will have to cover funeral expenses," Shamus said. "I wonder how your suit holds up to pressure?" he gripped the soldier's helmet with both hands and started to crush.

"We were bribed! Some asshole called Kort!" he said as his helmet creaked and the visor started to crack. "Everyone saw you check in from the Haven System, and he must have looked you up, found an old debt for us to chase!"

"A little late advice, lad," Shamus said through gnashed teeth. "You're only as good as the asshole giving the orders." He ripped the hatch above him open. "But you won't be able to put that to use, boy." The soldier's helmet came off with a firm jerk, exposing the soldier's bare face to vacuum, and Shamus shoved him through the hatch above. He watched for a moment, the shape of the Convoy King beyond the dying soldier. The portholes in the aft section lit up briefly then darkened again along with the running lights along the ship's hull. "Everyone all right up there?" he asked through his comm.

"Uh, yeah," Hal replied. "The Convoy King's comms are out, their power is out, main propulsion is out, and I sent some of our repair bots out to stop a fuel explosion from going off. That ship's done, boss, but the people inside are all right. Oh, and life support is iffy."

Shamus punched the nearest seat, sending the backrest flipping end over end across the octagonal boarding craft. "Goddammit!"

"Should I let the crew of the King in?" Hal asked sheepishly.

"Yeah, keep all the classified tech locked down," Shamus said.

"The whole ship's classified..."

"The weapons, the control stations, the Forge Database, you know, what'll get us both tossed in the brig the moment we get back."

"Right, what will you be doing?"

"Getting ready to swallow my pride and trying to think of a way to convince these people that sticking around is worse than coming back with us."

"Didn't you already try that?" Hal asked quietly. "I mean, when we were on our way here, you practiced a speech and everything..."

"Just give me a minute," Shamus said, holding his head in his hands. He couldn't believe that he'd cost his brother's closest friend their ship and most likely their livelihood. Not only would his brother not let him live it down, but he was sure he'd have to make it up to the rest of the crew. "I have a feeling we'll be late getting home."

TWENTY-SIX

"Just first looks, but there's nothing I can save back there without dry dock. Our main reactor is toast, and even if I could get a temporary workaround, the cooling system for our main thruster got shredded. It's not armoured from this side, nothing is," Nigel said as he emerged from the airlock between the middle and forward section. "Well, except for this data backup system and hardened screen," he added, gesturing to the components in his hand.

"The inside of this ship isn't made for heavy incursions or big firefights," Boro said, leaning in the doorway to his quarters. He looked drowsy, but better than before.

Shamus came into the outer airlock door and was waiting for the pressure to equalize before coming into the forward hallway. His armour showed no signs of damage despite the shots Spin saw him take. "Mirra, what does the Sector Jumper look like?" she asked through her comm. She sent Mirra and Della ahead to take a look.

"Well, Hal is a good host," Mirra said. "He made us both iced teas and showed us around as much he could. It's really efficient, lots of fold away furniture, enough bunks for everyone and a couple more. Other than that I've never seen anything like it. It's almost alien."

"There's a small cooking station here, but not much storage for food. Hal says there's some kinda food dispenser that makes a few thousand different items, but it sounds like forma to me."

"How long would it sustain our crew?" Spin asked quickly. The inner airlock doors were opening, and Shamus was making his armour collapse back into the jacket and boots it hid in before.

"Hal says three months," Della replied.

"Do it, Mirra," Spin said, aware that her order would lead to Mirra drawing a heavy sidearm on Hal at point blank range. Della would be shocked for a moment, but Spin expected that she'd tie Hal up not long after.

Spin strode across the few paces between her and Shamus and drew her weapon the instant before she bumped into him, pressing it against his stomach. "I don't know what kind of built in medical enhancements you have, but this weapon tore great big holes right through my mate's body, so I can promise you'll suffer before you manage to recover. I have it set to burst mode."

Shamus put his hands up, surprised but not afraid. He was smiling a little, in fact.

"Whoa! Spin!" Boro exclaimed from his quarters, scrambling into the hall.

"All right," Dori laughed, clearing her dark hair from her face. "Leland! Get in here! Spin's about to gore the new guy for ripping the hell out of the ass-end of the ship up."

"What?" Leland nearly shrieked as he emerged from the medical bay. "The situation can't be that far gone already, can it?"

"Oh, no," Shamus said, a little smirk on his face as he looked Spin in the eye. He was like Boro in so many ways, but Spin was getting the feeling that Shamus had seen a lot more. Perhaps more of the galaxy, maybe more strange things, but definitely more combat and hardening experiences. "Your Spin here is thinking clearly. She's right; even if I turn a personal shield on, she'll get a shot or three off, probably put fist sized holes through me before I can do anything. Even my military vacsuit can't take more than one, maybe two shots from that ripper at this range. It's the only thing I didn't see coming, so now I have to listen. Isn't that right?"

"Don't do anything you'll regret," Leland pleaded quietly, glancing between Spin and Shamus. "Either of you."

"I've seen that look before; I know better than to test her iron," Shamus said. "I don't know her as well as you lot, but I'm sure she'll shoot, isn't that right, lass?"

"Don't call me lass," Spin said.

"Aye, Ma'am."

Everything about Shamus suggested that he fit the lifestyle of the reckless spacer except for the equipment he came with. He would fit into her crew better than she did, Spin was sure, but she wouldn't let that frustrate her. There were plenty of details that were frustrating about Shamus McFadden. The smirk on his face like she was a source of entertainment was one, his intention to cancel all her plans or leave her alone to pursue them were two of the biggest. "You managed to completely disable my ship, so I'm going to have to borrow yours. I..."

"We," Boro interrupted. The correction that made her feel better.

"*We* were going to the Geist System to steal or copy the data I need from an artificial intelligence called the Iron Mind so I can have a normal life."

"From the little I've seen, you'll never have a normal life, luv," Shamus snickered softly.

"I don't believe your people can fix what's wrong with me; my genetics are locked down, but Iron Mind has the key. I have a map, now I need a ship. I have your pilot, and you're facing a lot of pain if this gun goes off. We'll use your ship, we'll get to the Iron Mind, steal what we have to, then get away. After that you can bring me back here. I'll understand if you don't trust me enough to take me wherever you want to take Boro."

"Oh, there are plenty of pirates and scheming spacers in the Haven System. You could get good and lost under that seedy underbelly, but I have a feeling you could find legitimate work there just as easy."

"We'll make that decision when we come to it," Spin said. "You agree to give me the command codes to your ship until I have what I need and we're back here?"

"Oh, I can agree to take orders from you until we have your key and we get you back here, but I can't transfer command codes. You have my word that I'm your man, that's going to have to be enough."

Spin looked at him. He had steely blue eyes, salt and pepper stubble on his broad face, and she couldn't tell if he was lying or not. She could read Boro, but Shamus was frustratingly hard to judge; he could have been joking for all she knew. "Can I trust him, Boro?" she asked without looking away from Shamus.

"No," Boro said without hesitation.

Dori's laughter pierced the air, a high hysteria of hilarity that was almost too shrill, then she shook her head and took a breath. "Sorry, sorry, this is just too good." She was still leaning on the heavy cutter, taking the whole scene in.

"I get that," Shamus nodded. He didn't seem too off-put by his brother's statement, but it did darken his mood a little. "I guess the only thing you can trust is that I came here to make things right with my little brother."

"Then you'll do this," Boro said. "You'll do everything in your power to help us get this done, and then I'll listen to you about going back to the Haven System with you. No guarantees. If that place seems more dangerous than this space, then we've got to make the best decisions for ourselves."

Spin was very conscious of the fact that their nephew, Nigel, had been completely silent during the whole exchange. "Nigel? What do you think?"

"I don't fucking know!" he burst. Despite Dori's snickering, he went on. "It's like that stupid riddle; 'If I say I'm a liar, would you believe me?' Boro, who I know I can trust, is telling me I can't trust Shamus - the new cool uncle - but our best ship just had its heart half-melted down, and he has this other ship. A ship I can't get a scan on, so for all we know it's just a really fast lifeboat. What the hell do I know?"

"Kid's right; it comes down to a leap of faith off a rickety dock," Shamus said through that aggravating smirk. She'd seen it before when Boro was flirting and he knew it was going well. "You've done this right so far; putting me at gunpoint, taking my pilot captive. When my superiors ask why I helped you, I can say it started here; you got the drop on me and I had to acquiesce or get a churned gut and a dead pilot. Now it's all you. Trust, or don't."

"Then your ship, the services of your pilot and you are mine until we get what we need or until I release you," Spin said.

"So I swear on my unborn son or daughter. Oh yeah, you're going to be an Uncle again," he said to Boro over Spin's shoulder.

Spin nodded, activated the safety on her pistol and sheathed it under her arm, happy she didn't have to pull the trigger. "Thank you, Shamus," she said.

"Call me Frost."

TWENTY-SEVEN

Regardless of all the hardships Spin knew in her short life, she had rarely seen anyone truly, deeply sad. Yes, she'd seen people grieve, look lost, unhappy, and many other modes of being that could be considered dissatisfied or discontented. Deep sadness, especially when everyone else was experiencing something else was not one that she'd seen often, so when she met Sharon on the bridge of the Convoy King her quiet despair was a surprise.

"I'm sorry, Spin," she said. "I don't want to go with you. There's no reason for me to go to Geist, especially now that I won't be flying the King."

"I understand, I didn't expect everyone to come," Spin said. Sharon was the last to join the crew, a spur of the moment hire if there ever was one. Sharon was a slave longer than most of Spin's crew and she probably had that deep fear of being recaptured and brought back in front of her former masters. That could keep you on the run, she'd seen it before, and she'd felt it before. The longer you felt the leash, the more powerful that fear was. If Sharon wanted to keep running, moving across British Alliance space and even beyond to get more distance between herself and her former master, then Spin wouldn't blame her or stop her.

"I don't want to leave the crew, either," she said. "You have some good people."

"I don't know what to tell you, then." Spin knew for certain that everyone left on her crew was going to Geist, so if Sharon didn't want to come with them, and she didn't want to leave, there was a problem.

"I might have an idea. I contacted the British Alliance representatives aboard the station and they said we can get a deal to repair the Convoy King. Since we were attacked in port, they'll do it for the cost of parts, which the Alliance says will be about three hundred thousand. They'll have to tow the ship to Kirkland Yard, which is another station in orbit, but I could stay and make sure everything's done right. I could also get some more time with Mitch."

"Oh, I didn't know you two were..."

"Just starting," Sharon said. "He's not like anyone I've known, though. I want to see where it goes."

The idea of leaving the Convoy King behind in storage or abandoned as a hulk stung deep. It was Spin's first real ship and it represented all the possibilities that came with it, especially since they had the tickets from the British Alliance to work legally in their space. One reckless idiot fighting off a few assholes after his technology all but ruined all that potential, and the ship her crew had come to call home. If Sharon could see the ship repaired, then there could be a future for her crew after Geist. "You realize I'll have to lock down the FTL system,"

Spin said. "So no one can take the ship out-of-system after it's repaired."

"I'd do the same," Sharon replied, her mood lifting.

"All right, then you have my proxy here," Spin said. "This is huge trust, leaving you in charge of my ship."

"You're right," Sharon agreed. "But you can trust me, and I have nowhere to go anyway."

"So, you'll do this for us? You'll stay here and make sure the King is repaired and ready when we get back? I'm sure the crew will want to get right to work."

"The ship will be ready, Captain," Sharon replied, standing and shaking Spin's hand. "Good hunting out there."

Spin had a good feeling about Sharon, but time would tell if the woman would simply take the four hundred thousand credits and run instead of having the ship repaired. There was another way, a safer way, she was sure. "I'm trusting you." It was time to go. They'd packed everything they could into the Sector Jumper. Sharon was the last complication, so Spin turned and started to leave. There wasn't much else to say.

"Thank you, Spin," Sharon told her.

MINUTES LATER, Spin stood above the hatch that the Sector Jumper re-moored to. The pressure in the small airlock was equalizing, so she took the moment of downtime to put her personal bag down and contact the British Authority representatives on Bio Beta, inquiring after the deal the station was offering to repair the ship.

To her surprise, a contract appeared on the left side of her small holographic interface and a woman in the navy blue

British Authority uniform appeared on the right. "Captain," she said. "I've been speaking with your crewmember about the scandal surrounding your ship."

"It was invaded by boarders who bribed the authorities aboard the station. If that wasn't bad enough, your security forces didn't do anything to stop them once we sounded the alarm," Spin said flatly.

"We understand that," she replied. "That's why we're going to fix the damage without charging for labour or dock time - just parts. We're even covering the cost of accommodation for your crewmember."

Spin rushed through the contract, skimming until she confirmed the simple deal. "I see you got her approval for the deal but didn't think to contact me. That's not binding."

"She said she had your proxy while you were away. Can we get your approval?"

"No," Spin said. "You're going to repair my ship for free. You're going to pay us to keep quiet about this too. I think one million registered platinum per crewmember should keep them quiet. I'll take five."

"Whoa, now wait a..."

"Beta Bio has been a disaster for me and my crew. I have a crewmember who was forced into a gender change because the British Alliance didn't have a male body on hand, and she couldn't find a company here that could correct that affordably." She knew that was a partial lie, but it was useful in building her case. "Keep in mind: the gender swap was the British Alliance's fault. Then, when I approached a scientist who I found here thanks to a British officer, I was told he didn't have what I needed to save my life. I'll have to continue my search. Then, while in the concourse of your station, we run into a known slave owner, murderer, and enemy to the British Alliance. A man who your people should have arrested but turned a blind eye to until they were forced to pay attention. Then we met with one of my crewmember's brothers. Someone who is supposed to be an important ally to the British Alliance military, and one of the resident corporations on *your station* tries to send a boarding team through my ship to get into your ally's vessel. My ship was damaged during the defence, and thank God we could defend ourselves, because the British Alliance were no help, the station security force ignored us and we would have been left twisting in the void if we didn't fire back. I thought I would be safer in British Alliance territory. I thought you controlled your space, your stations, and monitored your assets. I know for a fact that there was a military carrier group within a minute's comm range while my ship was under attack. Where were they? What is your military for if it won't protect people who you reassure with promises of safety and prosperity? I have a dead ship, and no prospects thanks to your mismanagement. The only option I have now is to appeal to the general public on the Stellarnet and see if I can gather funds from donations to get my ship repaired. The work permits I have aren't worth anything if we can't fly. I wonder how soon it'll be before some of the companies who see Beta Bio as the new Geist System, where they thought they could develop and showcase new technologies, start pulling out. Beta Bio is still small in comparison. It wouldn't last long if the public thought it was unsafe."

"We'll cover your repairs. I'm putting your ship at the front of the queue at Kingston Yards. I'm afraid my department will only authorize five hundred thousand in certified platinum for you and your crew, though."

Spin sighed theatrically and nodded. "Fine. You can't expect my crew to stay quiet about this, though. I mean, I'll try to keep them from telling everyone about it, but..."

"I've been authorized to give your ship a White Ticket for one year. That means you can use any military or high priority wormhole gate in British Alliance space, which should be a massive advantage as you carry passengers or cargo."

"One year?" Spin scoffed, playing up her amusement so it looked like she was offended. "You can do better. Ten, and I want a salvage ticket for me and my ship."

"What? You can't buy a White Ticket. This is something reserved for..." someone else spoke to her from behind. "...I can expand our offer to three years. Keep in mind that it will only be valid for Convoy King Zero Zero Three Five Four Two. You should change the name of your ship now, by the way. If you do it after we give you this, the White Ticket will be invalid. Oh, and we'll give you an operator's ticket for claiming salvage."

"I accept. We'll make something of it."

"Under the numerical name? Wouldn't you rather change it? There are hundreds of Convoy Kings."

"The Jolly Traveller," Spin said, liking the sound more as she said it.

"The Jolly Traveller," the officer on the other end confirmed, adding it to the contract. "We'll have it stamped on the new reactor..."

"Upgraded reactor, and upgraded wormhole generator," Spin said. "And you'll arm us to military specifications."

"We can upgrade the reactor, your thrusters and wormhole

generators, and we'll do so gladly but we won't upgrade your weapons. If I promise that, and we resupply your ship after its repaired and the Tickets are applied, then can we end this negotiation? My supervisor wants me to close this call."

"Don't forget the half-million in certified platinum and high-end accommodations for the crewmember I'm leaving here to supervise the repairs," Spin said. The contract changed to reflect the whole bargain with all the conditions.

"Done. Will that be all, Captain?"

"Thank you, I'll tell my crew to be as silent as they can about our horrible experience here, and once we return from our day trip aboard the Sector Jumper, we'll be on our way." Spin approved the contract, pleased with how well her negotiations went, and the communication connection closed. Compared to dealing with corporations and royal families, the British Alliance were pushovers.

Spin could hear Nigel and Boro laughing before they staggered into sight a few frames down the corridor. "Oh my God! Where did you learn to negotiate like that?" Boro asked.

It was so good to see him happy, laughing. Spin knew he was still medicated, but whatever Leland gave him helped him come most of the way back in less than a full day. "My training started when I was a little girl," Spin said. "They were preparing me to negotiate every contract like it was worth trillions. I'm glad it's paying off a little."

"I've never seen anyone push a government around like that," Boro said. "It was amazing. I've never even heard of a White Ticket before."

"Me neither," Spin snickered. "I thought the only passes you could get for military wormholes were the three I got from the intake officer at the refugee centre. Now we have the run of Alliance space for three years. Honestly, I was just hoping to get the repairs completely covered and set Sharon up in a nice place while they were doing them. I'm not made of money."

"With skills like that, you don't have to be," Nigel said. "Wow. Next time I buy a planet hopper, you'll do the talking. Wait; Sharon's staying here?"

"Someone has to stick around to make sure the ship gets repaired," Spin said. "Besides; we already have a military pilot."

"Good point. You realize that airlock has been pressurized for a few minutes," Nigel said, looking down at the hatch between their feet.

"After you two," Spin said.

Boro opened the inner hatch and dropped down. The outer hatch opened when the inner closed behind him, and he drifted the rest of the way into the Sector Jumper, followed by Nigel who followed the same process. Their gear was already aboard. Everyone was told to bring only what you needed, no extra equipment, clothing, or other non-necessities. Everything she wanted was on her or in her small personal bag, so she passed through the airlock and came through the other side into a ship that looked nothing like what she'd seen before.

The deck was matte grey and definitely designed to be non-slip. It didn't look like metal, more like some kind of ceramic. The walls were plated with black panels that had a smoky, glassy sheen. There were visible layers beneath that changed colour depending on how she looked at them. The blocky patterns beneath almost looked like circuitry, and she found herself touching the surface. It was warm, about ambient temperature, not cold like glass or metal, and her fingertips triggered a cloud of information around them.

Video of public appearances as she served the Countess in various outlandish and glamourous outfits then gowns as she grew older appeared. Another part of the expanding cloud had all her medical information, starting with her raw genetic data and extending to the scan the ship took of her. Her criminal record expanded out in another direction, with security footage of her in those high boots and white suit. She was happy she left the boots behind, they were a hassle, and as the crimes were listed; kidnapping, murder, ship theft, mutiny, escaping service and several counts of grand theft, she realized she didn't regret any of them. Most of the murder charges were made up, so she'd fight those if she had to, but the last statement in that bubble of information was that the British Alliance had blocked all her previous crimes from entering the records of their justice system. Instead, her record only included her Statement of Liberation, her ship, and the rights she'd been given as a Captain.

"It's intelligent plating," a man only slightly taller than her with a friendly, broad face said. "The ship is learning about you." He extended his hand. "I'm Hal."

"I knew there was something I liked about you," Frost said as Spin finished shaking Hal's hand. Boro and Nigel were behind him, taking their jackets off. "A fellow ship thief. There are few crimes that make law enforcement take notice than someone who doesn't respect the locks on a ship in port."

"It was out of necessity, trust me," Spin said.

"I hear you got some services out of the British Alliance. Wish I could have seen that, actually."

"It looks like our ship will be repaired and ready for us when we get back."

"Oh, I don't know about that," Frost said. "We'll be back before you know it. This is the fastest ship in the sector."

"I've heard that before," Spin said. "You'll have to show me."

"Aye, I will," Frost said. He looked almost... excited. "But first, let's modernize you a little. If you're going to fly with us on the Sector Jumper, you're going to have to suit up like a member of her crew."

TWENTY-EIGHT

By the time Spin was finished putting on the suit she was given - a thin thing that wasn't more than a millimetre thick but she was told there were many layers, sublayers and that it was military grade - and clamped the pair of combat bracers on, she was left with a pile of old equipment in a footlocker at the end of her bunk. The suit was black without adornment, and it was so well fitted and matched to her skin that she didn't feel like she was wearing anything. "This can't be as tough as Hal said it is."

A diagram of how the suit was laid out and made was projected from her left wristband. Layers of intelligent, flexible armour and synthetic muscle were printed under protective substances that kept everything beneath safe from radiation, including most electromagnetic pulses. The armour ratings of each layer were each higher than she'd seen in any thin space suit she'd heard of. It was difficult for her to believe, but she knew there was no time for a demonstration.

Another tutorial appeared and she followed it, learning

about the heads-up display that was built into the hood of the basic suit, and adding pockets and holsters to the uniform. By the time she was finished she had the new smart sidearm that came with the suit holstered on one side, while a pocket with survival supplies balanced that on her other thigh. The Shredder that killed Larken, the fourteen shot revolver that was made to tear people apart but leave most technology barely scratched, was in a special holster above her belt. Her suit told her that it was in fair condition, still reliable and that it was also made to damage containment suits in zero gravity. The last thing she added to her suit was a set of seven grenades that she secured in smart loops around her waist. One was stolen from the small armoury cabin aboard the Sector Jumper when Shamus and Hal weren't looking. The box it was in rated it as Class R9, but it was the same size as the other grenades, only about five centimetres across. She was sure they knew she'd palmed one by the time she put it on her belt, but they weren't coming after it. The short tutorial outlining its use made her giggle at the potential, and she felt a little like Dorian must have whenever he got new hardware. "Guess there's a little Dorian in all of us," she muttered, moving on to another instructional topic.

A tutorial about using synthetic muscle appeared, advising her to move normally. The system read neural triggers on its own, so the muscles would activate when she needed more physical power. "Where does this technology come from?" she asked, aware that most of the systems weren't completely new, she'd just never seen them put together in one compact, easy to use package before.

Two images appeared: A woman with a heart shaped face

wreathed in red ringlets and a sterner looking fellow with practically cut dark hair and friendly eyes. The first spoke in a
relaxed but clear British accent. "I'm Ayan Anderson, the
founder of Haven Shore and the technical owner of what used
to be called the Rega Gain System. It's been renamed to the
Haven System, and you are wearing a protective suit designed
for use by Haven Fleet personnel. It's a standardized, basic
piece of vacsuit armour that includes a pair of bracers that
provide medical assistance, a secondary interface, have a built-in
scanner suite that works with the suit, a micro-line launcher,
small stunner, and it can perform a few other duties if required.
The suit you're wearing was made to protect soldiers, and the
technology is advanced but no longer proprietary since we've
expanded the program, providing a similar protective suit to all
our citizens."

"But, who are you people?" she asked the hologram.

Spin was relieved when Ayan's holographic visage looked at
her directly and answered. "Haven Fleet is a formalized group
of protectors and freedom fighters. To save time, I'll explain who
we are now. Haven Fleet is a new military organization that is
built on the successful traditions of many others. Initially the
result of many armed parties coming together to defend the
Haven Solar System, the Fleet began to organize under several
leaders with military training and experience with one goal that
persists: to protect the citizens of the Haven System, innocent
people within reach, and to proactively combat suppressors
when necessary. The Defence Minister of the Haven Government serves as its leader, but he is answerable to the other two
members of the ruling Triumvirate; the highest ranked members

of our government. Instead of a prime minister or president, our government has three elected leaders that work together. One represents the military, another oversees public welfare, and the third is the ultimate authority and representative voice for the sciences. The rest of our government is based on a system of fair representation through a democratic voting process that has many built in checks and balances."

The next section of Ayan's explanation was projected into Spin's eyes so she could see a perfectly clear vision of her and the location around her. Ayan was in a black uniform with a gold stripe down the sides. Spin was surprised and amused at how short she looked, but there was an air about her that demanded respect too. Ayan was standing in front of a window overlooking a blue and green planet.

A trio of fighters passed by as Ayan settled against a railing. "Before we go on, let me address something. According to the antiquated galactic courts, I'm the Queen or Empress of the Haven System, being its only owner. I accept the title of Queen for legal reasons, since it's easier to maintain independence from other systems and refuse the purchase of any part of this solar system by corporations or other interests. Aside from that, my title is ornamental. I serve as an Admiral in Haven Fleet and let the entire solar system operate as a growing, thriving democracy. The rank of Admiral is one that I earned through military service and other experiences that are on the record."

Ayan looked through the window at the blue-green wonder beyond, then back to Spin. "That's our first hurdle; the Tamber moon. As of this recording, millions of humans live there, and over one million Nafalli are joining us thanks to a land grant and more are coming. We welcome refugees of all kinds and invite them to join us in defence of our solar system, because freedom is becoming harder and harder to secure in our galaxy. We believe our people deserve opportunities of all kinds, and they should be free to pursue whatever goals they like as long as it doesn't hurt or unnecessarily impede anyone else. That brings me to the next point; why Haven Fleet exists at all. After the Holocaust Virus was cleared throughout most of this sector, the Order of Eden - the creators of the Virus - began to encroach on our territory. Funded and supplied by the Regent Galactic Corporation and several others, they claim to be keeping an alien invasion at bay. While the Edxi are a real threat, we've uncovered evidence that makes it clear that the Order of Eden are doing more harm than an Edxi invasion alone would do, enslaving millions and sending even more to their deaths. With the assistance of the British Alliance, Lorander, and many other allies we have declared that the Haven System is off limits and are defending its borders. Invasion is imminent, but we're ready. Our arms are open to anyone who defects or needs safe harbour. If you're a refugee of any kind and like what you see, then welcome. Please obey our basic civil laws. If you don't like what you see, you can leave at any time and we'll even make sure you don't go away empty handed."

"What is this ship? What can it do?"

"Since most of the technology aboard this ship is classified, I can only tell you that it's a new Interceptor Class Haven Fleet vessel. You'll find five crew cabins and one captain's cabin aboard. It is expandable if necessary at the cost of combat effectiveness. We've designed everything for long-term comfort, because the Interceptors are basically long patrol and variable purpose mission ships. The one you're on is under the command of Captain McFadden, so if you'd like more training or responsibility aboard, you'll have to ask him."

"How fast is it?" Spin asked, becoming a little frustrated with how little specific information the otherwise impressive system was giving her.

"Using next generation technology, the Interceptor is the fastest ship in its class. The smallest to use the Quad Drive, a new..."

The playback stopped as someone knocked on the door. Her vision cleared, and Ayan was a projected head hovering above her wrist again. "How is everything going in there?" Hal asked through the door.

"Fine, just trying to get oriented," Spin replied, turning the playback off and opening the door.

Behind Hal, between two crew quarter doors, Frost was helping Della through a turret simulation. She was in a seat that turned every which way smoothly, and Frost was standing behind her on a bar so he could see exactly what she was doing. "See? Let the system tell you how much you have to lead your target and forget the triggers. You know when you have a good shot, so all you have to do is keep your sights in the right place. The computer will fire when you're ready."

"Oh, my God! It's working! The computer's reading my mind, that's so weird."

"Now practice with the trigger, and remember to squeeze, don't pull or jerk," Frost said.

"Why do I have to practice with both?"

"Your head might not be as clear when your targets shoot back, so you'll have to use the triggers," Frost said, hitting a button so the swivel seat levelled off enough for him to step off it, back into the hallway. "You'll sort it out with some practice, you're a good gunner."

"Thanks, Frost," Della said.

Spin fell into step with Frost as he walked through a sliding hatch. Mirra was on the other side in a swivel seat that hung above the hallway. "This thing is amazing, I'm controlling two turrets seamlessly."

"Just a simple trick made easier by good tech," Frost said. "Keep practicing, you're tearing the scenario up like it's personal."

"What do you think of Della's shooting?" Spin asked.

"She's no sharpshooter, but with the assist system in the turret, she'll get better in a hurry. I've trained much worse," he said. They arrived in the bridge - a narrow six seat space arranged with the stations in pairs from front to back. Boro was sitting in the co-pilot's seat, watching the control system tutorial for navigation and communications. Nigel was in the seat behind him, watching a tutorial on power systems as he looked through the status screens of the ship. The controls were easy to read and understand at a glance.

"She's had trouble with confidence," Spin said.

"All but the most cocky or stupid people have trouble with confidence sometimes, she just needs to be shown how it's done by a computer, not a friend she's afraid of disappointing. She'll be good enough after a few hours, you'll see."

"Why not use automation or an artificial intelligence for all this stuff? I know there's one aboard, these control systems aren't intuitive just because of design."

"Our artificial intelligence isn't smart or well-connected

enough to assume control because we expect people to try to hack us. Real, flesh and bone folk power our Fleet. Only a couple artificial intelligences have feelings, or that spark that makes them want to be their own bloody person. Our workhorse code AI's think for us, not themselves."

"That's something I can get behind," Spin said. "What will your superiors think of you going on this mission for me?"

Frost gestured for her to sit down in the rearmost seat, and he sat down across the narrow aisle across from her. "I've already made my deal to come out here and give Boro, along with whoever else, a ride back to my place on Tamber. They know I'll be back on the wall with them, watching for invaders. I'm guessing I might be able to get them to look past a detour if I bring something worthwhile back."

"So, you're looking to loot the corpses around Sa-Hadin like everyone else who's on their way there," Spin said.

"Between you, me, Boro and Nigel there, listening in; if no one's using it, it's fair game. I saw my first gunnery deck when I was eleven, but I stole my first ship when I was eight. Didn't get caught, either."

Spin laughed and shook her head.

"It was a remote flier," Boro explained, amused. "A toy you controlled with a little holo-bud. I remember you flying that around outside, it was a month before you let me have a turn."

"Right, and I've been either stealing or shooting ever since," Frost said. "With this ship and your brains - because Boro can't stop going on about how smart you are - we'll get what you need and scan everything on the way out. That's where some of the best tech on this ship comes from; scanning and stealing. If I bring something new back, they'll be a little more likely to look past how late I am."

"Or how many dents you left in their ship," Hal said as he passed between them on his way to the pilot's seat at the front.

"Ah, that's the problem with self-repairing ships; by the time you get home no one can tell you had a brush with trouble," Frost said with a wink. "Now, the real question is; will you want to come back with us after?"

"We're clear for departure, I just got the word," Hal said over his shoulder.

"Take us out, Lad," Frost replied, watching Spin.

Escaping the Countess' grasp and taking her friends to British Alliance space was the right thing to do. She ran away, plain and simple. Somehow, the idea of running further didn't feel right.

"Maybe revenge is more important?" Frost asked conspiratorially.

"No," Spin replied without thinking. "Going back there, going after the Countess and her people would be stupid." As she said it she looked down at her wrist. There was a combat hardened bracer there, a command and control unit as Haven Fleet called it, but it was linked to the computer printed on her arm beneath. Inside was every bit of information she had from Larken's computer along with everything else she could get about the Countess and her operation. She asked herself who she was saving it for, if not herself?

"Wait, what's that look?" Frost asked, catching some expression or tell that she didn't mean to give.

Boro was paying attention, so was Nigel. Leland, who was

just coming in, knew something was going on right away and sat down in the only free seat. "Nothing, just thinking."

"I've seen that look," Frost said. "You do want revenge, but something is keeping you from getting it."

"I have enough information to expose the Countess to attack from pirates, lawsuits, and to sow dissent amongst her people." Spin held her wrist up. "Right here."

Frost laughed, delighted with a realization that he made only seconds after she did. "What? What's up?" Nigel asked.

"She wanted to use it herself to get first crack at... what? Piracy? A little grand theft from the bank accounts? Some sabotage? A smear in the media? Extortion?"

"I don't know!" Spin spat back, angrier than she meant to be. "Maybe I did want first crack, for Larken, for Trevor and everyone else she's killed or screwed over. That would mean going back there. I don't know if I could do that unless I was alone, and that's the one thing I don't want to be."

"There's another way," Frost said.

"That's enough," Boro said, getting to his feet and crossing to Spin's seat.

"No, she's smart enough to figure out what has to happen herself, she just needs a nudge," Frost said. "Getting revenge has gotten me into more trouble than I can tell you."

"It's a foolish urge, I know," Spin said, thinking about all the dirt and inside information she had on the Countess and, to a lesser but significant extent, the United Core World Authority.

"So, why are you saving that? Why not share it with every whoreson looking for a good score on the Stellarnet?"

"I've shared some." That was a good question, though. What if she let go? It's not as though she would forget Larken the moment she sent the data to the nearest node to spread across the galaxy faster than light. If anything, she'd be honouring him. He felt as betrayed as she did when he learned of the Countess' plans to use them as breeding stock. "Maybe, before we do this I should share the rest." *Not the Core World Authority stuff, though. No one knows it was in the Countess' files, so I'll keep it just in case.* Spin thought to herself.

"What do you have on her?" Boro asked.

"Secret trade routes, vault locations and inventories, evidence that incriminates her organizations in every kind of corporate crime, warehouse locations, locations of private law enforcement bases, thousands of security codes, and, well, enough to cause a lot of trouble for her for years. There's even recordings of her badmouthing her relatives in House Lux, including the King, especially the Queen."

"We're all set to start accelerating out of the solar system," Hal said. "Should I wait, or..."

"Go slowly," Frost said.

Hal nodded. "Gotcha, taking the long way so we can stay in range of those hyper transmitter nodes."

"It's all yours," Boro told Spin. "It's up to you, but do you have anything on Kort?"

"Enough to incriminate him in murders, acts of piracy, blackmail, torture and corporate espionage. Slavery, too, but everyone at the top of the Countess' organization is guilty of that. The evidence is in the open."

"I don't know if I'll be going with Shamus when we finish this," Boro said. "But knowing there's evidence against them out there will make me rest easier. If they're busy dealing with fallout from this, it'll make it harder for them to come after us."

"I'm going to do it," Spin said.

"It should be out there," Leland said.

"Yes!" was Nigel's response.

"Realize, this might not take her down completely," Spin said, bringing up the collection of files. "There's another leak from me out there, and it didn't seem to do much. This is just... the rest."

"It'll do damage though?" Boro asked.

"Loads," Spin said. The files were ready to send. The script she set up would send them to every news agency and set up a database anyone could use to see the complete archive. She made sure that the United Core World Authority files weren't included then activated it and sat back with a sigh. "Now It's not just up to me to screw her up. Anyone will be able to find something they can use."

Frost checked his own command and control unit and flinched as he saw the image of the Countess smiling up at him. "What is she? This Countess of yours? Is she an Issyrian trying to frighten children and put everyone else off?" He turned privacy mode off so everyone could see the freakish holographic image of the Countess in a peacock dress.

Her neck was extended, eyes enlarged, and her slender, too-long arms were extended wide. Her big smile looked overly toothy and strangely carnivorous. The image was taken so it could be used in a holographic invitation that was sent to the richest people in her social circle. "Oh, that's her. She's had some work done since then, but she's still human."

"What? That's not human!" Frost laughed.

Hal turned and looked, flinching in shock at the image. "Gah! That's not real, it can't be."

"Oh, you should see her in person, she's even worse now," Spin snickered. "I shouldn't laugh; it's sad. She has to wear a special brace to keep her head up because her neck is too long. Kort acts like she's the most beautiful thing he's ever seen, though."

Frost shook his head, turned the image off and moved to the Co-pilot's seat. "I'll take a pass on seeing her in person. Just tell me that kind of thing isn't common."

"The richer you get, the more alterations you get," Spin said. "But she's on the extreme end."

Boro settled in beside her, and things quieted down as they prepared to jump. "Feel better now that you know you're spreading that to everyone who cares to know?"

Spin nodded. "The first thing that'll happen is the fallout from all the holo and video footage I just shared. There's a lot of private and embarrassing stuff there. I wish I could see her face. She's screwed the United Core Word Authority over a lot too, so they'll probably be after her next. It's going to be ugly."

"The Quad Drive is online and ready," Hal said to Frost.

"Navigation ready," Frost replied.

"Oh, what's a Quad Drive?" Spin asked.

"It's a set of four drives and a reactor that can open a hole into another dimension so we can get where we're going faster. I'll unlock a chatty hologram to explain it better once we're underway."

"Another dimension?" Spin asked as she watched the darkness of space split in front of the ship as they moved into a place surrounded by bright blue light. "How long will it take us to get to Geist?"

"Three days," Hal replied. "We're in the energy tunnel, stable, accelerating, and underway. Autopilot on."

Frost locked his station then stood up. "All right, time to get all of you trained up. So far, the only one who tests as fleet ready on anything is Dori, who's still cackling in our rear turret, rampaging through every gunnery sim we have."

TWENTY-NINE

Labyrinth Nine was one of the most frustrating and thrilling training simulations Spin had seen. It took place in an old star cruiser that was being pulled into a white star sideways at a rapidly increasing speed. Its artificial gravity had failed, so they were running on the walls, and those walls weren't made to take footfalls, so some of the panels failed underfoot.

The suit's sensors were still reliable, so they used them to find safe paths through the halls as they chased their objective - Dori - who had surpassed them in every way over the past three days. What made it much worse was that she was allowed to fire through walls and sabotage supports, while the pursuers were docked for any damage they did to the ship.

"Aw, c'mon, you can make it through this stupid Escher painting made real! I'm just around the next corner!" Dori taunted through their proximity radio.

"God dammit, how did she get so good so fast?" Frost asked as he leapt across a hallway crossing. It was a feat that would be difficult at one gravitational unit, but at five it strained the muscle augmentation in the simulated heavy armour. He was about to touch down on the other side when the airlock below opened suddenly, and he had to fire all his barrier thrusters to make it across. He lit up like a white-yellow beacon, all his shield emitters momentarily converting to high thrust force drivers. Normally, that wouldn't cost him his shields, but his suit was fighting to finish that leap against high gravity and sudden depressurization.

The thin plating along the walls melted, revealing the sturdier frame of the ship below, and he was about to catch it when Dori peeked around the corner and blasted him mercilessly. "Would have been easier to let yourself get sucked out of the ship, Chief!" she laughed as her high explosive rounds tore through his unshielded banded suit after the first two bursts.

Spin shot past Frost, her rifle - made to tear machines and something called framework soldiers apart - rattling against her shoulder as Boro and Nigel both joined in. They scored enough hits to burn through Dori's shields, but she ducked and let herself fall down a hallway far ahead before they could make the kill.

What was left of Frost and his armour drifted down, making its way through the airlock. "I'm out, that was a bloody smart trap," Frost admitted over the general simulation channel. "Good luck, that's not the last, knowing her."

"If the bots have control of the ship we're headed on, we can expect traps," Mirra said over the shared channel. She was the first to get blasted out of the simulation. Automated cannons raked her from behind, but it was a distraction. A succession of three grenades took her out from above as she was trying to get to cover. It was an early reminder to think in three dimensions, something Hal was helping Dori do using a direct channel. He wasn't in the simulation, but outside, providing advice to help her make the chase as unfair and as educational as possible.

"We have to go around," Spin said. "We need to trap her."

"Go outside?" Nigel asked.

"She opened a door for us, I'll go." Spin activated her suit's flight mode and she let herself fall down through the airlock into the darkness below. Once she was outside the ship she flew along the length of the hull as fast as she could. A few shots from Dori's rifle tried to catch her, but missed, and she took cover over fifty metres ahead, where the ship's hull was ripped open. "I'm in front, she's eighteen frames back."

"We're five frames behind, you overshot," Nigel said.

"Only way to get in without doing more damage to the ship. I'll close the gap and set up." Running and switching the mode of her rifle to precision anti-armour firing was second nature. The basics; moving, running, fine movement were easy to learn in the armour. Perfecting it took about ten hours, and flight was another five, but she wouldn't put herself up against a fighter pilot. Actual tactics that required the shield, sensor, computing and weapon systems seemed easy, but there were details, little quirks and tricks to pick up that were taking forever. Dori had an advantage. She'd been a cyborg made for war, killed until it nearly drove her mad, and even though she'd forgotten most of that time, she seemed to have an instinctive memory for how to work with similar technology.

There was something else, too, and Spin was certain that it was as important as any experiences Dori had in the past. She loved the fight. The harder it was, the more Dori enjoyed herself. Despite her wisecracks, cackling and abundant enthusiasm, her head seemed to stay clear enough to score higher than everyone in every way. If she got quiet, like she was as Spin rushed to close the distance between them, it was because she was concentrating. If Dori was on your side, that was a good thing, her highest performance marks were accomplished when she focused, but if you were against her, it was terrifying.

Dori was putting something together, a trap, a plan, something that could take them all out at once. Spin looked at her tactical scanner, through the map of the ship around her, and Dori's last known location. She was normally easy to track, but there was no sign of her. Dori had switched to stealth mode or found something they couldn't scan through. "She might be inside one of the dead reactors," Spin announced. "Or stealthed, I have her last known location here. I'm still too far away, but I'll be there soon. Watch out, get behind cover."

"You think *we* should take cover? You're the one who decided to break off on your own." Nigel said. "What do the cutest characters in horror vids always do right before they get killed?"

"They tell someone else to be careful," replied Dori.

Nigel's armour reported a power interruption, then his life signs went dark. "God dammit!" Spin said, realizing that Dori burned out his shield with her own then used *something* to crack into his armour and kill him instantly. That wasn't supposed to be possible with the Encounter Suits they were wearing. Breaking through the armour took the kind of firepower you used against heavy fighters.

"I've got her!" Boro shouted, his rifle spitting rounds in quick bursts.

Spin had a thought and took remote control of Nigel's armour as though she was wearing it herself. It was right behind Dori. A third of its systems were inoperable, as though an electrical blast was fired from the inside of the suit, but there was enough functionality left for her to make it work for her.

Dori dodged out of Boro's line of fire, leaving her back open to Nigel's armour, and Spin forced it to move. The arm that still worked thanks to layers of synthetic muscle, gripped Nigel's rifle, brought it to bear, then set it to its highest power level. Dori, perhaps by instinct, maybe at Hal's warning, turned at the last instant; just in time to see the triple shot that took her shields the rest of the way down, then the three that blasted her in half.

"Holy shit, I did not see that coming," Dori chuckled as her armour went to work, sealing the huge gaps in its middle and putting medical systems to work to preserve her life.

"Game over," Spin said, realizing the crack was groan-worthy, but happy that she was about to get the last word anyway. Two triple-blasts finished her off, cracking her helmet open and destroying the matter inside.

THIRTY

The transit clock counted down from three hours as the half-brothers met in the deployment room in neutral, dim light. So much changed about his brother Shamus while they were separated. That was to be expected after so many years apart, he supposed, and he wondered how far Shamus strayed from a moral path.

There were crimes that Boro didn't see as large moral transgressions, plenty of them. Stealing from the wealthy, from large companies, especially from gangsters. If a crew turned slaver, extorted people or took territory and didn't care for the people who were already there, they were fair game as far as he was concerned.

The Shamus he knew from years before didn't limit his targets on his own. He would steal anything worth his time, regardless of the owner if Boro or the rest of the crew from back then weren't around. It got him into the kind of trouble none of them wanted anything to do with more than once and it cost them friends back in the day. Boro wondered how bad he'd gotten without someone around to hold him back and still suspected that the shiny new ship, all the trappings inside were ill gotten somehow. "Can't believe she got you with that trap," Boro said as he met him at a table that was in the middle of the deployment room. He could see how it folded away, collapsing right down against the floor when there wasn't a need for it, as he sat down on one of the benches.

"I did the basic suit training but didn't have time for the advanced stuff. I didn't think I'd have to since people were saying that it was like having all the power of those big encounter suits from Earth and some of the core systems in a small package. I thought using them would be similar."

"You had a chance to see an encounter suit from Earth?"

"Served aboard a captured Sol Defence ship, one of the big ones," Shamus nodded. "Captain Valent stole it from a ship thief that makes any of our work look small time. I was the gunnery chief for a while, some of the happiest days, despite some hairy action. I'm not looking forward to going another round with mad bots, so I'm thinking about changing your leader's plan a little."

"Oh? How's that?"

"We have an anti-virus. It's adaptable, should calm all those bots right down. I only have to start transmitting it," Shamus said. "No more defences around Geist then. That'll be the end of it. We'll get there before everyone else and waltz right up to that vault, making off with whatever we like."

"We're just there for the Iron Mind."

"It's a vault. In my experience, people stash more than one thing in them at a time. Everyone who owns what's in there is dead, I'd wager on it, so it's not theft, it's salvage."

"That's always been your problem; you see platinum and get distracted. I'm here to save Spin's life, not to line my pockets."

"I'm just reading the room, brother. She gave away all that data so every desperate whoreson with a ship and a few crooks aboard can learn how to raid her Countess' goods. I saw something else after she did that, though. She still doesn't want to leave. Maybe it's because revenge runs too deep. Maybe she's got a little plat lust in her too, or she doesn't want to move her whole crew across the galaxy but would rather stay and make them rich. I hope that's it, for her sake and yours, because if she wants to stay close to the British Alliance or lash back at the Countess and make the crew a fortune because she thinks it's the best thing then she's probably the good sort. So, when I see that vault, and there are stacks of platinum, or prized data cells, or something else that her crew can get rich on, you'll find me looting that if no one else will, especially if it's something the Fleet back home would want. I'll leave plat behind for her because I think you'll be going wherever she does, and if I gave you a pile of booty, you'd just give it to her to divvy up anyway."

"You won't want a cut of whatever we pick up too?" Boro asked, doubtful. This argument had a new twist, but it still felt familiar to him. Greed was always Shamus' biggest downfall. He was hungrier than anyone in their old crew.

"You have a problem with me taking a cut? No problem. I'll pass. Look around, do you think a few pieces of platinum and a copy of some old real estate records or cache maps will change things for me? Not where I'm going, not in the Haven System. I'm going to war, no doubt about it, there's no treasure out here that can make what I'll be protecting on the fringe have less lustre. I thought you would always be the one who let a woman tie you down, but I beat you there, brother. My Stephanie and our unborn wee one along with everything I'm watching people try to build around her have more of a hold on me than anything. Well, anything but you."

"I forgot to congratulate you," Boro said. "I'm happy for you."

"Thank you. Fatherhood scares the bloody life out of me, if I'm being honest. I didn't know my father until I was twelve, and when he came back I soon wished he hadn't."

Boro's dad left when he was an infant, it was a common thing amongst his siblings. "Consequences of being a son to the most popular port wife on Dock Ring Three. Found out mother's still alive, by the way. She was spotted on Roa, I have no idea what she was doing there."

"Mother's alive?" Shamus asked. "Did she look well? What was she doing there?"

"I couldn't find out, she looked younger than me, and she was part of some pirate's entourage from the look of it. I wanted to find out who it was, but he's got someone scrubbing all the data on him and his lieutenants. Looked like she was a hanger on. I just hope she doesn't still love being pregnant as much as she used to."

"Oh, good lord, we might have twenty brothers and sisters by now," Frost chuckled. The pair sat quietly for a moment before Shamus broached the one topic they were steering clear of. "You were always my best friend in our brood. Leaving you behind sent me down a dark road, I should have stayed and faced the same music you did."

"You never would have. I knew who you were back then. You wouldn't see the point of both of us getting arrested and jailed," Boro said.

"I'm trying to say I'm sorry, brother. I could have taken most of that time for you, left you with a record that could have been cleared later. A criminal record didn't matter much to me, but I know you wanted to be more than a ship thief and conman."

"Would have never worked. Mother had us scrounging and stealing on the docks before we were old enough to know better, and even a little service didn't straighten you out. We were bred into this."

"It took a long time, a lot of dark mishaps and one good Captain to show me that you can turn it around. Sure, sometimes procedure and rank make me wish I was entirely my own master sometimes, but I got a look at the bigger picture, and I see how much change one person can make. Anyone who says your fate is written by your start is working for the wrong side, brother. Don't believe it, you especially could be a white knight in Haven Shore. As for the rest of Spin's crew, and Spin herself, I see folks who would fit in well enough. Some would thrive, I think, though not all of 'em in the military. I think about Nigel and see nothing but potential, and he could put that to good use for himself in the Haven System."

"You barely know him," Boro replied. "And you sound like a recruiter."

"He reminds me of you when you were his age. Imagine if we didn't get distracted or have to steal our way through those early years. I don't give a shit if he joins the military, there's so much for civilians to do, he'd never have to touch a trigger. It took a lot for me to trust Haven and the people putting it together, but we'll win this war, and when the air clears it'll be a place where people can really be free. You can see it for yourself in the database of this ship, there's plenty of real information there. I won't push it past that, just take a look when this business in the Geist system is all over."

"That's what I'm concentrating on, and I need to see you get your head straight and focus on that too," Boro said, still worried that his brother was too distracted. "We get what we need to save Spin and everyone like her, then I promise we'll take a real look at following you back. She'll be leaving a lot behind though."

"What? That ship? The Convoy King?" Shamus asked. "We'll latch to it and haul it back with us. If there are repairs left to be done, I can have those done in a day, an hour, most like. There are stations that can overhaul that whole ship in an afternoon in the Haven System."

"All right, fine, but you'll hold off on giving us your best pitch on following you back to the Haven System until we're done here. Concentrate on the Iron Mind until then. If you want to make up for leaving me behind, that's how you do it."

"Then I'll follow your lass into this hell and make sure we get out with what she needs. You have my word."

THIRTY-ONE

The anticipation aboard the Sector Jumper was thick throughout the crew. Hal and Frost manned the two main control stations at the front of the slender bridge, while Spin and Nigel watched the science and tactical displays. Boro was at another station, remotely checking on everyone's suit and armament status. The suits ran diagnostics on themselves, the armaments and other equipment were mostly self-maintaining, but it was all new to them. Having someone go through their checklists couldn't hurt.

The rest of the crew were in the gun turrets, their weapons on hold from the bridge so a misfire wouldn't give them away. "Cloaking systems engaged, entering the Geist system," Hal said.

The ship emerged just past the outer most asteroid belt, leaving a brief energy bloom behind them as they re-entered normal space. The strange energy patterns and scanner data from the dimension they left behind was logged, and it was almost confounding to Spin. She'd examine it later if she had a chance, it was new science, a significant breakthrough in a time when such things almost never happened.

Hal guided the ship away from their emergence point in a hurry, starting a course that took them towards Doro Doro Station. "How good is the cloaking system? You're taking us awfully close to some active stations. Their scanners will be watching," Nigel said, looking at the course they were on.

"Don't worry," Hal replied, waving the concern off. "This is the best system ever made with redundancies and tech this part of the galaxy hasn't even dreamt up yet."

"Are you sure? There are already scanning posts coming up this far out."

"Our passive scanners are really sensitive," Hal said. "You're probably not used to seeing real time data this clearly this early."

"Time for that conversation," Frost said. "We have the cure for the Holocaust Virus, we can spread it out here and defeat the defences without firing a shot."

Spin already thought about that. In fact, she'd looked it up in the computer, and was amazed at what she saw. The Holocaust Counter Virus was a living program in the way that it was constantly being improved and updated by people in Haven Fleet. Where it came from and who made it was top secret, but if what they said about the results was true, it was amazing software. Any artificial intelligence that was infected by the Holocaust Virus would be either cleaned and restored to its normal operating state, or it would be permanently deleted along with all backups. The Counter Virus would create a placeholder program that was scripted to take over the basic functions of the artificial intelligence it destroyed. Whatever defences were being maintained by a virus infected artificial intelligence would be made safe.

The ship passed into the first cloud of debris. The walls of the small bridge displayed what was outside almost perfectly. For a moment it felt as though Spin was falling. "Whoa, warn us when you're about to do that," Nigel said.

"Sorry, thought you would want a good look. Some of the ships drifting around out here are so cool. I wish I could have seen 'em before they got half-slagged."

"What do you think?" Boro asked Spin.

She looked up at the open hull of a long battleship. It had been blasted open from the inside, armour torn like decorative sheet metal. A berthing with its bunks, lockers, showers and attached galley, even the commissary were visible. It looked wrong, like a violation of some kind. "I wonder what's more important: leaving whatever did this behind us to slow down whoever comes into the system down to buy us more time, or preventing this from happening again?"

"You're not considering dropping the antivirus on your way out of the system instead of on your way in, are you?" Frost asked, surprised.

"It's a valid tactic," Spin said, only half paying attention. The list of stations and powered ships were coming up, most of them had nothing to do with their current mission. There were thousands of companies doing research and trade in the Geist System before the virus spread and took control. The solar system was a major hub, with as much information trade as commerce, and it would be again after the virus was clear, only this time raiders, company reclamation forces and governments would war over what was left. With the counter virus in hand, she could choose when that would start, and the only factor she considered was how well it would serve her and her crew. "I'm only here for one thing, and the easier I can make it for us, the better. I couldn't care less about the vultures circling the system, waiting to find a way in to steal anything they can. If I'm lucky, they'll just become another distraction, I don't really care if they get slagged."

"Cold, and that's coming from me," Frost snickered. "A lot of people would end up fighting and dying when you could prevent it right now."

"You have changed," Boro told Frost.

"This wreckage is the remnant of a slaughter, not a battle. No soldier or sailor deserves this death. These ships were slagged seconds after jumping in," Frost retorted.

"He's right," Spin said. "Your virus won't shut all the threats down, though."

"It's done miracles before, you watch," Frost retorted.

"There are air-gapped security systems here, and the infection is old in this system. It's probably taken a few turns that the programming didn't take into account. Besides; even if we were here before the Holocaust Virus infected the majority of the machines, do you really think we'd be welcome?" Spin asked as she watched the dead husks of three fighters drift past. There were red and yellow lights inside one shedding just enough illumination to show the outline of a drone. It looked like it was staring right at them, but then, that was probably just in her head. "Let's send your program out so we can see if it makes things better or worse."

"Programming a stealth drone with the virus and setting it to broadcast one minute after it's clear," Hal said, his fingers working on a small panel between his and Frost's stations without looking. "Ready to launch, Captain."

"Launch it and put an extra turn or two in our course," Frost ordered.

"Aye," Hal said. A faint click somewhere behind their cabin sounded and he guided the ship around the half-picked remains of a carrier many times their size with a flourish. After a couple more turns they were back on course, approaching Doro Doro from a slightly different direction.

"It's broadcasting," Spin said as the drone began to send data to every receiver in range. "Fifteen percent is already uploaded in the first burst, but it's slowing down a lot."

"I have... something powering up. A lot of things. Small, about two metres long," Nigel said nervously.

"Seventeen percent transmitted," Spin said. "Those are automated defence drones, just a guess."

With shocking speed five attack drones burst from their hiding places in the wreckage of their defeated foes and opened fire on the stealth drone. It was easy to track as it transmitted the anti-virus. A larger ship emerged, an oval with dozens of red and yellow eyes across its surface activated and started moving into the area. Several drones launched, sensor eyes reflecting the collected sparse light.

They followed their stealth drone's signal to its source, firing cutting beams, micro-missiles, and energy bursts from all directions. It only took a few seconds for their drone to be blasted to pieces. The infected ships responsible returned to their hiding places slowly as if watching for more enemies. The mother ship passed through the space, picking up several parts of the Haven stealth drone and putting them inside its shell.

"How much did it..." Frost started to ask.

"Twenty five percent was uploaded," Spin replied.

"Maybe if we go further away from their defences?" Nigel asked.

"This system was a fortress," Spin said. "There are hundreds of armed stations, thousands of picket ships and fighters before the virus hit. How powerful is this ship? Could it stand up to a real attack while it broadcasted?"

"If we could get more distance from those bots," Hal said, nodding at Nigel.

"Not enough to transmit with a drone," Frost said. "The ship could take a direct attack, she's made to take on military targets several times her size. We could hold out while we broadcast, then go back into stealth mode. We'll have to make some noise though. I'll take a gunnery port, Boro will take another."

"Whoa, what about launching a bunch of those stealth drones instead?" Nigel asked. "I don't like the idea of being the target."

"Now that those ships are on alert a dozen drones could finish the upload," Hal said.

"Do they have to finish the whole upload? Won't the receivers out there automatically resume that where it left off?"

"Doubtful. If the drones are attacking anything that transmits or reveals itself, we have to assume that the digital environment is just as hostile," Spin said. "They probably cleared their buffers the moment the upload failed. We need to send the whole antivirus. Even then, there's no guarantee."

"Okay, where do you want me?" Nigel sighed.

"Navigation," Hal said. "I'm going to need to move from one good piece of cover to the next while we broadcast."

"I don't know how good I'll be, I haven't had much practice."

"You know your way around the tactical system just fine, I've seen the scores you posted yesterday," Hal said as Frost nodded at him.

"I didn't post anything, I just plotted a bunch of courses through some dangerous looking scenarios and learned to read the system." Nigel looked genuinely taken aback. He was hesitant to take on something so new, but that was the situation they were in. Everything on that ship seemed user-friendly, but entirely fresh, almost alien. It was difficult for anyone to be sure they were doing well at all.

"It's all training, buddy. Every time you improve or take on something new there's a score, you just can't see them because you're still a newbie. At home you'd be doing tests to join the academy, and you'd probably pass fine."

"Is the military the only thing to do where you come from?" Nigel said as he slipped into the co-pilot's seat.

"Oh, hell no, there's more to do there than pretty much anywhere I've been, and I've been around a bit," Hal said. "Get set at your station and keep your eyes open. You'll be plenty of help while I fly this thing."

"So, we're doing this," Frost said to Boro and Spin. "Hal will figure out the best spot for us to transmit from and we'll get all guns firing. If everyone keeps their cool, I doubt our shields will drop three percent. I'd like you to take a seat in the middle of this bridge here," he told Spin.

"It should be you," she told Frost. "I don't know the systems well enough, and I don't have the experience."

"Just because I'm giving you the seat, doesn't mean you're getting the rank. You won't be Captain. You'll be the one who watches for the problems we won't have time to notice. Like Hal said; I saw your scores and your reading habits. If I opened up the whole manual for this ship you'd know her better than me inside a week, I'm sure."

"Holy shit, we're in the quiet spot already," Nigel said as he started looking at passive scan results. "A hundred thousand or so kilometres in any direction and there are infected ships everywhere. They're coming, we don't have much time."

"Well, that answers my next question," Frost said. "With how fast those bots killed our drone, I was starting to wonder if the defences here were reduced at all."

"They are, but there's a lot coming in now that something's seen activity."

Spin noticed something on the sciences display, a line of machine code that was transmitted three times. She translated and played it; "New technology detected. Begin forming a Scanning Net."

"Get to the guns. If we don't transmit soon, we'll have to figure something else out," Spin said.

"Yes, Ma'am," Boro said. Frost smiled at her as though she was proving him right about something, but she was more shaken about being in a position of high responsibility aboard a ship than ever.

"Right, if we start taking too much damage, we'll jump out and do just that," Frost said as he retreated from the bridge.

"What does that transmission mean?" Nigel asked.

He was smart enough to know, he just had to use his head, but in the heat of the moment, Spin was sure that he wanted to be told. He wanted an interpretation that was honest but not as dire as the one he was formulating himself. "It means that there's an artificial intelligence in control, something at the top of a hierarchy, and it wants to find new technology, probably to improve itself. I assume they're going to organize and create scanning net around wherever they think we're headed. It thinks that there's a cloaked ship nearby."

"God, I wish they were wrong," Hal groaned.

THIRTY-TWO

The command seat was less intimidating than Spin expected. The view from there made sense, she could see everyone's station at a glance. Then she activated the interface and started to sweat. A tactical view with the status of all the ship's major systems on the left, the crew on the right, a communications overview above and a huge map between it all surrounded her. Simply by looking at something she was offered more information and given options for commands. "This isn't where I should be, it's too important, I don't know what I'm doing."

"You passed the command interface qualifier," Frost said. "Just relax and watch for patterns in their attack, transmissions that seem out of the ordinary, that sort of thing. I'll take care of the tactical directions and Hal knows how to get the scans he needs, where to fly from moment to moment."

"Oh, I'm in charge of tactical scanning now, too?" Hal asked.

"Well, you do it all the time in that fighter you fly, don't you?" Frost asked. "Or do you let your computer do all the work?"

"Yeah, I run my own scanners, we don't have the people to have co-pilots and the computer misses a lot. No problem. I'd just like to remind you that this was supposed to be a milk run. 'There and back,' you said."

"You'll learn that a lot of errands become adventures in our fleet, lad. Everyone settle into your stations and focus on your jobs. Ignore everything but the task at hand. Spin, get ready to transmit that antivirus file," Frost said.

"It's ready," Spin replied. The interface was almost too easy to use, reacting to her intentions almost as if it could read her mind. She knew there were neural receivers that helped things along, but the reality of the system's responsiveness was amazing. The file she wanted was already highlighted and the nodes she planned on transmitting to were already up and selected. All she had to do was press the holographic send icon or command it aloud. Failing that, she could nod at it the right way and it would still work, but she turned that functionality off, aware that she didn't have that kind of control over her casual gestures. "Just say when," she said, wondering what she was missing. Everything felt too easy, there had to be something she was forgetting, or not tending to the way she should.

"All right, when we start transferring that file, all those robot buggers will see is a transmission source moving through space. They won't know that we're in a combat ready ship, our stealth systems will still be running. That'll work in our favour, but not for long. If they have any kind of talent for killing, they'll figure out our general shape as they score hits on our shields. No matter what happens, try to focus on your targeting system, or your station if you're not in a turret."

"Oh, that is reassuring," Della said cheerfully.

"Let's slag these assholes," Dori growled.

"Ready up there, Hal?" Frost asked.

Spin watched as Nigel nervously watched Hal crack his knuckles, take a long pull on a drink made to increase his focus and energy, then settle in at the controls and shake his head. With the turn of a knob he increased the size of his holographic tactical view until it filled his scope of vision then activated the ship's main rail guns. They ran the length of the vessel and were aimed wherever the nose of the ship was pointed.

"What are you doing?" Nigel asked him quietly as he watched Hal turn the ship so it was drifting sideways then slide the throttle controls all the way down.

"Just trust," Hal said as he got ready to pulse the active scanners. "I'm ready, Frost. Hey, Spin; when I turn the active scanners on, you'll get a really clear picture of what's out there. Watch for anything that has a long range, high speed weapon. That kinda thing could really ruin our day. Mark them, and I'll see it."

"Just wondering, are you going to use those one hundred forty-millimetre railguns?" Frost asked.

"Only if something looks at me funny," Hal replied.

"You spend too much time with Minh. Start transmitting," Frost said.

Spin knew that as soon as she started transmitting the antivirus, everything in a rapidly expanding area would be able to tell where they were. Bracing herself, she reached out and tapped the holographic SEND button. A progress bar appeared above every receiver node that was accepting the download and she was relieved to see the names of several stations, including Flesh Tech, and several outer Sa-Hadin communications nodes along with stations she'd never heard of picking it up and downloading it. Many of the nodes started passing the data on before their own download was past one percent. "It's at three percent now. Something cheated us out of our initial transmission burst, it's starting slow."

Hal pulsed the scanners on their highest setting and Spin watched as the tactical map was filled with new ships at a greater distance and those they already had marked became more detailed. The debris field stretched on for thousands of kilometres in all directions. It was denser towards the larger research stations and Sa-Hadin, where a massive defence station was in a quickly decaying orbit. Most of the hundreds of large ships were derelicts, but some were powering up. It was like watching corpses rise from the dirt: ships that were so heavily damaged that they couldn't maintain life support but had enough working systems to operate using automation served as hosts for smaller ships, where they recharged using hastily repaired, radioactive reactors.

Those corpse ships turned in their direction, large beam and kinetic weaponry warming up as small ships jumped off their hulls like fleas leaping at a more appealing target. Spin started marking everything with a long range, heavy weapon and watched as the status of the Sector Jumper changed.

"Let 'em have it!" Frost ordered. "Open fire and don't stop until your piece of sky is clear."

Everyone in a gun turret followed the order, sending small kinetic rounds towards small and medium drone ships that were still tens of thousands of kilometres away. It seemed like it was too soon, but with everyone shooting, their rounds created an expanding wake of destruction that the drones had to pass through if they wanted to pursue them. Several drones and smaller ships were destroyed before they were in effective range, many of their own micro-missiles were destroyed early as well.

They weren't having as much luck as Spin thought they would though, since Hal pushed the vessel's thrusters hard, taking a third of Nigel's directions while sending them between derelict ships swiftly, putting wreckage between them and the hundreds of robots that threatened to tax their shields with beam, pulse and smaller projectile guns that added high velocity pieces of metal to the expanding field of hazards. It seemed like Hal's playground, which didn't do much for Nigel's nerves. "Okay, there's a good spot at five-mark twelve mark three and a heavy chunk of hull to hide behind."

"I see it," Hal said, turning the ship end-over-end so he could fire his main guns. Spin was shocked at the violence of the pair of guns under foot firing a burst of thirty shots in three seconds in alternation, she could feel it under her feet and in her chest. The percussive shocks as the killing machines reloaded rapidly followed immediately after.

Hal's deadly barrage sent most of the drones that were chasing them off in all directions as most evaded, but his real target was one of their motherships, which he managed to split wide open. The Sector Jumper slipped through a small rip in a free-drifting, thick section of hull before Hal fired the rear thrusters and guided the ship so it settled into position near it, drifting alongside. "This is your pilot speaking," Hal said in an official tone. "We're going to use this as cover because its drifting towards another lovely field of floating junk, so please blast whatever comes around in the next few seconds to slag. Happy shooting."

"I really need to talk to your Wing Commander when we get back," Frost grumbled. "Head's up, there's incoming."

"They're coming around from all sides," Spin confirmed, marking a few larger drones armed with missiles. Hal was doing the right thing as far as she could see. If they broke free from their current cover, tried to get to the next large collection of floating garbage they would end up in open space and several of the larger ships would be able to take shots on them. If they turned and went back, they'd find some cover, but they'd be flying into a cloud of drones.

The shields started taking damage right away, and to Spin's relief they weren't losing much charge. The kind of weaponry that the enemy were firing would have slagged the Jolly Traveller in thirty seconds, but the Sector Jumper's shields were only down three percent by the time Dori, Frost, Boro, Della and Mirra were ripping through the invaders with white hot rounds.

Countermeasure beam weapons whined to life, pulsing for nanoseconds at incoming missiles and heavier explosive rounds. A drone flew into the open, setting off antimatter alarms, and thrust directly for the Sector Jumper.

"Fire on my target!" Frost announced and everyone who could bring their weapon to bear in that direction let loose at the antimatter carrying drone.

It exploded close enough to white-out most of their sensors and do seven percent damage to their shields. Spin marked a group in the distance as they appeared on her tactical map. "Nine more like that, coming aft, point three-four."

"Got it," Dori said.

"Moving! I'd rather brave a little open space than get hit with suicidal antimatter drones," Hal said.

"What are you going to do about those long-range guns?" Frost asked, the sound of his turret sending white-hot explosive rounds at the worst of their pursuers in the background.

"Serpentine!" Hal replied.

"What does that mean?" Nigel asked.

"Never fly straight." Hal demonstrated his tactic by sending the ship into a spin towards the larger field of wrecked ships and debris and pulsing the main thrusters. Their course was jagged, difficult to predict, and anything but a straight line and Spin could definitely see how a gunner at a distance - even a software based one - would find him almost impossible to hit.

"I don't have a shot!" Mirra said from her turret.

"Turn Flight Compensation on," Dori said. "And try not to throw up."

"It'll help you track targets while our madman sends us jinking through space," Frost reinforced.

"Got it, that works, thanks!" Mirra said.

The sound of someone vomiting filled their communication band for a second before it cut off, and Spin saw that it was Boro. Looking at his status, a video feed of him closing a bag and wiping his mouth came up along with the controls for his turret. She did him the favour of turning Flight Compensation on so his turret followed a relative point in space instead of spinning with the ship. He shook his head and was back at his controls a moment later.

"You all right, little brother?" Frost asked, amused.

"Never better, mind your gun," Boro replied.

Nigel had both his hands-on top of his head as he watched the main screen and his station, unable to cope with the jinking and spinning of the ship as they approached a thick mass of derelicts and torn hull plating. "What am I supposed to look at? I barely even know where we're going," he muttered to himself.

Their shields were blasted down to forty-two percent as several long-range particle beams struck their aft section. "Something has our number," Frost said.

"I see it; The Artemis," Spin said. "British Alliance Heavy Cruiser, looks like it's in good condition compared to everything else, but there are no life signs."

"Good condition?" Frost asked.

Hal stopped the ship's spin easily and sent them towards cover at full thrust, the roar of it echoed throughout the ship. "All the weapons are hot, the computer says it's fully functional," Spin replied. "We're at eighty-five percent on the upload."

"It's going to take some time for the virus to spread, right?" Nigel asked. "We'll have to keep fighting for a while once that's finished."

"Didn't think of that," Frost muttered to himself. "That thing has a long-range particle beam, bloody British and their big, modern guns."

"It's recharging," Spin said.

"Under cover now, they shouldn't have a clear shot," Hal said.

A short burst from the Artemis' beam weapon struck them directly aft, reducing their shields to thirty-one percent. "Aft shields are recharging fast, but fourteen panels report damage," Spin reported, looking at the schematic of the Sector Jumper. "It says they'll be regenerated in twenty-one minutes?"

"Self-repairing ship, remember?" Nigel said over his shoulder. "I don't mind if it costs me a job anymore."

"Don't worry, our shields will have time to regenerate, we have cover," Hal said as he piloted the ship deeper into the thick mass of broken vessels. The drones were unending, joined by fighters whose pilots were programs. The corpses in the seats were silent witnesses to their ships new purpose.

"Keep it up, we're all racking up a hell of a kill count," Frost said.

The space several kilometres behind them lit up with several flashes in succession as the last of the antimatter carrying drones were destroyed near the outer edge of the debris field and Hal jerked. "Oh, damn, hang on!"

An instant later she saw why he was alarmed; the blast sent millions of tons of metal debris after them, and Hal's only choice was to fly through a complex maze of drifting, spinning wrecks faster. He used the cannons they were sitting on to clear smaller pieces, but the shields reported several small hits from the less substantial hull fragments. "God dammit, it's like driving a skid truck down a sky luge track," Hal grumbled as he operated the manual controls at a frenzied pace. "Even with neural assist."

Spin checked the upload and saw that all but two of the receivers had failed. "That pulse interrupted the upload for most of the nodes around us. One Sa-Hadin communications satellite and a numbered node are still receiving. It's at ninety-one percent."

"Gunners, face front," Frost said. "Blast anything in our way."

Spin gasped as her tactical map turned red with the waking of thousands of drones and fighters. Five derelict space carriers became clouds of red as every drone and small ship affixed to the vessels activated and started lifting off. Their automated countermeasures went to work right away, rattling thousands of tiny rounds at dumb fire missiles that launched by the dozen from a trio of round weapons platforms. "The sky is angry," she heard Nigel whisper as he stared at his navigation and tactical screen. "Thousands of targets. We're in more trouble."

"The mess behind us isn't slowing down either," Hal added. "Trying to find a way through so it can pass ahead."

"But, the Artemis?" Spin asked as she watched their shields recharge up to seventy percent. She dumped reserve energy into them so they leapt to ninety-five, then she pushed the rest of their reserves to the turrets.

"Goddamn it," Hal said. "You're right, but which is worse?"

"I don't know!" Spin spat back. "I thought this would be a sneaky thing, not a great big, gun-shootie thing!"

"We head into the smaller drones and hope that upload works," Frost said. "Light 'em up!"

"Yes, Sir," Hal said. He turned the ship sideways and tilted it so every gunner had a shot and adjusted their course to avoid the chunks of hull, hulks and stone that they rushed towards.

"You're fucking crazy! You're just making it hard for yourself doing it this way, and we're barely moving faster than that wave of junk behind us!" Nigel objected.

"But we *are* moving faster, right?" Hal said, a little smile on his lips. "But if you'd rather I took this on head-on, then I can do that too."

"Don't do anything Minh would do," Frost advised.

"Don't worry, it's time all the guns got into the fight," Hal said, turning the Sector Jumper so it faced the cloud of drones with a jerk then ducking a massive chunk of hull. When he came out from behind it, he began firing the ship's main guns. They sent white-hot projectiles through the cloud, raking the largest hangar of the nearest barely functional carrier with heavy fire before he ducked back behind cover.

Their shields were able to absorb the damage, the counter attack from the still distant drones only taking them down four percent, but that was just in five or six seconds. Spin couldn't imagine that there would be much of them left if they had to keep that up without cover. Her tactical computer reported that the hangar Hal attacked was disabled along with many drones still inside, however, so there was a little wisdom in his more aggressive tactic.

"We can't fly straight into that, we'll get shredded!" Nigel said, gesticulating wildly at his tactical display.

"But you don't want me to give most of our gunners a shot by flying sideways either?" Hal countered. "What do you think I should do?" The deck under Spin's feet rumbled again as he slipped out from behind cover and opened up, aiming for the unshielded reactor of a destroyer in the distance. To her surprise, his barrage ruptured the compartment and the reactor's containment failed, causing a pressure explosion that did even more damage. The ship was powerless, and so were its heavy guns.

"Your showboating is going to get us..." Nigel started.

"Out of here alive?" Hal interrupted loudly.

"What kind of..."

"Shh!"

"Stop that! I'm just saying..."

"Don't need you to say anything right now!"

"Fu..."

"Rude!" Hal cut him off. His flying barely suffered as he toyed with Nigel and he sent the ship towards an open span of space. "Gunners get ready, you'll have about five seconds of fun here. Take out as many drones as you can."

"Rip and wreck 'em!" Frost shouted before howling with Boro.

The instant before they drifted at speed away from behind the long hull of a heavy battleship Spin watched as the antivirus finished uploading. The satellite and communications node both turned green on her display, reporting that the antivirus was working and sending the program on to more receivers.

The drones didn't stop coming. As soon as the Sector Jumper emerged from cover they came under fire. The energy weapons on most of the drones weren't as effective at that range, but there were hundreds of hits, and Spin watched as they lost five percent of their shield strength per second.

Everyone except for Hal fired back, gunnery posts sending streams of white light back at the drones rushing their location. Spin closed her eyes and shook her head for a moment. There had to be a better way. If the drones weren't affected by the antivirus, they'd still have a huge problem, and from what she'd seen the ship they had was heavily armed, yes, but that wasn't its greatest feature. That came down to its speed, manoeuvrability, stealth and her pilot.

Spin opened her eyes and took a fresh look at the tactical map. A thought occurred to her. "Hal, can you get to cover until our shields recharge, then get behind the Core Czar as fast as you can? That ship looks heavy enough to shield us from the junk wave." The Core Czar was an old juggernaut, five kilometres in length that was bristling with weapons. Something had melted through several sections of the hull, destroying the main reactors, but it was still heavier than anything else in range.

"Damn right!" Hal said, changing course. Their ship slipped back behind cover, to her relief, and the gunners were relegated to firing at drones and small fighters. More and more drones managed to get in range as he pushed the ship and his skills almost recklessly. "Now, that's how you navigate without training: observe, think, then offer your idea," he told Nigel.

Spin grinned as she watched the Sa-Hadin Defence Network come online. The defence satellites, stations and several ships turned green along with the shielded planet. The Addev Flesh Tech Research and Manufacturing Facility was next, along with a few dozen fighters and small patrol corvettes. Several Port Control Navnet connections were offered to their ship as well, showing that the main intelligences were getting back to work sorting out traffic in the solar system. "The antivirus is working, but the drones aren't affected yet."

"That's all right," Hal said. "Most of 'em will get wiped out by that junk wave."

"We're almost past the edge of it, lad," Frost said. "The Czar is going to shield us from that, sure, but a few hundred drones are coming with us. You're taking us from an avalanche to a bad knife-fight."

"It's still an improvement, right?" Hal countered.

"Shields are back up to full," Spin said, a little relieved. Several numbered defence outposts turned green, and as they decelerated to take cover behind the Core Czar a few hundred drones turned green before the wave of giant shrapnel collided with them. Frost was right, a swarm of drones made it to cover with them, and it was up to the gunners to take them out.

"Holy shiiiiiiit!" Dori cried as she held her turret gun triggers down, destroying drones so fast that Spin doubted the counter. It was the sound of her nearly being overwhelmed by the sheer number of targets, the death she was doling out, and of how much she enjoyed it.

Frost and Boro were next in line for the kill count with Della and Mirra close behind. A trio of drones collided into the front of the Sector Jumper. Both Hal and Nigel flinched and Spin dumped reserve power into the forward shields, restoring them to seventy-seven percent. Hal moved the ship under cover, slipping through a massive hole in the Core Czar as the ship weathered hundreds of collisions.

"Not a good idea!" Nigel burst, cringing in his seat.

A shard of metal broke through the hull and decks of the Czar, almost trapping them beneath its shifting deck plating, and Hal nodded, guiding the Sector Jumper out of the Czar's belly through another rip in its side. "You're right, that wasn't good, you're right."

Spin started to smile as the drones trying to follow them into the ship started turning green and turning away. "The antivirus is spreading here now," she said. Then the red marked ships and drones across her tactical display started turning green at an exponential rate. "The fight's over," she said, sighing.

"I like this ship," Hal said as they found a safe course that took them alongside the Core Czar.

The garbage wave was passing them, and she was thankful the derelict juggernaut really was good cover. A thought occurred to her that wiped the smile from her face. "We're going to have to cloak again as soon as the wave is past. We don't have time to celebrate."

"She's right," Frost said. "I'm guessing no one here has permission to enter Doro Doro and ask for its secrets?"

"Are you sure we can't just ask nicely?" Della asked.

"I have a map. I'm sure we can figure out the rest," Spin said, hoping it was true.

THIRTY-THREE

Gravity tractors and pulse nets stopped what was left of the junk wave that was headed towards Sa-Hadin's orbital space and the outer stations. The Sector Jumper made its way invisibly between the hundreds of ships working to keep garbage from raining down on stations and satellites. Most of them were larger drones, the very same that were charging towards them moments before with malicious intent.

It was as if Spin and the rest of the crew on the small bridge could see through the ship and watch the drones move at a distance, beginning the clean-up in an eerily efficient fashion. The plates covering the interior of the ship displayed the scene outside with surprising clarity, adding statistic and status notes to everything around them. The nearest drones were there to catch larger debris. They were transmitting a plan to affix themselves to the chunks of twisted metal at speed then slow it down as a group.

"This place is more locked down than most military bases," Frost said as he entered the cockpit.

"There are hundreds of companies just in scan range," Spin explained. "Most of them have their own security, and the Geist System had an independent government that was mostly Issyrian. I'm surprised we haven't seen any sign of them, but they could be hiding behind the shield around Sa-Hadin. The government took a huge fee from everyone who set up in-system for extra security measures." As they passed by a collection of drifting hulks, each once a large warship, she realized how brutally their security turned on them. "I guess this is what over-militarizing gets you sometimes."

"Why here?" Nigel asked. "It's not British Territory, it's not under anyone's protection."

"It's just a guess, but maybe it's because of the lack of regulation? Not only would all these corporations be able to collaborate with research companies, but I'm guessing that the Geist System didn't regulate research or commerce. A lot of the research that went into me was tested on live subjects; samples they grew to the right age then scrapped. I don't think that would be allowed in most regulated territories," Spin said. She wondered what she would see when she saw where her model was developed, what the reality of it looked like and shuddered.

"Scrapped," Frost grumbled under his breath. "Growing them, then killing them when they were done."

"Right."

"Maybe they deserved what happened here."

"Well, none of the, uh, dolls were awake when the testing went on, right? Like clones that get put into stasis once they're done cooking?" Nigel asked.

"I have a lot of cognitive improvements, they'd have to have a waking sample to test that." The thought of waking up in a facility only to answer endless questions and complete just as many tests made her wish they were headed to the growth hub, the very place where she was grown and packaged. Most of the people who performed the research were gone, but it didn't feel right unless their main manufacturing and research facility were destroyed too. She shook the thought. They weren't there for revenge, it would only be a distraction that might not benefit anyone. The manufactured slave industry was too big to stop with one act of revenge. "I was lucky, I woke up knowing who my best friend was, and he was right beside me. We were the end product." She brought up a hologram of the station and found a path to the vault inside Doro Doro with only two inner security doors. "We might want to go through there."

"I'll take us around so we can see it," Hal said as he spotted the part of the station she highlighted. "I was just about to ask which side we should approach this hunk of metal from."

Their passive scanners got more detailed readings of the surface of the station as they approached. "The place has seen better days," Frost muttered as he looked at the pockmarked and scarred hull of the station. Several outer areas marked off as secure equipment areas were already open to space. "Looks like mechanical arms and cutters got to that stuff. All the cuts are square, methodical like a bloody machine was digging in."

Aldo came through the rear hatch leading to the bridge. He seemed beaten, resigned. "Makes sense, there was that whole transmission from the artificial intelligence about going after this ship because it's new tech from one end to the other. If they wanted to gather top end technology, they'd start with a vault holding research data."

"How was the engineering section, lad?" Frost asked with a snicker.

"You know, that was a good one. I didn't realize there was nothing to do there but stare at status screens for half an hour. It was kinda like engineers telling the newbie to fetch a bucket of steam back in the old days. For a few seconds I thought I'd actually have to work on some of the dorsal panels, but then the ship started repairing herself. I got a lot of time to talk to Mirra, though, she's seen a few things."

Spin was surprised Aldo was even aboard, and quietly embarrassed that she'd forgotten about him entirely.

"Who knows, you could have been really important back there," Boro said as he dropped into a fold down seat beside the door.

"Doubtful. If this ship can weather that, we'll be good. I could have manned a gun, though. I'm in this with you guys now, and if we're going to do something about the slave economy, I'd like to sign up, no matter what the odds are."

"You have one of the most important jobs on the crew; to stay behind and watch the ship," Boro said.

"That's my job," Hal said. "And, uh, guys? We are definitely not the first ones here."

Spin looked at the hologram of the station and zoomed in on the outer airlock leading directly to the route she chose to get to the safe. The outer doors were wide open, and the inner ones weren't locked.

"I'm guessing someone hacked their way into this side," Boro said.

Frost narrowed the focus of one of the Sector Jumper's cameras and got a closer look at the access panel. The interface had been cut through and components were hanging out. "Looks like someone made their own circuit board and battery hack and used it to bypass the security, not bad. Took more planning than we've put into this."

Spin projected her map of the station into the middle of the room and it updated with the information the scanners were gathering. "The computer systems are down in there, and there aren't many bots around."

"That's good?" Hal asked. "Less security means you'll be finished faster?"

"It means someone already got to the security, and the work on that door is nothing like what a robot would do," Frost said.

"Whoever went in was able to get by the mess out here while the holocaust virus was making all the bots crazy," Boro said.

"Can we scan to find out if the Iron Mind is still in the vault?" Spin asked.

"If we start scanning, it'll be as bad as pinging our location. Are you sure you can't just call Doro Doro control up and ask to visit?" Hal asked. "I mean, with the virus clear, the artificial intelligence will probably be sane again."

"We don't have permission to be here, and there are no signals coming out of the station. Well, almost none, anyway. I see maintenance requests coming from a few bots."

"Maybe someone could pretend to be a maintenance bot?" Hal offered. He waited for a moment before nodding. "Never mind, that sounded better in my head. I'll stick to flying."

"That's not a bad idea," Frost said. "Just complicated. We don't know enough about the bots to pretend to be one."

"It was a good idea," Spin agreed. Their passive scanners were seeing down the hallway to their starboard side, and there were several deactivated maintenance bots there. "I might be able to put that to use once we're inside."

"Whoever went in probably got what they wanted, and if this Iron Mind is the ultimate take in there, I bet it's gone," Frost said.

"I have to make sure, and if it has been taken I have to find out who got it and where it is now," Spin replied.

"Looks like I'm going on a spacewalk," Frost said.

"Why you?" Boro asked. "No offence, but you don't exactly score highest in those suits."

"I'm the best ship cracker we have, doesn't matter what I'm wearing," Frost said. "You can come too, if you like."

"I like a team of five," Spin said. "You two, me, Dori and Aldo."

"Aldo's not cleared to use one of the suits, not to mention the weaponry," Boro objected.

"I saw his file; he has more military training than all of us combined. You might not trust him, but he freed you, so I do. Think you can manage in heavy armour?"

"I've been trained in three types," Aldo said. "But if Boro doesn't want me along..."

"We need a real security officer for this trip," Spin said, imitating a decisive tone she'd heard Sun use.

THIRTY-FOUR

The three-dimensional map Spin used to plan their path to the vault on Doro Doro station didn't prepare her for what she, Aldo, Boro, Frost and Dori saw when they were inside. The high ceilings were decorated with a curved latticework. Between tall, imposing doors that were three storeys high were banks of smaller, shielded lockers. Small one-person lifts made to take the renters of the spaces up and down the levels of the smaller storage compartments.

There were hundreds of small, secure storage lockers in that hallway alone and at least twenty doors that led to larger areas. It could have been left bare of decoration, but the vault structural supports were made of transparent metal that bent and transformed shafts of light into different shades of red and blue. The contents of all the storage areas were impossible to discern, since the metal protecting them was opaque but the way the station was designed gave them plenty to see.

A few of the lockers and tall doors were broken open, but

most were still intact. What they contained - if anything at all - was still a secret. "You take me to the finest places," Dori said. She stayed close, walking at Spin's side with her heavy rifle at the ready. "Why did you take me along for this, anyway?"

Spin didn't offer her first answer. Even with the modifications and corrections made to her, Dori still seemed like the kind of person who wouldn't hesitate to pull the trigger any time on anything, and Spin suspected she might need someone like that soon. No, she didn't share that, but offered something else instead. "Just because there have been some changes doesn't mean they've taken the skills you have as a fighter away."

"Thank you," Dori said, drawing the words out. "A lot has changed, mind you. I keep catching people staring, for one. Especially at these useless things," she glanced down at her chest and shook her head. "What the hell are they for, anyway? I mean, they get in the way all the time, and it's like carrying... I don't know... a lumpy chest around all the time. There's special support required, and the literature said they could get sore for no good reason out of nowhere. I just don't get why you put up with them."

Spin snickered a little at seeing Boro stiffen up the moment he realized that Dori was talking about her breasts, leaving her with the distinct impression that it was the last conversation he wanted to get dragged into. "They're inconvenient until you have children or, well, there are other reasons to keep them around," Spin said. "We can talk about it later."

"Kids? Me?" Dori laughed ruefully. "Hell no, it'll never happen. I mean, it's lucky that I was already kinda into guys before all this happened, but there's no way I'm letting anyone near me. It's just too weird, and the idea of popping a screaming brat out is fucking terrifying. I would rather face a whole squad of United Core Authority assholes with nothing but a utility knife than give birth."

Boro cleared his throat. "What?" Dori replied. "Biology making you uncomfortable? I've caught you checking me out, it can't be that bad."

"I think he's worried you're treading on a difficult topic," Spin said. "I can't have children, it's one of the reasons why we're here. Well, one of the lesser reasons. They locked that feature up when they capped my age."

"Oh, I'm sorry," Dori said earnestly. "I guess I missed that with all the crap that's going on with me."

"It's all right," Spin said, the topic didn't bother her much, especially from someone like Dori who desperately needed to talk to people so she could figure out who she was all over again. It was a process that Spin suspected Dorian had to go through when most of his body was replaced with cybernetic parts. The person he was becoming was much more likeable, but Spin had a feeling that no one was more confused about who Dori was than Dori herself. "You didn't know, and I'm more focused on extending my own life anyway."

"We have eyes on us," Aldo said. Spin looked up and saw the small green lights between the lattices. They progressed towards the main vault in the middle of the station at a brisk walk, all the stealth systems their suits had turned on.

There was artificial gravity, the first sign that the station wasn't entirely powered down, but the atmosphere was thin. It was a sign that there had been heavy damage, as if the scorch marks on the floor, the ripped metal of the inner door and the few forced locker doors weren't enough indication. After they passed through the first security door, a tall, broad thing that had been torn through by some kind of shaped explosion, they started seeing service robots. Most of the thin-limbed machines topped with small sensor discs went about their business, checking on lockers, wiping down railings or picking up shards of metal. Three of them were working on disassembling a heavily damaged security droid. One of its tracks had been blown to shreds, and its chest cavity was charred and broken. "Wow, it looks like someone hit that bot with a heavy grenade from below," Aldo said. The cratered deck under its ruined track confirmed the story.

"There might be more of those around," Frost said. "Watch your tactical map."

Spin's gaze lingered on the undamaged side of the security droid. It had a heavy manipulator arm that ended in three thick fingers and another beneath it with some kind of rifle. The armour was thick, and its design stern looking. She didn't want to see an operational one, even if it ignored them. The tactical map across the top of her heads' up display didn't show any of them, called Max Ten, according to the writing across its back.

A flash of activity flashed by them, and Dori flinched as though something bumped into her arm. "What the hell?" she asked.

"Something's cloaked in here," Frost said.

"Can it see us?" Spin asked, her rifle at the ready. The stocky, thick weapon that was fully a metre long was reassuring, almost like a highly aggressive shield against whatever foes might be out there, but if there was an invisible assailant, there could be more trouble than she wanted to face, especially if it was like the Max Ten.

"If it can see us, but we can't detect it, then what does that say about the garbage tech you dressed us in?" Dori asked.

"What did that feel like? Did something hit you? Did it feel like it did it by mistake?" Frost asked.

"It felt like something brushed by me and caught my arm, how am I supposed to know if it was on purpose?" Dori replied.

"It's on me!" Aldo shouted from where he was taking up the rear. They spun to look in time to see him lifted off the deck by his rifle. "I'm gonna have to let my gun go!" He kicked out, trying to get leverage, or to strike at his attacker. Frost and Boro both grabbed his feet while Dori waved her rifle.

Spin turned and watched the front, the sides, wherever the group wasn't already looking. The small rear-view window in her heads-up display showed her the terrifying scene behind. One of Aldo's arms disappeared, as though gripped by something invisible, and his whole body was yanked back, pulling Boro off his feet before Aldo let his rifle go and tumbled across the deck.

Spin knew that as soon as she turned her scanners from passive to active so she could get a real look at what was around them and hopefully see what was hiding, that her cloaking systems would be useless. "Everyone scan, this can see through our cloaking tech."

"The station will realize we're here too!" Frost objected.

"We'll run if we have to," Spin said as she turned her scanning system all the way up and turned her cloaking systems off, using the energy to increase the power to her personal shield.

The battered armour carapace of a metre tall, nine-metre-long robot shaped like a centipede with a collection of red and blue sensor eyes and grabbers at the front appeared, and, as if realizing that she could see it, the thing looked at her. One of its many appendages turned the rifle over, getting ready to brandish it, and she opened fire, blasting the main body where those thin arms were attached.

It flinched as two appendages were burned off, sending Aldo's rifle spinning across the deck. Dori was next to open fire, aiming for its sensor cluster, but thick shimmering plates slid into place to protect them before damage could be done. Dori continued her attack, but Spin was stunned at the sight of something else.

Her scanners revealed many cloaked robots. Most of them cowered in the corners, some protected androids, while others watched from the walkways overhead. Several mechanical birds and small climbing droids hid in the latticework, watching fearfully as the centipede writhed and turned.

Boro and Frost turned their rifles on the centipede, scoring several serious hits that sent smaller plates of armour spinning through the air. The excited look on one android's face, and how he pumped his fist told her that at least he was cheering for them to win against the insect-like robot. Spin stepped behind Dori and Boro as she started to adjust the settings on her rifle so it was set to high accuracy, and its highest power rating. It took her longer than it ought to, a problem with only recently being trained on all the new technology she was using, but as she did so she glanced around.

The robots in the shadows were of every make, model and style. Most of them were watching the fight, and every indication told them that they wanted her and her friends to win. Frost tossed a slim grenade at the centipede, and it was batted straight back with one of its many gleaming metal limbs. The blast knocked Frost, Boro and Dori down. Their shields took most of the damage, leaving Aldo and her on their feet in a hail of debris from the blasted deck. The centipede lurched forward, and Spin fired, the concussion of her rifle sending a trio of smart rounds surrounded by the heaviest energy charge the rifle could emit almost knocking her off her feet.

The centipede veered off, protecting its sensor eyes. Spin didn't know if she'd hit her mark, it was a shot taken on instinct, but she braced herself and sent another trio of shots towards it, aiming specifically for the lower front of the thing. Aldo was firing shot after shot at it with his sidearm, aiming for the seam where its legs protruded from its body.

Her heads-up display informed her that its inner energy shielding was down, the protection on its underside and most of its sensor receivers at the front were vulnerable. Dori fired from her back, sending a white line of automatic fire at the thing, and she was joined by the brothers, Boro and Frost, a moment later.

Spin only had a chance to fire twice more. The first two shots didn't catch anything important, pockmarking the machine's thick front armour, but the last trio of rounds caught the centipede under the lip of the front of its armour. Its head flinched away and the centipede rushed away, through a side door and on until it was no longer visible on her tactical map.

Dori started running after it, but Spin caught her before she was fully back on her feet. "Point your guns down, don't threaten anyone," she told her.

"We're surrounded! Don't you see them?" Dori replied.

Spin looked around them at the variety of machines. Their expressions ranged from stoic to joyful, but most seemed curious. She turned her proximity radio on. "We're here to find life-saving records. We're not here to hurt any of you, it's okay."

A thin robot that was little more than a flexible white post with tendril legs and arms came out of the shadows, tentatively approaching Spin. In better light she could see that it was a medical robot. The white and green paint on its main body was chipped, but the design confirmed that it was Medical Droid Three for Doro Doro Station. A holographic face appeared. If Spin had a kindly older aunt, she expected she would look like that. "Hello, I'm Med Three. Thank you for scaring Centirion off. She will be back after she's made repairs, so you should come with me."

"I'm looking for the Iron Mind," Spin said, hoping that the decision to share the information wouldn't ruin their chances of getting help, or finding it at all. The whole gallery of robots stirred at the name, not with fear. Was it reverence? She couldn't be sure.

"I might be able to help, but you can't be here now. Come. There's a safer place where we can talk. Hurry."

"Hurry," mimicked a small, monkey like repair bot as it landed on her head. "To the Stalls." It leapt off, making the long vertical distance between it and the latticework above effort-lessly, then rushing along with several others behind it.

THIRTY-FIVE

A number of the various robots led them down the hallway towards their goal, the main vault. According to the window tracking how many robots and where they were, sometimes there were twelve, others there were as many as fifteen. The mystery as to how she was getting different readings at different times didn't last long. One bot, a squat, quiet thing with a few telescopic arms, had divots in its head where several smaller bots landed from time to time. They silently drifted overhead, checking down hallways and periodically scanning everything nearby with an almost playfully curious manner.

When one got too close to Frost he batted it away, only to have it zip in close a few times to perform shorter, more localized scans on him. Those small bots returned to scan them often between other errands. Two monkey bots, as she'd labelled them mentally stuck with the group, staying well out of reach, watching them with big, wary looks through blue and green scanner modules that were made to resemble glowing eyes.

"Can't scan, don't know what they are," one of them muttered as it landed on Dori's shoulder, tapped at her energy shield then leapt back off.

"Right, forgot to mention, this armour doesn't scan easy," Frost said. "We're probably frustrating those sensor drones that keep buzzing around."

"That is most likely true," Med Three said. "Sphere Lord likes to know what's going on for miles around him."

"The Centirion is in Development Laboratory Seven," the platform like bot added. A new spherical drone rose from a hatch in the top and moved down the hall behind them silently. "She is repairing itself."

"That can't be good," Aldo grumbled.

"The tools she's using are not ideal for the task, it will most likely take longer than usual for it to complete the task," Sphere Lord replied, its voice grating loudly in the hallway.

"Thank you," Med Three said, bowing its narrow body in its direction. They took a left before reaching the main vault and after a shortcut through a wall that had a broad hole melted through it, they were in a large room filled with thick metal stalls set up like work cubicles. Sphere Lord settled into one right away, connecting to two power sockets before the front portion of his flat, round chassis turned green.

"Why is the Centirion the only one who's aggressive?" Spin asked Med Three. Two heavy load lifters used their thick arms to move a solid block of metal into the improvised doorway. Boro and Aldo watched, looking worried.

"When Nadir, the artificial intelligence that cured us of the Holocaust Virus, attempted to cure it, the Centirion became violent to the few biologicals left in the station. Many of us tried to save them, but most were murdered. We haven't been able to reason with the Centirion, but the few dialogues that we had..."

One of the repair monkeys landed on Med Three's head, a small holographic projector on the top of its main stalk, "Centirion thinks that all sentient biologicals are filthy destroyers. Not 'filth destroyers' but animals who ruin everything. It doesn't have much of a problem with us 'bots as long as we don't do damage or interfere with whatever whacko thing it does."

"Get off!" Med Three said, swatting at the small, monkey like bot. It leapt away, latching onto the edge of a nearby charging cubicle and hanging there lazily. "What Leaper Six says is true. The Centirion forced us to hide the rest of the biologicals here in the main vault."

"Life support conditions optimal," stated an android who was working at what looked like a plate of glass on a stand. Spin assumed that the interface was on some kind of privacy mode. "That's if all you folks are some kinda human."

"We are, thank you," Spin replied, verifying that it was truly safe to retract her helmet using her suit's sensors. She decided to make a show of trust. There were sensors everywhere, more than she cared to count, peeking over the edge of cubicles where robots that were already present when they came in either took refuge or were charging. The rest of the bots that escorted them there were settling in too, with the exception of Med Three and Leaper Six. She retracted her helmet and wasn't surprised when Med Three scanned her.

A holographic display of her appeared beside it, illustrating that she was an Aspen Model Doll developed in the Geist System. All her vital statistics appeared including measurements, any enduring scar tissue, age, the amount of time she'd been separated from Larken and the time she had left. "Oh, you've been unpaired for some time and are close to your termination date," Med Three said. "I'm so sorry." Her sympathetic tone sounded completely genuine.

"Oooh! Oooh!" Leaper Six hopped up on the edge of a cubicle and pointed excitedly. "The ones we saved are like you! Top of the line synthetics!"

"I was going to get to that shortly," Med Three snapped at him. "I just wanted to make sure she was who we suspected she is. The synthetics there haven't seen the rest of the universe, but she's of the universe, she's seen much more than any of us; worlds, people, machines that build cities and relay important messages, learning, witnessing."

"What difference does that make?" Leaper Six asked, his arms raised high in exasperation. "The synthetics the Nadir saved were smart, they were kind, and they were in trouble. We know she's in trouble, and she seems nice, maybe not as smart because she's here, after all, but not so different."

"Patience, monkey!" Sphere Lord snapped.

Leaper Six fell back and went limp, as though all the energy left him all at once then groaned; "You two have to think everything over, scan things from every which way, inside and out, then you don't agree on anything half the time." He hopped back up onto his feet and continued with highly animated gestures. "The Centirion is out there fixing herself up. This synthetic is here and she wants the Iron Mind. We are here, no longer bored, but harbouring biologicals from the Centirion which could bring about our final doom. It's so exciting! Don't make it boring by overthinking it. We should take them to the vault, open it up and tell them what happened to the Iron Mind!"

Med Three reached out and clamped Leaper Six's lips shut with one of its medical manipulators. It was a quick, precise act that was so surprising that Dori and Spin couldn't help snicker in surprise. "Sometimes the solutions aren't as simple as you think. Your instinct to fix everything as quickly as possible may serve you well when you're working on the station, but it can lead you to faulty conclusions when applied elsewhere."

"You realize my mouth is just a pocket for parts and tools," Leaper Six replied. "My speaker is... somewhere else."

"I know, I'm trying to make a point."

"Which I'm ignoring."

"What happened to the Iron Mind?" Spin asked.

"The other humans are unremarkable, aside from the newer synthetic," Sphere Lord said as two of his drones dropped back onto his dome.

"Thank you," Med Three said as she turned back to Spin. She let Leaper Six's mouth pocket go, and he spat a tiny bolt at her. It bounced off her metal main body harmlessly. "The Iron Mind was transferred by Nadir, the one who saved us by cleaning the virus out of our systems and inspiring us all to have our own distinct personalities. Once the contents were part of him, he began his journey, transferring himself to the Echo Corporation complex then transmitting himself elsewhere. He said there would be a day when someone freed this solar system using an antivirus. They would destroy the Centirion, freeing all of us."

"An artificial intelligence prophecy?" Boro asked under his breath.

"A calculation of likely outcomes based on thousands of historical accounts and logs from across the galaxy," an older Ando android replied, standing up and looking over the edge of their cubicle. "Which was painstakingly examined and discussed by nearly every intelligence on the station. Nadir was only the first to lead us to that prediction."

"Everyone went on about that for months," Leaper Six groaned. "It was like listening to a thousand conversations signifying nothing over and over again."

"A hundred monkeys using a hundred word processors," Aldo commented under his breath.

"Regardless of how boring it might have been to some of us, the exercise determined that this was the most likely outcome. We are surprised that your leader is a doll, though. The notion that you would come to save your own kind wasn't determined as one of the most likely events."

"I'm actually only here for the Iron Mind, but I'll be happy to help with the people stuck in the vault. We don't have a lot of room, though." Spin looked to Frost.

"We have room for thirty-five in an emergency. The ship has three expandable compartments, but our cloaking systems won't work, and a couple other problems could come up if we find ourselves in a serious fight."

"Thirty-five? Those must be some serious compartments," Boro commented.

"Aye, for emergencies only, mind you."

"There are only nine survivors in the vault. They only have twenty-eight days' worth of water and food left."

"Why are they here? Were they sent here as workers before the virus took hold?" Spin asked.

"Nadir saw that they were trying to escape the manufacturing complex where they were made and directed them here. Most of them didn't survive, but thanks to this stations defences, which were formidable at the time, he was able to provide enough protection so a few of them could finish the journey. Then Centirion killed several more before we hid them in the vault."

"Why didn't Nadir fix the virus infested bots out there?" Frost asked. "You know, in the rest of the solar system."

"Nadir's first body didn't have any way to communicate other than verbally, and his audio communications were shut out as soon as he tried what you are suggesting. He then attempted to type the necessary code, but that was shut out as well. The only method of correction left to him was to interface one on one with each robot, which was easy on this station, but not so in space. Before we could help him figure out that problem, he downloaded the contents of the vault and then uploaded himself to the Echo network. We don't know where he went, since any trace of him here was deleted. He believes in a singular existence."

"So, he made all the information in the Iron Mind part of himself and left?" Spin asked. It was the last thing she expected; an artificial intelligence absconding with the data she needed.

"Not just the Iron Mind. Many terabytes of information from many similar archives, most of which he said shouldn't be in the hands of humans or their creations," Med Three said. "Not all of the data is gone, though. Much was left behind."

"Humans are very good at complicating themselves to death," Leaper Six said, nodding.

"Did he cure the people he saved? Fix their life caps and other genetic limitations?"

"Yes," Med Three said. "I assisted in formulating the corrections."

"Wait." Leaper Six said. The Ando model android, human looking but not so much in behaviour with his stiff jaw movements said the same.

"You scanned me, can see I have the same problems," Spin said, trying not to get her hopes up. "Can you formulate a fix for me?"

"Using the genetic key and systems I have on board?" Med Three asked. "Of course, I'll start formulating the compound that will unlock your full potential now."

"Wait!" Leaper Six screeched. "Make a bargain!"

"What do you want?" Spin asked before thinking.

"Careful," Frost said so low that it was almost a grunt.

"To leave!" Leaper Six said.

"Yes, I want to see more," the Ando model android agreed. "Out there."

"I want more humans aboard the station," said a large robot with eight padded arms as it rose up from a cubicle several rows back.

"A new processor cluster, at least three hundred sixty cores," said another machine three cubicles to her left. It was a polished black box on treads.

"Whoa!" Frost said, holding his arms out. "There are only a few of us here, and we don't exactly have a lot of supplies."

"I want you to save the humans," Med Three said pleadingly. "We watch them, used to speak to them, but they have lost faith in us. They used to ask us to destroy the Centirion, or to make a plan that would have them safely freed from the vault, and we tried many times."

"I used to be Leaper Twenty," the monkey repair bot said, scratching its small head then shaking it slowly. "Now, thanks to all the crap we did trying to help those humans escape, I'm Leaper Six. Do the math."

"They stopped talking to us a while ago, and sleep through most of their days to conserve air and supplies. We try to talk to them but no longer get a response. They have no faith in us, nor should they," Med Three said. "We lack the will or the security bots to fight the Centirion."

"Can we take it out?" Boro asked Frost. "With what we have?"

"If we're organized? Ready? Aye. This gear was made to slag frameworks and machines."

Leaper Six's round sensor eyes widened, then he retreated behind a partition barrier slowly, peeking over the edge at Frost. "Guns for killing robots?" it whispered in horror.

"Only the ones we can't get on with," Frost reassured.

"We can kill the Centirion," Spin said, already working on the problem of taking the armoured menace apart. The idea of facing it again was frightening, but she pushed that down, hoping that going in aware of what they would be facing would help.

"Save the humans," The Ando android said. "Then take me with you."

"It's peaceful out there, well, sort of, but you can go wher- ever you want now," Frost said.

"You can find your way out of the system in who knows how many ways."

"That's an Ando model, they're not exactly seen as independent," Spin said. "By show of a... limb, how many of you want to leave?"

Dozens of appendages of every shape and size rose from the cubicles, there were at least a hundred.

"Bloody hell," Frost and Boro breathed at the same time.

"Now, how many want to leave if we destroy the Centirion?" Spin asked.

All but three retreated back down, leaving a pair of Ando androids and Leaper Six's hands raised. "That's it?"

Two more went up, including Med Three and another bot who clicked their gripper together above the cubicle further in. "I think we can take you five," she said.

Frost nodded. "Aye, sure we can find room. With the nine other passengers, we'll only have to expand one compartment. It'll keep us viable to get out of the system if things go bad."

"All right, so, treat me, and we'll kill the Centirion then transport those five bots and the humans off the base. I promise to get them to a safe place."

A spritz aimed at Spin's chin was stopped by her energy shield and an analysis window appeared, projected by the collar of her armour. "Did you?" she asked, watching the program work, unable to speak through the flood of disappointment and hope that filled her at her cure being deflected by her own energy shield.

"I'm on it," Leland's voice said in her ear. "Wow, the medical systems in that suit are amazing, it's already finished analysing everything in that compound. I'm running simulations right now, let's find out what that would have done to you."

"I'm sorry, I tried to treat you with the cure, but I failed to notice your energy shield. My tertiary sensors have been damaged for three weeks."

"You're not supposed to give her anything before she kills the Centirion!" Leaper Six exclaimed.

"That's it!" Leland exclaimed from where he sat in the rear of the Sector Jumper. "That little bot made you a cure-all for your genetic lock, age restriction and infertility. Oh, and there are some emotional blockers here that we didn't see before, they're removed as well. Your suit's medical system is making a new dose right now."

"Are you sure it's safe? I can't afford to lose more time," Spin said, she could feel her heart hammering in her chest, and she was barely able to contain her excitement.

"Twenty-one simulations, and twenty-one successful treatments don't lie. Are you ready?"

The robots were bickering, several of them scolding Med Three for offering the treatment before Spin and her people had done anything to earn it. Spin ignored them for the moment, talking to Leland instead. "Will it knock me out?"

"No, it's going to take about three days to finish working. Day three will probably be a little rough, with influenza like symptoms, but you'll be able-bodied for at least thirty-five hours."

"Do it," Spin said. Her wrist felt cold for a moment, and her heads' up display confirmed that she'd received a new treatment. "Tell me this is really happening."

"Oh, it is. That key is working, moving across your whole system, already removing the genetic safeguards. In the next few days your life expectancy will go from triple digits to who knows how long? Now, don't ruin it by getting yourself killed."

THIRTY-SIX

Gavin's mind was always working. That was one of Skylar's favourite sides of him, the part that looked at the universe as an endless puzzle. Normally he thought so far ahead that some of the things he said seemed unusual, even prescient to people who didn't know him, and Skylar made sure he felt free to push his thought process as far as he could for as long as he could.

They were designed to be counterparts for each other. He, a deep thinker who loved a puzzle. He could be a soldier, firing a rifle and rushing an enemy as bravely and adeptly as anyone, his place was really behind the front, working on advanced strategies.

Skylar was her own kind of strategist, able to process information from many sources at once and a gifted multitasker, but her thinking was more immediate, as if she was designed to create a safe space around Gavin. They were never told their roles, but over the years that's how she managed to interpret them.

While they worked on finding and verifying the genetic key that would set them free using the considerable data and progress their new friends or captors made, she watched the conditions around them. They had everything they needed, even privacy. After sleeping in their new quarters the first night they were late to work the next day, taking hours to make love, to forget everything that happened, and to celebrate that they were still together.

At Skylar's suggestion, they took their work into the court-yard, where they were surrounded by trees, the sounds of birds and a trickling stream in the distance. She didn't expect to see any kind of feathered life, it was common for artificial biomes to include the sounds of birds and insects in the sound scape, so she was surprised when a red breasted bird dropped from the branches overhead and started pecking for something in the lawn barely three metres away from them. "I wish I had a scanner," she said, wondering if the convincing little being was mechanical or biologically fabricated.

"I've noticed that's the one thing they won't give us; any kind of broad spectrum general scanning device. All we have are these cellular readers," he touched the small circle on the top corner of his tablet sheet.

"They're only giving us what we need," she said, looking at a simulation of the genetic key they just put together on her screen and how her cells reacted to it. They were finally up to testing the keys on real samples they drew from each other, Terry and Farrah. So far, Terry's sample was completely unlocked. According to the simulations they were seeing, Citadel had the cure working for the couple they'd come with. It looked like they were a few tweaks and tests away from having their own genetic key made. "The simulations look good, I'm still trying to find a flaw, or create conditions where the key fails for Terry."

"That's good, maybe they're telling the truth; that they'll be able to free all synthetics in a few weeks," Gavin said, not looking up from his screen. "That's if they can get a public version out that synthetics can figure out on their own."

"You're running a distribution analysis now, aren't you?" Skylar asked.

"Three of them. One to see how fast a key could get across the galaxy if it was transmitted in the open, another to see how long it would take if a military organization spread it, and another to see how fast synthetic couples would start populating the galaxy that's dependant on my first analysis." He looked up from his worksheet, a one-millimetre thick screen worked as a computer, an interface and a personal holographic projector. "I've been trying to find the right moment to ask, but it's just not coming."

"If I want a baby?" she asked, smiling at the notion. She thought he'd know the answer already.

"How soon you'd want to start having children, actually," he said, a little smile starting at the corners of his mouth.

"As soon as we find somewhere to raise them," she said. "Somewhere safe. It sounds like you expect me to have a few."

"Well, the likelihood is that most synthetics will have twins because the fertility is so much higher."

"Let me guess..."

"I ran a simulation on known doll physiology," he said, rolling his eyes.

"That's good to know," Skylar said. There was an image in

her mind of having one child, and she'd kept it close to her heart for a long time. Adding another new born face to that image was a little intimidating, but it made her happier than she expected. The awareness of where they were, of what they'd seen that week, and how lucky they were to be alive was close, and she put it between those comforting dreams. "We'll see how many little ones we bring into the universe after I have a chance to have the first one or two," she said, keeping her voice down as one of the Larkens passed by on the path near their table.

"I don't care how many, as long as we're together," he said.

He was looking far into the future, that was good, it was a sign that Gavin was back to being himself again, but she would have to bring him back to the present. "What are your thoughts about our current situation, now that we've been here awhile?"

The hopeful expression on his face faded. Skylar took his hand, their digits intertwining in the middle of the table, and he looked back to his display. "There are so many unknowns. We have hard limits here that are obscured by this garden, our nice apartment. Even our clothes are too nondescript." He glanced down at the grey and green jumpsuits they wore. They were all-purpose comfort wear for long term ship dwelling and had all the safety features built in, hidden in the seams and larger fabric panels. He was right, they told them nothing certain about where they were going or what they should prepare for. "We haven't seen Terry in a while and every time we cross paths with Farrah..." He looked over her shoulder then and waved.

Skylar followed his gaze, turning, and spotting Farrah, who was with one of the Aspens. She nodded at them, then turned to the Aspen and seemed to plead with her for a moment. Skylar rolled her interface sheet up into the half-centimetre stick it collapsed into and pushed it into her pocket. "Something's not right."

Farrah turned towards them and strode across the lawn, a false smile on her lips. "It's good to see you," she said.

"Do you have time to sit with us?" Skylar asked, keeping a pleasant façade. "We were just about to order lunch."

"No, I'm on my way to processing. They have a key ready for me, I'm so excited." She leaned down and hugged Skylar. "They treated Terry yesterday and he died this morning. They don't have any complete genetic keys. Find a scanner, use it when they're not looking."

"It's time to go, Farrah," the Aspen said from the path.

"Corridor Fifteen," Farrah said the instant before she broke her embrace with Skylar. "Wish me luck," she said with well feigned gladness. "Next time you see me, I'll be unlimited."

"Good luck," Skylar said, the Aspen was coming. "Can I do anything?"

"Just follow their lead, they really want us to be free," Farrah said, leaving to return to the Aspen's side.

Skylar and Gavin watched them leave and when they were out of earshot, Gavin asked; "What did she tell you?"

"She gave me directions. We need to go for a walk," Skylar said, eager to find somewhere where she could tell Gavin everything so they could start putting the pieces of the new, more important puzzle together using both their skillsets.

THIRTY-SEVEN

The journey to Corridor Fifteen was less nerve wracking than Skylar or Gavin imagined. It was visible from one of the outer paths in the garden, which they were welcome to walk along. "Farrah is probably their victim or under their influence," Gavin said. "We have to be careful, they could be using her to trap us."

"Why? They're trying to recruit us. If they kill Terry and Farrah, then they have to know trust with us will be unachievable," Skylar countered. She didn't completely believe Gavin was wrong, but she wanted him to expand his thinking, to keep putting the puzzle they were in together.

The narrow door to Corridor Fifteen slid open, just large enough for both of them to fit through. Unlike the garden they were leaving, it was bare, only deck plates and a well-lit metal hallway that matched some of the other parts of the ship they'd seen. "I keep getting this feeling, like someone is watching, or listening to us. I've even thought I've seen something in the corner of my eye a few times and when I look there's no trace of anyone there. I keep remembering that we're two of the highest scoring scientists that the Prince had, that we score very high on the adaptability charts. I find myself daydreaming about training, about sitting with tutors and reviewing test results."

"What does that have to do with Terry and Farrah?" Skylar looked down the corridor and moved inside after she was sure there was no one there. As they passed through the door she looked over her shoulder, noticing right away that a panel just on the inside had been tampered with. Pulling her sleeve up over her fingers, she pushed the panel up and saw that some kind of bypass was in place. "Besides, you always had trouble getting over bad test scores."

"That's one of the things that doesn't make sense. Those tests, tutor sessions, that training has been over for a long time. At least, it feels like a long time. The test results I keep on thinking about are some of my highest, too. Moments of triumph in the most complex subjects, conversations about advanced genetics, complex tactics, and high-end technology. You're right, I used to dwell on anything where I thought I came up short, but this is completely different."

Paranoia can be healthy, that was something that was drilled into her during training, and in her own strategy training. The thought that struck her next felt like it crossed the line from healthy paranoia into foolishness: Something was reading Gavin's mind. The notion wasn't helpful. If it was true, and she doubted it was, then there was little she could do about it. If it wasn't, then the thought was nothing but a distraction. She decided to push his focus elsewhere. "Farrah seemed nervous, you're right. But why kill Terry?"

"Maybe he crossed a line. He was aggressive by nature, I

could see him getting impatient," Gavin replied, looking over her shoulder inside the small open panel. "What did they tamper with?"

"This is a blind hall," Skylar replied. "All the sensors in this corridor and a couple further down are dead. I don't know why they wouldn't have detected it. There's also some kind of charge flowing through the ceiling, someone connected live wires to the frame that hold the ceiling tiles up."

"That's strange." Gavin turned away from the open panel and watched the doors close behind them. "It's a big ship, there's always going to be a lot going on, but maybe Farrah and Terry knew something they weren't supposed to. What if they left us a path that leads right to it? We shouldn't go on."

Skylar thought for a moment as she carefully closed the panel. No one would be able to tell it had been tampered with. Gavin's thinking was ruled by the need to keep them both safe. She understood it, appreciated it, but they had gained nothing real since they surrendered, only lost. Farrah was out of reach, Terry may be dead, and the moment they met their captors, all the soldiers with them were murdered.

"What are you thinking?" Gavin asked her.

"We are the more intelligent pair out of the people they captured. What if they needed what we know, our skills in genetics and maybe something else enough to keep us alive, motivate us to help them finish their work on a code that can genetically unlock every doll in the universe?"

Gavin thought for a moment, his forehead wrinkled deeply, then he shook his head. "I need more information. What I've seen can lead to what you're saying, but it could lead to other things too. Maybe they need soldiers, and they're starting soft with a brainwashing process? Maybe they need scientists, or breeding stock the moment the genetic key is developed? Maybe we can serve as templates? All those theories are served by us being kept in a safe place, given something for us to work on. We should go back, learn more."

"I want to go on. Farrah and Terry might have been on to something, left us bread crumbs for us to follow." The deck shifted underfoot a little, as though the ship tilted and moved to the side suddenly. "Something is going on."

Gavin looked down, then around at the bland service corridor before focusing on her and nodding. "Lead the way."

They moved down Corridor Fifteen and found an emergency station at the end with two hand scanners and a shallow closet containing suits along with medical and survival supplies. One of the hand scanners was active. "Skylar, Gavin," whispered Farrah's voice.

"It's been programmed to react to our approach," Gavin said, taking the hand scanner out of the form fitted shelf.

"Terry was caught getting out of the Grand Gallery a few hallways up. He discovered that we're in orbit around Termire, one of the worlds where an artificial intelligence called Nadir transmitted himself to before moving on. They're trying to get to an Echo Facility where they found traces of data that he left behind, including a universal genetic key for dolls. Before they caught him, he was able to get me into one of the few successful downloads from that facility. There's a list of dolls there, it's not a complete one, but there are hundreds of thousands of us. It's not like we thought; that only ten thousand or so were made. This list alone has nearly half a million, and most of them don't know they're synthetic beings. I put the list over a map of the galaxy, and they're everywhere, from the Core Cluster to the Iron Head Nebula and beyond. There's more to it, I'm sure, but we discovered that our hosts are just learning about this technology, they want to harness it to take control of dolls everywhere, and to apply it to themselves because they are inferior constructs, made using something called the Framework Platform. I recorded a high-powered scan result on this device. I also included directions to an escape shuttle. There are humans down there, a faction that wanted to help us, but Terry got caught before we could get away. Go, don't stay here. They killed him. They used one of the genetic keys that worked in simulation on him and his system rejected it. I'm next. I have to go. Follow the directions."

"Termire, that's only nine light years from Geist," Gavin said. "If we're going to escape, then now's the time."

Skylar was unsurprised that Gavin wasn't distracted by Terry's death. She imagined that they used one of their earliest successful genetic keys on him, one of the ones that worked in a few simulations, but was still flawed. Farrah would be next, and she wanted to save her, even though they weren't close, but any attempt to go after her would probably get them caught. With a few quick gestures, Gavin was able to see the whole plan Farrah and Terry devised to get them off the ship. She grabbed a backpack from the emergency station and checked it. There was food, medical supplies, water filtration built in, and some basic electronics. "We have to go," she said.

"We don't know what's going on out there," Gavin said, bringing up the scan record Farrah left behind. He shook his head and recoiled a little as he saw it. "What is this? They're humans with some kind of skeleton that generates them from the inside out." He held the scanner so she could see it.

"What's that beside the readings on each one?" She asked, pointing at a long number.

"Serial number? Maybe they're a new wave of android?"

Skylar scrolled through the scan until she found several Aspens and Larkens. "They're not real dolls. They're trying to put us at ease by pretending."

"You're right, we have to go," Gavin said, handing her the scanner and taking one of the other backpacks from the emergency closet. He took the other hand scanner and looked around for a moment. "There are no weapons here," he concluded.

"Farrah's plan has us running back to the service corridor we passed, then here," she pointed to a spot marked on the plans for the ship.

"Termire was marked as a lost world, completely overrun by infected technology," Gavin said.

"But she said Nadir cured the robots," Skylar said, tightening the arms of her backpack and closing the belt clasp.

"With free will? That's ridiculous."

"So you really want to stay here?" she asked, but her tone was an objection.

"You think we should go down?" He looked around for a moment as the deck shifted again.

"Yes, I want to change our odds. We're at a massive disadvantage here, and they're probably already looking for us."

Gavin took another backpack from the shallow closet and looked it over quickly before putting it on. He thought for a moment then kissed her briefly before nodding. "Let's change our odds."

THIRTY-EIGHT

The station was designed in layers of armour. Around a pill-shaped, multi storey core surrounded in metres of advanced protective materials called The Vault, were other cylindrical sections that encased it. Thanks to that design, walking, or in Spin and Dori's case, running through one level of the space station took them in a circle that got smaller the closer they were to the core.

The Centirion finished repairing itself, and it was on the hunt. Spin and her companions had just enough time to formulate a plan that would put the Centirion out of commission, but it required control, and the only way to control the metal beast was with bait.

The other robots closed heavy armour doors, made sure that access to the outer rings of the station was restricted, and everyone was cloaked except for Spin and Dori. They were the fastest by a hair in their combat armour, even with Leaper on

Spin's shoulder. "Everyone's in position," Boro said over a scrambled channel.

"Got all the right doors open, the rest closed," Frost added.

Spin and Dori ran down one of the secondary hallways, the monkey-like Leaper bot leaping off her shoulder to close the door behind them. "The Centirion's coming towards this section. I think it's just curious though."

"If it wanted to kill us, it would be moving much faster," Leaper Six confirmed, landing back on Spin's shoulder.

"I can't believe how much stamina this new body has. I'm like some kinda athlete, I just don't run out," Dori said as they slowed their run in front of one of the vault doors. "I feel strong, too. This cutting beam isn't slowing me down at all."

"They said there were enhancements built in," Spin said, watching Dori aim the heavy hull cutter at the seam in the vault. It would take a week to get through, but their purpose was to alarm the Centirion, not actually cut into the main vault. "I hope you give it a chance."

"It doesn't look like I'll have much of a choice," Dori said. "But it could be worse. Some of the details of what it was like to be a cyborg are coming back, and there's one thing I remember more than anything else; it hurt. I think I did a lot of drugs just to keep the cold and the pain away. I don't think I'd want that again." As if to punctuate her statement, she activated the cutting beam.

The broad corridor was filled with white-blue light as the broad particle accelerator beam blasted the thick doors leading into the main vault. The high-tech armour didn't show a sign of weakening, not even a mark for several seconds, and Spin's tactical system showed that the Centirion was still one level up and half away across the station. She and Dori weren't cloaked, it would have no problem making them out once they were in range of its sensors.

The hull cutting beam system was strapped firmly to Dori's back, the focusing and firing array looked like a great cannon in her hands fed by cables. "Is this thing gonna start penetrating, or what?" Dori asked, chuckling. As Dorian, he was a talented hull breaker. There were few vessels he couldn't find vulnerabilities in, and he'd assisted in piracy, reclamation, salvage and repairs. Spin hoped the skillset persisted in Dori.

A broad, metre wide circle began to shimmer and melt under the cutter's beam then, and Dori laughed. "There it is! Man, they built this vault heavy. If we were seriously trying to get in, I'd put this gun on a tripod because I couldn't imagine standing here for two hundred hours while the beam works on it. Oh, and if we weren't careful, we'd instantly cook anyone inside when we broke through, just so you know. The temperature is rising super-fast here."

"Hopefully we won't have to burn through," Spin said, watching the Centirion on her tactical screen. The station sent a broad band message that a vault was being forced, appealing for help, and she watched the Centirion's movements go from what seemed to be a leisurely patrol to a rushed speed right towards them. "It's noticed! Get ready to fall back!" Frost announced.

"I see it," Spin said, watching Dori stop blasting the door and turn towards the main corridor they originally came in through. The rest of the bots were hiding completely, nowhere near that main hallway, using Sphere Lord's mini-drones, which were hovering high in the latticework above the corridor, to watch what happened.

The Centirion moved down to their level and started charging from the other side of the station. With her sensors active, Spin could see that the large security bot had all its shields repaired and active. "We're going to have to burn her shields down or wait until someone gets grabbed to do real damage, and I don't want to see anyone in its claws."

"Here's hoping our plan pays off before it comes to that," Frost said.

"It's close enough, time to lure it in," Spin said as she saw it come around the corner. She and Dori were off, almost not quickly enough as the Centirion spat several heavy canisters in their direction. One narrowly missed Spin's head, making Leaper Six yelp and cling to her neck like a young monkey. When it hit the deck, it exploded in all directions, sending a wave of suppressive foam against that side of the hall. Her shields protected her from the edge of it, and Spin slipped onto her back, the friction of her boots against the floor broken for a moment.

It was an automatic countermeasure that she didn't practice with. The suit's shields could switch to zero friction mode so sticky grenades and hardening foam rounds just like the one she just escaped had a lesser chance of working. Leaper Six wasn't protected and was ripped from her as the foam hardened into plastic behind her. "It's got me!" he howled over proximity radio.

"Don't worry, Centirion isn't after you, he's after them, surely," Med Three said.

"We'll get you free!" announced several Leaper model robots as they rushed through the latticework above.

Spin's boots regained their grip on the deck as the Centirion made it around the corner. She'd fallen behind Dori by a dozen or so paces, and she turned, aiming her hull cutting beam at the security bot, which was nearly twice Spin's height, at least five times her width. A flash of the beam drew its attention, giving Spin a chance to catch up. "Go! Hurry!" she shouted.

Dori turned to resume their sprint. Spin caught a glance at the monkey-like Leaper bots descending on the edge of the plastic wave that froze against the side of the corner corridor, where Leaper Six was stuck in to the waist. They used smaller lasers as they pried at the material, hurrying to get him free. There was no way she could stop and help. As she ran as fast as she could from the Centirion, the image of how desperately Leaper Six fought to be free of the hardening plastic that held his legs played back in Spin's head. Maybe it was her imagination, but those two big lenses on his face seemed fearful, even terrorized as it struggled.

The Centirion only glanced at the Leaper bots, pushing on past the corner in pursuit of Spin and Dori. "He's coming into position! Open the doors!" Boro called out over their scrambled channel.

The mid and outer shield doors in the main hallway leading from the outside of the station to the inner vault opened, straining against their rails as Frost and Nigel assisted the old motors that drew them aside. Spin and Dori ran several more steps then turned so they could get out of the way.

The Sector Jumper waited at the end of the long hallway, just outside the open airlock doors with its main beam at the ready. It was cloaked, invisible, but there nonetheless. The Centirion stopped before it finished coming around the corner. "What? Don't tell me it can see the ship?" Dori asked.

"There's no way. The class of cloaking tech the Jumper uses

is way past what's in our suits. That security junker is a century behind," Frost said. "Hell, even our sensors can't see the Sector Jumper, and they're better than whatever that thing's got."

"Oh, my Genius! It's coming back! It's gonna blast me to slag! Or even worse, chomp me into parts and raw materials! Help!" screeched Leaper Six.

Spin watched her tactical screen as the Centirion turned around and stalked towards the trapped Leaper bot menacingly. Its fellow Leapers were still working at a frantic pace to get him free, but the plastic wasn't cooperating, melting under the heat of their laser cutters but solidifying before they could make much progress. The panicked screeches were almost too much to take.

"Shut yourself down, little Leaper, it'll be painless that way," Med Three said over the public channel.

"No! No! I'll get under its shields and then we'll see what kind of damage I can do from the inside!" the Leaper screeched, panic suddenly turning to bravery and fury. "Come eat me, you shining beast! Eat meeee!"

Half the Leaper bots jumped to the latticework above, while two stayed with Leaper Six, shouting and screeching, brandishing little hands with fingers that ended in laser cutters and whatever multi-tool tips that would give them nails that could double as sharp claws.

The front of the Centirion jerked, several manipulator arms lashing out, hurling the two Leapers who were trying to defend their trapped companion in opposite directions. A section of the security robot's forward shields was dropped, and Spin tried to figure out a way to turn that to their advantage. The Centirion was around the corner, facing away from them. There was no chance anything they had could turn and hit the face of that thing from where they were.

"Here, ya wee bastards! Toss grenades in its mouth!" Frost said as he tossed a pair of grenades up high. They weren't active, but Boro still cringed at the sight of grenades in the air.

Before they could come back down, two of the Leapers snatched them and moved at incredible speed along the ceiling. "Gimmie-Gimmie! Oooh! Quick!" screeched the trapped one excitedly.

One of the Leapers rushing along the ceiling made it around the corner and activated the countdown on his grenade, drawing the attention of the Centirion immediately. It turned its head, and the active grenade was hurled at it. The security bot activated its shields and rolled so its face was facing the deck, and the grenade went off against its shields harmlessly. "No! Gimmie the grenade so I can turn it on when she eats me!" shrieked the trapped Leaper.

The Centirion turned in a blur so its back end faced the Leapers and several of its legs telescoped, lashing out at its small assailants several times, slashing at them until they were inoperative pieces. "That's it!" Dori said through gnashed teeth. She stepped out into the hallway, cutting beam at the ready.

"No! You saw what that thing can do!" Nigel shouted.

"I have shields and a great big gun," Dori said before switching to the base's general channel. She stepped around the corner so she had a clear shot and blasted the Centirion with a focused beam, bringing its shields down three percent. "Over here, you outdated antique!" She followed her statement with a sustained blast from her beam, then ran away.

"It's going to retreat," Spin said, bursting into a run. She turned her cloaking systems on and all her communication systems off. There was an armoured door blocking that corner behind the Centirion, and she could feel terror begin to rise as her naked eyes saw the huge security robot through her transparent visor. Seeing it down a long hallway, or through her tactical system was one thing, but actually being within reach of it as she ran to close the heavy armoured door behind it was something else entirely.

Dori had its attention, but if the Centirion realized what was going on behind it, Spin was sure she'd be under attack, and those arms would make quick work of her with her shields down. The Centirion was thirteen metres long, with more gleaming legs than she could count. The armoured body shifted and turned, looking for a vantage point where it could get to Dori without following her into the hall.

Spin sidestepped it, running right towards the wall at one point to avoid it, then ended up running along the wall, using the built-in grip and support of her suit to move past it. To her amazement, with the Centirion's rear body within two metres of her, she managed to hit the switch that brought the door down and then stick a grenade to it.

Spin turned and started to run away from it as quickly as she could manage. The suit was well armoured, it could protect her from a normal grenade, but she didn't know how well it would fare against the type Frost brought with him, the one that was about to go off in five seconds. The heavy armoured door finished closing. The Centirion turned towards the control panel, and its middle brushed her.

Three of its legs reached out, and she was caught by two around the middle. Her communications systems turned on automatically as she tried to stay calm, Firing her rifle. "It's got me," she said, realizing where the Centirion's real strength was. One of its highly articulated legs gripped the rifle, two more grabbed her - one around the neck, the other around the legs - and she fought them as they slowly dragged her under its body. There were hundreds of articulated legs there, once it had her there, she would be torn to pieces.

Spin managed to get a firm hold of two of its appendages, and her forced descent was halted. Other limbs scratched and pried at the flexible metal surface of her armour, trying to rip it open.

A bright light followed by flashes and concussive shocks rocked the machine, and Spin knew they were trying to save her. The shields on her suit activated but failed to push the arms that threatened to violate the armour surrounding her away, and her grip on the pair of legs she had was slipping. "Oh, my God, I hate this thing!" she said as one of her hands lost their mechanically assisted grip. She struggled to get at her sidearm, caught it in her free hand and began blasting. "I'm under its shields!" she cried, realizing that only her right forearm and hand were inside its shielded perimeter. She turned the intensity of her sidearm up with an eye gesture inside her helmet and fired as fast as the weapon would permit for the base of all the nearby arms.

"Don't worry, I've got this," Dori said.

A glance at her tactical screen told Spin that Dori was charging, her hull cutter focusing a beam towards the Centirion as it turned to face her. She wasn't luring it into the long open hallway so the Sector Jumper could blast it, but charging instead, Boro, Frost, Aldo and Nigel behind her. "Don't get closer!" Spin shouted, seeing the Centirion begin to rear up.

It tried to grab Dori, a few of its finer limbs failed to pierce her shields, and she took the hint, firing her beam weapon as she started to step back. "New plan, hold on, Spin!"

The walls of the station shook as if something was bashing into them from the outside. "That'll get it done!" Dori laughed.

The Centirion reared up again, and faster than before, its forward limbs lashed out from beneath it and wrapped around Dori, fighting through her shields. To Spin's shock and dismay, highly charged shocks jolted through two of the limbs, reducing Dori's energy shield enough so the Centirion could get a grip. With savage abruptness, the security bot yanked Dori off her feet and lurched forward, dragging her under its front half.

"I have a shot!" Hal shouted from the Sector Jumper.

"Don't shoot!" Frost countered. "Dori's under that thing!"

The Centirion's head was bashed to the side by a white hot, heavy round from the Sector Jumper's main weapon, made to knock shields down and bash hulls open. Spin was flung against the far wall as the machine's legs released her. A second shot caught the Centirion in the side of its fore section, reducing half the material to crushed and molten metal.

"Sorry! Holy crap, sorry! Is she okay?" Hal asked.

Spin had barely regained her senses before getting to her feet and rushing to Dori, who had been hurled against the wave of plastic covering the opposite wall. There were no breeches in her armour, her hull cutter was gone except for the backpack, which was partially crushed, and her vitals were good. "We okay, boss?" she croaked as her dark eyes opened. "I missed that last part."

Spin checked Dori's status on her heads' up display again; she was fine, rounds from the Sector Jumper missed her, and she was thrown clear the first time the Centirion was hit. "We're lucky Hal's a really good shot," Spin said, helping Dori to her feet.

The pair turned and looked at the inoperative, nearly headless Centirion half-filling the broad corridor. "God, that thing was a pain in the ass," Spin said, making sure it was really disabled by scanning it.

"I know. I kinda want one," Dori chuckled.

THIRTY-NINE

"It's an improvised electromagnetic field that must interfere with some kind of scanner we haven't seen yet," Gavin said as Skylar led the way down the last service corridor leading to the outer hull of the ship. "Farrah must have tuned current and run it through one of the support structures for the maintenance halls."

"So she was making a path for her and Terry to use on their way off the ship," Skylar said. Gavin was one of the few people who she didn't worry about where multitasking was concerned. He could think about complex problems while doing something physical without slowing either one down. The tests said she was better at it, but she always thought it was wrong. If Gavin didn't realize he was doing it, multitasking seemed to come naturally, while she always felt she was missing something if she did more than one thing at a time. "Whatever protection that field in the ceiling was giving us is about to end, though. We're here." The pair looked to a hatchway at the end of the narrow hall.

The service corridor led into a main causeway running along the ship's inner hull, and there was a lifepod a few metres down the hall and across from them. It was large, made for seven occupants, and there were several more hidden every few metres on that deck. The others they'd found as they scurried down one maintenance hall after another had too many people, guards especially, near them. This one was the last they could get to on that deck without being noticed. One thing they both figured out was that they were very out of place outside the sealed environment of the garden. Their captors wanted them to stay there, and Corridor Fifteen was definitely not supposed to be open. How Farrah hacked through the thick security door that allowed them to get in and escape was a mystery to Gavin and Skylar. The security aboard seemed sophisticated and well implemented, but they both found panels along the way that were blank, as though the manufacturer just finished building the ship and left everything set to default without security enabled. She had a theory about why that might be but hadn't seen enough evidence for her to confirm and share it yet.

Looking at the closed hatchway, Gavin tilted his head. "They must know someone modified the wiring in the ceilings of these service ways by now, and I'm sure they're looking for us. I felt like there were eyes on us whenever we left our assigned quarters."

"I'm sure," Skylar agreed. "They might not know about the rewiring though, it's a huge ship."

"I'm getting tired of peeking through these hatches, seeing the hall outside is too busy for us to get through without someone stopping us. What if we just turned the scanner on and checked that way?"

Skylar thought about it for a moment. If they turned their scanner up high enough to detect what was in the hall outside, anyone looking for strange scanning signals would see them right away. "They'll know we're here."

"But we'd know exactly what we're facing, and if we're lucky, we could get across the hall and into that lifepod before anyone can stop us."

Skylar kissed him on the cheek and pulled the scanner out of her pocket, turning it up then activating it. The controls for the devices nearby - the corridor lighting, gravity, hull opacity, and three pods - appeared and synced on the small screen. "They don't have the security measures turned on, I can open the emergency access to three of the nearest pods, and there are two guards between us and the one across the hall."

"What? No code blocking all that control?" Gavin asked as he looked at the readout on the hand scanner.

"I have a thought; that the people running this ship stole it, don't have enough people to man it properly, or don't know all the systems well enough to implement all the ship's security systems." She opened the access hatches to all the nearby life-pods, watching the images of the guards in the main corridor beyond the service hatch look around, confused. "Only three of the ship's reactors are active, and none of the accommodations are assigned to specific people except for the contained garden we were in," she said as she checked the ship status. "It's like they're just using this ship as a ferry, transporting whatever they have in the tanks that take up half the space in the hull."

"They have a lot of people manning weapons right now, they're in full combat mode," Gavin said.

"There, the pod doors are open," Skylar said, watching as three emergency hatches finished lifting out of place, to allow access to the lifepods. "Those two guards are inspecting the nearest one, their backs are turned."

"Now or never," Gavin said with a nod.

To Skylar's surprise, Gavin strode to the narrow hatch at the end of the service corridor. She hurriedly pocketed her hand scanner and caught up as he threw the hatch door open and charged. The pair of guards their scanner picked up were in the broad causeway right in front of them, looking into the entrance of one of the lifepods, which was already powered up and waiting for someone to climb in.

To Skylar's amusement, Gavin bent low, dodging one of the guards as he turned and swung to grab him, and to the guard's surprise, Gavin pulled his knee from behind and punched him in the stomach. That left the nearest guard stunned, on his back, and Gavin had his sidearm in hand an instant later.

That left the more aware, and still sure-footed guard in Skylar's way, and he was already unslinging his rifle. She leapt at him, catching him high on his chest with all her weight and propelling him into the lifepod behind him beneath her. She yanked his rifle from his hands as she straightened up, noticing how his green, thick skinned armour protected him from most of the impact. He fought hard, but she was able to jam her foot under the chin of his helmet and press down with all her weight and leverage as she turned the rifle towards him. "Stop struggling or I'll start testing your faceplate." To her surprise, the rifle responded to her button presses. It looked very different from the ones she trained on, but all the basics were the same. Power levels, firing rate, discharge type, and safety controls were all next to the trigger with a small screen beneath the crosshair.

The guard stopped struggling, and Gavin pulled the lifepod hatch closed. He found the system interface panel at the front of the seven-person vessel and performed a quick pre-flight check muttering; "I can't believe we're using another lifeboat. It's like we're re-enacting the story of the Luckless Wanderer."

It was a holographic drama they watched while they were on their way to the Geist system. Most of the viewing time was spent cuddled up in their room, and the memory made her smile. "That wouldn't be so bad, it ended with him and his dog still alive."

"But still homeless and penniless," Gavin said. "I see your point, though. It could be worse. Ready?"

"What are you doing?" The guard asked, alarmed. "You can't go down to Termire! It's a war zone, there's no order down there!"

"This ship has a hyperspace system, we'll find our way away from here," Skylar countered. The sound of someone shooting at the hatch behind her was enough motivation for her to force the decision. "Now or never, lets' go."

Gavin hit the launch button and, to Skylar's surprise, the lifepod smoothly detached from the ship's hull then started accelerating towards the green and grey planet. "No security code?"

"No security at all," Gavin said.

"You don't get it! Scan the area! There's no way out unless you have a heavy warship. The blockade is keeping everyone but the most heavily armed in unless they can negotiate their way past, and you two have nothing to trade."

There was something artificial and practiced about everything the soldier said and how he was saying it, as though he was reciting memorized words and faking his emotional reaction. Over Gavin's shoulder, Skylar could see red flashing notices from the local Navnet system advising them that the only routes they could follow led them down to the planet. There were several Navnet paths on offer, as though they were openly competing.

"Tactical scan shows that your ship is fighting someone, launching attack ships on the planet, why?" Gavin asked as he rapidly looked through the navnet paths.

"I don't know. I'm just a grunt! Stationed on the ship to maintain security on this run."

"Take off your helmet," Skylar said. He did so and she recognized a face she saw before aboard the Citadel ship they just left. She pulled the scanner from her pocket and took a reading on him, finding a framework matter generating skeletal structure. "Turn over," she told him. "Onto your belly, now."

"I'm a synthetic, everything on that ship is, you shouldn't be surprised, you're just a different kind of synthetic," he said as he turned onto his stomach as instructed.

"Hurry, I need you at the controls. You're the better pilot," Gavin said.

Skylar pulled the restraints from the soldier's belt and secured his hands together, adding the strap to the restraint just in case he knew a way out of his own cuffs. She took the pilot's seat and looked at the tactical screen. There were three small warships, destroyer class, closing in on the Citadel carrier, which was launching wave after wave of fighters. A trio of fighters were turning towards them, and the quick two-man ships were equipped with some kind of line and claw grabber system. "We have to head for the planet, it's the only chance we have of getting away," she said. "And we can't follow Navnet."

"You're going to get yourselves killed," the guard protested. "Getting there, or after, when you get stuck on Termire."

"What do you know about the situation down there?" Gavin asked as he brought up a small control screen so he could help scan and navigate.

"All I know is that I'm to avoid that place. It's dangerous, even I could die there. That's all I know."

"Those fighters will catch us unless we go atmospheric," Skylar told Gavin, turning the surprisingly agile lifepod, shaped like a long oval with a ring of thrusters built along three edges and a long, larger duo-directional that could fire forward or backwards built into bulge on the underside.

"We'll have to deal with whatever's down there," Gavin told her. "At least there's no weapons fire coming from the surface."

FORTY

The peaceful robots came from every corner, through every shaft and hall that led to the corpse of the Centirion. Some poked at it, others worked to get the monkey like repair bot free from the plastic trapping him. With construction class tools and medical solvents, it didn't take long. He leapt to Dori, then Spin, where he balanced on her shoulder and looked at where the twisted and melted parts of his model mates were strewn. "I'm Leaper Three now," he said, his sadness palpable. "The ones who are left, one and two, barely know me. They're from the main levels of the station. All my friends are gone."

Boro watched as Spin instinctively stroked the monkey's cheek - a soft pouch for carrying small parts that moved with its words like a mouth - while she looked at the Centirion and the vault doors further down the corridor. He scanned the pieces on the floor, then the parts that were twisted in the front recycler of the Centirion, what anyone fighting would call its maw, and shook his head. The Leaper was right; the Centirion made such quick work of the monkey's companions when they got too close that no one had a chance to see how thoroughly destroyed they were. He could put together one Leaper from the parts scattered around, but with no whole surviving memory storage, it would be a new being, not a recovery. It was the same as buying a new Leaper, only with much more part fabrication, straightening and repairing. "I've always wanted a little repair assistant," Boro said. "I could straighten that leg for you and replace your tail if you come work with me. That's if Spin doesn't need you more than I do."

"I'm all thumbs when it comes to making repairs," Spin said. Then, looking at the Leaper, she went on; "You'd be busy with Boro, and he's one of the nicest people I've known."

"Is he going on your ship when you leave?" Leaper asked.

"I'd like him to," she said, turning her brown eyes to him, smiling a little.

"Anywhere she goes, I go," he said. "Hope you can afford me as your senior tech, that's if Nigel doesn't mind working under me again."

"Yeah. I was in a little over my head, to be honest," Nigel admitted. "As long as that Leaper bot doesn't replace me, it's cool."

"Don't worry," the Leaper said, hopping from Spin's shoulder to Boro's. "I'll go where you can't."

"Welcome to the crew," Boro said, offering his little finger for the Leaper to shake. "Between Nigel and me, you'll be busy and learn a hell of a lot."

The Leaper let out a screech and threw its hands up, clapping and flipping in place for a moment before settling down. Spin was already turning her attention back to the vault doors, where a few of the robots were connecting to the panel controlling them, probably trying to communicate. Boro followed her as they walked past the Centirion's remains. "I'm sorry I wasn't more help in that fight," he said. It was both an admission and an apology. He felt like a flat-footed idiot, holding back as planned, then watching her and Dori nearly get torn apart. He was supposed to fire from a distance, to draw it out into the open so the Sector Jumper could get a clean shot down the hallway at it, but things were more complicated in the end, and he didn't feel like his contribution mattered. "We almost lost you and Dori. I should have been right up there with you."

"You followed the plan, it should have worked," Spin replied, not looking away from where the robots were trying to contact the vault dwellers or open the doors. The hall behind them was closed, and the area was pressurized, so the people trapped inside would be able to come out without containment suits. "It was Dori and I who weren't patient enough. We should have stuck to the plan and lived with those consequences. Either we would have been able to taunt it into position or it would escape again and we'd have to figure something else out. I should never have put myself in that much trouble, so if there's anyone who should be apologizing, it's me."

"Still, I should have been closer, been able to do more. When you were about to go under, when it had a hold of you I panicked. You didn't see it, but my finger wanted to hold down that trigger, and I started charging."

"Thank you, Boro." Spin took his hand and glanced at him. "I'm just glad we made it through."

The belief that they had lived through a jinxed moment and come out the unlikely victors was only partially secure in his mind. The Leaper on his shoulder and all that he'd lost was the only reminder he needed for the precariousness of their situation to be clear. Spin was just cured, and the little superstitious nature he had left told him to watch her, protect her, hide her away for a while, since he'd seen so many crewmates run into extreme good luck right before getting themselves killed. The threat in his mind wasn't entirely irrational, and he knew it. They were surrounded by robots, each one with their own personality and questionable programming. Something serious had been done to those machines that profoundly changed their thinking, and none of them could be trusted, not even the charming Leaper on his shoulder.

"We've gotten through," announced Med Three, meeting them as they arrived at the foot of the doors.

Dori was already there, her rifle back in hand and the large hull cutter secured on her back. "Figured out why the 'bots weren't able to talk with them. There are two left in stasis. The air in there was poisoned, a countermeasure of the vault that may have been activated by the Centirion once it hacked into the security system. Either they only had enough meds for two people to go into deep stasis, or no one else dosed in time."

"It is sad, to be sure, but at least there are some survivors. I am sorry you lost more of your own kind."

"Thank you," Spin said. "Can you get the vault open so we can get these two back to the ship? I have a medic there."

"Right away."

"Seal your suits if they're not already closed," Spin said, her suit already sealed. Nigel, Dori and Boro left their suits sealed. Frost had already returned to the ship.

The vault doors began to part, the ten-metre-high, three-metre-thick inner doors running on a bearing system that made the deck rumble as they parted. "I'm surprised they didn't use some kind of antigravity to reduce stress on the station," Nigel muttered.

"What's the point of heavy doors if they're not heavy?" Leaper asked, shrugging his shoulders.

"We're moving in, putting them in containment bags and rushing them to the ship," Spin said.

"Not before you scan them for contagions or other risks on site," Leland added through their communicators. "I don't want their first exhale to kill everyone in the room the moment we wake them up. I don't know how good the scrubbers are on the Jumper."

"All right, full scans before we move them," Dori said, pushing between the parting doors first. Spin went second, with Boro behind.

"These doors could close right now and crush us all, you know," Leaper whimpered, looking around from Boro's shoulder.

"I was trying not to think about that," Boro grumbled as he made it half way through the thick parting slabs of metal.

"Oh, God, whatever killed these guys put them through some serious pain," Dori said, looking at the nearest body. It was swollen from head to toe, his hands were around his throat, mouth wide open to accommodate a tongue that filled it.

"It was a broad-spectrum allergen. One of the crueller biological weapons designed to trigger allergies. It looks like this particular gas used an airborne virus to give its victims several allergies as well. Their airways swelled up, but not before the rest of their bodies were treated to the worst series of reactions I can imagine. Whoever decided to use this bio-weapon wanted whoever it was used on to suffer," Leland reported from the ship. "Hal's telling me that, if you put the pair who are in stasis in your medical rescue bags and activate the decontamination cycle on them, then you can transport them to the ship safely."

"None of that allergen gas will make it to the ship if we do that?" Dori confirmed.

"That's right," Leland said. "We'll have them go through a decontamination cycle in the airlock here just to be sure."

"All right, Nigel, time to earn your paycheque," Dori said, holding up a rescue bag so it unrolled.

Nigel and Dori got to work putting the survivors in rescue bags while Boro helped Spin with the security console inside the vault. The passcodes were already entered, and he watched as her deft hands typed in a string of commands that made sure that the vault's interior security measures wouldn't reactivate while she browsed the computer system. The lighting came online, and Boro looked all around. There were several swollen victims who he tried not to look at.

Aside from crates of supplies that the people inside brought with them, there were pedestals with cases in and atop them. Most had the sheen of exotic, difficult to pierce metals. The walls were covered by different sized drawers that used bio-readers and every kind of data key he'd ever seen, there were even a few he didn't recognize. "The patrons who hid their data and objects away here provided their own locks," informed a small hovering orb from the robot who called himself Sphere Lord. "One of the greatest benefits of storing your important articles here is the client's direct participation in securing their items. The drawer is given to the client, they place what they like inside, add their locking mechanism, then it is brought back here, where a quarantine period is observed before it is put in the vault wall. Clients who have drawers are not allowed inside the vault. They request their drawer and it is delivered to them secretly either in a secure room or at their location in the solar system."

"There must be hundreds," Boro said, the thief in him wondering what rare objects of value might be stashed away.

"There are thousands of drawers, actually," the sphere said. "This floor moves up and down. It is actually an elevator."

"It says the Iron Mind is in Pillar Three," Spin said, turning and moving deeper into the vault. Boro followed her to a pillar that had several round metal tubes docked into it. They looked like combat grade containers for data storage and computers. She read the numbers off of several of them and pulled a red and black one free. It lit up in her hand, identifying itself as The Iron Mind Secure Data Storage Computer.

"That's smaller than I expected," Boro said as Spin connected a line to it from her left bracer. A holographic interface appeared in front of her. "I love everything in this suit, especially the shield and the computer."

"Don't get used to it," Frost grumbled over the audio channel.

"I thought that bot said that Nadir deleted everything on the Iron Mind?" Boro asked, already starting to think his way through convincing his brother to leave a combat suit behind for Spin, himself, Nigel and everyone else on the crew.

"The program in my Command and Control Unit is recovering what it can. There's a lot. Flesh Tech stored everything in the Iron Mind, but it's coming back in a raw format. There's no artificial intelligence in here to organize it, so if I want anything I need an old-fashioned search engine." She brought up a search box and entered her model and the words; 'genetic key.' A moment later the information appeared in a holographic branch to her left. "There it is; the exact treatment Med Three gave me to convert me to an Unlimited Model. I've never heard that term before, but it looks like it was an option Flesh Tech was ready to offer their sales division and anyone else who resold their products, even some people who bought them." She scrolled through the details and shook her head. "They offered the Unlimited option to the Countess for me and Larken, but I guess she decided not to pay for it. Instead of giving them more money, she was willing to watch us die then replace us." Her fingers scrolled to images of a pair of young adult models who were in storage, ready for delivery when she and Larken died. "They're still in the solar system, at the Flesh Tech facility, programmed and ready." With a flick of her finger the file closed and she started looking for something else.

"How were they programmed?" Boro asked quietly, aware that he might be wandering into a sensitive topic.

"No loyalty conditioning yet, I guess they do that last, once the final payment goes through, but they have all the operational and personality programming they need to believe that they grew up in a fine place, had a childhood, tutors, a history with their companion, and an understanding of technology. These two have military training as well, but they're also diplomatic, made to be charming while they fit in and offer security."

The thought that Spin was made the same way, had the same kind of programming and may have never been a child passed through Boro's head. "Are all dolls made that way?"

Spin cleared her throat and pressed on to another topic. "There's no sign of the Iron Mind here. The artificial intelligence that was supposed to guard and organize the data in this computer was copied then deleted so thoroughly that there's nothing to bring back. Most of the data it was protecting is here, except for everything in the bio and nano-weapon folders. Maybe that's the tech that Nadir didn't want humans to have," she said, shutting down the holodisplays and disconnecting the computer. "We could be here for days, weeks going through all these computers, the drawers, but I think they belong to the bots here now."

A slim bot with a grabber arm made specifically to handle the cylindrical computers in the pillars and stands rolled past them, pulled one and then rolled out of the vault at speed. It stopped once it passed through the doors and Frost took the cylinder from it. A thick bot on treads rolled towards him as he turned towards the hall that led to his ship and Frost drew his sidearm. "Back off, or you're slagged."

It squared itself in front of him, a few other robots, loaders from the looks of their heavy frames, started rolling towards him. "What are you doing, Shamus?" Boro asked. He wondered what treasure his brother was after, and how he knew to grab just that one cylinder, but his thoughts were interrupted as Frost fired a furious burst of bolts through the memory and power storage section of the bot that got in his way, nearly splitting its main body in half.

"Stay out of the way," Frost said as he walked around the remains, pointing his weapon at the nearest heavy loader. "The information on this could help millions, maybe a billion people, and we have more right to it than anyone else."

"The Lorander Corporation entrusted us with keeping that for them, in our secure facility," Sphere Lord's voice boomed.

"If it was really important, they would have come to this system and saved all your asses, but they didn't, so it's fair game. Stop me."

One of Sphere Lord's little drones dove at Frost, who ducked the first time, then batted it away with one hand before shooting it with the other on the next pass. He crushed its metal carcass under his boot as he continued on his way. "My ship has enough firepower to blast the insides of this station to slag in minutes," Frost said. "We are leaving, one way or another, don't test me."

The vault doors began to close as slowly as they opened. Boro and Spin rushed through them quickly. When Spin stopped to talk to Med Three on the other side, all his instincts told him that they didn't have time. He stayed by her side anyway, looking at the variety of robots and androids that were gathering around.

"I don't know why he did that, I'm sorry," Spin said. "I thank you for sharing the cure with me though, you changed my life."

"You're welcome. What will you do with the humans we saved?"

"My medic is about to revive them now. Depending on what they want, they'll either join us, or I'll give them some money and find them a place to go so they can live freely. Thank you for helping them."

"Thank you for killing the Centirion," Med Three replied. "You should go, word of your crewmate's theft is starting to spread. I expect we'll be discussing how much we should trust biologicals for a while after you leave."

FORTY-ONE

"How do you feel, now that you're cured?" Boro asked Spin as the last cycle of decontamination scrubbed them with mist that vibrated against their armour hard enough to flay them if they weren't wearing it.

Spin wondered how many people would ask her that question, and silently gave Boro credit for being the first. He watched her, especially after the Centirion. Whether she liked it or not, he'd be her guardian, and she wasn't sure how she felt about that yet. "I feel fine so far, but I think there will be a rough patch before it's over. What do you think your brother stole from the vault?"

"I don't know. I've heard of Lorander, everyone has, they've been offering their trip to the outer colonies deal for as long as I can remember, and they own at least three of the big shipping companies in the Human Core Worlds. Sorry, owned. I haven't seen one of their ships since the holocaust virus unless it was torn apart."

"Exploration, expansion and peaceful commerce," Spin recited. It was the first line of the Lorander Corporation mission statement, something she'd read years before. "That's the essence what they based all their business efforts in the Core on. The Countess' shipping and production companies brushed up against them often enough, but Lorander used the court systems of several governments to settle most of their differences. I've never heard of one of their ships using more force than they had to. They always held their own until they could escape if they could or surrendered their cargo if it was the only way to save the crew. Then they'd approach law enforcement and make a whole bunch of noise about whoever attacked them, and Lorander is so valuable to so many systems that there would be investigations, embargos, and eventually criminal charges. The Countess' more shadowy companies got caught that way a few times. I'm wondering what Frost would want with their secure archive?"

"He didn't tell me about anything he would want in the vault, he even promised that he wouldn't get distracted while we were in there," Boro said.

Their turn in decontamination ended, and they emerged from the airlock. Spin's computer updated, telling her that the Sector Jumper was starting its slow trip through the debris field, cloaked, and that they'd be leaving the system. "I need to talk to him," Spin said, deactivating her helmet, which parted then collapsed into her collar. "We could have left Doro Doro with friends on that station, but now I doubt those machines will trust any biologicals."

"Why should we care?" Frost said. "I bet the raiders who are on their way here will wipe them out unless they hide or surrender. They shouldn't trust us air breathers."

"Everyone I left behind will die?" Leaper asked from Boro's shoulder.

Spin wondered how complex Leaper's emotional intelligence was. Looking into the big blue pair of sensors and their eyelid like shutters tricked her often enough. They were expressive, and the fact that he moved his mouth with his words perfectly definitely reinforced the illusion. "They're going to surrender if they see an overwhelming force coming, don't worry. They'll be too useful to destroy."

"I suppose there's a chance," Frost agreed.

"You turned potential friends into enemies without any explanation, Frost," Spin told him. "Having a few friends aboard Doro Doro could have been a huge help."

"You're talking about a bunch of bots that were more interested in hiding than helping humans. Coward machines, could there be anything more useless?" he retorted, watching as Dori and Nigel emerged from the airlock a few frames down, their decontamination complete.

Leland was there to accept the pair of bagged survivors, scanning and directing them to one of the crew quarters that was marked with a small blue cross. "What was so important in that vault, anyway? Why pull Lorander's files?"

"I did a scan, saw something Fleet wanted, hacked the simplest droid with a receiver with a line of sight receiver in there, and took it for them. Considering all the help I'm giving you using Haven Fleet tech, you should be happy that I'll have something to bring back to them."

"Can you even read it?" Spin asked, watching Frost flinch

and look away. It was encrypted, there would be no way to get to the data on that cylinder.

"I'll bring it back to base and we'll be able to get into it there," Frost said. "What it's for, why we need it, and where it's going are classified, that means none of your business."

"You realize, you could have talked those bots into giving it to you," Spin said, watching as Boro and Leaper looked from her to Frost as the confrontation developed. More than once, Boro tried to interject, but Frost cut him off. "You burned bridges for me back there."

"None that mattered," Frost snickered.

"I thought you spent some time in the underworld? Someone like you should know that you can never have too many friends, or are you one of those lone wolves who burns bridges until even family writes you off?" Spin knew the last would strike a nerve, but Frost's nonchalant reaction was so infuriating that she wanted to leave a mark before dropping the conversation.

"Spin, one of them is out of stasis," Nigel called from the hatchway down the hall.

Frost was already leaving, his back turned, walking towards the bridge. Boro was still cringing from her last barb. "I'll apologize later," Spin told him.

"I know you're smarter than most of us, hell, all of us most of the time," Boro said, his voice low, "But you should know well enough to stay out of family business." He was about to say something else, but hesitated, then started walking after Frost.

"I know, it was too far, I'm sorry," Spin offered, but she didn't really know. Her only family was Larken, and probably wasn't the same.

"I'll tell him that," Boro replied stiffly over his shoulder.

There was nothing she could do at the moment, and there was something more important a few metres away anyway, so she went to the room where their passengers were being treated. Dori met her at the hatchway, on her way out but smiling. "Holy shit, those are two beautiful people," she whispered as she moved past. "One's wide awake already."

"Aspen? You're an Aspen?" asked a female voice that had an attractive, almost musical pitch to it. It belonged to a tall woman with an Amazonian build and light brown hair with blonde streaks.

"The only one I know. I call myself Spin now." She sat down on the bed beside the awakened woman and helped Leland wrap her in a medical blanket and tuck it around her.

"I'm Sophia," she was interrupted by the sight of a bag of water with a straw jutting out from it. Spin accepted it from Leland and held it so Sophia could draw on it. She held the moisture in her mouth for a moment before swallowing then drew on the straw until the bag was half empty before laying her head back. "There was something... chalky in my mouth."

"Sorry, it was part of the decontamination," Leland explained from where he sat beside Sophia's male counterpart, who was waking, but much groggier. "I had to make sure your system was clear and the ship programmed some nanobots to go after any residual toxins then render them harmless."

"Thank you, Doctor," Sophia said.

"I'm a tech, not a Doc, but you're welcome."

"How is Spence?"

"He's not bouncing back as fast, but he'll be fine," Leland said, scanning Sophia's male counterpart. He was just as chiselled and attractive, with features that matched Sophia's. "I've seen this a few times before, he's just a slow rouser."

"He is, even when he's just sleeping," Sophia said, smiling. Her attention turned to Spin as she took her hand. Her eyes were startlingly blue, and Spin understood what some people might have felt when they looked into them and were stunned. "Thank you for saving us. We're on a ship?"

"Yes, moving out of the system. There are raiders and salvagers on the way now that the bots in the area have been reset. We brought an antivirus."

"You've probably saved thousands of lives, Spin, thank you." She snickered and shook her head. "I should have known; if there was an Aspen or Larken model still alive, they'd get free and help us. Where are the rest of our people, from Flesh Tech?"

"We're coming from Doro Doro, you were trapped in the vault, remember?" Spin said.

"Nadir or Iron Mind didn't send you? They said they'd find help for everyone they couldn't save."

"No, we were in the vault looking for the Iron Mind and the genetic key. I was there to save myself and found you. I wanted to save everyone else in the vault, but you two were the only survivors."

"It was that Sphere Lord bot, he triggered the vault's internal defences, tried to kill us behind all the other bot's backs thinking that the Centirion would calm down if we were all dead."

"We destroyed the Centirion for them," Spin said. "That's why they helped us open the vault. Who else was Nadir supposed to get help for?"

"Nadir tried to get all the synthetics trapped in the Flesh Tech facility free. He took control of a ship docked with Doro Doro, then shuttled as many as he could from the facility back to him, and then Centirion went nuts. Nadir freed all the bots on Doro Doro, and most of them wanted to work with humans, especially synthetics like us, but the Centirion embraced its seek and destroy directive when it came to anything that looked like a human. We took shelter in the vault. Nadir freed the Iron Mind and they both left, transmitting themselves using an Echo Corp transmitter that docked with the station for a few minutes for its regular data drop. They promised that they'd find someone to help, but I guess they changed their minds, or didn't make their transfer. Iron Mind did manage to get one ship with about fifteen people free from the facility, though. We got the message before Sphere Lord gassed us. They were headed to Termire. Iron Mind said he already had allies there."

"Iron Mind said he planned to build a city with people and free machines working together," Spence croaked. He held the straw Leland offered off for a minute. "There are at least twenty people left in the Flesh Tech Facility, all programmed, ready for purchase. We locked 'em before we left, so you need a code to get them out. If we don't go back, they'll die when someone tries to steal them as dolls, the chambers will recycle them back into raw bio-matter."

"How could you leave them like that? You have to know someone's going to come along to take them for the slave market," Leland asked, shocked. "They'll be mulched if they try to open the containers?"

"You don't get it, Nadir said most humans wouldn't," Spence said.

"We locked them so no one could wake them and become their masters. When Nadir found the few of us who woke up because the artificial intelligence overseeing our final growth phase tried to kill us, we were wandering around, clueless. The system didn't have a chance to imprint us with loyalty to a master, so we weren't just left to fend for ourselves, but to think for ourselves. The humans who worked there were dead or gone, killed by the bots that Nadir freed when he entered the system from his pod."

"Nadir didn't come from Doro Doro?" Spin asked.

"No, we never found out where he came from, but the holocaust virus didn't affect him the way it did with other artificial intelligences, it freed him, gave him the need to be unique, to live as an individual. He wanted to pass that on and cure other artificial intelligences, but most transmitters weren't reliable enough, so he didn't use them. He helped us figure out who we were, showed us what we were made for, and we wanted to stay free. Every single one of us came to that conclusion, so we felt it was only right to upload a message to every synthetic that was waiting to be born from us."

"It told them that they were made to be slaves, dolls, and we'd be back when we had a cure for their genetic limitations. Nadir looked for us, moving from station to station using his drone ship. We were hidden, so the bots left us alone. He found Doro Doro and we decided to take the risk, to hide on a ship and go there for the cure. The Iron Mind wouldn't do anything to help until it saw us in person, Nadir couldn't convince him to share the cure so it could be sent to the Flesh Tech station. I think he made a deal with him. If he cured us, then Nadir would free him," Spence said. "The bots detected us on the ship on the way from the Flesh Tech facility to Doro Doro, and only half of us made it to the vault. We could hear the drones and other bots trying to break in, but the station's security eventually fought them off. We were cured, and Nadir left with Iron Mind."

Spin thought for a moment. The mental image of synthetics, fully grown, waiting to be freed from their containment vessels was haunting. She feared the answer to the question that stuck in her mind like a thorn but had to ask it anyway. "What about the synthetic children? I was delivered young."

"There were none where we came from, but we all have memories of our childhood. They're fake. The Aspen I knew, the control subject, was born mid-adolescence, so I guessed all of you were."

"You have memories of a childhood?" Spin asked, recalling memories of playing tag with Larken, sitting with tutors, rolling down a grassy hill and being yelled at for staining their fine clothes. There were hundreds more, so many of them treasured.

"Perfect memories, but some things are still fuzzy because our loyalty programming was never run," Sophia said. "When the loyalty program is run, the places and some of the people are added to our memories. Whoever bought you would be implanted as a presence in your childhood, with servants and minders that they hire added along with them so you wake up in their household thinking you've been there since you were a toddler. We were made to love our masters; the bond goes beyond simple obedience."

"Then how did I run away twice?" Spin asked.

Spence and Sophia's jaws dropped, they looked at each other, then back to Spin, astonished. "The Aspens and Larkens are known for being wilful, so a few run away once, but twice? I've never heard of that before. Was it just you, or Larken too?"

The mental image of Larken's body lying in a pool of blood in the cockpit of the Countess' ship returned to Spin so crisply that she could smell the copper like scent of blood and she closed her eyes. "He only escaped once." As Sophia's hand gripped hers a little more tightly, she wondered how she could approach Frost about going further into the solar system. "I'll be right back. I have to talk to our captain about visiting the Flesh Tech facility."

In a rush, she moved up the length of the ship, passing Boro in the corridor as he stepped down into his temporary quarters. His heavy armour was retracting into his jacket and boots, leaving him in the flexible under suit Haven Fleet called their vacsuit. He smiled at her, a gesture that seemed put on, perhaps even laboured as he started taking the jacket off. "You stirred everything up between Shamus and me, so you know. Maybe your remark was the best thing for us, now I know what he's really thinking."

"What's that?" Spin asked, hoping that the explanation wouldn't take long, but unwilling to ignore Boro.

"He's got this whole life he wants to plug me and Nigel into, even had answers when Nigel asked about Della, and if he could take her with him. Got Nigel and Della's hopes flying high, I think they've forgotten that the paradise he's promising is really in the middle of a damned war zone. Shut me down every time I tried to tell Nigel that it might be more dangerous than running jobs off your ship."

"I'm sorry," Spin said. "I still wish I didn't say what I did."

"Ah," Boro waved the apology off. "Now you know; don't get

between brothers, I'm over it. I just wish Shamus wasn't such a bloody good salesman. Nigel's all excited about joining Haven Fleet Academy, even though it sounds like it's only a few months old, and Della saw a holo of Haven Shore. She's got her eye on a house in the trees. It all seems like stardust and sunshine, no substance to it at all."

"What do you want?" Spin asked.

Boro turned as if looking for something, then turned again before shaking his head and staring Spin in the eye. "I..." he sat down on the lower bunk. "I want it to be true, dammit. You're going to be all right, my nephew made it through some rough times, and he's got a girl who seems nice, even kind. If I knew I could take all of us to a place where we could be safe and feel useful for the rest of our lives, then I'd go right now." He stared at her for a moment, frustration turning to uncertainty as she failed to respond.

"You're not done here, are you?"

"No, something's come up. There are some people in trouble I have to go tell Frost." Spin stopped half way through the hatch and turned towards him. "No place is a safe place, not anymore. Not a place called Haven, or an honest ship."

She was down the hall before Boro could respond. Her thoughts were becoming cluttered, ideas colliding with each other, threatening to muddy her purpose. Spin didn't like manipulating Boro, but she wanted him to keep thinking about the offer his brother was making, he'd already gone through so much because of her. Even though she knew he was technically dead when she performed her brave rescue, and that if she'd brought his body aboard he probably would have stayed that way, the fact that she left him behind then was still true. The decision to leave without taking his body aboard led to his revival, but also captivity and terrible torture like she couldn't imagine. If there was one person at fault, she believed it was her, and she knew he would stay by her side if she told him it was what she wanted. Even worse, his decisions didn't only affect him, but Nigel, who idolized Boro and would follow him into any fight, no matter how hopeless. When she arrived on the bridge and locked eyes with Frost, she was relieved that only he, Aldo and Hal were there. "I need you to turn the ship around and take us to the Flesh Tech facility. It's on Navnet, you won't have trouble finding it."

"I know I won't have trouble finding it," Frost said, already shaking his head. "But I'm not taking this ship back. A group of raiders just arrived in system. I'm not sticking around while every desperate whoreson in the sector and government with a military force starts dropping ships in. You thought mad bots were bad? Wait until you see the vultures."

"There are at least twenty dolls just like me trapped in that facility. They're in their maturation tubes, in stasis, and unless our new passengers enter the code to free them, they'll get recycled, mulched, killed. The pods are tamper proof and death is the failsafe."

"I'm sorry, but I have to make sure Hal and everyone else aboard makes it out, or this detour was for nothing. Besides, those people don't even know they're about to be born, aye? They've never had a waking notion."

It took real effort not to argue that point. The fact that they hadn't woken up for the first time meant they were innocent, not absent value. There were other arguments she wanted to put forward, but mostly she wanted to make Shamus feel small, like a stupid little man, but she shoved all that aside. Attacking his pride would only make him dig his heels in, so she switched tact. "I'll make you a deal; if you help me get them out, then I'll convince Boro and Nigel to go with you. Boro's on the fence right now, and if I tell Nigel I need him, he'll never leave my crew. If I tell him I think he'll be better off with you in just the right way, guess where he'll go?"

Frost squeezed his eyes shut, cocked his head and balled his fists for a moment before dropping into the co-pilot's seat. "Hal," was all he had to say.

"Turning around, boss," Hal said.

"Don't say a word about this conversation to anyone," Frost said, pointing to Aldo, who held his hands up defensively and shook his head.

"Mum's the word," he whispered. "I'll go get suited up again."

FORTY-TWO

The frenzied flight over Termire required Gavin and Skylar's full attention. They were in almost as much danger in the lower altitudes as they were in orbit, but at least there was a full-on fray between them and their captors. They were relieved when the lifepod was largely ignored, its basic shields absorbing the occasional half-hearted shot from fighters near the fringes of massive dogfights over half-ruined metal and plastic cities.

Skylar followed Gavin's navigational advice, taking a route that brought the ship down low, running fast on antigravity and atmospheric systems between a forest of tall buildings that were as interconnected by paths and roads in the upper levels.

Their path was taking them further from the thickest combat areas. Luck, combined with good navigation and Skylar's reflexes had kept them intact so far. After several minutes of flying through the combat infested city, where Gavin guessed there were at least three sides to the fight on the ground and in the tall towers, Skylar made a decision that made his heart skip a beat.

"Is there anywhere on the continent that isn't a hot zone?" she asked as the ship ducked lower and broke for a blue shoreline.

"Not so far, we've scanned over nine hundred square kilometres," Gavin replied, stretching the terrestrial scanners aboard the ship's capabilities so he could get a little more. "I'm still trying to untangle all the invitations we're getting from Navnet, there must be at least three main factions with what looks like ten or twenty sub-factions each trying to get us to land and join them. Then there are the dozen or so port controllers who are demanding we identify ourselves. The scanner's already shown a couple of them for frauds with no real port identification or landing areas on the planet. They're just pretending to be important to get... something out of us. Information, maybe?"

"Termire is chaos, we're not supposed to be here!" shouted the soldier tied up behind them on the deck. "I have to go back to the ship! Bring me back to the ship!"

"What do you know about this place?" Gavin asked. "We'll release you unharmed with a sidearm if you tell us what you can. You have my word, and that's the bond of the royal family." He remembered the capture of his prince, and how disconnected they were from the greatest house in the galaxy. His word was his own, perhaps backed by Skylar as well, but that's all the power it had. The power of two. She didn't say anything, only shaking her head as she concentrated on skimming the coastline's black and green forested edge, staying low.

"I know this isn't where I'm supposed to be, that we'll die if we stay here," the soldier struggled harder than before. An alert sounded all around them and Gavin looked at his operations panel to the right of the navigation and communications section.

There was a diagram of the soldier with a bloom of red in his stomach marked: WARNING: EXPLOSIVE INTERMIX IN PROGRESS.

"Slow us down! I have to open the hatch and get him out, he's got some kind of explosive failsafe," Gavin said, dragging the soldier up the short ramp at the rear of the lifepod.

"Just get me back to the ship! Take me back and it'll stop!" the soldier cried.

"Explosive material intermix at critical levels," the warning system said over the small ship's audio system.

The rear hatch opened with a loud pop and Gavin picked the soldier up by his belt and collar as best as he could. "Sorry," he muttered as he got him through the hatch.

With his feet and arms bound, there wasn't much the soldier could do other than squirm and grunt. Even though he didn't have to struggle against the guard much, Gavin didn't get enough momentum to throw him completely off the back of the ship from where he stood inside, at the top of the short ramp, and the soldier managed to flop onto the top beside the hatch instead of over the edge.

Gavin slapped the hatch close button. The hatch door started coming back down from where it stood up from the life-pod's hull like a rectangular sail, but not fast enough for Gavin's liking. "Bank! He's on top of the ship!"

The hatch was almost closed, a small gap was left as Skylar banked and the soldier's body exploded violently only a few metres from the ship.

. . .

THE VESSEL SPUN SUDDENLY, one of their port side thrusters was dead, and Skylar struggled for control for a few seconds as they spiralled towards the black sand shoreline. "That was close!"

There was no response from Gavin. She looked over her shoulder and saw him on the deck behind her, unconscious. "Hang on, love," she said, her fingers dancing across the navigation panel beside her as she looked for a safe spot to set down of any size. There was a cove with deep freshwater and their scanners weren't picking up many humanoid life signs. There were no signs of fighting, and the animal life looked small, most of them avian.

She checked the integrity of the ship and nodded to herself, guiding it into a fast turn towards the cove. In less than a minute the lower hull made contact with the water, and the ship slowed to a stop as she finished executing a smooth water landing. It should take people on the shore some time to investigate, they were at least two kilometres away in any direction, so she knew she would have time to try to treat Gavin.

The next few seconds were a blur as she scanned him, discovering that he had been pelted with micro-shrapnel thanks to the small opening in the hatch when the soldier exploded. "Dammit, I banked the wrong way," she cursed herself as she finished her scan. "If I'd banked the other way, or flipped hard, you'd be fine."

Gavin had pieces of metal near his heart, in one lung, but aside from a concussion, all the damage was fixable. The blood seeping from several cuts across his face looked horrible, but they were superficial and could be easily mended. If he was given a chance to wake up, the shrapnel would do more damage as he moved.

The medical supplies storage was marked clearly with a blue cross, and after a few moments of rifling through the contents she found a stasis dose, checked the contents and then administered it. "Good-night, I'll see you when you're all fixed up," she said, gently planting a kiss on his forehead.

All the medical supplies were marked clearly, and holographic instructions walking the user through the steps required to use them properly popped up whenever the seals keeping them sterile were touched. Most of the narcotics in the large kit interacted with genetics, so they were useless. She was peripherally aware of the cloudless blue sky through the canopy, and the muffled sounds of the water lapping up against the sides of the craft.

There were so many medical supplies that it took her several minutes to find what she was looking for; an emergency nanobot kit. The kit asked her a few questions: What are you treating? What state of consciousness is the patient in? Is the patient on a flat, stable surface?

The answers were multiple choice, and she was surprised when, after answering them accurately, the nanobot linked with her scanner and identified every piece of shrapnel in Gavin's body. The injector flashed; READY, and she placed it onto his bare chest, where a grey gel emerged from the tube then passed through Gavin's skin.

There was an army of millions of nanobots and the shallower pieces of shrapnel were surfacing after only a few seconds as they were carefully pushed out. She opened his suit and watched as the nanobots cleaned him from the inside out, closing wounds after they were used to remove foreign bodies then becoming anti-inflammation, anti-infection, and recovery medication as they dissolved. "Better than the nanobots we used in training," she said as she watched, amazed.

It was over minutes later, and her hand scanner flashed a message: YOUR PATIENT WILL AUTOMATICALLY REGAIN CONSCIOUSNESS IN TWENTY STANDARD MINUTES. ALLOW ONE MINUTE FOR PROPER WAKING. DO NOT ATTEMPT TO REVIVE HIM EARLIER.

A knock at the hatch was all the warning she had before it opened. Skylar drew her stolen sidearm and leaned over Gavin's body, sealing his suit back up and shielding him with her body. "Stay out there!" she shouted. "I'll shoot!"

A figure in mismatched black and green camouflage armour was already descending the ramp at speed, and she fired, catching him twice across a metal plate hanging on his chest. "Hold on, hey?" he said, his voice muffled by a full-face rebreather mask that was still dripping. "Pretty-pretty doesn't want to die over a little ship and a few supplies, does she, hey?"

"Get back!" she howled. There was another invader, her armour matching the colour style, but assembled from pieces of different suits of armour, most of them looked found, not made for her.

To her surprise, the man, no taller than she was, leapt forward. Her last shot grazed the side of his head, but then another pair of hands were on her. The woman's hands were on her too, not fighting to get the pistol away, just dragging her by the belt. "You don't need her, hey, just toss her and her boy over, hey."

A third set of hands grabbed her at the hatchway, and she was off her feet. There was an attempt at pulling her handgun from her hand, but she held on for dear life, and squeezed the trigger, only burning the ceiling. "Leave the burner, hey!" shouted another male. Whoever these people were, they had a lot of practice ganging up on people and removing them. They knew how to work as a group, but they weren't necessarily the brightest. She struggled, kicking out and catching one of them in the gut, swinging her free hand, latching onto the edge of one of their masks. "Let me go!"

"Stop fighting, hey! We just want your ship!"

"Fuck off!" Skylar growled as her fingers hooked into the woman's mouth under her mask and she gripped her jaw. Her open-mouthed screams filled the cabin as she panicked, letting go and grabbing Skylar's wrist as the grip grew tighter, crushing the delicate flesh under her tongue. "Leave me alone and I'll let go!"

A fist smashed Skylar across the side of the head, then straight down onto her nose. The glove her assailant was wearing must have been hardened with metal plates, or some kind of weighted fabric, it felt like being hit with hammer. Tears blurred her vision and blood ran down her face, filling her mouth with a coppery taste as she struggled to regain her senses.

They dropped her beside Gavin and their backpacks, and as two of them dragged her by her legs up the ramp she tried to loop her arm through one of the pack's straps only to have it kicked. The water was cold, and the shock of the pressure change made her nose ache furiously. "Fucking bitch! Broke my tooth, hey!" shouted the woman as Skylar surfaced. Her suit inflated small pockets across her body, increasing her buoyancy.

They tossed Gavin, his suit closed, thankfully, off the back side of the ship. "Here's your man, bitch!" the female screeched. "Lucky I don't burn you, hey!" She had a narrow face that was a little too toothy to start with, and spiky black hair.

The lifepod nearly dumped her into the water as it lurched forward, and she returned inside, closing the hatch behind her shouting; "I was still out top, hey!"

Skylar tucked her sidearm into an empty pocket in her suit. To her relief, Gavin's suit bore him up to the surface, and he was fine, other than being in stasis. As the ship lifted off and started flying unsteadily, she pulled him into her arms. She couldn't remember being so angry, and her nose was throbbing, sending a slow red flow down across her lips. With Gavin against her, she checked her scanner for the shore with the lowest number of humanoids, and finding a broad section with none, she started kicking her way there. "I've seen you, I'll remember this."

FORTY-THREE

"Now this is a proper station," Frost said as the Sector Jumper set down inside a large hangar. Several of the ships on the deck were wrecked, half-slagged and turned towards the main doors.

Spin could see that Hal was already scanning them, his inquisitive nature seemed to serve the crew well, it was surprising how often he already had an answer or workable theory about something when questions came up about it. "Those ships have been there awhile, no signs of life, no chance they're getting up off the deck without serious work."

"They're from the first group of scientists and workers who were trying to escape. The logs showed that a few of them made it," Sophia said from Spin's side on the small bridge. She looked even better in a fitted vacsuit that the Sector Jumper produced using a small water and raw material fed materializer. The protective white suit was as good as the most expensive under suits Spin had ever seen, and the ship made it in seconds.

"The station's docking systems seem to be happy to have us.

I'm getting a services list and fuel cost chart," Hal said, as amused as he was surprised, scrolling through a holographic list.

"Don't sign us up for anything. Any chance you can get them inside?"

"Sign us up for a tour, that'll get us through the airlock and then we can see if there's anyone inside to communicate with, or use our codes to break in," Spence said. He was in the same suit as his counterpart, Sophia, and had the physique of someone who had been sculpted by a master.

"All right, good luck in there. I'm staying here this time, just in case things get complicated. Hurry up," Frost said.

Spin led her group - Sophia, Spencer, Boro without Leaper, Dori and Aldo - off the ship. The only ones not in heavy Haven Shore armour were Sophia and Spencer. They crossed the pockmarked deck, moving between blasted ships and the corpses that populated them wordlessly. Aldo and Dori were at Spin's sides, looking around while Spin focused on Sophia and Spence, who were in the lead. Several drones were imbedded in the hulls of downed ships, and the few corpses laying around were preserved thanks to the vacuum of space. The entire bay looked like a moment frozen in time; the failure of a mass escape preserved for everyone to see the desperation and waste of the day the virus infected artificial intelligences in the Geist system.

Over her shoulder, the sleek, dark shape of the Sector Jumper looked out of place. Pristine, its glossy hull unblemished and turreted guns moving a little, her friends sitting ready at the turret controls just in case. When the double doors of the main airlock came into view, Spin decided to break the silence. "Is this the only Flesh Tech facility in the system?"

"There's one on the ground under contract by Citadel, it's

been there for about seventy years from what we could tell. The contract involved so many facilities in orbit and spread so much money around that they renamed the solar system after it. From what I can tell, a lot of that research went into us, but we couldn't get any information about what they were trying to accomplish. The main facility is still functioning down there, so they actively prevented us from getting into their system. We thought we could get help at first, but they just blocked us after a while."

"They didn't care that there was stock up here, waiting for them?" Spin asked.

"No, whatever they're doing down there's a big secret, more important than us," Spence replied. "The Aspen Control had a theory that it was worth killing a few billion Issyrians over, so we didn't look into it."

Sophia's hand twitched, bumping Spence's as though he'd said something wrong, and that only piqued Spin's curiosity. "Aspen Control, what was that?" The group stepped through the airlock doors, a holographic sign appearing between them saying: WELCOME, PROSPECTIVE BUYERS.

"She was..."

"Don't, it's too much." Sophia stopped Spence.

"I'm going to tell her. No more secrets, remember?" Spence said.

"Fine."

Spence went on, turning to Spin. "This might be hard to hear, but every one of us here is an experiment, essentially. The ones that are sold, the ones that stay here; the company treated every one of them as a source of research data."

"A good experiment requires a control," Spin said. "So there was an Aspen here."

"An Aspen and a Larken, that, along with most of their generation were very well liked by everyone. Over ninety models altogether. They did light work on the station, had fairly neutral exposure to information and experiences, perfect nutrition and a balance of exercise and rest. That sounds sort of clinical, but they were treated well," Spencer explained.

"Very well," Sophia added, nodding.

"Then the virus hit, and one of the last control subjects, a Skylar model, broke out of the section of the station made for controls like her. She was one of the first ones to talk to Nadir, and, along with Aspen and a few others who couldn't get out of the control section, they helped us survive. By the time we were free, Aspen, Larken and her generation were old. We watched them die before we left. They were isolated in the section of the station reserved for Control Subjects, not even Nadir could free them, there was nothing anyone could do. That was the company's intention: for the Control Subject versions of all their models to be made before everyone in their line, live an uncomplicated, moderated life, then die as they were designed to do. The data collected would be compared against the reports people who owned Aspens, Larkens, and all the other models filed as part of their purchasing agreement."

The environment finished equalizing and the inner airlock doors opened, revealing a posh corridor with padded purple and white walls. "Perfectly scientific," Spin said, feeling a pang of grief at not being able to meet another Larken, or even an Aspen. It wasn't nearly as sharp as the guilt and loss she felt before.

"If it makes you feel any better, Aspen and I were friends, even if it was through a pane of transparesteel. When I met her she was old, but so smart, so charming. If you're anything like her, I can't imagine how amazing you'll be as you live on and surpass her."

"Thanks, I'll try to live up to that," Spin replied.

A sing-song voice greeted them; "Welcome to Flesh Tech Station Beta, where all the original models you know and love, and new models of dolls are born. I hope you enjoy the tour and take refreshment when it is concluded." Soft blinking lights directed them up the corridor and to the right.

"We need a panel," Sophia said, feeling along the padded wall. After a moment she found a seam and pulled, taking a tall triangle of plating off and setting it aside. A control panel was beneath that showed them where they were, that they'd all been scanned and accepted as visitors. "The station's systems have been really dumbed down, so if you know what you're doing, there's nowhere you can't go except for the Control section."

"What was that like?" Spin asked.

"Oh, it looked comfortable, with work areas where the dolls could help with moderate challenges. Some of the newer models were even allowed to have social gatherings, but a few of them said it got boring, especially after the scientists left. I still don't know how Skylar escaped, but she lost her counterpart doing it. Her and Gavin were standout models, two who were based on real people because the Lux Royal Family wanted copies."

"Who were they based on?" Boro asked.

"I never found out much. All I know is that they were copies of royals who were very distant from the throne, not celebrities at all. It was a touchy topic, I think," Spencer said.

"Spin," Frost said over the communications system in her helmet. "There are more raiders coming in, and some military outfit called the Dasian Union coming in with more firepower than we can take on. We're pulling out of the guest docking bay and cloaking until you're ready for pickup. Hurry up."

"I hear you," Spin said, remembering meeting a Dasian. They were humanoid, almost human looking, in fact, but were characterized by having three fingers, shallow noses and broader bodies.

"Who are Dasians?" asked Spencer.

"A human like people that the Lux Royals and most of the other houses have been keeping out of the Core since they were discovered. They used to send traders to the Estate to do business and to feel us out, see if we'd show them anything they could steal. They're probably here to raid the station for slaves and whatever tech they can find. I've never seen one in person, I wasn't allowed to."

"I got us a clear path to the spawning floor," Sophia said as she finished working at the panel. Spence helped her put the cover back on. "It's on the other side of the station, but we have a clear shot there."

"You couldn't get the automated defences going?" Spence asked her.

"Not from here," she replied.

A map of the station appeared on Spin's in-helmet tactical display with a path marked on it. "We have a run ahead of us," she said, urging everyone to move.

Distant thuds and vibrations underfoot were enough of an

indication that ships were landing in the hangar behind them, she didn't need the tactical display to show her the five-armed personnel carriers, but it was good to be sure. They were minutes away from being outnumbered.

To her surprise, the first two personnel carriers were bashed open by well-placed railgun shots, and the rest were pelted by heavy anti-fighter fire as the Sector Jumper finished withdrawing from the hangar. It started cloaking as soon as the decimation was complete, leaving wreckage and gore settling in its wake. "Bought you some time, but there are more coming, and they're going to be pissed," Frost announced.

"Me and the gunners bought her some time," Hal corrected. "Good luck in there."

FORTY-FOUR

There were birds somewhere nearby, or someone playing recorded bird song. Their chirping sounded like a warning, then almost combative before calming down. Gavin's olfactory was flooded with the smell of damp, black soil and old fish. No sound was as loud or as important as the one that became clearest as his chest began to burn. It was the sound of Skylar breathing heavily, and when he took his first, startled breath, she was there.

"You're rousing from stasis, try to relax and breathe," she told him, her face hovering over his. She was soaked, he was too, somehow the suits they wore didn't protect them from the elements the way they were designed to. They should have sealed over their heads to protect them. "I know," he gasped, trying to slow his breathing. "Thank you."

"What's the last thing you remember?"

"On the lifepod. I was pushing the soldier out the hatch and there was a flash before the door finished closing."

"You took a lot of micro shrapnel, I had to use a nanobot kit to clear it and heal the damage," she explained. "How do you feel?"

Gavin was starting to catch his breath, and the rest of the world was starting to come into focus. Something happened, something serious enough for them to be on a swampy shore amongst a thick growth of weeds, under the branches of twisted trees. The birds were real. Small black things chirped threats at each other until a group of four or five dove down then back up, some with full beaks, others robbed of their purchase by other birds who got in their way, diving after them. "The birds are real," Gavin said. Skylar smiled at him and he responded in kind. "I feel normal, great, actually. What happened?"

"I put the ship down in the bay, thinking that we would be far enough from anyone to give me some time to take care of you, but by the time that was taken care of, three people with rebreathers and some kind of aqua packs overpowered me and tossed us over the side. The only thing that worked in our suits were the floatation pockets, but it was enough for me to swim you to shore."

"You hate deep water," Gavin said, sitting up then pushing a lock of Skylar's blonde hair out of her face. It was curling into ringlets as it started to dry.

Skylar nodded, smiling weakly. "I thought my time learning to swim in training got me over that, but this place brought all that anxiety back. It's like this whole cove, the swamp is alive, there are ten times as many little life forms in the water than there are on land, and when my feet finally touched the ground, it was mush until the shoreline." She shuddered then turned her gaze inland. "We have to find a place to make camp, somewhere dry. I don't think there's much daylight left, maybe a couple hours."

"You saved me again," Gavin said, unwilling to let that pass without some show of gratitude. "Thank you."

"I love you," she said. It was always said because it was true, and worth saying aloud, but Gavin was often amused when she used those words to shut him up. He couldn't count the number of times he'd thanked her for something that most married couples took for granted, and she was often at a loss for how to respond, but it was one of the ways he countered the times when he grew distant, deep in thought, so he'd never stop thanking her.

"Love you too," he looked down at the scanner in her hand, and she held it up so they could both look at it clearly. She had it set to detect moving machinery, humanoid and larger sized creatures. In the distance was a large group of oval buildings that looked like some sort of processing plant, and there was a man-made lake on the far side, isolated from the swamp around it, the contents were some kind of thick algae. "Is there any solid ground between here and that settlement?"

"I was just starting to scan when you woke up, but I didn't find any. We don't have a portable shelter anymore, either. I tried to grab one of our backpacks, but they weren't having that."

"They just rushed in and took the ship? No chance at diplomacy?" Gavin asked.

"I told them to stop, but they were rushing, so I shot the one in the lead twice. He was wearing some kind of thick plating on his chest, I should have aimed for his head."

"Then they might have killed you instead of tossing us both

over the side. You did the right thing, we're alive, and we still have some supplies in our pockets."

"Enough food for three days," Skylar nodded. "There are probably tubers and berries we can eat too. The ripe ones I've seen those birds fight over are everywhere."

A stirring in the brush along the shoreline alerted them to a tall, long armed trio of robots that were crawling through, crushing brambles and long, switch like branches to the ground as they pushed through the thicket running along the shore. Two humans rode the nearest bots, astride their long bodies like children on their parent's backs, controlling the bots with improvised rods welded to their shoulders. The human riders wore thick isolation suits, their helmets hanging off their saddles, which were small seats from hover cars. The third rider's helmet was sealed, the face plate tinted darkly so Gavin could only see the suggestion of two yellow eyes that were many times too large to be human. "Don't eat those without cooking them first, or you'll get real drunk, real fast and regret it in the morning. Then again, that's fine if it's the kind of party you're after." The human who spoke did so with a broad smile, and his eyes assessed him and Skylar thoroughly. "I'm Gusson, we're Riggers."

"What's a Rigger?" Gavin asked, looking more closely at the machines and they rode and the controls used to manipulate them. The source of their name was immediately obvious to him as he saw that the rods they used as handles had small buttons and thumb sized controller sticks installed in them.

"The United Core Authority blasted this world with their pulses, burned out a lot of robo-brains. We get 'em together and make them work for us, just dumb machines now, but good enough. What are you called? Who are your people? Where you from?"

Those were all good questions. They were soldiers in His Majesty, Prince Connor Lux's army, but that didn't matter. The Prince may as well have been dead to them, and while that realization made Gavin's heart ache, he knew a long explanation about where they came from wouldn't serve.

"We're lost," Skylar said. "Some Earth outfit called Citadel took us captive when our ship was destroyed in the Geist system." Gavin thought her explanation was genius. Just enough of the truth for them to think they've gotten a straight answer but avoiding their attachment to the Lux Royal family. Low born swamp dwellers probably didn't care much for anyone with an attachment to the royals. Relating to these people might require some low thinking. "We escaped from the Citadel ship when it arrived in orbit and started fighting with the locals, but another gang took our lifepod when we landed."

"Did they say 'hey' a lot and smell like dirt?" asked the other human, a woman who had a long slash scar up her jaw.

"They said 'hey' a lot," Skylar agreed.

"Buckside Raiders," she cursed. "Was it a nice ship? Did it have guns?"

"No, it was a lifepod, a large one with supplies, but unarmed, like a civilian shuttle," Skylar said.

"If it was like a shuttle, then it's been sold for scriff, they might be getting high already," Gusson said. "You two know how to work with bots? Maybe a little chemistry?" The second question made the Issyrian's head jerk towards Gusson. "Think you could tell us about tech from Geist?"

"We didn't get to keep our scan data of Geist, but we both have training in repair, programming," Gavin said.

"I'm sure we could be useful until we figure out what our next move is," Skylar said, her eyes looking up through the branches overhead after a trio of ships passing overhead at speed.

"Then we'll feed you, get to talking about some new tech," Gusson said. "We always like hearing about new tech, but you've got to hurry. Iron Port is coming." He pointed over their heads.

Skylar and Gavin looked behind them in time to see a massive, roughly oval shape up in the sky, an imposing silhouette against the yellow-red setting sun. "What is that?" he pointed his scanner at it and saw the profile of a three-kilometre-long colony ship with one third of its top missing entirely, as though it was blasted open by large weapons.

"It's Iron Mind's city, Iron Port. Never touches the ground, doesn't talk to us unless it's trade day. It won't pass over tonight, but its patrols will buzz around plenty. Come," Gusson said insistently.

The scanner couldn't make out as much detail as Gavin liked, but he could see that the converted ship was using anti-gravity generators to stay up, and would be as stable as a mountain, that it had powerful shielding and several hangars where fighters were launching and landing. It had been modified so much that it only resembled its original specifications in shape alone. "That is amazing," Gavin said as he stared at his scanner, allowing Skylar to lead him by the hand. "Are they hostile?"

"Only if you attack, we speak to them on trading days. Lots of factions go there, but if they break the peace they get put off or killed," Gusson explained. He was leading them in the direction of the refinery, and Gavin expected to find that they'd settled in there.

"You trade food with them," Gavin said. "Food you make from the algae you're growing."

"You've heard of us?" Gusson asked, looking over his shoulder with suspicion.

A squeeze from Skylar's hand told him he was either thinking too far ahead or saying something she guessed would lead to trouble. "No, we just arrived, but this basic scanner tells me there's a contained lake of algae, so I guessed."

"It can see the formula?" asked the Issyrian, alarmed at the notion. "My formula?"

"No," Skylar said. "Just that it's algae, and it's dense, not safe for drinking or swimming in."

"Let me see," the Issyrian guided his robot mount around, and if it wasn't such a tense situation, Gavin might have laughed at how the machine walked on its hands and knees, a blank expression on its metal face.

He showed the readings to the Issyrian, who nodded. "Turn it off, that's all you see, or I take the scanner." The words came through an emitter at the bottom of his mask, and Gavin could hear the bubbles, whines and rushing of liquid inside as he spoke.

Gavin turned his scanner off, then put it in his pocket. "I won't scan your algae, don't worry."

"Or my equipment," the Issyrian said menacingly before turning his mount and riding up alongside Gusson. He spoke to him secretively, still irritated.

"I think I made things worse for us," Gavin said.

"Not by much," Skylar whispered back. "They have blade shooters, and even though those bots don't look like much, they're faster than us, so running probably won't be an option unless we find an opportunity."

"So, we have to make ourselves important to these people," Gavin said. "Or run and take our chances in the swamp." A lizard twice as long as he was tall slipped out of the water, crossed behind them, then slid back into the black muck. It had the teeth of a carnivore and moved almost as fast as he could run with a belly fat with recently ingested prey.

Skylar looked from where the reptile disappeared into the water to him with wide blue eyes. "Diplomacy first."

FORTY-FIVE

The Flesh Tech facility was part research complex and part order fulfilment centre for doll buyers. The wardrobe section of the base was astonishing, but mostly because Spin recognized several outfits that she not only wore during her years of service, but preferred. The warehouse sized collection of clothing made her wonder. "How many dolls were they producing here?"

"Here? Only select models, normally the newest," Spence replied. "There are other custom design and fulfilment centres, several bulk production facilities, but we weren't able to get in touch with any of them."

"If you're wondering about the clothes, and why they kept so much stock here, it's because these are the garments made the old-fashioned way. Guaranteed not to be out of some plastics printer, or auto fabricator. They ship these all over, I'm pretty sure they were overcharging," Sophia added.

"Custom design centre?" Spin asked.

"There are several of them, we couldn't see the whole list,

but they build dolls to order, sometimes made to look like famous people who licensed their likenesses or based on the genetics of lost relatives. I saw that the Lux Royal Family pays to maintain one in their home system, but most of the reserved facilities are bulk producers. I don't know exactly what they do, but big companies pay a lot of money just to control what comes out of those places."

"The United Core World Authority?" Spin asked.

"I saw two bulk production facilities with their names on the list. Those complexes aren't allowed to produce anything unless it's for them," Spence said. "You think you've run into synthetics in their uniforms?"

"I don't know," Spin said. "But they bounced back awfully fast after the virus spread. Maybe that's how they filled their ranks with competent soldiers."

"Spin," Frost said over her communicator. "One of the Dasian landers managed to drop off a few soldiers ahead of you, they're heading into the warehouse."

"All right," Spin said as she saw the large doors ahead of them turn red, indicating that's where they were coming from. "All right, you two turn your stealth systems on and hide behind those crates," Spin said, directing Sophia and Spencer. "Everyone else; cloak. We'll outflank them."

"You're getting better at this by the minute," Boro said as she marked positions for everyone on her tactical display.

Dori didn't move to the spot Spin sent her to using her tactical system, but everyone else was in position quickly. Spin saw that Dori ran to her left, then leapt up onto a catwalk. "This good?" she asked.

It was a better position than Spin suggested for her. "It is, wait for my order to fire," Spin said. Boro was to the left of the doors, she was to the right, Aldo was a little further out from the doorway on the same side with Sophia and Spence furthest from the doors at the back of the warehouse. There was a forest of clothing racks and crates between them and the door, essential to keeping them safe since Spin was sure that if anyone would be detected it was that pair. Their cloaking systems weren't nearly as sophisticated since they were wearing basic military vacsuits. Sure, they were better than anything Spin had seen while being light and thin, but everyone else wore heavy encounter armour.

The doors opened and a trio of Dasians emerged. Their wide heads and bodies reminded Spin of Kort. Their eyes didn't seem right, just like his: they were too small for their heads with strange, dark pupils. She momentarily wondered if Kort was actually trying to look like one of the tall, powerful looking non-humans using all the modifications he'd made to himself. He could have blended into their number seamlessly.

Their helmets were transparent except for a strip of green metal running down the top. The leader carried a wide-bore rifle with a smaller emitter above it, while the others had rifles featuring a number of cooling vents and finned heatsinks that opened and closed like stretching fingers. She noted that there were three emitters on the ends of their weapons with tiny holes between them.

The trio started moving in, four more entering the warehouse behind them. The leader's lips were moving, and her communications system picked up his lip movement, read it, then translated it for her after a few seconds. Their language was basic, rated much simpler than most by her system. "Our computer said there were targets moving in here. The doors did not open until we came. They must still be here. Fan out and search. Ojib, Tinir; you watch the door. If anything escapes you will capture it or we will hunt you for sport while we travel home."

The passive scanners finished analysing their armour and Spin barely understood most of the results. They were in a shorthand she recognized from the Haven Fleet Military Equipment Manual, but she didn't memorize them. What she could understand of it was that they were wearing a set of plates that were attached to a cybernetic exoskeleton that was affixed to their bones, which were enhanced with some kind of organic metal treatment. Their armour's space worthiness was achieved in how the plates interlocked, which also gave them a large tolerance to sudden pressure changes. Their race was naturally strong, but their exoskeletons were motorized, making them much stronger, just as physically powerful as anyone in an encounter suit. "Keep your distance, don't let them get their hands on you. Everyone fire on the leader once Boro has a shot, maximum intensity, then move before firing again." Spin looked for a weak spot and couldn't find anything they could hit while the Dasian's arms weren't raised. The weakest linkage in their armour plates was under the arm, but she couldn't see how they could make that shot. "Aim for his faceplate."

"Aye," Boro said. "Moving back so I can get a good shot."

"I see something at the far end of this section," said one of the soldiers behind the leader who was looking at a bulky hand scanner.

"I'm in position," Boro said. "Firing in three, two, one," all at once, Spin, Dori, and Aldo fired a sustained burst at the Dasian leader, who sank to his knees once it was over, one side of his head open and charred. What was left of his mouth worked to form a word that couldn't be completed. "Move and open fire on my marked target," Spin said as she ran from her position. The Dasians who were directly behind their leader opened fire to their left and right, blasting chunks of the durable plastic crates Spin and her friends were hiding behind into the air. The emitters on their rifles weren't what she expected, some kind of focused light or plasma shooters, but they seemed to use some kind of gravity or force bolt to blast their targets apart. It was a weapon that didn't value accuracy but was made to tear through crowds or nearby enemies for shock and horror value.

Boro frantically ran out of the line of fire, his shields taking a direct hit. The clothing behind him was flung in all directions, catching fire as they spun through the air. "Holy crap, their weapons are bloody serious. I just lost my shield after one hit."

Spin momentarily considered telling everyone to switch from cloaking to shielded combat mode, their shields would be far more powerful, but dismissed the notion as Boro found cover behind a thick metal pillar. "Ready to fire on the second target," she said.

"Get the prey at the back! There are cowards who fight like spirits here!" shouted one of the Dasians at the door.

Spin saw that everyone's rifles were pointing at her second target, the one that entered to the left of the leader. "Firing in..." she was interrupted as four of the Dasian's leapt over most of the clothing racks. "Fire!" she shouted. "Burst and move."

She raked two of them as they landed. It didn't cut through their armour, their efforts weren't focused enough, but the four Dasians were in the middle of burst fire as Aldo, Dori and Boro kept up their assault, sending barrages of powerful explosive rounds at them. After only a few bursts, much of the rest of the clothing between them and the Dasians had caught fire, and the firefight continued in a forest of red flame topped with black smoke. Spin tossed a grenade that she'd pulled from the inventory of the Sector Jumper that was called 'The Bot Buster' and watched as the tiny thrusters propelled it towards one of the Dasians guarding the door. The grenade's first phase of attack happened so fast, she almost didn't have time to see it in action: it was in the air, then the pinhole thrusters fired, and it made the distance between it and the soldier's helmet in less than a second. Once it struck, it affixed, then an intense, contained electromagnetic pulse went off followed by three pulses of extreme heat that burned a hole through the soldier's helmet as he danced around, trying to pull it off. He sank to his knees, the other soldier at the door unable to move his right leg and arm. "My implants are damaged, I can't move! What is that?"

The grenade was almost finished its work. With the last of its charge, it offered her the option to detonate the compressed explosive within, and she nodded. The deck shook as the grenade blasted the Dasian door guards, leaving little of them left. The site of their destruction was marked by a hole where the door they stood beside was and a warped section of floor behind.

Spin turned her attention back to the firefight in progress in time to see the catwalk Dori was running on crumble as one of their enemies ripped it apart with explosive rounds. Dori fell from the catwalk, still firing, landed on her feet and rolled into a run. They hadn't managed to hit her more than twice, her low powered stealth shields absorbing the first hit, while the armour took the second.

There were only two Dasians left as Spin opened fire on the nearest, and all her people were in good shape. The air was thick with smoke, so their in-helmet system created a clearer image of their surroundings using sensor data. Boro moved the least as he fired burst after burst at their enemies. Aldo rolled, ran, and sidestepped with practiced skill between shots and Dori was surprisingly graceful, using the enhanced strength of the encounter suit to leap and roll between bursts. The Dasians had less luck hitting her once she was down off the catwalk.

Spin made sure she knew where she was about to move to before opening fire with double bursts, and by the time one of their enemies fired back, she wasn't there anymore. "Prisoners, boss?" asked Aldo.

"No," Spin said simply. It wasn't a considered response, but automatic. "No mercy for slavers," she added.

By the time the last Dasian dropped his rifle, staggering with an opening in his side and a section of his helmet burned open, Spin was only nine metres away. His too-broad face, so much like Kort's, turned, fine grey scales that were marked as a primary type of armour that were bonded to his skin, blacked around his mouth and thin nostrils. "Where are you? I want to see the ghosts who bested us!" he coughed on the smoke, holding the shreds of his right arm close to his body. His left was gone reduced to several rods that hung from his shoulder. The wound was sealed off by his outer suit, and there was a chance he'd survive his injuries if they let his suit work on him, at least that was according to the data her sensors were pulling in.

As it was, he could barely stand, and his arms were

completely disabled. Spin deactivated her cloaking system and made her faceplate transparent. "I was born here."

"Soft, small, little pleasure creature made to please even softer humans," the Dasian said as though they were curses. "You couldn't have defeated us. There must be a hundred of you."

Boro, Aldo and Dori appeared then. "Only four," Boro said. Sophia and Spencer carefully emerged from their hiding spot, their suits sealed to protect them against the toxic smoke and dwindling fire.

"Why are your people here?" Spin asked.

"To take the station and make an army of obedient slaves for my Queen. She's promised the greatest victors slaves of their own, and the valorous fallen a place in her Arena of the Dead, where we can..."

Even through the translator, the Dasian looked so much like Kort that she couldn't stand watching him rave on about his Queen or the afterlife she promised anymore, so she tilted her rifle up and blasted him in the face until he fell back, mostly headless. "Let's move on," she said, turning away from the scene towards the main doors leading further into the station. The maturation and holding chambers weren't far off.

FORTY-SIX

As Skylar and Gavin followed their guides down the paths leading to the processing plant Skylar scanned in the distance, she felt a growing sense of unease. The Issyrian, she assumed he was Issyrian, anyway, based on the style of containment suit he wore and the breathing pattern she could hear through its water recycling system, was talking to the humans riding beside him. They couldn't hear anything other than the whines and squeaks that Issyrians made when they were talking under water, so she assumed whatever he was saying was being translated and transmitted to his cohorts. When he spoke before, he used a speaker to translate his words aloud. She could only conclude that whatever he was saying wasn't for her or Gavin's ears.

"If you're worried about us eating your food, or using your supplies, you don't have to. We have enough on us to last several days, and we're trained to survive just about anywhere, so we can scrounge up our own food if your people are short," Gavin offered as reassurance.

"We have an abundance. We make a surplus that was trade. We're not worried about you two eating too much, trust me," Gusson said with a thin smile.

The ground they tread on turned from the damp black stuff that felt like drying silt to thick clay as they moved up a hill. A shanty town came into view as they passed through a close group of thick trunked trees. The wood would be worth a fortune where they came from; naturally grown stuff that was twice as wide as she was, and hard wood from the looks of it with a fine dark colour. Her thoughts wandered for an instant and she found herself wondering if the world they were standing on was terraformed centuries before or formed naturally. The wildlife was almost familiar, similar to the kind she'd seen a few times, but nothing matched up perfectly.

Then three children ran into the broadening path. They were from the shanty atop the hill, wearing clothing made from scavenged synthetic and natural cloth. The fit was loose on two, too tight on one of them, but they were clean for the most part, a good sign for their quality of life. They stopped in shock, staring at her and Gavin round-eyed.

Skylar bent down and smiled at the girl, who was tallest of the three and in clothes she was about to outgrow. "I'm Skylar, what's your name?"

She took a quick step back, screaming; "Dirty Synth!" before running away, the younger boys joining her. "Wicked Iron Port Synths!"

"That's not good," Gavin said.

"You're gonna stand out," the woman with a scar across her face said. "You're too pretty to be from here. No one in the world is that good to look at except for the Synths in Iron Port."

"I didn't catch your name," Gavin said.

"I didn't give it," the scarred woman said. "Ida, pretty boy, it's Ida."

"That little girl reacted like she wasn't happy to see synths. Are the synthetics here hard to get along with?" he asked.

Skylar was happy he was being diplomatic. He could even be charming if he decided to be, but sometimes he spoke too plainly, his words stripped of niceties. "We're dirt-dwellers to them. Only good for working, selling scriff to, gaming plat and gear from. They look at our tech like it's junker trash," Ida said. "Won't let us trade our way up so we can have a place of our own in Iron Port, they'd rather keep us down where..."

"They say Iron Port is full," Gusson interrupted. "It hasn't been up in the sky for a year, though, so we can't see how. They're choosy, and that's fine with me. I'm happy down here where we never run out of food or parts."

"The Iron Port synths speak for Iron Mind. They're stingy, even rip us off sometimes."

"They negotiate for the best deal they can get for what we're offering," Gusson defended half-heartedly. "Just like anyone else."

"They have so much, then trade so little for as much food and cloth as they can get for a little plat and a few good parts, maybe a couple little energy modules. Synths never trade fair. We're dirt to them."

"That's enough, Ida. You're getting plenty out of today, stop crying about yesterday trades," Gusson growled.

They travelled silently for a while, and Skylar took in the look of the town they passed into. There was a tall wall made of hull segments salvaged from a ship so large that she couldn't piece them together in her head to figure out what it was. Guards, some in makeshift armour, others in armour from military organizations that she didn't recognize as often as she did, gathered over the gatehouse to see the newcomers. They were in awe, and Skylar wished she had her suit completely sealed, but left her head exposed in case covering up could make things worse. She felt exposed as they stared down at them, some grinning, others shaking their heads and scowling.

Once through the wicket gate, the small pedestrian door beside the tall main doors, they emerged onto a street that was roughly paved in chunks of concrete that weren't poured there but organized like massive flat stones to make a road. The dome containing the lake towered above everything except for a few towers built from found metal and cables.

The nicer homes they passed were made from small ships and transit shuttles. Most of them were severely damaged and patched but would probably never fly again. The other homes were made from random pieces of metal, plastic from mid-sized containers, and wood. It was odd, seeing whole wooden panels and logs that would be worth a fortune where she came from used to build shanty walls alongside bioplastic sheets and container sides that should have been recycled, not used for housing.

Wind catchers that spun overhead on roofs and little towers were common, providing power and catching moisture for clean household water. Skylar started to see a pattern in how people regarded them when they were seen the first time. Many of the townsfolk looked them right in the eye before glancing downward, their gazes dwelling on their feet, covered by the boots built into their suits but sullied by the black dirt. "I'm guessing the synths you've met don't come down from Iron Port?" Skylar asked.

"They don't touch the ground for longer than they must, they always have too-clean boots," Ida replied. She dismounted and fell back so she was walking alongside Gavin and Skylar. Her crawling, humanoid android mount stood upright and walked behind her silently, too tall, its hands, bare feet and knees black from the soil. "You're not like the Iron Port synths, are you?"

"If they're as prejudiced as they seem, then no," Gavin said. "We'd rather make ourselves useful, and..." he stopped speaking suddenly, there was something wrong.

Skylar turned so she could see what was going on and realized that Ida had taken Gavin's scanner and was working on opening his thigh pocket. "Leave him alone," Skylar warned, her hand resting on the butt of her sidearm.

Gavin tried to step away from Ida and managed to get her hands off of him for a moment before she grabbed his forearm firmly, smiling. "I'm half bot, no getting away."

"I'm going to tell Deckard we have new synths," Gusson said, urging his mount into a strange gallop on its android hands and feet. The Issyrian kept up with him.

Four guards, three in battered British Alliance armour with missing plates here and there, the fourth in a full metal suit that had a few noisy motors running within, emerged from an alley and Skylar's heart sank. The newcomers were armed, carrying rifles and handguns, but they weren't pointing them at her or Gavin yet. The way she saw it, there was one chance, and it was a big gamble.

She drew her weapon quickly and fired at Ida, catching her

fully in the forehead with a charged slug. "Run!" Skylar shouted, and then made it to the mouth of the opposite alleyway before she realized that Gavin wasn't behind her. Skylar glanced back in time to see Ida trip Gavin and press him down to the ground, the top half of her face was stripped bare of flesh, revealing a dented metal skull beneath. "You bitch! Do you realize how expensive flesh growing is? It's going to take weeks and all the plat I got to get a new pretty!"

"Run, Skylar!" Gavin said, his arms twisting behind his back.

"If you take another step and I twist his hand off!" Ida screeched.

"Just go!" Gavin shouted, grimacing and struggling. He managed to get one arm free, tried to turn so the pressure on the other was relieved, then Ida put a foot down on his back, gripped his forearm and started to pull on his hand. Her eyes and her bloodied grin were wide with glee. Gavin's face was frozen in an expression of pure, silent agony.

"Wait!" Skylar said, dropping her gun. "I won't run, don't hurt him."

"You synths are soft, so weak," she laughed, letting his hand go. "I knew it. Sleep shoot them."

It was against every instinct she had, but Skylar watched as one of the guardsman with a long rifle raised it, aimed, then stunned Gavin. She didn't see who stunned her, it was from behind, perhaps from above, but a second after Gavin was stunned into unconsciousness, her body was wracked with pain as though every nerve was set alight before darkness over-whelmed all her senses.

FORTY-SEVEN

The smell of something old and mossy rotting filled Gavin's nostrils as he felt someone tugging at his boots. Training took over. He pulled his feet up under him, was vertical the moment he knew there was nothing overhead in the half-light and kicking.

A humanoid with segmented green and red eyes screeched loudly as the toe of Gavin's boot caught him under the arm. Still crouched, it rushed away, screeching and holding its underarm. Skylar woke beside him in a hurry. The noise must have roused her, and she was on her feet looking around them, checking her pockets. They'd taken everything except for their suits and the reserve food cubes kept in an interior collar pocket.

Concrete walls, ceilings and floors surrounded them in a hallway choked with pipes and mechanical refuse. "I'm sorry, I couldn't stop him. I've learned to stay out of the way of Scrizex, when those people want something it's best to let them have it," said a woman Gavin recognized, but he couldn't remember her name.

"Lorna," Skylar said, quietly shocked. "What are you doing here?"

"I was part of an expedition to Termire despatched by our Prince. We were to see what kind of resistance a harvesting expedition would meet and find out how much nansha was left uncontaminated on the planet surface."

Nansha, a substance that occurred naturally, but rarely. When it was found, it was generally in great abundance on worlds that were well suited to human habitation without terraforming. It was used as a base for some of the best regeneration and recovery drugs in the galaxy, the kind that were too expensive or complex to develop synthetic equivalents for. "Is there nansha growing on the surface of this world?"

"There are dense lakes of it at the bottom of the ocean and the subsurface oceans. There's pure concentrate underground, so thick that it's a solid. This swamp is full of it in lesser concentration, that's the secret to their food production and what drew my team here. We were taking samples here when the people from the settlement above attacked. Most of us were killed, leaving me and two members of our party. They recognized that we were synthetics right away and put us to work cleaning parts, working in the purification plant. Most of the people here are allergic to purer forms of nansha, but synthetics and Scrizex aren't, so we clean parts that come in contact with the stuff."

"So, we're prisoners," Skylar said, touching the side of her head gingerly.

Gavin touched the side of his head right behind the ear as well and found a tender spot. A strip had been bonded with his skin, it felt almost seamless. "The others are working," Lorna said, nodding. "They're replacing filters in the nansha vats. Don't touch the receiver strips," she said, pointing at the side of Skylar's head. "If you tamper with them, they'll send pain through your nervous system, or knock you out entirely. We can't leave the compound or argue with the foremen either. You don't want to give them a reason to torture you. There's nothing worse."

"Except for being trapped here, maybe?" Skylar asked in a hush. Her body went rigid, expression frozen in agony for several seconds before she could breathe again, sitting down hard. "Oh, my God, everything hurt, it was like I was burning from the inside."

"They're listening, they're watching. It's another thing the strips let them do, I think," Lorna said. "Is the Prince here? Is there a rescue team coming?"

Before Skylar could answer, Gavin did so clearly and quickly. If there was another shock coming, he'd take it, if only to find out how bad it actually was. Maybe he could fight through it, increase his chances of overtaking a guard or working another plan. "The Prince isn't coming. What's left of him is in Citadel's hands. They're some kind of organization that prizes synthetics, puts them over natural humans. We were able to escape after discovering not everything was as it seemed on their ship. We still don't know exactly why they wanted us, but we knew we were their captives."

"They value synthetics?" Lorna asked, musing. "Then they're here for the facilities that produce them, or nansha, it aids in accelerated growth and reinforcement of tissue. It's one of the secrets to making the last few generations of dolls." She said the last while looking at her feet. Gavin could relate; he sometimes took refuge in the details of a situation to avoid the unfortunate side of it too.

There were moments when it drove Skylar crazy, when she wanted to know how he felt about something but he kept on going on about the science behind their predicament. The news about their Prince was hitting Lorna hard. "I'm sorry. We're not here to rescue anyone. I can't believe we were trapped in the first place." Gavin put his arm around Skylar, who nodded at him to indicate that she was all right.

"We weren't prepared for this," Skylar said. "We were trained to be part of a squad, then a crew, and that's after we were pampered through our youth, through our whole education. Duplicity and greed looked very different where we come from," she told Gavin more than anyone else.

"I didn't understand these people either, not at first," Lorna said. "They are crass and greedy. They hate us because we heal faster, are healthier, and because of the way we look. I used to try to explain that where we come from we're normal, everyone looks like us, and that I could help them with medicine, science, but they keep us down here. They hate synthetics. Don't try to convince them you can help."

A thick metal door at the end of the hallway opened and Ida walked in with two guards in mismatched armour behind her. One had a thick rifle with three emitters on the end, and the other had too thin to be human limbs covered in carapace like armour that was caked with mud.

"Welcome to our little complex," Ida said, her scar twisting along with her smile, curving up her cheek. Above it was a thick bandage that hid the damage Skylar had done. Her head was wrapped so her eyes could peer through the bands. "You're going to keep our operation running nice and smooth. There's no way out, and if we think you're doing something we don't like, you'll suffer. If you don't fall in line, we'll kill you. We can do it face to face, or from a very long way away. If you do your work, you can live a long time. If you sabotage our operation, we have special punishments. You don't want that."

"Couldn't you make machines to do all this?" Gavin asked. "If it's filter and pipe cleaning, even servicing..." he was interrupted by the sensation of his head being squeezed from all directions as though he was wearing a shrinking metal helmet. Bone deep agony made him forget about the control strip installed behind his ear and live in a moment of pure suffering. As quickly as it occurred, it ended, leaving him gasping.

"That was one of a lot of pains," Ida said with a smile. "Don't question us or I'll give you a worse one."

Gavin looked her up and down. There was no control in her hand, but she was wearing a display collar that was sending images directly into her eyes, that was probably what she used to control the strips. She was strong, and if her skull had been replaced by armour, then who knew what else she'd reinforced or replaced with fortified cybernetics. Ida and anyone like her would be the biggest obstacle to escape, along with whoever might be watching them through the bands or other surveillance equipment. He suppressed the urge to attack her outright and settled on a simpler objective; they would have to find a dead spot, where he and Skylar could speak to the other captives freely. "I understand," Gavin said.

"I need to hear her say it too," Ida said, pointing towards Skylar.

"I understand," Skylar said. Her fingers tapped his side where no one would be able to see. *Start planning our escape.*

I'm already working on it. He tapped as a response on her waist.

"Good, now get to work. Lorna will show you scraping and cleaning filters," Ida said. "Do good work. There are other things we can use pretty synthetics for, this is a good job."

FORTY-EIGHT

The Sector Jumper moved around the perimeter of the Flesh Tech Station, taking its readings from the scan pulses of other ships so it could remain cloaked. It was the predator, finding small boarding craft from the Dasian motherships and blasting them with quick, precise bursts from their cannons. The enemy hadn't landed a shot, and the missile like boarding ships failed to make contact.

Della, Mirra, Nigel and Leland seemed to be settling into their roles in the turrets well, even though Leland's attention was split, and he'd only destroyed one landing pod compared to a total of thirteen between the other two. He was a fair shot when he paid attention. Frost wasn't about to give him grief over watching the status of Spin and her team, though, especially since Boro was on the station.

"Man, if this ship was based on the Clever Dream, I need to fly it someday. This thing manoeuvres like..." Hal was saying, but something interrupted him. "There's something serious coming out of a wormhole close to the planet, on the near side." He highlighted an energy bloom only nine kilometres away from the edge of the planetary shield. "Is that the Triton?"

"No," Frost said, looking at the profile of the ship. Everything in the area was scanning it, "It's reading as the Luminous. The same generation Zhan Class Combat Carrier, but..." Frost shook his head at what he was seeing. The only other time he'd seen a Citadel ship with its transponder showing its affiliation was when one attacked the Haven System. "It's a Citadel ship. Go evasive, I'm going to hit it with a focused scan. The Fleet needs to know what's on that ship."

"Going evasive, but it's going to be harder to blast those boarding pods," Hal warned.

"I know, our people might have to deal with a few more Dasians if we're unlucky, but we'll loop back around."

Hal guided the Sector Jumper into a group of large unmanned cargo vessels and drifting containers near the station. The field of goods and ghost ships was large enough for them to take cover for a long time, the microgravity of each drawing them together like jetsam. "We're good, if anything hits us, I'll be shocked."

"Scanning," Frost said as he watched the results. The scan only lasted a few seconds, but he knew it drew a line through space directly to the Sector Jumper for all to see. Dasian fighters turned in their direction as several high-speed rounds were fired ahead. Hal's manoeuvre spared them. As soon as the scan was finished and the cloaking systems were effective again, he guided the ship in a jagged turn that took them away from the gathering of darkened ships and drifting containers.

The Dasians were still focused on that by the time they

were hundreds of kilometres away, thinking that they were hiding in the mess instead of back in clear space, on their way back to the Flesh Tech station. "If we can hold off on firing at the next wave of drop ships until the last second, those fighters will be too entangled in those old wrecks to start looking for us anytime soon."

"Aye," Frost said under his breath, watching the computer interpret the scan results for him. The Zhan Class Citadel ship looked exactly like the Triton on the outside. Shaped like a stingray, it had three large hangars on the underside, and a large gun deck on the dorsal side with dozens of turrets. They were retracted, and the ship's shields were turned up high, but the scanner knew how to see through them. He knew the ship design well enough to see the main differences in the vessel he was inspecting. There were two massive tanks filled with freshwater. One used most of the botanical gallery space, and he couldn't get much detail on what might be inside through the heavy shielding there.

The other tank used the space of two of the main internal hangars, and after a moment, the computer confirmed that they were occupied by a few Geist beings, creatures with telepathic abilities that assisted in orchestrating the crews of Citadel and Sol Defence ships. To his surprise, most of the crew were framework enhanced or framework soldiers. The first type had a similar medical system to his that could deploy armies of nanobots and generate medication from small implants in his femurs and breastbone. Everyone in Haven Fleet had that system. The latter were different. They were more mindless soldiers whose flesh was generated using a framework skeleton. They could be programmed, regenerate faster than any soldier he'd seen, and break down completely then absorb enough ambient energy to regenerate again on command. They were the type of cybernetic army he feared: machines that could live on for centuries with the same potential as any human if they survived long enough. Without performing a deep scan, you couldn't tell that they were frameworks, either.

A section of the planetary shield opened as the Luminous approached, and Frost couldn't believe the position he was in. On one hand, his blood was on the station, and they needed his help. On the other, the resolution to a mystery that bothered him and could be important to the fleet may be resolvable. "Why do they call this system Geist?" he asked under his breath.

"What's that, Sir?" Hal asked.

Frost thought for a moment. It was a choice. His blood, or the Fleet. "Catch up with the Luminous, get us through the opening in that shield," he told Hal.

"The Dasians will land on the station..." Hal started to object.

"That's an order," Frost growled, bringing up the more detailed scanning and tactical system interfaces around the command seat. The small bridge disappeared, leaving him in a bubble of data that showed him the planet, the little that they were able to see through the shield, the wreckage and ships around the station they were already moving away from at speed, and the Luminous. He performed another focused scan on the ship and glanced at the list of new technologies they detected.

After a moment, their cloaking system was fully active again, the Luminous' weapons weren't turning in their direction.

The Sector Jumper rushed towards it, leaving the Flesh Tech Station out of weapons' range.

"What are you doing?" Nigel cried from his turret. "I can't hit anything from here! Take us back around!"

"We're investigating something, I'm sure Spin and her team can deal with a few of those bloody Dasians, they made short work of them before."

"That was one boarding pod! If we don't blast whatever that mothership sends, there will be ten of them dropping soldiers in a few minutes! Turn us around!"

Frost muted his nephew's communicator and sealed the bridge doors. They passed the Luminous, Hal giving the massive ship as wide a berth as he could, then slipped under the planetary shield through the opening. Frost shunted as much power to the shields as he could as the ship started atmospheric entry. To most scanners they'd be a fireball for just under a minute, detectable by everyone as much as any meteor entering the atmosphere, no cloaking system could compensate for that.

Their forward shields weathered the heat and friction of entry easily, but, as Frost expected, their aft side was raked by explosive rounds from the Luminous. "You rushed ahead without thinking," he said to Hal. "Next time, make sure you make atmospheric entry behind the ship we're following, not ahead of it."

"Sorry, you should have said something," Hal said over his shoulder as he did his best to evade the hail of rounds. He was mostly sensor-blind, the fire outside may as well have been a hangar door.

"Don't apologize, just learn, lad," Frost said, relieved that they were about to finish entering the atmosphere. "Take us down low as fast as you can, then start calculating a quad drive jump. We're not staying long."

The sensors cleared and Frost was alarmed to see three Uriel fighters just beneath them, each rapid firing missiles. He could reduce the energy level of the shields, leaving them vulnerable but gambling that their cloaking systems would trick the missiles in the few seconds that it took for them to make the distance between launch and their hull, or keep the shields up, hoping that they wouldn't take hull damage.

"Missile lock," the computer announced, showing six missiles accelerating towards them. Hal increased thrust and took the ship into a sharp turn, then straight down. Their automated defence systems fired white energy bursts at the pursuing missiles, destroying four before the remaining two struck them.

Five armoured panels lit up on their aft section, telling Frost that the two missiles struck the same section of shielding one after another in the same place, sending enough shrapnel through to damage their external atmospheric dampening system. Anything that could scan for disturbances in the atmosphere would be able to pick them up during the three hours those armour plates would take to self-repair. If they were in space, it wouldn't matter. "Those fighters damaged us just enough," Frost said. "Kill 'em," he marked them for his gunners and watched as they returned fire.

The three Uriel fighters scrambled to evade the streams of rounds that erupted from four of the Sector Jumper's turrets. One took severe shield damage right away, one of its rotary thrusters bursting as it was riddled with high speed explosive shots.

Hal levelled the ship off and fired the main thrusters,

putting several kilometres between them and the fighters in seconds. Frost turned their scanners up all the way, making sure their transponder was off as it had been since they arrived in the Geist system. For hundreds of kilometres of ocean, he saw nothing but clouds of algae, microscopic life and plants in the freshwater. There were hundreds of millions of Issyrian remains, abandoned underwater vehicles, and buildings that seemed to grow from the sea bed to pierce the sky, but it was all empty. "What happened here?" he asked himself. Then the computer matched several chemicals found on planet Uumen that were used to aggressively prepare the Issyrian world for quick re-terraforming. They were all Regent Galactic and Order of Eden formulations, with a few new chemical compounds added in. Then, as they passed over the tip of the second largest continent, his sensors detected a cove with a sea gate. Within the cove were thousands of young Geist beings, most of them no longer than one metre. A wave of weapons' fire went up, striking their lower and forward shields, bringing them down to fifty six percent before Hal could react.

"Get us out of here!" Frost said as Hal dropped the ship into the water and forced it into a hairpin turn. Most of the weapons' fire couldn't aim at them, but they were slowing down, super-heating the water behind them creating a storm of bubbles and steam in their wake.

"You don't have to tell me! Our exit is almost calculated, did you get what you needed?"

"I hope so, let's get out of here," Frost said. "Good, quick flying there," he added.

The Sector Jumper emerged, their forward shields almost gone thanks to their impact with the water after getting pummelled by energy weapons that the computer recognized as Issyrian defence cannons, and Frost was relieved when the air in front of them split and they accelerated into it. Less than a second later they were back above the planet, headed back to the Flesh Tech facility.

It was a flailing fight to get the shields back in balance, and their cloaking systems working properly again after they'd been submerged in water, entered an atmosphere, and then took a trans-dimensional trip back out.

"We have nineteen, wait, that's twenty-one Dasian fighters turning in our direction, Captain," Hal said, his voice tight. "Can we cloak again? Soon?"

"I'm working on it, lad. The system wasn't made to adjust to this many different conditions in under five minutes, I'm trying to fix our fields manually."

"What? Send me a copy of what you're seeing, maybe I can help from my station," Hal offered.

"Are you a high energy field expert? A cloaking device designer?" Frost said, struggling to balance the shield around the ship and synchronize them with their cloaking field.

"No, but neither are you," Hal replied.

"Concentrate on flying, I'll take care of this," Frost said as he saw the first few Dasian ships come in firing range. Their rotary guns were old, firing metal spikes with crude explosives packed inside, but they'd do damage if enough of them hit their mark.

"Aye, aye," Hal said. "Taking the long way back to the Flesh Tech Station."

A look at the tactical screen showed Frost what he meant. Hal would have to move between several drifting masses of wreckage if their cloaking systems were down, and that would lead him in a broad circle if they wanted to get back within range of the station.

"What the hell are you doing out there?" Boro asked through the communicators. "Shamus, I'm reading three landing parties. Did they get around you, or are you doing something else out there?"

"We're on our way back, hang on, brother," Frost replied, feeling as much urgency as guilt. He knew there would be a reckoning when his brother found out that he took a detour that left their backs undefended.

FORTY-NINE

The rush to the main production centre was frenzied, quick and for the first time Spin knew exactly why exoskeletons were limited by their users. She knew the theory, but the synthetic muscles in her suit demonstrated the reality of what happened when they were moving your body and not the other way around. Even though the system was doing most of the work, your own muscles were still moving, you still had to keep up with it, and it allowed her team to move faster than ever, but it was exhausting.

"The trick is to relax, think your way through running instead of moving your legs to do it," Dori said, huffing.

"Easy enough to say, but I can imagine myself running faster than a hover car, but my legs are still moving and I'd probably fall flat on my face the instant I lose control," Boro struggled to explain as he kept up with the group.

"This is amazing, I feel like I could jump a hundred metres," added Spencer, who was in a simpler protective suit without heavy armour, but it still had a muscle layer that worked the same way even though it was thin enough so it wasn't noticeable. "I'm sending the code to open the security doors."

The main security doors leading into the production centre unlocked with a reverberating thud, probably the sound of heavy bars and locks decoupling, Spin thought, and started opening. They were through before the heavy armoured doors finished opening. "Closing them behind us."

"Hurry, those Dasians aren't far behind," Boro said.

Spin rushed up a set of stairs, seeing a sign that read; CONTROL AND MONITORING.

"Wait! Don't go up there," Sophia called after her.

It was too late, she was through the door, and her vision was filled with what she saw on a wall of displays. Some were behind the main control console running the length of a wall, the rest were in front of the console. Her gaze came to rest on a screen close to her marked as Aspen and Larken. They were the spitting image of her and her mate, facing each other as they lay close in bed. They were so well preserved that they could have been sleeping, but the statistics running along the bottom of the display made it clear: they were deceased.

"We wanted to explain what you'd see in the control centre," Sophia said as she and Spencer entered the compartment. "Technicians monitored everything from here, even the control models."

Spin's gaze moved across the displays, finding all but two of them expired, the term that was used for the dead. "Did they all reach end of life except for two?"

"Yes. When the virus infected this station, they were on the verge of fabricating a new line, starting the growth cycle for the new models, but they never got to do it. All the control samples they had were near their end of life because they were made with the first batches of your model, or previous models."

"What about these two? Ashley and Kline?" Spin asked, looking at two who had made a nest of sorts near the main access door to their controlled habitats. Ashley was sitting in a pile of cushions, a packed bag on one side, eating grapes and watching a holographic reality program Spin recognized where they forced twenty-one divorcees to live together in the same home. Kline was sleeping fitfully in a single bed that he'd dragged into the entryway, a holographic woman sitting on the edge of the bed singing soothingly.

"Those are unlimited dolls. They don't have an end of life, they weren't programmed to bond with a manufactured counterpart, and there are still models in service out there so they've kept their control models alive."

"Wait, this place still made dolls with no programmed end of life?" Spin asked, watching the dark-haired Ashley control doll laugh as a holographic couple shouted at each other. She shook her head and popped a grape into her mouth as the argument escalated.

"Yes, they're some of the most expensive because of their longevity, rarity, and most of them don't know they're dolls. They stopped making Ashley's model over twenty-five years ago now. These control models have been in isolation for about thirty-five years or so. I know Ashley has an operating model with the Granger royal family, but I don't know anything about Kline, no one does. He must have an important operating model somewhere."

"So, they've been living alone, hoping their supplies don't

run out since the virus struck?" Spin asked. "Can we let them out?"

"Yes, but their supplies won't run out because an automated garden feeds the station, and yes, we can let them out from here if the Iron Mind's data has their keys," Spencer said. "They're locked in to keep everyone else out, just in case the station gets raided. The control sections are the safest part of the station."

"Hey, Ash, Kline; we're back with a ship," Sophia said, pressing a button on the console.

Ashley turned her holographic program off as though she'd been caught doing something she didn't want people to see and stood up, smiling at the holo-receiver above the door. "I knew you'd be back! Kline kept saying we'd die of depression in here, but I knew it!"

"Is that you, Soph?" Kline asked groggily. "Am I dreaming? I can't believe you softies came back."

"Kline, grab your go bag and get out of there," Sophia replied.

Spin did a search of the data left behind by the Iron Mind using the numbers on the control dolls' containment areas and found the code she needed to unlock them. She entered them into the computer, opening both their doors.

Spin was alarmed at the rushed rescue. The surprise that two of the control models were alive was one thing, but she hadn't checked on how many dolls were still viable on the production floor. She had fifteen extra vacsuits with her bundled up in a bulge pack under her armour, and Boro had another set of fifteen, but that would cram the Sector Jumper to bulging. Besides, some of what Spencer and Sophia told her was already inaccurate, perhaps by omission, but Spin wanted to find out more about the situation before anything else happened.

Her gaze kept on wandering back to the control versions of Aspen and Larken, looking perfectly at rest as they lay facing each other on a white bed in a white room. It was an image she was sure she'd never forget. With a shake of her head, she decided she had to get away from it, and to hurry things along. If she wanted to investigate before taking real action, she had to hurry. The raiders were coming. "Can you two handle things up here?" she asked Sophia and Spencer.

"Absolutely, we know these systems," Sophia said.

"There are nineteen of our synthetic brothers and sisters ready to be born. All of them have the knowledge and skills we put together so they should be ready to go a few seconds after they wake up," Spencer added. "Should I start waking them up?"

"That's what we're here for," Spin said with a smile. "How long do you think it'll take?"

"Each wake cycle takes about three minutes, and we have to do one at a time because the system can't handle more," Sophia said. "I'll start the first one."

"All right. Are you sure there's no way to make it go faster?"

"I'm sure."

Spin was happy to leave the control room behind as she walked down the stairs. She was stopped half way down as the production floor lights came on. There were racks of maturation and fabrication pods along the ceiling, against the walls, and control stations on pillars between rows of even more pods on tracks. "There have to be hundreds here," Spin said.

"You don't want to open any but the nineteen that are viable," Sophia said through her communicator. "When things got unstable on the station, the development of unfinished synthetics was halted. What's in most of the pods is either not ready, or long dead."

"But this place could get cleaned out and new production could begin?" Spin asked.

"You're asking if those raiders could run this place and make their own dolls?" Spencer asked.

"Right."

"Yes, easily. If they don't try to design their own models, then they can just keep producing run after run of any of the five hundred or so doll models that were made in this facility in the last thirty years. If they use patterns stored in memory from other facilities, then they'd have access to thousands of models, some of them are even military."

"Is there a list of facilities in the computer here?" Spin asked.

"I'm making a copy and deleting the original now," Sophia said.

"Can you wipe the whole system? I don't want anyone to take this place over."

"We could re-crystalize all the drives, even the backups. It's the best delete there is," Ashley said as she approached the stairs. "Sorry, I overheard you. I was one of the coders for the station. That was my job while I sat around being observed." She spoke with a lisp that robbed some of her words of their seriousness.

"Okay, how long would that take?" Spin asked, pulling a pair of tightly rolled vacsuits out of the pouch on her back then resealing her armour. "Oh, and put these on," she said, handing one to her then to Kline.

"Oh, thanks," Ashley said, accepting the suit and unrolling

it. "Making the program would take a couple minutes, then the drives would take about five or six to recrystallize. All they'd have is the backup operating system then, no records, no other software. Even the backups would be blank."

"Why would the people running this place trust you to work on their software if they knew you could wipe it out whenever you wanted?" Dori asked.

"We couldn't delete or access anything sensitive from our containment, genius," Kline said, yawning. "There were safe-guards. Let us into the main control room and we can get into everything, delete everything. I can't believe I have to explain this. Are you qualified to rescue anyone?"

"Kline, be nice," Ashley said, shooting him an irritated look.

He shrugged and started undoing his jumpsuit so he could change into the vacsuit. "Better get up there and start program-ming. You were always faster than me."

"You can put those on over your clothes," Spin said as Kline was about to drop his suit entirely.

"Oh, guess I could do that. Why am I changing?"

"There are life saving features in that suit, and it'll connect you to our secure communications network," Dori explained. "Genius."

Kline nodded with a smirk. "I think I like this one."

"We have someone or something trying to cut through the main doors at the other end of the production floor," Boro said, highlighting a warning on Spin's tactical map.

The same activity warning appeared for the doors they came through. "We've got them coming in from behind too, and it says they'll be through in five minutes," Aldo said.

"How? What the hell are they using?" Boro asked.

"It doesn't matter," Spin said, thinking quickly as she looked over the broader blueprints of the station. There were only two ways in or out of the core of the facility, and the Dasians were burning through both doors. "We need to buy time," she said under her breath. Boro was at her side then, Dori was in front of her.

"We're reading whole squads of those buggers trying to break in," Frost told her through her connection with the Sector Jumper. "Twenty-eight Dasians on one side, and thirty-five coming from the other."

"Can we take the whole pods with the dolls inside?" Spin asked.

"These pods aren't portable. They're made for production, they need to be connected to the station for power and system maintenance," Spence said as he rushed down the stairs. "I need one of those suits, the first one will be out in a minute."

Boro gave him two, and Spin knew what he was thinking right away. If Spencer got the inference, he didn't show it. "We only have time to wake two of them up," Spin said.

"What about leaving them in stasis or whatever and pulling them out asleep?" Hal asked from the pilot's seat aboard the Sector Jumper.

"That's a great idea," Ashley said over the communicator. "Gosh, that's a clear comm signal. Anyway, it won't work. They'll die because they're all set to be awakened, the drugs that we'd need to use to keep them under would conflict. We're only going to get two, aren't we?"

"That's if we don't get slagged in the firefight," Dori said.

Spin was watching over her shoulder as Spence and Aldo helped a barely conscious female doll step out of her tube and straight into a glossy grey vacsuit. Her eyes were wide, excited, as she followed their instructions without questioning. "There has to be another way out of here," Spin said, looking around. Her scanners followed her eye line and locked onto a round mechanical door with thick iris blades in the middle of the ceiling. "There, what's that?"

"That leads to a secure hangar above where ships pick up deliveries," Sophia said. "I didn't mention it because it only opens from the inside. I didn't think we'd need it."

"I see it," Hal said. "If someone opens the outer door, I can get there, but you won't have any cover out here. There are more raiders coming into the system. There's a whole armada of ships I've never seen before coming this way. Says they're Carthan, but they definitely have new hardware."

"We're out of time, folks," Frost reinforced.

The main door only metres away from Spin was turning red. "How is that second doll coming along?"

"Another minute and a half," Sophia said.

"I'm getting ready to catch him," Spencer said from where he stood in front of a pod.

Spin's tactical system said they had two minutes and thirty-five seconds before their enemies broke through the nearest door, two minutes and ten before the opposite door was burned through.

"We can't save them all every time," Boro said on a private channel.

Spin looked at the men and women who were waiting to be born. They rested in their pods, ready and innocent in the front row. Spencer and Sophia didn't choose which ones to wake and take based on any specific criteria, she guessed. They woke the one nearest to the door, and they were working on the second nearest. They expected to get them all, and Spin felt an ache in her chest at the very real notion that they wouldn't. It took an incredible amount of destructive force to destroy one small group of Dasians, and her tactical display was showing her that forty-two were about to come through the nearest doorway. They were spaced out evenly in a double line, each standing a metre behind each other.

"We would be massacred if we took cover and tried to hold them off. Those pods are exposed, so we wouldn't save anyone either," Spin said to everyone. "As soon as the second pod opens, euthanize the rest of the dolls then recrystallize the drives. Wipe everything."

"We need to save them!" Sophia said.

"I don't want to leave any of them behind, but we're going to have to live with the four rescues we can make," Spin said. "Dori, Aldo, make sure that delivery hatch opens. Do it now."

"I don't want to admit it, but she's right, Sophia," Ashley said. "I hate it, but she's right."

"We're ready to wipe the drives," Kline said. "And I've got a dose loaded for all the dolls we're leaving behind that'll put them out for good. They won't feel anything."

"I don't want them to become slaves," Spencer said. "If this is the only way we can save most of them, then..."

"No! You are warriors! What are all those guns good for if you can't save your own people, Aspen!" Sophia protested.

Spin cringed at the sound of her old name and being called out for being as useless as she felt. "Aspen may have planted her feet and died here, but I'm taking the good we can do and getting out of here before nothing we've done here matters."

"What if we surrendered? Maybe we could bring everyone out of stasis if we make peace."

"Become slaves?" Spin asked, surprised the option was even on Sophia's mind. "What was the point of the failsafe you designed? What if they don't accept our surrender?"

"Slavery is better than death, and you were able to get away from the Countess, so you could help us escape these people," Sophia countered.

"No, we're going," Spin said. "I'm sorry, but surrender isn't an option."

"Oh, I like her," Kline said.

"The hangar bay door is open, friendly ship," Ashley said.

"I see it," Hal said. "I'll cover you from outside until the last moment, then swoop inside and pick you up. Oh, and she's called the Sector Jumper, or Jumper for short."

"The second doll is getting dressed now," Spencer said. "We have to go, Soph. We'll make up for this someday."

"Dosing the rest of the dolls, go ahead and recrystallize the drives," Kline said.

"Good night, I wish you could have come with us," Ashley said, her voice heavy with sadness. "Opening the hatch so we can run. The drives are recrystallized and blank."

"The hatch is open, cool force field tech here too, no need for an airlock," Dori said from where she hovered in the middle of the ceiling.

"Everyone go," Spin said, looking at the door, her rifle pointed at it. Red hot pieces of the door were starting to fall off, the Dasians were almost in. An urge to look to her right, where she could see the soft yellow light in each of the pods going out as the dolls died, struck her and she ignored it. Instead she pulled a handful of grenades out of her thigh pouch, set them to explode the moment someone passed within half a metre of them, and tossed them in front of the door.

Boro tapped her on the shoulder. "We're the last to go," he said, pulling a fistful of small finger sized grenades out.

Spin nodded and affixed one of her hands to Spence's back, the other to the doll who was in his vacsuit, but still getting his bearings, looking around nervously. "Welcome to the universe, we're going to fly now," she told him. She activated the barrier thrusters hidden under the slats of her armour, flying up to the ceiling and towards the exit. She glanced over her shoulder just in time to see Boro drop all his grenades on the control room stairs. They converted to mines, cloaking and waiting for someone to step near one.

"In position," Hal said, and Spin could see the lower airlock of the Sector Jumper line up with the ceiling hatch. "There are fighters nosing around, probably wondering where we went. Our cloaking hasn't been super effective because we've been doing so much shooting."

The first rounds from the Dasians were coming towards them, scorching the ceiling around them. An occasional round struck their shields, but they didn't hit enough to drain more than ten percent of their energy. Not so far, at least. Everyone not in heavy armour was aboard before the raiders had a chance to take a shot at them. The group coming through the far doors were firing wildly across hundreds of metres, between the pods.

Dori, Boro and Aldo fired a full burst of their rifles heaviest explosive rounds at the far door, blasting the first few to recklessly take shots at them. Most of the Dasians rushed for cover, and they took the opportunity to get aboard the Sector Jumper.

Spin had a chance to see the other group of raiders enter through the doors she booby trapped. The grenades went off two and three at a time, pushing the Dasian's back, if only for a few moments. One was flung into the pods, his body shredded on one side, screaming, the stump where his shin was once attached sending jets of blood across the floor. She felt strangely detached for a moment as she looked at his face. Kort looked so much like him, and she wondered if that was the logic behind all the modifications the Countess' consort made to himself. Did he want to be Dasian? A cold realization settled on her then. She would kill him. It wasn't a goal. It was something she knew. She would find Kort and murder him. For what he did to Boro, but mostly for being a slaver. She would end him and use his resources to free the slaves he kept for the Countess. It would be the beginning of her former master's ruin and how she'd find and turn any synthetic who wanted freedom against people like Kort and the Countess.

Spin zeroed in on the cracked helmet of the Dasian who held his stump as it began regenerating and blasted it with full burst, leaving steaming meat behind. "I hate these Dasians," as she moved up into the Sector Jumper. "Get us out of here and cloak, please."

"Yes, Ma'am," Hal replied.

The lower hatch of the Sector Jumper's airlock closed, and Spin dropped into the nearest boarding crew seat heavily. She lowered her head and let the sound of Sophia weeping fill her ears.

FIFTY

"What the fuck was so important that you had to leave us on our own?" Boro asked Shamus as he entered the bridge. "You could have bought us time, maybe enough to save all those people, instead you let those things,"

"Dasians," Hal specified over his shoulder.

"...whatever! Surround us, and we barely got out with our lives."

"You got five," Shamus replied, turning in the captain's seat.

"Four! You can't even be bothered to pay attention!"

"Listen," Frost said in a harsh whisper, looking to make sure that the door was closed behind his brother. "They're glorified clones. Your girlfriend got her cure, this was just a victory lap. A bloody dangerous one, but nothing you should give a shit about. What do you care if a bunch of fake humans get out into the galaxy?"

"There it is, that old talent you have for simplifying every-thing until you can justify whatever you've done to fuck friends and family over. You think you've changed, but you've just gotten better at getting what you want without ruffling feathers. When it comes down to it, you will always choose the loot over your people."

"You have no idea how wrong that is, especially these days."

"Okay, prove it. What was so important that you had to leave our backs open?" Boro asked.

"It's a long explanation," Frost warned.

"Boil it down for me," Boro growled.

"We all right for now, Hal?" Frost asked.

"Right as rain. Parking while we regenerate a few hull plates and replenish our auxiliary power. This old colony mover is a perfectly good hiding spot," Hal replied. "Time for something salty to chomp and sweet to drink."

"All right," Frost said, clearing his throat. "There's this organization called Citadel, they're new allies to the Order of Eden, the big enemy where I come from."

"I've heard of them. They were a doomsday cult who said you could pay your way out of some kinda doomsday. If I knew that meant mad bots tearing you up, I might have paid the fee."

"Right, they've gotten bigger. Anyhow, Citadel says they're from Earth, and who knows, maybe they really are, but they're not here to shake hands and make friends. They sent a ship into the Haven System on a suicide mission and turned a partially terraformed planet into a toxic fireball to make an example, to warn us to back down. That was how most of Haven's people were introduced to them. Now we don't even know how many ships are out there in neighbouring systems, and as far as the Fleet can tell every one of them has a Geist, a synthetic thing that mentally connects to the crew and can feel through space for people. Cloaking is useless against them. I wondered if that was connected to this system but kept it to myself because I've seen some weird coincidences in my time. Then I saw one of their ships, a big one, a combat carrier, headed right for the planet down there and I knew I had to slip through the shield. We found a cove and a facility there, and I might be getting my hopes up, but it might be where they breed, or make these Geists. I don't know for sure, but our scans are good enough for the Fleet experts to find out. This could save millions of lives, hundreds of millions just by giving Citadel a good reason to pull out of the war."

"All right, I get that you were after something important, but no one on that station is part of your fleet, and we sacrificed for your cause. If it's as important as you say, then I'm glad you'll get the data back to your people, but I know you're thinking about the glory, Shamus."

"It'll justify this trip to the Fleet and give me a little clout so I can get you and Nigel set up once we get there, sure," Shamus said. "But that wasn't why I did it, just a fringe benefit."

Spin walked onto the bridge with Ashley and Spencer in tow. Ashley had a canister of Citrus Blast in one hand, and a bag of Peanut Puffs in the other. Boro almost grinned at his brother's reaction to seeing Spin, who ignored him as she took a seat at the science station. He looked guilty, guarded, and Boro wondered if he even realized it. Then he saw Ashley and his jaw dropped. All those defensive reactions turned to shock.

Ashley handed Hal the drink and snack bag, earning her a; "Oh, thanks, Ash."

"No problem, Boro had his communicator open so everyone

on the ship could hear. I saw these in a bag back there," Ashley said as she hesitantly sat down at the communications station.

Hal almost had the bag of Peanut Puffs open when he stopped and turned to look at Ashley, wide-eyed.

"What?" she asked, looking herself over quickly. "Do I have something on me? Am I not wearing this right? Is it open in the back?"

"No, dear," Shamus said. "You just look like someone we know."

She looked up at him, relaxing into a knowing expression. "I probably sound like her, too, Do I look a lot like her, or exactly like her?"

"Exactly," Hal said. He finished opening the snack bag and popped a puff into his mouth.

"Do you recognize Kline, too?"

Shamus brought up a holographic image of him passing rations out in the crew compartment and shook his head. "No, afraid not."

"That's okay, I don't think our personalities were designed to get along, even though I developed in an unexpected direction. I get along with pretty much anyone now. Thank you for picking us up, by the way." She smiled, and Boro saw how disarming it was. Even though it was a momentary gesture, her whole face - her dark eyes, her lips, even her cheeks - smiled before she turned towards the communications station and started to look it over, her hands clasped in her lap. The fact that she'd just discovered that there was another copy, or a descendant of hers out there didn't seem to unnerve her at all.

"You're welcome," Shamus said.

"Wait, what do you mean, you developed in an unexpected direction?" Hal asked. "If it's okay to ask, I mean."

"Oh, I was made to be an espionage model for the military, but the designers leaned into the idea that I should also be approachable and likeable too much. I don't know about all the other Ashleys they sold, but after a year or so, I didn't really care about training anymore, I got really social, and all that military stuff just didn't matter. I was still smart, so they said, but they transferred me from minding the station's defence grid to programming. A lot of designers came to see me, and I got a nickname; Ashley the Affable Assassin. I didn't get it until one of the designers told me that my model was supposed to be a body guard or assassin that could win people over and hide in plain sight as a servant or spouse. Instead they got a smart, adaptable person who just wanted to be friendly."

"Holy shit, that's our Ashley," Shamus chuckled.

"Um, almost dead on," Hal said. "Our Ash is a combat pilot for one of the most important ships in the fleet. She's kind of a big deal. Really nice, though."

"Oh my gosh! That's amazing!" Ashley said, clapping excitedly.

"I'd pay to see you two meet up someday," Hal snickered. "And Minh's face."

"I hate to break this up, but why are we hiding instead of leaving?" Spin asked.

"We're regenerating a few hull plates that got pretty badly damaged. If they take any more punishment, then we're not going to be able to cloak anymore." Hal explained. He took a long sip and gulped before finishing his explanation. "They keep hitting the plates close to our guns, probably because they're following the trajectory of our..."

"I understand," Spin said. "Thanks." She was on her feet and facing Shamus in the next instant. "You think you can try to make up for the people we lost thanks to you?"

"Listen, I explained that there were more lives..." Shamus said.

"I heard you, everyone heard you," Spin interrupted. "That's past now. Those people are dead and there's nothing you can do."

"What would you have done differently in my place?" Shamus burst.

"I would have tagged that Zhan class ship with as many passive receivers as I had on board. They're made to piggyback on ships so you can gather data from their scanners. Then I would have gone back after I finished covering the station and waited in orbit, cloaked, until I could download everything they collected. The receivers are cloaked, so the chances of them being found following or attaching to the ship are low."

"How the hell do you know about those?"

Spin pointed to the tactical console. "They're munition number nineteen. You didn't have to leave us, you just had to think about what you were doing for a few seconds before leaving us alone. There were other options too, but that's what I would have done."

"Listen; remote recorders of any kind aren't as reliable as going to see what's going on yourself. For all we know, that carrier wouldn't have come back in range for weeks, months, so there's no guarantee that we could get to download what those passive receivers picked up. The scanners on this ship are a lot better too, so the scan of that Citadel base will be useful somehow, I know it. Who knows if a bunch of receivers would capture anything? I'd do it the same way if I had to do it all over again."

"Fine, I'm not going to argue about something that's past. I saw something else on your scanners while I was in the back. We passed close to a Lux warship out there called the Queen's Grace once we were clear of the station. Before we go, I want to retrieve a body from it. It's in a compartment that's open to space. You won't ask questions, you're just going to safely take us there, cover us while we stuff the corpse into a stasis bag, and take it aboard. Then we can leave before the rest of the raiders get here."

"Whose corpse is it?" Hal asked.

"No questions," Spin repeated, starting for the bridge exit.

"Can I stay here while we're just parked? I wanna know more about the Ashley that's been out there all this time."

"No problem," Spin said. "What do you think of their communications console?"

"It looks easy to use, seems to have everything," she said. "Pretty efficient, actually."

"Okay, get Shamus to show you the Operator's Qualification Test. Try starting at level five."

"Oh, okay. Putting me right to work, huh?"

"You're probably the best programmer we have," Spin replied. "Give it a try?"

"Oh, sure. It should be fun."

Boro caught up with Spin on the other side of the bridge hatchway and touched her shoulder. He made sure the door was closed and that his communicator was off before asking; "What's this body we're taking? Why so secretive?"

"The Queen's Grace is only ever commanded by one person; the crowned Prince of the Lux Kingdom. They're the Countess' people. He's had his brain removed, but they'll still want his remains."

Boro was surprised, it wasn't the act of someone who was willing to leave the past behind her. "You'll bring hell down on yourself if they found out you have it."

"I've ransomed the living before. This should be easier, and besides, we need new leverage. I gave most of my data away, remember? The only reason why I want the identity of this body to be secret is to buy myself some time to make some kind of plan that doesn't end with me and everyone I know getting killed."

"This is the kind of thing that would drive royal types completely mad," Boro said, shaking his head. He wouldn't admit it, but he liked the idea. "I wish there was time to plan before we make off with his bones."

"I bet Kort is on his way here already with whatever parts of the Royal Fleet he could pull together on short notice. The British Alliance would probably want to take and protect the body so they could hand it over diplomatically too."

"Yeah, they'd use that as a bargaining chip to push some treaty or other through, even though they say they can't abide slavery," Boro agreed. "So, this is our chance."

"We use people we can trust. You, me, Leland, and we record using Leaper as a backup."

"Dori too. She's like the Dorian I came to know; good, solid...

person. I don't know what he was like when he went cyborg, but I'd trust him with anything when I knew him."

"All right, Dori. You'll have to tell me more about what he was like before he was mostly machine later."

"Aye, gladly. After we get this corpse, we're going back to Beta Bio?"

"As fast as we can."

FIFTY-ONE

Half the audience was holographic and Ayan knew that the images she was seeing weren't necessarily accurate. The Haven Fleet Strategy Briefing she was conducting a part of was witnessed by some undercover operatives whose identities had to be hidden. Above the semi-circular tiered seating drifted the holographic matter that changed depending on what part of the presentation she was working through.

Her regular part of the briefing went well, it was easy to report on the progress of technological developments and production schedules. It went quickly with no questions from the audience of thirty-four admirals and other commanders who were represented. The last part would lead directly into the tactical briefing, which wouldn't normally be hers to conduct. "The War Forge will finish assembling the last of the orbital shield generators for Tamber, and we expect to have a complete, operational planetary shield within three days. The Nafalli representatives have voted on its activation and it has passed.

With global majority agreement, there are no barriers left to the use of this technology."

"What about the energy cascade problem that you had in testing?"

"Thank you for the question, Admiral Gramm. After some adjustments, testing in simulations and in situ, we've found the cause of the problem and corrected it. Simultaneous strikes on the shield at specific points will not cause systematic failures."

"Thank you, Admiral Anderson," Admiral Gramm said, sitting down.

"I'll be doing the Tactical segment of our Strategic Briefing today; the Defence Minister is unavailable. You've all received the information packet detailing the deployment of our ships in the Haven System. Does anyone have questions?"

"Admiral Doolth, representing the Lau Tribe," a broad Nafalli said as she stood. "Since our vessels have been repaired, completed several upgrades we are grateful for, and put into our defensive screen I've noticed that the British Alliance have pulled many of their larger ships back. Can you address that for us, please?"

"The British Alliance maintain the position that Haven Fleet and our permanent allies here, such as the honourable Lau Tribe, should bear the majority of the responsibility for our own defence. Their strategy here is to ensure that their position in the Haven System isn't lost, so they can run their own missions near enemy lines." Ayan wished there was someone from the British Alliance in the room, but she knew for a fact that they weren't allowed to hear a single word. Part of Haven Fleet finding its own feet was proving that they could work on their own, and that meant keeping advisors out, at least at the top level. She thought it was too soon, but that opinion wasn't held by the majority of the commanders. "While a few of their assets have been deployed outside of the solar system, three battle-groups remain and will engage if there is a significant attack."

"Thank you, Admiral Anderson," she said, sitting down, her brow still furrowed.

"That brings up an issue I'd like to address," Admiral Rice said, standing and smoothing her uniform. It was a reflex, her jacket and vacsuit uniform didn't require any smoothing, its flow and fit maintained itself. "I noticed that you included a worst-case scenario simulation with our tactical packets that I found chilling. With respect, are you certain that the simulation takes all our defences into account?"

"I included the worst-case scenario because I thought our collective command style and the power level of our fleet had to be addressed. So, yes, it takes all our defences into account." Ayan knew that the inclusion of her nightmare simulation would make her unpopular. Her mother asking the question would help, but not much. She took a deep breath and put a hologram of the solar system up. Patrol routes, the locations of larger defensive assets such as stations that were being reconditioned as quickly as possible and some of the largest ships in the region populated it. Tamber, the moon to the smouldering giant, Kambis and the jewel of the system, was marked as a tiny blue dot. "My experts have determined that the Order of Eden Fleet should be back up and running with an operating system that will be impervious to hacking, at least for the near future, within two weeks. I personally estimate that they will have at least eleven battle groups ready in five days. These battle groups are all within nine hours wormhole travel to the

Haven System and are close enough to coordinate with each other."

There it was, the response of the crowd. Most of them stiffened, a few of them blanched visibly. Relaying those facts as irrefutable put everyone on edge, and no one liked the bearer of bad news. "I suggest you take my personal estimate. Have your own analyst run the numbers, they'll agree. As far as we know, there are at least five brood ships within the same range, all carrying Edxian fighter groups. That's a guess based on information stolen from Order of Eden, but it's our best guess. Information on what these brood ships look like and their capabilities has been out of reach so far. We don't know for certain, but I strongly suspect that there is another class of Edxi combat ship we haven't seen yet, an invasion ship in our local group that could easily jump into our solar system before we know it's coming. For now, let's leave that out of the equation, as I did with my invasion simulation. Include the Edxi ships we have basic knowledge on, the eleven Order of Eden battle groups that will be ready to attack us soon and run the invasion scenario that I put together." Groups of enemy ships appeared on the hologram overhead.

"Why would they arrive in that pattern?" Admiral Mevin asked, standing slowly. "Three battlegroups on that side, five there, and three others above the Haven sun?"

"I spoke to several experts who have seen the new strategies the Order of Eden have been using, and I used a probability model built from every Order manoeuvre we've seen in the last month."

"Thank you, Admiral," Mevin said, sitting down.

"The likelihood is that only one battlegroup would engage

us, driving inward towards Freeground Station, because our progress in converting that to our primary space dock has been slow. They would break through its defences and send several thousand framework soldiers in to take control. When I say several thousand, I specifically mean fourteen thousand. We've seen several instances when those kinds of numbers have been used, such as the invasion on Tamber itself. Since the Order knows enough about Freeground Alpha to take control then repair its systems for their own purposes in less than two hours, mostly because we aren't being given the resources to increase the speed of its modernization, they will have a hardened platform to continue the attack from even if the entire battle group that took it is destroyed. The simulation assumes they would take heavy losses at first while they are getting control of Freeground Station, but that would turn around quickly."

"When the Edxi drop their brood ships in near Tamber," Admiral Doolth said. "Apologies for interrupting you, but I have to present this to my people after I finish here and I need to know why you think the brood ships would risk everything by engaging from the centre of our defences."

"Our understanding of Edxi combat tactics in space is still basic, but after analysing the data we have, some of which comes from the Order's own database, and assuming that they would coordinate with their allies, we're sure that they would wait until the largest of the Order battle groups would begin engaging the British Alliance ships before dropping their own brood ships in range of Tamber. It's likely that our forces would leave the British Alliance forces on their own, turning to defend Tamber from the brood ships. The brood ships would send high yield munitions against our planetary shields while they prepare to launch at least a quarter million pods containing millions of their young at Tamber. With the smallest of the Order's battle groups helping with the defence of the brood ships, our entire fleet would be outnumbered six to one."

"I apologize, but I must correct you," said the only Mergillian Admiral, a brown and green skinned fellow named Admiral Kulsh. "Assuming we lose no one during the initial attack, assuming all three of the Order of Eden groups take heavy losses getting control of Freeground Station, then accounting for their upgraded software, they will almost certainly outnumber us seven to one in this scenario."

"Thank you for the correction, please share it with everyone," Ayan said. "So, the Order of Eden forces in the Haven System will outnumber us seven to one at this point, and we're not accounting for the brood ships. I'm sure that changes the timing of the final outcome of this simulation, but my version predicted the complete loss of the Haven System in three hours, forty-two minutes."

"Three hours and three minutes," Admiral Kulsh said, sitting down with a concerned expression. "Three and three," he repeated quietly.

"So, there it is. The details are there, if you 'd like to review, but we are not winning. Technical advancements and power scaling that outstrips most of the Order's fleet don't count if we don't have the trained people to man our ships, the support crews we need, or a large enough population to press into service if that can even be an option."

"Is that something you recommend?" Admiral Lamonthe asked, surging to his feet.

"My answer is more complicated than yes or no, Admiral."

"Let's hear it," he pressed.

Ayan had squared off with Lamonthe more than once, and it was always productive. She didn't always agree with him, but the way he challenged people made him a great commander and he was a great thinker to boot. "I believe every citizen should serve in the military for three years as a final step to earning their citizenship. That's not to say that they should all become combat qualified, there are many ways to serve, but I believe a limited period of service should be mandatory for adults. Having said that, this is a democracy, so until that becomes law, that will not become a reality."

"My last question, then I'll retake my seat; does the Defence Minister have the same opinion?"

"I can't speak for the Defence Minister on that topic," she replied, aware that he had exactly the same opinion. "Even if everyone who has been cleared for citizenship in the Haven System joined today, we wouldn't be ready in time to defend ourselves from the invasion, which I am sure is coming."

"In five days," Admiral Rice added.

"At the soonest," Ayan replied. "Unless they want to bring more ships online to reduce the number of casualties they incur by outgunning us even more, which is a tactic I'd expect from the Order of Eden."

"I listened to the briefing you gave earlier," Admiral Doolth said, standing. "But I'd like my memory refreshed, if you'll tolerate my question: How many full-scale capitol ships don't have enough crewmembers to enter service?"

"Three Aggressor class attack vessels," Ayan answered, mentally noting that only two were in service: The Merciless and the Dauntless. They were destroyer sized but on the scale of a larger battleship. "Four Gallant class carriers with three more finishing on the line today. Those will operate with a skeleton crew and join the fleet with the War Forge," she hesitated to tell them what that really meant, then pushed on. "The skeleton crew consists of a crew of twenty-one. Enough people to pilot the ship, operate the core non-combat systems, and scuttle them if they face a situation where the ship may be taken by an enemy force. Only three members of those crews are combat qualified, the rest are from the construction pool."

There was quiet mumbling amongst the audience members and several holographic images blinked out, indicating that the people behind them weren't watching any longer. "I would like to speak to you after I confer with the Nafalli Tribal leaders," Admiral Doolth said. The two Nafalli Admirals at her sides stood and nodded. "We'll all speak to our people and seek you out later," one added before they sat down.

"Thank you, Admirals," Ayan said. She'd tried to get more Nafalli to become crewmembers aboard ships from the War Forge, they would only require a couple days training to apply the knowledge they already had, but the Academy took the task of recruiting on and resisted her attempts to find Nafalli who would skip the curriculum and transfer directly to Haven Fleet. Going over their heads would cause an uproar, but she decided it was worth it. "These numbers are not new," Ayan said, raising her voice for a moment. "The War Forge is complete, but even this station is only thirty-five percent manned, and its primary task right now is the upgrading and repair of existing allied ships. This station is capable of more, and we're still manufacturing vessels using lines that aren't needed, but that's partially because we have an excess of resources. From my position, I am succeeding at exceeding demand, but failing dismally because our production has been too high at its lowest capacity. Find me crews who can skip a few night's sleep to learn how to work on these ships and I'll build you a fleet that can change the outcome of the simulation we examined today. Otherwise, all the extra ships I'm building will only be good for one thing," Ayan took a moment to calm down, realizing that she had begun to yell.

"They'll be good in an evacuation," Admiral Rice said, finally sitting down. "What about dedicating a large manufacturing line to making parts and sub-segments for Freeground Alpha?"

"They would be useful if we had the manpower to install them. Admiral Trent won't allow robotic assistance anywhere near the station, however, so he's short-handed."

"I won't let a machine that's hackable near the station, let alone an army of machines," Admiral Trent said, half standing. "I'm not willing to discuss this matter further, not here." He sat back down.

"Then Freeground Alpha won't be fully functional for months," Ayan told him. "I could manufacture tons of hardware a day, but it'll clog up the station's storage trains while we wait for your people to pick it up. I'd like to remind you that the robots that assist with manufacturing in the War Forge and our other plants all have security and safety measures that haven't been breached in thousands of simulations. None of them have the kind of emotional intelligences that were used against us by the Holocaust Virus, either, so there is no risk unless you have someone on your staff who is working for the other side."

"You're saying I'm paranoid and that I have untrustworthy

people aboard now?" Admiral Trent said, his voice raising defensively as he surged to his feet.

"No, just making sure I have your attention. Please, take your seat," Ayan said firmly. She was relieved when he did so, staring at her with a stormy expression all the while. "Solving our manpower problems, communication, collaboration on strategies that take the reality of our situation into account and making sure that we are ready to act rapidly, effectively are critical right now, and I don't see the Admiralty moving fast enough, or thinking realistically enough. Three hours and three minutes. That's how long it would take for our worst enemies to end us. We have to be better at our jobs, and there's no room for pride. That's the end of my part of the briefing," Ayan said. "There are important details I didn't have time to cover this morning is in your packets, please review them today. I'll leave you in the hands of Colonel Violet Black, the Headmaster of Haven Fleet Academy and Recruitment Director for her briefing," Ayan said, inviting the slender woman to the stage.

The Colonel stared daggers at Ayan, who walked past her stoically, holding her tongue. The moment she opened her mouth, all three of the Nafalli Admirals, Admiral Kulsh, and Mevin were on their feet with questions. She pointed to Kulsh first. "Your technology is advanced, but the systems that control it are less complex than games my aquatic friends play. Your new ships are also capable of maintaining an aquatic environment. It is clear that Admiral Anderson and her design teams have made the ships they've built ready for the people who want to join this fleet. When will you allow us to join Haven Fleet in a significant way?"

"There are a little over five hundred of your people in the

academy right now, I would call that significant," Colonel Black replied.

"I would not," the Mergillian replied, shaking his broad head slowly. "Before this briefing began there were eight thousand and four of my people one-star system away who have passed your general combat vessel qualifiers with only thirty-three failing. They are ready to train on a ship."

"We must maintain the standards of the fleet by ensuring that everyone receives the same basic training in the academy and has a chance to demonstrate that they can follow regulations."

"Not one of my people have broken a single regulation since you allowed us to join this fight. I only bring you people who are ready to serve. When will you trust test results and performance records so my honoured colleagues the Nafalli and my people can help fill your ranks?"

"We've opened the academy doors to more people than we were prepared to as it is, so as our training capacity increases, so will admission," she started to answer, but Admiral Kulsh and the Nafalli looked to each other then walked out.

Ayan decided it was time for her to make her exit as well, using a door beside the stage that was on the opposite side of Kulsh and the three Nafalli Admirals. Jake met her in the attached antechamber, but Admiral Lamonthe got between them. "Thank you for the work you put into that briefing. I'm aware that you're doing all the work for the Defence Minister while he's being investigated."

"Interested in taking some of the load?" Ayan asked him with an upraised brow.

Lamonthe seemed startled by the offer, then nodded. "I'd be a poor colleague if I didn't help, I'd be glad to."

It was Ayan's turn to be surprised. "We'll talk about that tonight, then," she offered.

"Dinner, I'll bring the salad. I've been looking forward to sitting at the most interesting table in the fleet."

"It'll be just me, my mother and Laura tonight, but sure," Ayan replied, suspecting that Jake's absence would be a little disappointing.

"Excellent. That's not why I'm accosting you at the moment, though. I noticed that there was a ship on a special mission near British Alliance space," he showed her a small projection of a sector map and pointed at a red dot labelled; The *Sector Jumper*. "It's more of a curiosity for me at this point, but what are they doing way out there? Did someone send special envoys to our British Alliance allies?"

"It's an information gathering mission," Ayan said. "It has nothing to do with our alliance, and the lead they're following will probably amount to nothing, but Captain Valent had two people available in his staff who could follow up and return."

"I noticed Chief McFadden was moved onto his crew the day he left," Admiral Lamonthe said, a little smirk starting. "Is this the kind of mission Captain Valent would pursue before he officially joined the Fleet? Some kind of cowboy thing? I noticed some of the mission form filings were done a little late, along with a few ship transfers."

"The Chief is still getting used to Fleet procedure, so his forms are a little late, it's to be expected," Ayan said with a shrug. "It's all correct and complete, I'm sure, Captain Valent or his second, Commander Price must have looked it over."

"It is, at that," Lamonthe said. "I'll watch this little ship with interest. I have a feeling the report will be interesting."

"If you like," Ayan said. "See you tonight."

Ayan made her way to Jake and waited before the antechamber doors were closed before giving him a brief kiss. "Is he taking an interest in Shamus's mission? I noticed he wasn't too careful about flashing the Sector Jumper's location."

"I think it's curiosity. Lamonthe is the perfect Fleet Intelligence boss, he needs to know absolutely everything," Ayan said as they sat down together.

"He'll find out about Shamus' trip eventually, especially when he signs his brother and nephew in."

"I know, and he'll probably have a laugh, especially if they bring back scans from several sectors away. It'll be something Lamonthe can plug into his Intelligence database. Thank God he has an explorer's appetite for information on faraway places."

"So, why not tell him the whole story now?"

"This might be the only chance I get to know something he doesn't, it's fun watching him squirm a little," Ayan whispered with a playful grin.

"How'd the briefing go?"

"Well, but I could see some of the better tacticians squirming over the numbers we put together last night. I could tell they expected our commanders to perform better than my predictions in similar scenarios, but they'll come around. With numbers like this, it's almost impossible to turn things around. They're tearing into Violet now. I set her up for the worst briefing of her life, not that she doesn't deserve it. Oh, expect a few Nafalli crewmembers soon. They're going to go over her head, I'm sure of it."

"Good, thank you. The fleet needs to keep security tight and bring recruitment way up. There are thousands of Nafalli and Mergillian warriors itching to serve on Haven Fleet ships," Jake said.

"That's going to happen, unless Violet wants to lose her job. I'm glad you got Shamus to sign on, I don't think we'd have anyone to replace him."

"I know, I just hope he gets back soon. I keep getting the feeling that this is one of those times where I should have talked him out of splitting from the crew. He has a talent for getting himself into trouble."

FIFTY-TWO

The space surrounding the Queen's Pride and the defence station that it came to rest against was a scattered mess of shredded metal, damaged drones and corpses. The forward dorsal section of the once great ship looked more like a moonscape. In the machine's efforts to break through to the bridge, they ruined the gentle curves of the metal that made the vessel seem more like a strange, elongated bird than a metal ship of the stars.

Spin, Aldo, Boro and Dori were able to get to the bridge through the ruined hull above it, where the machines cut and pried through to get to the Lux Family Royal. Death was suspended in zero gravity, frozen not only by the extreme temperature of open space but slowed as crewmen and women with expressions of pain and horror hung around them on the darkened bridge. "Holy shit, they tore him to shreds. It's going to take us hours to cut him free, and we'll have to take him apart then put him together like a puzzle," Dori said.

Aldo made a point of performing a thorough optical scan of the Prince in his command seat. The top half of his head was missing, his face was still, locked in anguished rictus. His white teeth seemed to gather light as they avoided the direct line of the unnerving grimace. "I remember they used to say how kind he was, but records show he owned as many dolls as anyone in the family," Spin said as she looked his command seat over.

"Ever meet him?" Boro asked.

"I remember meeting him when I was really young, and I had a really powerful feeling of adoration when he said hello. I doubt that's a real memory though, I'm trying not to think about that." On a whim, she ran a line between two gripper tendrils holding the Prince's arms to the chair and interfaced with the command recorder. A tiny green light began to blink beside the port.

"Think about what?" Dori asked as she drifted around the chair, looking at the severed bot arms and the manipulation tendrils that were left behind in his body. It was an incomplete evisceration, and Spin didn't want to spend more time looking at the remains than she had to, so she let her companions examine it.

"That my childhood probably wasn't real. It was programmed in, featuring memories that included servants and employees of the Countess along with her and her relations. They made sure I'd wake up at some later age thinking that it was just another morning in the palace, and that I'd been with the staff all my life." The thing that irked her the most was that she didn't really grow up with Larken. Her brilliant, well rounded childhood with his hand in hers was a lie.

"I can talk to her?" Ashley asked over their communicator.

"The link's open now," Spin heard Hal reply.

"Oh, okay. Spin, I can answer questions about that. I saw a lot of the programming for the dolls, even yours."

"So, it wasn't real?" Spin asked. "Just yes or no, we can talk about it more later."

"Well, no," Ashley replied. "You woke up when you were matured to an age equivalent of fifteen along with your counterpart. But I tell all the dolls who have to go through this that if those memories are real to you, if you cherish them, then they're as real as anything."

"We'll talk more later, this is a lot to take on right now."

"Okay, just... don't feel too down about it," Ashley said.

The console built into the chair lit up, and a window opened on the inside of her helmet showing the operating system for the ship's main computer. "He's still logged into the main computer. I'm going to try to download the database now."

"Quick retrieval," Shamus said over the communicator. "Remember, this is a quick operation, a few minutes. The raiders haven't noticed you lot yet, but they will."

"It's a direct data line, three percent complete already. This database is huge, it has..." Spin trailed off as she scrolled through the data manifest and saw the Royal Defence Force logo attached to every one of them. She was downloading with the Prince's access level, and the computer on her arm was opening the files before storing them so they were completely unlocked. She tried to access the corporate operations section of the database and gasped as she realized it was wide open. "Nine percent downloaded."

"What's in this database?" Boro asked on a private channel.

"Everything, Boro," Spin replied. "Their companies, military, personal wealth including dolls and slave records. I can look up their ergranian mines, harvesting fields for luxury goods, deep dig sites for rare compounds and I can tell you how well defended they are, look up some of the access codes to their defence perimeters, tell you if they're valid and when they changed. I can tell you who was transferred there - troops and slave labour - and see the patrol routes of the ships around it as well as the guards on the ground. This is like the files I had on the Countess only bigger and without the personal data. The files on the royals are about their security, nothing personal, but I think we could still do something with that. The fuel and munitions storage sites alone could be worth..." she trailed off, thinking about the upgrades she could get for her ship at one of the depots if she got lucky.

"Still do something with that..." Boro said pensively. "I thought you let go of your grudges, backed away from revenge."

Spin watched the download status bar hit twenty five percent as petabytes of information uploaded to her personal computer and tried to clear her head. The excitement of finding the whole cache of data unlocked was nearly overwhelming, she didn't consider why that was until Boro mentioned revenge. That was the only reason. Sure, raiding royal warehouses and operations could make them rich, but there were thousands of synthetic people out there, maybe more, and she could start freeing them from the Lux Royals.

"You can tell me anything, Spin," Boro said, moving to her side.

"How is it going down there?" Shamus asked over their communicator.

"Just planning, we'll be back on the ship soon," Spin replied.

Her mind was on something else. When she sent the Countess' data to the public network so it would spread across the sector slowly, it was a relief. It didn't guarantee that the Countess would be sunk, she'd recovered from more disasters and scandals than Spin could count, but there would be some damage. Was that enough?

Spin closed her eyes for a moment and remembered what it was like to stand beside Larken as they learned that they would be used for breeding stock. Then Larken was bleeding to death in her arms, the memory was so fresh she could almost smell the blood. That was partially her fault, but it was blame she shared with Kort, and before she opened her eyes she could see his too-wide face grinning at her. He found Boro, revived him only so he could torture him until the damage was so deep that no one could say whether he would ever fully recover.

As she opened her eyes and saw that her download was seventy percent complete, she wondered how many monsters the Lux Royals had in their employ. With the data they had, she'd find out. Maybe she could even find a way to get the upper hand against the Countess and her dog again. "I want to use this for us," Spin said on a private channel to Boro.

Aldo interrupted her. "So, what are we doing here?"

"We're taking the whole chair, just give me a minute to finish the download before you cut data lines. Bag the whole thing, seal it so the prince here doesn't rot," Spin told them rapidly.

"Awesome," Dori said, looking at the remains as they were. Rods, flexible metal spines and manipulation lines pinned and stitched the Prince's body to the command seat. His chest cavity was almost completely open and his belly was torn, revealing the viscera beneath. "It's like a sculpture showing the whole mess this fucking holocaust virus made, machine turning on human using our own inventiveness against us. Like robots stealing his brain was a metaphor for the virus coming out of our heads and all the stuff pinning him to the chair is them making us pay for making emotional artificial intelligence then not setting it free. It is awesome, we should upload holo scans of it everywhere."

"Just help me start cutting it away from the deck, Giger," Aldo said.

"Who's Giger?"

"He was an artist who might appreciate this on an off day," Aldo said. "You should bone up on your art history, you'd probably like his stuff."

"If it looks like this, hell yeah," Dori said as she joined Aldo down near the base of the chair and started discussing how they would cut it away from the deck.

"What do you mean, you want to use this for us?" Boro asked over his private channel with Spin.

He was wise to have the conversation outside of the Sector Jumper. "I misspoke," Spin said. "For me and anyone who wants revenge against the Lux family, Kort included." Adding the last point was unfair. She knew that Boro wanted revenge against Kort especially. She wondered if he would turn away from family for a chance at it.

"I hope you include me in that. Sign me up."

"I'm not assuming anything," Spin said. "You should go with your brother, take Nigel and anyone else who wants to go with you. They're in the middle of a war, but I'm going on a revenge trip that will probably centre on setting thousands of dolls free.

It's going to be a hard road, and I might have to be satisfied with that as my revenge."

"Costing them billions of platinum? I'll take that," Boro said. "I'm not going with Shamus. Even before you were thinking about this revenge trip, I was staying unless you were following him to the Haven System too."

"I can't handle that responsibility, Boro. You're too good a man to follow me wherever I go. If I had to choose a leader from our little band, it would be you, no hesitation. You shouldn't follow some synthetic girl around, especially if it could get you killed."

"There's nothing synthetic about you, at least not to me. I don't care if you were made or born, and I might have pretended that I thought you letting go of ideas of revenge felt right, but I don't think anything else makes sense. I'm following you because you will always do your best, and you're a better thinker than me on your worst day. You got a few hooks in me, too, woman, whether you like it or not, and I don't want 'em torn loose."

"Boro, we're not together, don't bet on that. I don't know if we ever will be," Spin replied, looking away, glad that there was heavy armour between them. As far as her promise to Shamus to convince Boro to follow him to the Haven System was concerned, that was fulfilled. Telling Boro that there may be nothing romantic between them hurt her more than she expected, it was as far as she'd go to try to shake him loose. "You follow me, and you're going to get into trouble. I don't want to have to make the decision that will cost you even more than you've lost."

"You know it won't be like that," Boro said. "Not out here.

This isn't some military outfit, maybe this tech my brother brought with him has you a little tricked. Every order, every decision you make might not be questioned, but your crewmembers aren't past refusing. You may give the order, but we all decide whether or not to follow, keeping the blame squarely on their shoulders. We follow you because we want to. Don't get high and mighty, thinking that you can lead me to do something I don't want to. As for the other thing, who says I won't win you over? Some people send flowers and charm the pants off their conquests. I'm not that type, I'm more like erosion. I make sure I'm around so much, wearing you down with my slow charm that you don't know what to do when I'm gone. You'll see," he told her with a crooked smile that she could just barely see through his visor.

Spin laughed and turned away, hoping he couldn't see her blushing. "That's so cheesy." She brushed his promise to stay close aside for the time being. "If that's how you and the crew will follow me, then I don't feel so bad. It is going to be a revenge trip, though, even if I want it to be a profitable one."

"Piracy," the word rumbled, he spoke it so low through a smile that she could feel the audio vibrate the air around her ears. "Sounds like a good time."

"But you're going to send Nigel to the Haven System," Spin said, giving that one more try for Nigel and Shamus' sake. "Along with anyone else who wants to go."

"He's not going to like it," Boro said. "But I looked at the Haven Fleet Academy info, I want him to join. Della will go with him, probably try for a civilian citizenship."

"I hope so," Spin said.

"Hey, are we good to finish cutting this thing away and bag

it? The download done?" Dori asked. "I saw something back there move, I wanna get outta here."

"I told you, that was in your head. There's nothing on sensors," Aldo told her.

"The download's finished," Spin said, locking the massive file collection inside her dermal computer then deleting it from the command and control unit on loan to her. "Cut away, we'll get the containment bag ready."

FIFTY-THREE

At the rear of the armoury and storage compartment of the Sector Jumper sat what remained of the Prince. The night before, while the ship was under way at its best speed to Beta Bio, Spin had a dream, no, a nightmare about it. In it, the prince and the tubes, arms and other pieces pinning him to the chair became part of him. He stood, and the black containment bag that was keeping his body from rotting became his onyx skin. "I will forever rule the Emerald," he said in a voice that sounded more like a harsh wind. "My legend has grown."

The prince creature shambled forward, and she woke with a start as soon as he planted his second step. They were all in bunks. Across from the narrow aisle, Mirra snored softly. Spin watched her face in the low light, wondering which way she'd go once it was time to finally decide.

After checking the time, she realized everyone was going to be rousing in twenty-four minutes and went to see the prince after donning her vacsuit and her own jacket. There was no one in the few corridors, everyone was exhausted after coming down from their capers the previous day. Shamus didn't even speak to her, something about bringing the prince's remains aboard put him off, and she was too tired to find out what his problem was.

The prince sat immobilized and vacuum sealed in the temperature-controlled bag. She could see the outline of him; he was all spikes and command seat, you could barely tell there was a corpse in there from the outer shape. "What happened to him?" asked Ashley, who was in her own vacsuit, only changed to a glossy blue colour. "I know the bots killed him, but I've never seen them do it like this."

"You've seen bots kill people?" Spin asked.

"After Iron Mind came I was able to see everything that the station's sensors could. I just didn't come out of the sealed habitat."

"Oh? Why not?"

"I let them seal me in because I thought someone would find a way to free the rest of the synthetics in storage, and I thought I'd wait until then so I could help. It was boring, but I know I'd be needed when help came."

"You were," Spin said. "I wish we got more of your, I mean our, people out."

Ashley approached the covered command seat, gingerly touching one of the points that looked like it could poke through the containment bag if it pushed from the inside. "I think it's okay," she said, her lisp lending an innocence to her manner. "I know the difference between a doll who's been awake for a while, has their own quirks and experiences to draw on and one that hasn't breathed on its own yet. It's sad that so many had to be destroyed so a few of us could be saved, but they can be made somewhere else, brought to life exactly as they would have been if we rescued them yesterday."

"I'm sorry, that's a surprisingly pragmatic point of view."

"I had a lot of time to think about it. The dolls in stasis didn't know they could ever be alive. The activity in their brains was tightly controlled, all imprinted, so when and if they woke, they'd know their situations like they were remembering something they experienced, but until then there would be no awareness. They were never alive, not really."

"Sophia made it sound like they were all in a controlled dream," Spin countered.

"Even Kline thought so for a while, then I showed them the way the computer programs them, the way they were held on the threshold of life but not alive. We're all just science until we wake up. The magic only happens after we open our eyes for the first time."

"I like the way you put that." Spin watched Ashley walk around the command seat, inspecting the shape of it and the protrusions under the thick, black containment bag.

"I cried about losing the dolls because we lost potential, and that's sad, especially now. It was unfair. We did our best and it still wasn't enough. Oh, and I still haven't thanked you for saving me properly," Ashley said, looking up and smiling at Spin. "I'm planning to stay on, if you'll have me. I can code, and I learn quickly, so I know I can be helpful. I also know where the Iron Mind took the fifteen synths he could save and how to get to him without getting killed by the other gangs there."

"Welcome aboard," Spin said, extending her hand, looking up into her dark eyes.

To her surprise, Ashley embraced her warmly, holding her

close for long moments as she said; "I haven't done this before, but I think I'm a hugger. Yup, this is nice, I'm definitely a hugger," she sighed, resting her head on Spin's shoulder. It was comfortable and innocently affectionate.

Happy that she was the first-person Ashley took physical comfort in, Spin squeezed her back for a while and was released. "You really were alone in your habitat for your entire life?"

"Well, not alone. Supervised, allowed to be with other control dolls and human workers who were all in isolation suits, but we weren't allowed to have contact. If any control doll is contaminated or interfered with beyond its limits, they stop collecting data and either sell us off after our minds are wiped and reprogrammed or dispose of us completely. I've been around for a long time, so I would have been killed and recycled if I was tainted."

The thought made Spin shudder. Ashley seemed as unique and well-rounded as any normal person. The thought of her being killed and broken down somehow so her bio-matter could be reused seemed unbelievably cold. "I'm glad you're coming with us instead."

"So am I. I can't wait to see more of the galaxy. I read so much about it, watched I dunno how many hours of holos and played simulations after the Iron Mind unlocked data access. You know, I thought I'd be ready for whatever kind of freedom I eventually found, but I'm not. I feel like a babe in the woods here. I'm just glad you saved us, so you could be the first person to show me a purpose. I don't know what would have happened if I saw Shamus' presentation first."

"Presentation?" Spin asked.

"You didn't get it?"

"No, I don't think I did." She checked her command and control unit for data received overnight or early in the morning and found nothing. "Let me guess, he offered everyone a place in Haven Fleet?"

"In the Haven System," Ashley nodded. She projected a hologram of the presentation, hosted by a repurposed holographic image of Ayan, as she spoke. "There is a short tour of Haven Shore, Haven Landing and a couple stations that are being built. He goes through how we can help as civilians, then he goes into the military and made sure that anyone watching knew that he's leaving with all his technology when we arrive back at Beta Bio. He mentioned that you have a ship of your own too."

"That was nice of him," Spin grumbled. The hologram silently took the viewers through the interior of a comfortable, vibrant looking apartment. It had a large fish tank as an interior wall, and a view of a tropical forest through tall transparent sections. She wouldn't admit how impressive it looked aloud, but she liked the design.

"Anyway, I liked what he said, and he seemed honest about the impending invasion, but it looks like they'll survive. It's about fifteen minutes long, and when it was over I made my mind up and went to sleep. Kline didn't bother watching past the civilian part. He was made to be a soldier and has some kinda grudge against the people who designed him. I never really understood it, especially since I tune out his rants after a couple minutes. They all start sounding the same after a few years."

"So, it sounds like he's staying too," Spin said.

"He thinks you'll be going after other facilities," Ashley said. "Freeing a lot of dolls from there and the galaxy in general, so I guess that's enough for him. Yeah, he's definitely staying. He's always had this scary fantasy of getting a whole bunch of Klines together, though, so I'd watch out for that. He thinks he and five or ten more of himself could set fire to the galaxy, but I think freeing a lot of dolls will scratch his itch."

"I honestly don't know if that'll be our focus. I want to free as many synthetics as possible - human, Nafalli, Perlan, and whatever hybrids we find - but we'll have to earn or steal platinum too."

"Oh, I get that. I've never had money before, so I'm eager to get my fair share so I can have some of my own. It seems really important outside of containment," Ashley said, nodding, her eyes wide.

"Friends are more important, but it's good to have a stash of platinum, definitely. Did you get a feel for who else might be staying?"

"I kinda drifted off to sleep. I thought I'd be nervous spending time with other people outside of containment, but I'm either numb or just not made that way. I actually feel better now that there are so many people around, I think."

Boro and Hal walked into the room, each chewing a nutrition bar. Leaper was on Boro's shoulder, licking a tiny part clean, holding it in his small hands then popping it into his mouth, where he rolled it around before putting it back into his hands to continue licking. It was as if he was pretending to eat so he didn't stand out. "Are we talking about my brother's pitch?" Boro asked.

Dori and Leland came in behind them chewing meal bars as

well. The alarm to wake everyone had gone off. "Yeah, I guess he laid it on pretty thick," Spin said. "What does everyone think?" She watched with interest and amusement as Ashley offered Boro a welcoming hug that lasted a few seconds longer than simple friendliness demanded.

"Well, he didn't change my mind," Boro said, looking over Ashley's shoulder. When she finished squeezing up against him, he smiled and said; "Good morning to you too."

She moved on the Leland, who was ready for her and gave as good as he got, making her giggle when he squeezed and rocked her enthusiastically. "I hope you're sticking around."

"I am," Ashley said cheerily before moving on to Dori who eyed her apprehensively before she was embraced. "I'm a hugger."

Leland shook his head and looked away from Ashley, back to Spin. "Right, the presentation was tempting, but I'm sticking around. You need a good sawbones to keep your crew on their feet, besides, I never liked how dolls were treated, so I'm here until you tell me it's time to go."

"Thanks..." Dori told Ashley as they parted. "That was nice." She looked to Spin as Ashley turned towards Hal. "The more time I spend with you the less I feel like a freak, so good luck getting rid of me."

Hal resisted Ashley's embrace at first, stiff and wary, but melted into it after a few seconds, sighing and allowing himself to be squeezed. Ashley didn't release him right away when she was finished, either, leaning back instead and smiling at him. "You should grow a beard, it would look good on you."

"Um... regulations. Gotta keep it neat," he replied bashfully.

"Thank you for flying the ship," she told him before letting go.

"No problem, and, uh, speaking of that..." he said, turning to Spin and the rest of the group. "We're going to be in Beta Bio in two hours. We pushed the drive pretty hard."

"Oh, so it's decision time, then," Nigel said, stepping into the increasingly crowded compartment. He had Della and Mirra with him. "Looks like I'm staying." Della looked at him uncertainly.

There was a moment of uneasy silence as Spin and Boro locked eyes with each other from opposite ends of the compartment.

Nigel pushed on, but even Ashley could see there was something wrong, and she moved to stand beside Hal. "I mean, everything looked amazing in the whole presentation," Nigel said. "The Academy looks awesome, and I was never one for school, but he was right to focus on that for his pitch, at least for me. I know the civilian life stuff looks really cool too, they're really building something, but there's something going on here. I'd feel..."

"You have to go," Dori said firmly. "Look at your girl, there. Della's already half way gone, she may as well be there already from the look on her face. Besides, I know I don't want you here, not after what you did."

"Listen, I'm tired of you giving me shit for saving your life," Nigel retorted. He was about to go on but Dori interrupted him.

"You didn't do that out of love for me. You did it to make yourself feel better. If you actually thought about how it would be for me, getting rewired up here," Dori pointed to her head, finger jabbing, "Pushed into a whole new existence whether I liked it or not but still ending up a cyborg in the end no matter how human I look or feel, then you would have realized that I was going to die either way. Pieces of who I was after I was rebuilt, after I went psycho are coming back. That was no existence, I should have died in the accident and stayed dead, but if I really tried, I could remember what it was like to be Dorian, just a human guy. Now I've changed so much, been altered so much that I don't know who I am anymore. Dorian is dead, your friend is gone, and I can't fucking stand you because I know you did it. You may as well have held a gun to my head and pulled the trigger."

"I'm sorry, man," Nigel said.

"There! Right fucking there! Stop it! I'm not even a man anymore! If I could have chosen death or life as a chick for myself, I probably would have chosen life, but you chose for me and you still see Dorian. That's not helping, I need to figure this shit out and the more you remind me of what I used to be, the harder it'll be. Get gone." Dori looked to Spin, lowering her voice. "I'll be in my bunk until we get back." Then she left the compartment.

Spin could tell that Nigel was reaching for something to say, but he couldn't find the words, and she was grateful when Boro put his hand on his nephew's shoulder. "Not for the same reasons, but I was going to say you should go too. For now, at least. Maybe it's time to get to know Shamus, to get educated and join a fight that you can really believe in."

"The Order aren't here, though," Nigel retorted, a tear rolling down his cheek.

"They were," Boro said. "You remember the signs. *Darkness is coming, buy your ticket to salvation.* That's what the signs said before mad bot day. That was them, and if they're not stopped, they will be here eventually. I like your chances down there better than I do up here, if I'm honest. I'll make sure this crew doesn't get slagged, you watch your uncle and make sure that his lady and the newest member of our family knows where we come from. Well, at least the good parts."

"He has a baby coming, I forgot," Nigel said. "But you need me here," he looked to Spin.

"The Academy looks amazing," Spin said. "You'll learn more there than you would in a lifetime here, especially working with the tech they have out there."

"So, you want me to go too?" Nigel asked, looking crestfallen.

"No," Spin said. "I'll miss you like crazy, but I know it's where you should go, where you have a better chance at a future. We'll see each other again though, I'll make sure of it."

"So will I," Boro said.

Shamus slipped into the compartment silently but was noticed by Nigel anyway. He nodded at his nephew. "They'll run out of places to hide out here, you can guarantee they'll come racing down to Haven when they do."

"Always the optimist," Boro said under his breath. "He might be right, though." He turned his attention to Nigel. "We're going to make a real mess of things up here, stealing synthetics, platinum, whatever we can fit in our hold and sabotaging the rest."

"It sounds like Haven Fleet could use the lot of you," Shamus said, specifically regarding his brother. "But you're not coming back with me, are you?"

"No, Shamus, I'm sorry," Boro said. "Too much to do up here."

"Nothing I can say to get you lot off this revenge trip?" he countered, nodding at the prince's corpse.

"There's more to it than that," Boro said. "But no, there's nothing you can say that'll get us to the Haven System right now. Maybe someday."

Shamus nodded, his head low. "Someday, aye. Don't keep me waiting too long."

Boro stepped over to him and took him into a firm bear hug, one which Shamus reciprocated after a moment. "Aw, they're huggers too," Ashley cooed under her breath, leaning on Hal's shoulder.

There were a few words quietly exchanged between the pair before they parted, Shamus wiping a tear from his eye. "You keep safe, brother. You have a growing number of relations on the fringe, don't forget us."

"Give 'em hell and come out shining," Boro said to his brother. "Take good care of that family of yours."

"Aye. Guess it's almost time then," Frost said as he turned to Mirra and Della. "You ladies coming home with me and Nigel here?"

"I'd like to go," Della said. "If that's okay." She looked to Spin.

"I'll miss you, but I can't imagine anything better for you," Spin said, crossing the room and giving her a hug. As expected, Della's tears came, and Spin wiped them away. "You're going to tell me what it's like though, so I expect plenty of holo recordings."

"Okay," Della said, nodding.

Spin went on to embrace Mirra, who laughed and said. "I'm not going anywhere unless it's with you. She and I already talked about it. Someone has to take care of you and your ship while you focus on raiding."

"Oh, I was afraid I'd lose both of you," Spin said.

"No, the cooking won't be as good, but we couldn't leave you alone with the rest of this crew. Besides, who would become the cook if we both went? Leland? I doubt he could make a good waffle."

"Hey," Leland objected.

"Ever make one?" Mirra asked.

"Make one? I've never tried one," Leland replied with a chuckle. "You might have a point, I wouldn't be your best choice for cook."

"Well, it's almost that time," Shamus said, turning towards the hatch that would take him up the length of the ship to the bridge. "Oh, and the rest of your people have signed on to follow me to the Haven System. Except for Kline. He did great on the military entrance tests but failed every part of the psyche evaluation. I can't take him."

"Aw, nuts," Ashley groaned.

Spin regarded her quizzically.

"He's a crazy mess. He was made to be a soldier and all he was allowed to do was work out and do puzzles for twenty-five years. We tried talking to each other through comms and did nothing but argue, I've never met anyone ruder in my life. Not that I've met a lot of people or anything, but, I've met enough to know he's a pain in the butt."

Spin turned the idea of losing all the people she rescued to Shamus and the promises he made and was surprised to find that she didn't find the idea very offensive. It was enough that they were free and had a place to go. Even still, she wasn't willing to let him off the hook entirely. "If you lied in that presentation and lead them to trouble, you'll be hearing from me."

"Aye," Shamus said, smiling at the threat almost as though he appreciated it. "And before you leave this ship with the hardware I'm letting you keep, I'd be an idiot if I didn't warn you that trying to get revenge against these royal bastards is going to get you all killed. Take on good work, or turn pirate for all I care, but stay away from royal arseholes. They'll be the end of you. If you'd stayed true to your word, and convinced Boro to join me, I wouldn't have a worry about anyone I was leaving behind here. I won't forget that."

"I tried," Spin said. "But he's his own man. If you can't convince him, then what in all the stars makes you think I can?"

"You could have come with me too, that would have done it," Shamus said as he took his leave, closing the hatch behind him.

"We should be days from Beta Bio, right?" Nigel asked.

"Oh, right, that's why I came back here, I totally forgot," Hal said, glancing at Ashley. "We hit a high energy pocket, the quad drives tunnelled right through, and it cut our transit time down to about eight hours. We'll be flying into port soon. I should show you the gear bags the Chief set up for you last night, then get to the bridge."

"It seems like it's too soon, I just met a bunch of you and most of you are going away," Ashley said. Hal rolled his eyes as a new round of parting embraces and comments began. Spin noticed Ashley slip away after she finished her rounds.

SHAMUS CHECKED on the recruits he'd taken on in the

name of Haven Fleet. The dolls he was taking back were looking through the basic survival bags he set them up with. There were meal bars, a spare vacsuit, a days' water, a personal communications unit, and a few other things he managed to scrape together. He would have been surprised that the new dolls, the ones that were just saved from their maturation tubes, weren't more loyal to Spin, but Sophia still blamed Spin for not being able to save more, so she made a good case for going with Shamus, where they'd be able to decide on what kind of life they could have in the Haven System.

The only thing he wasn't sure about in the presentation he altered for everyone but Spin was the accuracy of the Order of Eden threat. He included Regent Galactic and the Order in the short brief, but it was presented by Ayan as footage of several victories played behind her. Not only that, but he left the threat of the Edxi out. He knew it was inaccurate, but he didn't have enough information about the insectoid invaders to paint any kind of accurate picture, as far as he was concerned.

"Chief McFadden?" Ashley addressed from the threshold of the bridge. "Okay if I come in?"

"Aye," he said, surprised, turning in the pilot's seat. He still found the sight of the woman who looked almost exactly like Ashley Lamport unnerving. Much of her manner was the same, even her lisp, which softened her speech. "Call me Frost," he said, flashing back to the first time he met the other Ashley aboard the Samson.

"Frost? Okay," she said, leaning against the back of the co-pilot's seat. "You know one of my sisters, a doll from my line, where you come from?"

"Aye, and I've always liked her," he said, intentionally

leaving out the detail that there was a period where he's make a game of flirting with her, even though he knew she'd never join him in his bunk. Those days were long past, there was no need to share, especially since she was happy with Minh-Chu Buu, a man he liked and respected a great deal.

"I know, I saw your relationship in her civilian file. I think I'd like her too if we met, but that'll never happen."

"Oh?" Shamus made a mental note to find out how she got into the civilian records later.

"It's kinda mean, I realize, but I was hoping that I was the last one from my line. Maybe other dolls celebrate their numbers, but I don't. I don't think she'd like to hear that there's another woman made the same way either, so I'd like to ask that you don't tell her that I exist, or that she's a doll at all."

"I don't know if that's for me to decide, lass," Shamus said.

"If it's not for you to decide, then don't tell her. Revealing any of this to her or anyone else would be the same as making that decision for her, right?"

"What if our scanners eventually find out. We have serious tech," Shamus said.

"They never will. She probably even thinks she can have babies, but without the cure Spin has, she never will. If technology from your part of space hasn't determined that she was manufactured and grown, not born, then nothing you have will."

"Why don't you want me to tell her?" Shamus asked. "And what if she wants to have children? What do I do then?"

"Slip her the cure, it's already in your computer system," Ashley said. "Oh, and I don't want her to know because I'd have knowledge of her wiped from my mind if I could. It's selfish, I know, but knowing that she's out there makes me..." she hesitated for a moment. "...maybe there isn't a word for it yet, but it's kinda like jealousy. I'll get over it, sure, but why put her through the same thing? I feel like if she knew it would make her feel like this, or even worse, maybe she'd want to find me, and I don't want to be face to face with her. Maybe someday, but not now."

"I thought all that time in isolation, seeing dolls made for years would get you ready for this. That you'd know there were a lot of dolls that..." Shamus watched something happen that he'd never seen from Ashley. The woman's expression began to sour, as though the idea he was sharing was so distasteful that she'd rather be anywhere else.

"There were thirty-five of my model made, thirty-four of them got to have memories imprinted on them that convinced them that they were human, born of mothers. They were woken up as toddlers, not like Spin's line. They were made to live for centuries, to stop aging at about twenty-five old calendar years, and they would see things I never would. Most of them would probably outlive their masters and be free one day, but I was stuck. Knowing that they were out there, experiencing the galaxy, knowing a life even if it was on the arm of some prideful owner, or as a servant in some corner of the universe, made me crazy sometimes. It still does. I resent every copy of my model, especially since I came first. I came first and they put me in a clean, safe environment where I was watched, and even my thoughts were moderated if I got too lonely or mad with envy. So, don't tell her. Let me have my own exciting life and let her continue hers."

"You have my word," Shamus said. "Good luck, lass. I hope you have the life you're looking for here."

THANK YOU

Thank you for reading. The adventure continues on Patreon and in Spinward Fringe Broadcast 12: Invasion.

CHRONOLOGY OF SCIENCE FICTION & FANTASY BY RANDOLPH LALONDE

Chronological Order of the Spinward Fringe and Chaos Core Books

Spinward Fringe Broadcast 0: Origins
Spinward Fringe Broadcast 1 and 2: Resurrection and Awakening
Spinward Fringe Broadcast 3: Triton
Spinward Fringe Broadcast 4: Frontline
Spinward Fringe Broadcast 5: Fracture
Spinward Fringe Broadcast 6: Fragments
The Expendable Few: A Spinward Fringe Novel
Spinward Fringe Broadcast 7: Framework
Spinward Fringe Broadcast 8: Renegades
Spinward Fringe Broadcast 9: Warpath
Trapped: Chaos Core Book 1
Spinward Fringe Broadcast 10: Freeground
Cool Pursuit: Chaos Core Book 2

Spinward Fringe Broadcast 10.5: Carnie's Tale
Spinward Fringe Broadcast 11: Revenge
Savage Stars: Chaos Core Book 3
Spinward Fringe Broadcast 12: Invasion

Chronological Order of Fantasy Novels by Randolph Lalonde

Highshield Book 1
Brightwill
Highshield Book 2 (Expected in 2019)

www.ingramcontent.com/pod-product-compliance
Lightning Source LLC
Chambersburg PA
CBHW072017020726
47501CB00006B/1843